REIGN OF LIGHT

Also by Amanda Briar

The Dawnlin Trilogy
Dawn of Hope
Blade of Truth
Reign of Light

Reign of Light

AMANDA BRIAR

FUN SIZE
PUBLISHING

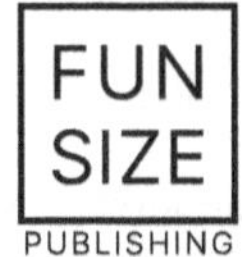

Reign of Light
Text Copyright © 2025 by Amanda Briar
Cover Copyright © 2025 by Amanda Briar
Map Copyright © 2025 by Amanda Briar

Fun Size Publishing is an imprint of Fun Size Media LLC.

Fun Size Media LLC
Antioch, CA 94509
business@funsizemedia.com

Editing by K. Morton Editing Services

Formatting by Fun Size Publishing

Cover Art by Fun Size Publishing

Map Design by Fun Size Publishing
Original Illustrations from Map Effects Fantasy Map Builder

Epilogue Chapter Art by Morgan Valdez @illustratedbymorgan

Library of Congress Control Number: Pending

Paperback
ISBN 978-1-964819-13-6

Hardcover
ISBN 978-1-964819-14-3

Special Edition Paperback
ISBN 978-1-964819-15-0

Special Edition Hardcover
ISBN 978-1-964819-16-7

Ebook
ISBN 978-1-964819-12-9

Audiobook
ISBN 978-1-964819-17-4

Published in November 2025

www.amandabriar.com

To my sister.

And to anyone who has ever had to,
or is currently trying to make a life altering decision.
You are not alone.

It may feel difficult but you are strong.
Light always finds a way.

AUTHOR'S NOTE

Reign of Light is a New Adult Fantasy Romance novel filled with adventure and high stakes. The story includes mention of loss of family and friends, death/illness/injury of loved ones, death and burial of a parent, adult language, imprisonment, violence, strangulation, abandonment, mental and emotional abuse, life or death situations, alcohol use, physical injury, explicit sexual content, and death. Readers who are sensitive to these themes please take note.

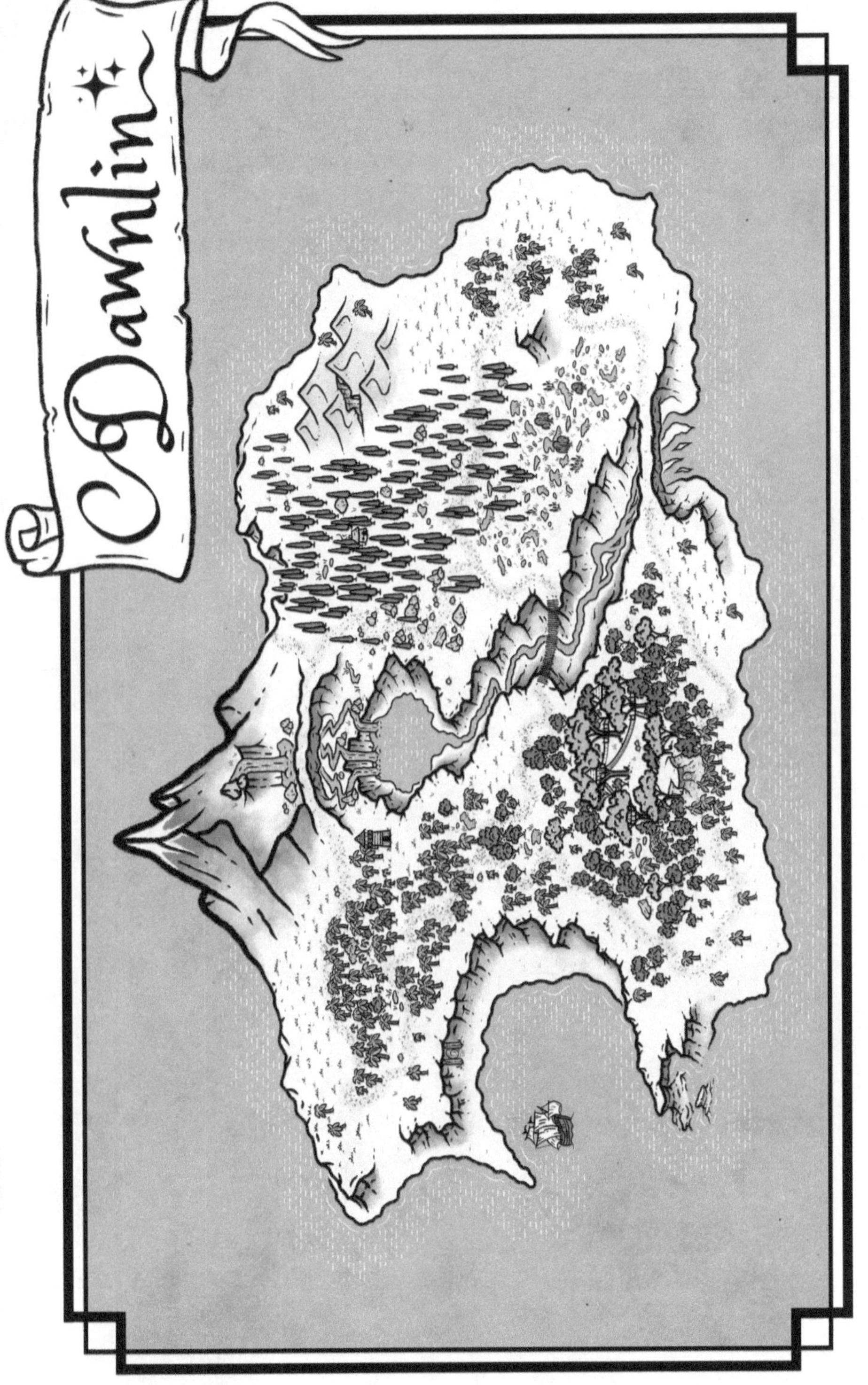

Dawnlin

REIGN OF LIGHT

PROLOGUE

Time is constant, as reliable as the surety of death. Time had never concerned the man before, not when he knew there was nothing he could do to change it. It would pass whether he wanted it to or not. He had learned early on that time did not matter as long as he surrounded himself with those he loved.

Time was of no importance.

Until he saw her lying there, and knew deep in his soul that her time was running out.

Suddenly, time was the most important and precious thing in the world.

Walking away from her was the hardest thing he'd ever done. This woman was the light that brightened his life, but if he did nothing, if he stayed, her light would be snuffed out for eternity.

He had to try.

The man traipsed through the dark streets, the fog and gloom particularly thick tonight, mimicking the despair and helplessness he felt as he stood over her almost lifeless body. The roads were empty at the late hour, and he thanked the gods for that small blessing amid what felt like the biggest curse.

Not a soul would be around to see what he was doing, to follow him, and possibly destroy his chances of saving her.

Dawnlin.

He'd heard the stories, passed along in the whispers of childhood, shirked as a folly and fantasy in the beginnings of adulthood. But he never forgot it. A land said to hold a cure, one that would bring her back to him, exactly where she belongs.

He would not lose his love, no matter what trials this life had thrown at them, trying to keep them apart. He would fight it, and he would cure her. He wouldn't let his hope die.

If only he could find it.

The man's boots pounded on the pavement, a metronome signaling his race against time, when something caught his eye, just as he passed the dark entrance to an abandoned alley. His body jerked to a halt, and as if it was calling out to him, he turned to find something he knew deep in his soul was the answer. White stone glowing against the gloomy, dim light, water flowing freely and musically, this beacon called to him, and he knew this was it. The way to call the Guardian.

The man stepped into the alley, a welcome calm coming over him as he gazed upon the sight that would change his life, that gave him hope.

The fountain.

CHAPTER ONE

The thought of having a future beyond the cold stone walls of my castle in Blackwood was always just that. A thought. A dream. Something I spent my entire life imagining, especially when I lost myself in the pages of a book. My life would never look like those of the heroines I admired. My future would never be mine. Love would never be within my reach. The duty to my kingdom that had been settled on my shoulders from the moment I took my first breath would always take priority.

I'd lived for years with the longing and desire for a life and future I wanted, but knew I could never have. My acceptance of that reality changed the moment my boots sank into the soft soil of Dawnlin.

In a way, it felt like a dream itself. The warmth, the smells, the sounds, the suns. I was transported to a world opposite in every way from the one I'd been trapped in, all because I had hope.

Hope for a future that I could choose, one different from what fate promised, led me to this place. It opened my eyes to a new life that could be molded by my own actions, a future of my own creation, not only here but also when I returned.

Now, that hope is gone.

Dane stole it.

He robbed not only me, but every single person on this island of the hope that brought them here, hope that they could alter the trajectory of their life and save someone they couldn't live without. The evidence of his betrayal is right before me, hanging from the white-knuckled grip of someone else who, not long ago, also hurt me, just in a vastly different way.

Shallow breaths stutter in my chest and pain lances through my fingers as I fist Weston's clothes. I'm trying with everything I have to stay upright, despite the ache in the depths of my chest telling me to fall to my knees and break under the weight of the new reality that we are trapped here.

Forever.

Without the passage of time on the island, all of us here will live forever in an endless monotony. We'll have no purpose, no future, no hope that we can return, with only each other to rely on and build a semblance of normalcy.

The sound of metal slicing into the soft soil at my feet cuts through the dull roar in my ears and snaps me out of my spiraling thoughts, though I'm unable to look away from the empty pouch Mara still clutches. The very same lump of fabric that only days ago still held a golden glow, filled with the dust I had almost taken. If I had, I wouldn't be staring at her now, trying to make sense of how this could have happened. If I had, it never *would* have happened.

"Lennox."

Warmth settles on my cheek, and the brush of the rough calluses from years of Weston's training jars me from my trance. I wish it were just that. A trance, a hallucination, a nightmare. Anything that would mean all our fears aren't currently coming to pass.

I pull my eyes from the pouch, and tilt my chin until our gazes meet, the deep pools of teal reading everything I'm feeling. I can't hide anything from him; he already knows. Tears well, and his face blurs as I feel my strength crumbling. As much as I don't want them, I can't stop them. Tears that represent every single inadequacy that's weighed down on my shoulders for years pool in my vision, marring the one thing that has felt solid and sure since I've been here.

Useless.

Dane was right. I feel useless. I couldn't even accomplish one thing and take the dust that would have given at least a few Castaways a chance at going home. If I'd been strong enough to fight Dane, smart enough not to let him catch on, I could have changed some of our fates. If I had, at least being trapped would have been bittersweet.

"Lennox, sweetheart," Weston mumbles, and I blink rapidly, clearing the tears and begging them not to fall. "Be strong for just a little longer."

Barely holding back a choked sob, I nod slowly, our eyes staying locked on each other as he assesses me. It's as if nothing else exists when Weston looks at me, the face of pure understanding, as he waits to make sure I am alright, that I will not break.

Not yet.

A flash of movement catches my eye as Mara takes a step closer, and Weston reacts. His arm lifts quickly, his sword leveling at her without taking his focus off me.

"Don't take another fucking step," he growls. "She may trust you, but I don't."

My chest swells as a vision of what he would be like as the First Guard back home flashes before my eyes. The way he would protect me, the way no guards would ever think of challenging him or speaking to me in a condescending manner, the way no suitors would ever want to come near me. But now, that is a future that will nevercome to pass.

"She's fine," I whisper, but it's only when I take a deep breath and unclench my hands from him that he turns away, focusing his full attention back on the Voyagers that brought us this fate-altering news.

"I'm not trying to trick you," Mara calls. "Or attack you, or whatever betrayals are running through your head."

"After the way she came back to me the last time she met up with you, I'm not taking any chances," Weston calls back, his brows drawn low and jaw tight with the same look of fury he had the night I stepped foot onto the ship, exhausted and bleeding.

The night everything changed between us.

"I'm sorry. I was wrong, and I can't take it back. Can we just forget it happened?" Mara asks.

"No."

Weston's harsh response echoes in the air around us, making his feelings about the situation clear. He does not forgive Mara for throwing knives at my back, whether her actions resulted from Dane's manipulations or not.

He yanks his sword from the ground, both his blades relaxed in front of him despite his shoulders sending off waves of tension as he squares his body to them.

"We'll need to figure out where we go from here, and what our next steps are. It won't be accomplished tonight," he says. "Meet us tomorrow at the plateau. Only bring one other person, and don't even think about trying to pull anything. You won't be prepared for it."

"Who the fuck put you in charge?" Mara snaps, crossing her arms over her chest. With both Dane and Storm gone, Mara is the most likely person to step into the role of leading the Voyagers, especially since I'm no longer one of them. But she's never met Weston before, never seen him protect his people, so she has no idea of the respect he has from every member of his crew.

"Dane did. The second he stole the magic from the Guardian and tried to kill me for it." Mara's eyes go wide, and her mouth falls open slightly, and I feel my jaw slacken as well. Weston hid that information from me for a while, but now that Dane's gone, maybe he feels we have nothing to lose from her knowing.

He continues. "Dane may have filled your minds with lies, but that doesn't change that I am the one in charge here. You'll agree, or we don't have to include you. It's your choice."

Her head snaps to me. "Lennox—"

"Do what he says, Mara." The edge in my voice makes her jaw slam shut as her head swivels between the two of us.

I'm grateful for her apology. I'm glad she realized what she did was wrong and how she treated me was unwarranted. But she doesn't know everything, and if she thinks she can step in and try to tell Weston and the rest of the crew who have been in hiding for years how and when they are going to have access to the island, she is mistaken. Weston will never let anyone else dictate what's best for the crew, especially since she hasn't proven that she isn't still willing to harm us. Apology or not.

"What if more of us want to come after they find out?" she asks.

"Be a leader, and tell them no."

Her eyes narrow at Weston, and irritation itches in my fingertips. I didn't expect her to like him, or even be cordial, but her resistance to him trying to negotiate a meeting that is safe for everyone is frustrating.

"So what, we're just supposed to risk our own safety if you show up with more Castaways? How am I supposed to ensure that there will only be two of you, too?" she snaps.

"It doesn't matter how many of us there are. No one will harm you, unless you make the first move," Weston says. "There will be two of you. Once we come to an agreement, if others want to meet and talk, we will deal with that then."

Mara shuffles uncomfortably on her feet and lets out a low huff. "Fine," she grinds out.

Despite the initial resistance, I'm relieved she isn't fighting Weston's requirement harder. I don't think she ever truly wanted to be in charge of the Voyagers, despite being so vocal about how everyone should view me as a traitor. For someone who isn't used to having authority to step in when there is no one else, it can be an adjustment.

That day would have been in my future, but now I'll never know.

Before I left to return to the Voyagers, Weston and I discussed the possibility of a truce if the dust ran out without discovering how to replenish it. We expected that conversation to be with the Guardian, not with Mara, who must adjust to this new role she has taken on, as well as someone who doesn't know everything Dane kept hidden, or the location of the waters.

Weston's head swivels toward Roley, and the boy's shoulders raise in a slight cower. Abandoning whatever he was going to say, Weston's chin drops to his shoulder, his gaze finding mine as his voice lowers to a barely audible mumble.

"He's scared of me. He can choose to come with us tonight, or wait until after we meet, but the option should come from you."

I nod and clear my throat, trying hard not to betray the emotion that is still trapped in a knot there.

"Roley," I call out, and his eyes dart away from Weston toward me. "You can still come with us tonight if you want, or you can wait until we figure everything out. It's up to you."

His eyes flicker back to Weston as he mulls over the choice. "Um, I think I'll wait," he says weakly.

"That's alright, Roley," Weston says. "Fin will be happy to see you whenever you decide."

Roley's face perks up at the mention of his friend, and he nods, a small smile playing at his lips. "Okay," he says shyly.

"When are we meeting?" Mara says, pulling our attention back to her.

"Midday. When the suns are highest. We'll see you then," Weston says as one sword slides into its sheath. His free hand finds my lower back, and the firm pressure is conversation enough.

Let's move.

Bending to pick up my discarded bow, I don't bother with the dropped arrow or slinging it over my shoulder. My arms feel too heavy, and the movement feels pointless. If Mara can be trusted, there's no threat anymore. No Dane or Storm hunting us, no ambush waiting in the trees. There's no one to protect ourselves against any longer.

"See you soon, Roley. Mara." I catch her stare and give her a curt nod before turning my back and striding away. After our last encounter, I didn't think I'd ever turn my back on Mara again. By no means am I letting my guard down. Weston would be furious with me if I did, but the devastation on her face when she admitted Dane left gave me hope. After everything that happened tonight and the reality it forced her to accept, I truly don't think she'll hurt either of us.

"Don't follow," Weston orders before falling into step behind me, his heavy footsteps catching mine easily. We move quickly but quietly, putting as much distance between us and them as we can. Just as the portal comes into sight, Weston's mumble breaks the silence.

"Keep walking. I won't risk Mara's curiosity."

Shadows from the towering trees of the dark forest fall over us as we briskly walk past the portal, following the curve of the path until we are no longer in their direct line of sight. The firm press of Weston's hand disappears from my back, only to be replaced by his fingers lacing through mine, squeezing my hand tightly.

"Near the falls," he says, and we quickly weave through the boulder-lined pathways until we're standing in front of the trapdoor. Weston halts, his arm wrapping around my back and his hand settling on my hip as he looks around, making sure no one followed despite not hearing any trailing footsteps. He bends and lifts the lid, ushering me inside, and follows closely behind.

The roar of the falls disappears the moment the trapdoor shuts with a thud, and thick silence fills the dim tunnel as the weight of what just happened settles over us.

The moment we are alone, cracks splinter through my facade, and the strength Weston urged me to hold on to shatters.

Short, rapid breaths rise in my chest as the finality of our situation threatens to suffocate me. I clench my fists tightly, trying to squeeze away the numbness in my fingertips and focus on slowing my breathing, but it's too much. I can't stop it. Spinning around, I look up into Weston's face, unsure if I'll find a mirror to the emotions cascading through my body, threatening to burst.

His brows draw in, and worry and concern coat his features as his eyes dance between mine. A hint of shame settles in my chest as I watch him stay strong, but when his gaze flickers to my quivering chin, then back to my eyes, I see there's more hiding beneath the surface.

Understanding.

Weston knows exactly what turmoil I'm trying to contain because deep down, he feels it too. He knows what it is to hold the responsibility for those around him and the sacrifice it takes to put everyone else first. He feels the failure of our attempts to get home, and the crushing defeat of losing our last shred of hope, but he's not succumbing to it. He's staying strong so that I don't have to anymore.

Wordlessly he steps closer, opening his arms wide enough so I can fall into them.

And I do.

My bow clatters to the ground as the first sob rips from my throat, breaking the fragile dam I constructed in front of Mara and Roley. The tears and cries come freely then, sobs rolling one after another as the weight of my body and everything it has been holding up falls into him. Uncontrollable strangled noises echo through the tunnel, hardly recognizable to my own ears. Tears stream down my cheeks, and my eyes squeeze shut, as if I can will this all away by pretending I didn't see that empty pouch.

Weston wraps his arms around my shoulders, pulling me into him and holding me tight. His fingers weave through my hair as his hand cradles the back of my head and presses my face into his chest. I barely feel his lips on the top of my head as he holds me upright until his words fall on my ears.

"I know."

Two words. In just two simple words, he's given me more acceptance and acknowledgment than I've ever had in my life. He isn't telling me how to feel or what to think. He isn't trying to smooth the situation over or forcing me to believe everything is going to be alright. He's letting me feel everything, letting me have this moment and these emotions, and giving me a safe place to let go in his arms where I know I'm cherished and understood.

He's feeling the same way, even if he refuses to show it.

I don't feel him move from being too lost in the heaves wracking my body and the chaos flooding my mind. My swollen eyes and gasping breaths make it hard to focus on anything other than the guilt and despair taking over me.

Weston slides his back down the wall of the tunnel, pulling me with him, and gathering me onto his lap. I curl into a ball, my cheek pressing against his firm chest, trying to use the pounding of his heart to calm me as I shake.

With one arm still wrapped tightly around my curved body, the other moves and his hand glides gently over me, stroking my hair, my face, my back, trying to ease away my pain with his touch.

"I tried," I manage to choke out. "I—I—"

The sobs don't subside, and I suck in breaths through my mouth before another wrangled cry takes it away again.

"Breathe," he murmurs. His hand settles on my face, and his thumb gently strokes my cheekbone, swiping away the rivers of tears that haven't stopped falling.

Prying my swollen eyes open, I tilt my chin to look up at him, only to find him gazing down at me, watching me break. The tension in his jaw is the only clue that he's still holding everything in and staying strong for me.

"If I hadn't…gone…he wouldn't…he wouldn't have known," I stutter, hiccuping and trying to push the words out. "He used it because he knew…he knew…I made him strand us all here. I failed, and it's my fault."

"No, Lennox. You didn't do this." His hand flattens against my cheek, and his eyes beg me to believe him. "Dane fucking did this. Not you. He could have left at any time. He could have taken you with him. You tried to give hope to some of the crew, and those actions did not cause him to turn on everyone left on this island. He'd already fucking done that."

A tiny granule deep inside me knows Weston is right, that the moment Dane chose himself over the magic, he'd turned against us all, and he would have continued to choose himself and his reasons over anything. Dane had admitted as much to me when revealing his plan to use me and anyone else who found the healing waters, but my actions changed his plan.

Now I have to live for eternity knowing that it was my choice that took a chance away from someone else, and condemned us all to the same fate.

"How do I tell Sig? And Stass? Jorn? Everyone. How could they do anything but hate me?"

"No one is going to hate you." His voice is low, and I know he's doing everything he can to soothe me, but I'm too far gone to be affected by it.

"Come here." He lifts me as if I weigh nothing, shifting my body so I'm straddling him and he can look me in the eye. His hands wrap around my face, holding me firmly as my body still convulses with harsh sobs and rapid breaths that aren't able to catch up.

"No one will hate you for having hope. You risked yourself to help them. It doesn't matter how things turned out. We all came to this island on our own, and we were lost here before you even arrived. Dane's dust was never an option until you tried to make it one. You gave them that hope, but you weren't the one to take it away. *He* was. No one will put that on your shoulders, do you hear me?"

His face is stern, but not angry. He wants me to hear his words, to understand and accept them. He's trying to prevent me from living the rest of my life saddled beneath the guilt of failing everyone around me, and a fresh wave of sadness washes over me knowing he cares enough to make sure I see it.

I hiccup again before nodding tersely, my eyes falling down to where my fists clench his vest.

"I wish it were just that," I say, clenching my fingers tighter. "I hurt you, and it wasn't even fucking worth it. I took away your hope." My words are a barely audible whisper, and new tears well in my eyes at the admission. "After all this time," I say, my voice cracking, "and everything you did for me, I took it away from you."

"Look at me," he says, his tone harsh and serious. His fingers pinch my chin and lift gently until I can do nothing but stare into his fierce eyes.

"The moment you stepped onto this island, you gave me more hope than you could ever know. You're still here." He leans forward, closing the distance between us. "You didn't take anything away from me. You gave me everything."

My face crumbles as a fresh wave of tears spills over and onto my cheeks.

The muscles in his face soften, and one side of his lips turns up in a small smile.

"That wasn't supposed to make you cry," he murmurs, and runs a thumb over my bottom lip.

"I was already crying," I say, sniffing loudly. I reach up and swipe my sleeve across my face, trying to wipe away the evidence of my weakness. "No one has ever said anything like that to me before."

"And no one else ever will." He chuckles softly, then strokes the pad of his thumb across my bottom lip again, his eyes never leaving mine. "If I have to be here for eternity, I'm grateful for whatever magic let me have you here too."

"Maybe it's what Dawnlin wanted all along," I whisper, and realize that I truly believe it.

Every step of the way, the magic of the island brought me to the mountain. It led me to the healing waters, which dropped me into Weston's hands. It helped me find the truth, trapping me among the victims of Dane's actions and forcing me to truly see and trust them. It let me off the ship, allowing me to enact my plan to steal the dust, but I don't know if the island accounted for this change in events.

Is this the end it foresaw? The one it wants? The one we need?

Has this been the goal all along?

And if so, why?

I honestly don't know, and I don't know if we ever will have an answer for why we are all stranded, while the man who cheated the magic walks free. We can speculate and try to figure it out, but nothing will change. It is our ending, and now all we can do is move forward and be grateful that it wasn't worse.

"If this is what the island wanted, remind me to thank it," Weston says as he leans forward, closing that last breath of space between us. The soft press of his lips into mine breaks the tension in my body, slowing the onslaught of guilt and fear and worry, or at least distracting me from it for a moment.

I lean into him, wrapping my arms around his neck, pulling him closer, craving the sturdy and safe feel of his body against mine. Understanding what I need, he wraps his arm around my waist and crushes me against him before angling his head and deepening the kiss. I lose myself in the moment, the steady rhythm of his tongue stroking mine, the tightening of his muscles around me, the feel of his chest grumbling as my fingernails brush his scalp.

Breaking away, breathless, I pull air into my chest ready to lean in for more, when he presses a brusque kiss to the corner of my jaw, then murmurs in my ear.

"Let's go home."

CHAPTER TWO

alking through the tunnels back to the ship is the slowest I've traveled since stepping foot onto Dawnlin. We have no reason to hurry. Time is on our side, and neither of us is rushing to break the news to the crew.

Weston weaves his fingers between mine as we silently traipse through the dim tunnel. The casual comfort feels wrong after the cyclone of emotions that we just went through. With each step, my apprehension escalates as the coming conversations play out in my mind, and I watch the faces of my friends fall. The tears. The loss of hope. The anger. Everything I just felt, I know they will too, and the two of us are going to be the ones who have to deliver the news.

The hardest part is that we've done this before, except this time is final.

The dust is gone, and over twenty years of effort has been futile.

There is no returning to our world.

After letting myself feel everything, an odd sense of calm washes over me. I know it is fleeting, and the tears I shed moments ago in

Weston's arms will not be the only ones I cry, probably not even the last of the night, but right now, I have enough strength to move forward. Weston held me together while I shattered, and now all I can do is try to pick up the pieces until they start to heal.

Time is the only thing that will heal these wounds, and time is the one thing on Dawnlin we have plenty of.

Waves roll gently onto the beach just outside the portal, and the luminescent glow followed by the calming crash is comforting, knowing we're almost home. This time when we step out of the portal, it will be different. We don't have to be on alert. We don't have to scan the surroundings to make sure no one spots us. We don't have to bolt back to the gangway. As we cross through the dense magic, it feels like we're stepping into a different Dawnlin than the one we left not that long ago.

Our boots sink into the sand with each heavy footfall, and the speed of our gait slows ever so slightly, as if we're trying to avoid the possibility of having to tell anyone what happened for just a little longer. The gangway still juts out onto the reef, and the deck is quiet, with no echo of conversation. There's no glow from the lanterns, only the reflection of the moonlight off the dark wood, indicating everyone is likely already below, and I let out a sigh of relief as we step onto the jagged rock.

Weston's arm settles across my shoulders, and I sink into his side as he presses a kiss into my hair. Wrapping my arm around his hips, I look down at my feet, trying to step over the glowing creatures settled into their hidden pools.

"I feel like I could sleep all the way through tomorrow. Maybe I should," I say, the hint of melancholy in my voice too difficult to hide.

"Sleep as long as you want. You don't have to come to the meeting. You can stay back on the ship."

I nudge him sharply with my shoulder. "Nice try. I'm coming."

He lets out a huff of a half-hearted laugh. "It was worth a shot."

"I'm not letting you go alone."

"I won't go alone."

His face is stoic when I tilt my head back to look up at him. "You're going to tell everyone? Right away?"

"I think they'd want to know. Like you said before, they deserve to. It also might be concerning if I just disappear in the middle of the day."

"We could come up with something if you need more time."

"I thought about waiting until I ensured it was safe for them to leave the ship, but that requires talking with Mara. So, I don't think I have much of a choice."

"Leave the ship? You mean live on the island?"

He nods slowly. "Yes."

I gape at him, too distracted from the thought of anyone leaving when my foot catches on a point in the rock, throwing me off balance. Weston's arm cinches tighter around my shoulders, keeping me from falling forward before slowing our pace down just a little more.

"You don't think they'll want to stay here? You really think they'd leave? This has been their home for so long."

I feel the shrug of his shoulders. "Some might. Some might not. It'll be their choice. Either way, I need to make sure it's safe for them, and that they *have* the choice."

I shake my head. "I don't want to go back to camp."

A low chuckle rings in my ears over the crash of the waves, making my stomach flutter. "I'm glad to hear that because that offer is only for all of them. *You* don't have a choice."

I huff loudly. "What are you going to do, tie me up to keep me from leaving?"

We stop abruptly, and his thumb is under my chin, tilting my head back as he lowers his face. A glimmer of mischief shines in his eyes as one corner of his lips turns up in a smirk. "Only if you ask me to, my queen." My mouth falls open only for him to push it closed and press a firm kiss to my lips before pulling away quickly. "Otherwise, don't threaten me with a good time."

He turns back toward the gangway and continues our trek. My feet can barely keep up with him because of the images now flashing through my mind and the heat gathering in my abdomen.

I clear my throat, trying not to be obvious about how much his words and the meaning behind them sent my head spinning.

"If you remember correctly, *Captain*, I already left once. I don't think you could stop me if I wanted to again."

"Don't remind me," he grumbles and pulls me more firmly to his side. "And don't call me that."

"*Weston.*" He lowers his chin so his gaze finds mine, and despite the joking I still see the hidden sadness from the day peeking through. "I don't want to leave. Just in case you needed to hear it again."

"Good."

The single word is reassuring as we ascend the gangway toward the quiet deck. I can already feel the tension in my shoulders releasing the closer we get to disappearing into our room until tomorrow afternoon, but as we crest the top, ready to step onto the wooden floorboards, my stomach falls.

The deck may be quiet, but it isn't empty.

Two figures sit in the darkness, their backs pressed against the mainmast. I know them well enough now that I don't need any light to pick out exactly who it is. Nerves roll off of Sig as she sits with her hands clenched, forearms resting on her bouncing knees. Jorn sits beside her, his eyes on the stars above, and his arms crossed over his chest.

She waited for us to return.

When she disappeared below deck as we prepared to leave, I didn't think there would be any reason that I wouldn't want her waiting for us when we came back. She was anxious about our return. We all were, and now I know we won't be able to move forward without telling her.

If she knows me half as well as I know her, she'll be able to tell anyway.

I feel the moment Weston spots them, because his back stiffens and the muscles in his arm tighten against me. A lump is already forming in my throat, trying to prevent me from saying the words out loud that I know are going to devastate her, probably more than anyone else.

I am not prepared to face her tonight. I thought we'd at least have a little more time to let everything settle and tamp down the vortex of our own emotions before having to tell anyone else. By the feel of Weston's tense body pressing into mine, it seems like he had the same expectation.

Sig glances over at us and looks away, before her head snaps back in our direction, as if she didn't process we had actually returned. She springs to her feet and crosses the deck swiftly, relief sagging in her shoulders.

"You're alright," she breathes, and stops just an arm's length away from us. "I told you everything would be fine." Her hands settle on her hips as she peers past us down the gangway. Her forehead crinkles as her eyebrows raise, and she cocks her head to the side. "Where's the kid?" Her gaze flickers up to Weston's face, and I know what she finds as she drags her eyes to mine before her expression falls.

"What's going on?" Her voice wavers as Jorn strides across the deck, stopping just behind her.

"Cap?" he says, as his head tilts and his brows crinkle together. One look from each of them is all it takes to know something is wrong, and it's a testament to how close they all are.

But it means we can't hide anything. We have to tell them.

A single tear escapes and slides down my cheek, followed closely by another, and Sig's stare follows their trail, watching my calm facade crack once again. She turns back to Weston, the tension in her jaw fierce despite the pleading in her eyes.

"Tell me," she urges. Pain laces her strained voice, and I can't help but think she's figured it out. She knows what Weston is about to tell her, and she's steeling herself for the blow of his words.

Weston lifts his arm from my shoulders and takes a step closer as she stares up at him, her eyes shining in the moonlight.

"He left, Sig. He used the rest of the dust and is gone." His voice is low and soft, like even though he knows what he is saying will hurt her, he's doing everything he can to prevent it.

"Shit," Jorn hisses, and throws his hands up, scrubbing them through his hair.

A pained cry erupts from her throat, and she slams her palm over her mouth trying to stifle it. My chest aches as I watch her crumble, just as I had, beneath the weight of Weston's declaration.

"So that's it then? This is forever?" she whispers.

Weston's jaw ticks, and he only nods.

Silence falls over us as her eyes dart away from Weston's face, settling somewhere on his vest. Her chest shakes with shuddering breaths as she tries to collect herself, to process how her greatest fear has now come true.

"Well," she says after a few moments. Her chin wavers, and her eyes fill with tears as her head turns and her eyes fall on me. "We tried."

A laugh mixed with a sob erupts from my chest as I nod at her. "We tried, Sig."

Her chin sinks into her chest as she begins to cry, and I can't stop myself, the pull of my hurting friend too much to overcome. I close the space between us and throw my arms around her and squeeze. She does the same, clutching me tightly, and we both let go, crying in each other's arms.

Sig helped me see the importance of getting back home. She made me realize how many life experiences I would miss if I didn't, and opened my eyes to the understanding that I wasn't ready to give those up. She helped me remember that living with a purpose and having experiences that only time can give you are more valuable than monotonously living forever.

After the island deemed me unworthy and denied me the healing waters, I decided in that moment to stay on Dawnlin forever. With my knowledge of their location, I thought I would help anyone who came to the island looking for the cure. It was a fate that felt like it gave me more than returning home would.

I had a purpose and a reason to be here. Day in and out, I would help the Guardian guide others to the waters, then send them back home.

But now, with this fate, I have no purpose.

None of us will ever return home, and no one seeking the waters will ever step foot on this island.

Our cries slow, my tears drying from the amount I've already cried tonight, and Sig lifts her head off my shoulder from where it had fallen in the throes of sadness. I release her, taking a step back as both of us swipe at our eyes and faces, hiccuping and sniveling.

"It'll be alright," she says. "We'll figure it out. Right, Cap?"

"We will," Weston says from beside me. He opens his arms for her, just as he had to me in the tunnel, and she steps forward, pulling him into a hug. She squeezes him once, fiercely, before backing away and curling into Jorn's chest.

Jorn reaches out and claps his hand on Weston's shoulder.

"Love you, brother," he says, and Weston mimics the gesture, squeezing Jorn's shoulder once silently, before both their arms fall away. Jorn looks at me and reaches out, mussing my hair quickly with a faint whisper of a smile on his lips. "At least you're here too, Little Lennox. We'll make it all count."

I shoot him a tearful smile as he wraps his arm around Sig and pulls her body into his, leading her across the deck and down the steps.

As I watch them walk away, I can't believe I ever questioned how they felt about me, how I ever wondered if our friendship was real, or if it was yet another one borne of my status. But now as I look at their backs retreating across the deck, after I've watched them cry tonight, knowing we will be each other's companions for eternity, any doubt I had disappears. They all care for me, just as much as I do for them, and we're in this together. Forever.

Once they disappear into the belly of the ship, I feel Weston move behind me, his hands weaving through my arms and settling across my hips. He rests his head on mine, and I can feel the prickle of his cheek pressed into my hair.

"That went better than I expected," he grumbles, but he can't hide the sadness in his voice.

I rest my hands on his forearms and feel his muscles ripple beneath my palms as he holds me tighter. "She knew it could happen. The dust running out, I mean. We thought we had more time. I don't think any of us were expecting it this soon after I left."

He lets out a deep sigh, and his fingers flex on my hips.

"Now to see what shit Mara tries to pull tomorrow." The sadness is gone, replaced by his firm tone, the captain already slipping back into assessing every threat.

"Do you think she'll try something?"

"Maybe. I've spent twenty years protecting the waters from anyone who hasn't found them, and I will not give up anything to her or anyone else just because we're stranded. If the island trusts them, that's a different story."

The waves crash around us, and a cool breeze picks up, causing the skin on my arms to prickle, but it isn't just the cold. It's also the nerves for tomorrow, the worry about everything going wrong once again, the fear that someone will get hurt.

"How will we know if it does?"

"We'll know. The island will make sure of it."

Dawnlin has its own unique way of communicating with us, whether it is one of the more dangerous forms, giving someone things they ask for, or literally locking a door. Back inside the mountain, it plainly said 'In the magic of Dawnlin you must trust.' Trusting the island has been difficult time and time again. Moving through all the challenges and struggles that arise without knowing what is the right path or why something is happening has been one of the most difficult parts of living here.

But more than trusting Dawnlin, how am I supposed to trust anyone back at camp? How can we know Mara wasn't part of Dane's plan all along, and that she isn't fooling us into feeling sorry for her? She hated me only days ago, and was trying to convince everyone to turn on me. Could she have absolved so much hatred toward me that quickly? Was Weston right to keep the tunnels hidden from her and Roley?

And most importantly, will tomorrow be the trap instead of tonight?

My stomach rolls as I think of all the possibilities and betrayals that can happen at the meeting tomorrow, and I don't know if I'll be able to let go of the dread. If this was an elaborate scheme to draw us out, to get us to let our guards down, and then attack so Dane could have access to the waters, Weston won't want to risk anyone else's safety to go with him. And if it was, why was Roley in on it?

Questions and worries cycle through my mind, and I can't hold them in any longer.

"I'm nervous about tomorrow. I'm worried it could be a trap."

"We'll be prepared. I don't trust her either," he says as he straightens and steps around me, taking my hand in his. "And if it is, well, I've had a long time to think about how I'd pay him back for this." His free hand brushes his abdomen, settling on his scar for a second before rising to my neck. His fingers wrap around the side and his thumb strokes my skin, the same way it did what feels like forever ago as he used the magic of the island to heal me. Eyes darkening as they fall to where his skin brushes mine, his voice lowers, the possessive grumble creeping into it and sending a shiver up my spine.

"And that was before he hurt you."

CHAPTER THREE

lames flicker in the sconces of the dim Captain's quarters as the latch of the door clicks behind us. The lanterns don't brighten as they usually do when we enter, and I'm grateful for the darkness. It feels fitting for tonight's events, and the shadow coated room matches the darkness I still don't know how I'm going to overcome. Each time I face another Castaway with the truth, the mending wound will tear open again and again.

I sneak a glance over my shoulder at Weston, but he's turned away, closing the door behind us. Twice tonight I've had the chance to let out the storm of emotions brewing inside of me, and I only could because he was there to let me. He was there to take away some of my burden, to let me feel everything and soothe the fragments of my guilt and fears, but he has shown nothing.

It feels like a lifetime ago now when I sat on the beach in the Oasis and watched Weston be strong for the entire crew in the wake of Jorn's drowning and subsequent revival. So much has happened since that day, not only on the island, but between us. I will never forget the clench of his jaw, the haunted look in his eye, and the stuttered answers he gave when I asked questions to comfort him. He stayed strong, hiding his own fear and hurt so no one else would worry, so that life could go on unchanged.

Back then I wondered who he had to lean on, or to help him when he needed it, but when I sat by his side on that beach and looked around, no one was there. It was only me.

The same as tonight.

The same as it now will be for all of eternity.

Lifting the bow and quiver over my head, I lean them against the wall behind the door before crossing to the desk. We came straight to the room instead of stopping at the armory, so my new vest is full of weapons that I pull out and drop onto the wood.

Weston steps beside me and silently follows suit, ridding himself of all the deadly blades he carried to protect us tonight. I unbuckle my belt last, and loop it over the chair just like his before turning to look at him.

The shadows on his cheekbones make it even more clear how much he's holding in, the tension almost palpable as my eyes trail over his clenched jaw. Gaze fixed on the desk, Weston unsheathes his last blade before dropping it with a clunk on the wooden surface. I reach out and take his hand, tugging gently and trying to pull his attention away from whatever is running through his mind.

His disheartened eyes rise to meet mine, and my chest squeezes. I have so little experience comforting anyone, but with my whole heart I want to help him. I *need* to help him. I won't be able to sleep knowing I did nothing to make him feel he isn't alone, that someone understands, just like he did for me.

Taking a step closer, I set my hand atop his. "What do you need?" I ask.

He shakes his head, but his eyes never leave mine. "I don't need anything, sweetheart."

Lifting my chin, I give him the same stern look he gave me back in the cave, the one that says I'm serious and he needs to listen.

"I don't believe you."

His throat bobs, but he says nothing. I don't accept his silence, not when I know it's how he keeps everything locked away beneath the surface.

"A long time ago, you told me that out there, you were the Captain, but in here, you were Weston. Just be Weston." I take another small step, closing the gap between us, and crane my neck back farther to hold his gaze. "You don't have to hide it from me. I know you're holding it all in, but you need someone to be there for you too. Someone to tell you everything will be alright."

The muscles in his jaw clench, and his assessing eyes move between mine. His fingers twitch between my palms, and I hope he's perceiving everything I'm trying to show him.

He doesn't have to hide from me, or stay strong in every moment. He can feel and be weak, just like he allows the rest of us to be. He can be unwell about our situation, even if it is only behind these doors, only with me.

"So tell me. What do you need?"

A heavy sigh escapes his chest as his eyelids flutter shut. He doesn't speak; he just moves, and presses his forehead to mine, our breaths mingling as I watch him try to keep hold of everything.

"You," he grumbles, and his eyelids rise slowly, as his focus bores into me. "I need you."

The breath catches in my throat as I lift my hand and set it on his chest, feeling the pounding of his heart beneath my fingertips.

"I'm right here."

In barely a blink, his hands find my face, tipping my head back as his lips crush mine. It isn't hurried or frenzied like it was before. Instead, he soaks up each movement, like he needs the caress just as much as I do.

I revel in the feel of his hands on my skin, hands that used to reach out even when I didn't want them anywhere near me. Since the moment I told him he could have me, that I didn't care about our titles back home, and that I only wanted him, he hasn't hesitated to touch me, to pull me in close, to make sure I was there and safe beside him. My body almost falters when the realization hits, and a deep sadness washes over me.

His touch. It's the way he shows he cares. The first time I came back from a shift, his hands were on me without hesitation, searching for any injuries, the same way they had in the infirmary. I noticed every time he was holding himself back, following my wishes after telling him to keep his hands off me, but he wanted to. My heart breaks as I think about what it meant for him to be unable to touch me or to have anyone that he could. Weston has been starved of physical connection for so many years. He clearly craves it, and I know it's exactly what he means when he says he needs me.

He needs to feel, to hold, to know he isn't alone, and I won't deprive him anymore.

With a gentle nudge, he walks me backward across the room, and my fingers grip the leather of his vest to steady myself. His lips never leave mine until his tongue parts my mouth, and his strokes deepen the kiss. He guides me through the room, and my breaths shorten as flutters low in my abdomen urge me to grip him tighter. The back of my legs hit the bed, and I break the kiss to look down at the laces of my vest and tug at the knots he tied so snugly earlier.

His hands wrap firmly around my wrists, lowering them gently away from the laces. My head snaps to his and tilts slightly, confusion written all over my face. Did I misread his intentions? His needs? His desires?

"No." He drops my arms to my sides, and I stare into his darkened eyes as he reaches for the vest, his fingers twirling around the ties. "I'll do it."

My heart pounds in my ears, the same beating rhythm mimicked between my thighs as he pulls the long cord slowly. His fingers weave through the crossed threads, and he tugs until they loosen in his hands. The dark leather falls to the ground, only to make my heaving breaths more obvious as his gaze sets fire to my skin. It's met with his fingertips a moment later, the spark of fire beginning to blaze along with flutters of anticipation between my thighs as he grips my shoulders. Rough calluses slide across my skin as his hands trail down before palming my breasts, and my nipples peak beneath them.

He's taking his time, and it takes all my focus to keep myself from reaching out, and hurrying him along, wanting to feel him beneath the fabric of my now stifling clothes.

My lip catches between my teeth when he reaches the waistband, his fingers working to bunch up the fabric. He tugs gently, fisting it in his hands and lifting, and I take the silent direction. I raise my arms over my head, and it's gone in a moment, followed by the sound of it hitting the ground somewhere across the room.

Weston's eyes won't meet mine, instead staying focused on his next task. They slide over my bare skin, and he moves faster, as if the sight of it has fueled his desire and increased his impatience. Thumbs hooked into the waistband of my pants, he tugs them down, leaving me in nothing but my undergarments and the prickle of goosebumps across my body.

His vest is untied and off, and buttons pop and bounce across the floor as he rips his shirt from his body, not caring at all about ruining it. He tosses it away with mine before I can even register how quickly he's moving. In the next moment he drops to his knees, lifting my feet one by one to pull off my boots and untangle the pants from around my ankles. Firm hands wrap around my hips, and he tugs me closer. I almost stumble when my body jerks forward, but he steadies me, and tucks his chin, pressing his forehead into the flesh of my stomach.

Thick, corded arms encircle me, and the muscles ripple as he squeezes tightly, pressing his face deeper into my abdomen. When his shoulders heave with a shuddering breath, I feel a pang in my chest.

Fuck it. I can't keep from touching him any longer.

My nails find his scalp, and I run my fingers through his hair, over and over again, massaging and soothing until he lets out a low groan and squeezes me even tighter. I slide my fingers down the sides of his face, and his beard prickles my palms as I tilt his head back so I can look into his eyes.

He rests his chin on my stomach and stares back at me. There are no tears, but the normally bright and challenging teal eyes that brought me to life are now filled with sorrow.

It's the first time I've seen him hopeless.

Even when he hovered above me, begging me to breathe, he didn't look as hopeless as he does in this moment. An ache courses through my body, and I feel like I could crumble under the weight of his pain, but I don't.

He's held strong for years. Now, he can let go, and I will be the strength he needs.

I trace my thumb over one of his eyebrows, smoothing away the bunched muscles and watching as they flatten. His eyelids fall closed in a slow blink before rising again, his gaze locked on mine. I push my hand into his hair, dragging it through the strands until my fingers slide down his cheek.

"I know," I murmur, offering him the same words of acceptance he offered me, giving him the same silent permission to let go.

His eyes darken as he lowers his chin, his stubble scraping down the skin of my abdomen, only to be soothed a moment later by the brush of his lips. Kisses pepper my stomach as he presses his face into me, weaving his way across my body, until he settles on the sensitive skin just below my hip. He presses a deep kiss there, sucking the skin gently into his mouth, and the throbbing between my thighs intensifies.

His arms unwind, and his hands meet at the top of the lace below his chin. A gasp rips from my throat as his shoulders flex, and the fabric tears through the center, falling to my feet and leaving me bare before him.

Frenzied fingertips press into my hips as his lips finally release me, only to guide me back to sit on the edge of the bed. Weston remains on his knees, walking on them toward me, his eyes trailing over my entire body before falling to my lap.

"Open up for me, beautiful." The growl of his voice breaks the silence in the room and makes my skin heat, but his words make my chest swell. His hands skate slowly up my calves, my thighs, then back down again, my skin tingling in his wake, before his palms settle on the inside of my knees. He slowly pushes my thighs apart, exposing every bare trace of me to him, and his focus is on me alone. I squirm under his gaze, the heat in his stare giving me an idea of everything he plans to do to me. As if he can't hold himself back any longer, his face falls to my core, his tongue starting its tantalizing assault, and I cry out at the explosion of pleasure that licks up my spine.

He growls against me at the sound, the vibration causing me to whimper as my fingers fist the bedding on either side of me. His tongue swirls through me, the speed increasing as he laps up my excitement.

"You taste…" A low growl rumbles again, and my head falls back, my eyes screwed shut as my legs shake beneath his palms. He lifts away, and my eyes fly open, staring down at him, wondering why he stopped, but I only find desire in his gaze. Stubble scrapes against the sensitive skin of my thigh as he nuzzles me with his chin and cheek before lowering his mouth just above me again.

His face darkens, and I get a glimmer of the Weston I saw back in the cabin, the one who threatened Dane, who put himself at risk to protect me. It makes my breath catch as he stares up at me, a predator who is claiming his prey.

"You taste like you're mine."

Something inside him snaps, and he lets go of whatever he was keeping leashed. His hands slide under my ass, dragging me to the edge of the bed. Pressing into me with a bruising grip, he tilts my hips up, giving him better access to my throbbing core before his lips and tongue find me again.

"Fuck, Weston," I gasp, and clutch onto his shoulders, the heat of his skin almost burning my palms. "I'm yours. I'm yours." The words come out breathy as my chest heaves and my toes curl. He is ravenous, coaxing the pleasure from me in wave after wave. Tears prick at my eyes as the throbbing between my thighs is met by the pressure and wet heat of his tongue.

I can barely handle the intensity of his strokes and what they are doing to my entire body. I need to feel him too, to get closer and ground myself to his skin. Sliding my hands down the back of his neck, I grip his muscular back, feeling the rippling tension as he moves and clutches my body. My nails dig into his skin when his tongue flickers over my most sensitive spot, and I cry out as my body convulses beneath him.

"This was supposed to be for you," I pant and bite my lip to stifle another cry.

"Trust me, sweetheart," he rumbles against me. "It is."

The world falls away when he sucks my clit into his mouth, flicking his tongue over it, and moving his hands to grip my thighs, spreading me wider for him. All I can feel is Weston, fingers digging into my muscles, face buried in my core. Pressure builds so quickly that I can't hold it back any longer, and my head falls back as I break apart. The muscles inside me flutter and clench repeatedly as I shudder and tremble beneath him, and I can't control the whimper that escapes at the overwhelming desire to have him inside me.

"Weston," I beg, and like he always knows exactly what I'm thinking, he heaves a deep sigh against me. With one final slow caress of his flattened tongue, he stands, his steady hands immediately finding the ties at his waistband. He loosens them, tugging and pulling quickly without ever taking his eyes off mine. Heavy pants rise in my chest, the pleasure he just enraptured me with still overwhelming my senses, but I feel the slick heat of excitement between my thighs again as I watch him undress himself.

My tongue runs over my bottom lip when the ties finally fall free, loose enough to allow the pants to drop to his ankles. His hard cock juts forward, pulling all my attention to it, and I understand why he said he was enjoying what he was doing as much as I was. But I meant what I said. I want him to have what he needs, and if that is me, I want to give it to him.

Without thinking or worrying, or focusing on my inexperience, I lean forward, letting my desires guide me, hoping to give him everything he just gave me. Reaching out, I wrap my fingers around his firm length, and gently drop to my knees before him.

"Lennox," he murmurs, and I feel the brush of his fingertips on my face, pushing my hair back and tilting my head so I'm looking up at him. "You don't have to."

"You don't want me to?" I ask, trying to keep the twinge of self-consciousness from creeping into my voice, but he huffs a low laugh and shakes his head.

"I didn't say that."

"Then let me."

He lets out a sigh as his other hand finds my face, and his thumb slowly caresses my bottom lip.

"My queen should not be on her knees for anyone. Especially not me."

I raise an eyebrow at him, the flooding feeling of a challenge overcoming any self-conscious thoughts I had mere moments ago.

"I made it clear that this was supposed to be for you, and as your queen, I dare you to stop me."

His pupils widen as our gazes stay locked together, and I lean forward, just enough so I can run my tongue along the tip of his cock. The hiss of a sharp intake of breath makes me swell with pride, and

I watch as he can't take it anymore. His head falls back, and his eyes screw shut as his chest rumbles with a deep groan.

"Fuck."

Just one word ignites a fire inside me, and I'm consumed by the desire to elicit more sounds like that.

Now I understand why every time I cry out, it urges him on.

Desire pools between my thighs now knowing what this does for him, so I lower my mouth further, taking the tip of him inside and sucking gently.

This groan is louder, and one hand lifts off my cheek and settles on the beam of the four-poster bed. He leans forward onto it, and I take him further into my mouth, licking and sucking, trying to imitate the motions he does to me. A flicker of worry that I'm not doing it right is squashed when his fingers weave through my hair, gently tugging and silently urging me to continue.

"Fuck, Lennox. I can't..." He grunts, and my eyes flick up to him, taking in the pleasure-filled expression on his face. "So good, sweetheart."

I moan in response, taking the encouragement and pulling him in deeper, sucking, licking and swirling, loving the way his body responds to my touch. His fingers clench again as I move back and forth, and I reach out to steady myself on his trembling thigh without slowing my movements or loosening my grip.

His breaths heave above me, but his hand is gentle, until it falls away and I feel him straighten.

"Enough," he says firmly, and I pull away, daring to glance up at him, my previous confidence wavering.

Until I see the heat in his stare.

Hands encircling my ribs, he lifts me to my feet, and his lips crash to mine in a searing kiss. His tongue invades my mouth, stroking and thrusting deep, and I moan into him, wrapping my arms around his neck and pulling him closer.

"I don't want to come in your mouth," he growls against my lips as he kicks his boots off and steps out of his pants, walking me backward. "I want you wrapped around me. I want to feel you gripping my cock when I'm buried inside you. Now."

He kisses me again, lifting me by my thighs and crawling forward onto the bed. The kiss doesn't break as he lowers me down, lining our hips and pressing his pelvis into mine. His broad shoulders and muscular arms envelop me, and his hot, bare skin sears me everywhere we touch. A palm finds my breast, kneading it hungrily as his tongue still invades my mouth, and my hips grind against his. His fingers move, wrapping over the lace and snapping it, the same as he did moments ago. My breasts barely fall from the garment before his mouth is on my nipple, pulling it into his mouth and sucking hard, making my entire body writhe.

Between my thighs is molten as his fingers slide through me, eliciting a grumble from his throat.

"So eager for me to be inside you, my queen," he says, and sucks my breast into his mouth harder.

"Yes," I cry, and grip the hair on the nape of his neck, mentally begging him to move faster. He releases my nipple and reaches between us, lining the tip of his length to my entrance, but he doesn't move, only wraps me up in his arms, the bulging muscles tightening and crushing me to him as if he too can't be close enough. Then with a flex of his hips, he slowly pushes inside.

"Gods," I moan into his lips, my eyes squeezing shut as the agonizing stretch drives me wild. The muscles in my core flutter, already clenching him with the anticipation of him filling me finally realized. His lips move to my jaw and down my neck as he rocks into me, pushing deeper with each tantalizing stroke. Hips grinding into mine, the rhythm sparks the pleasure, but keeps it at a constant hum that makes my body move against his, begging for more.

I know he needs this—the contact, the understanding, the control. I need it too. I need to know that despite everything that happened tonight, our life here will be the best it can be. I need to know that he is going to be alright, and that he knows I'm his.

Forever.

His mouth finds mine again as his hips continue their torturous rhythm. Tongue matching the deep thrusts of his cock, it's as if he just wants to relish this time, our connection, and only feel.

I let him.

Time passes as we lose ourselves in each other, without a thought of anything outside of the feel of our bodies moving together. I barely realize when he moves, rolling us to the side, and settling me on top so my legs straddle his body.

"Oh gods," I cry as my hips settle, deepening the press of his cock, the angle hitting something inside and eliciting a pleasure only he's ever brought out of me. My eyes screw shut and my jaw falls open as my hands reach out to his abdomen, clutching his tensing muscles as he stills beneath me.

"Open your eyes," he says, and they fly open, immediately finding his and seeing the fire still present. "I want to watch you as you come all over me." His hips buck into me, and my cry is closer to a scream as his cock sinks impossibly deeper.

Flattening my palms on his abdomen, I feel the rough scar brush against my skin as I look into his eyes. I can't hold back. My hips roll over his, rocking back and forth, feeling the slide of his length with each of my movements as my fingers dig into his muscles.

I watch him watch me; his jaw tight, his eyes hungry. His hands find my hips, and he moves me on top of him, lifting me and rocking me harder onto his cock, every movement growing more fevered than the last.

The pressure builds, and my jaw falls open, trying to contain it and let this last longer, for him and for me, but he's too attuned to my feelings. One hand slides from my hip, drifting between my thighs until his thumb finds my core, pressing into the spot that makes me shake.

Pleasure explodes through my body, the waves crashing through me with each rock of my hips and pressured circle of his thumb. A cry tears from my throat as the explosion wracks through me, and the muscles in my core clench and squeeze him, fueled even more by the look in his eye as he watches me fall. His pace hastens, the muscles in his abdomen tightening as he chases his own release, his grunts mixing with the sounds of our bodies moving together. With one final pulse, his body stiffens, his jaw slackens, and his pupils barely leave any color left in his eyes.

I fall forward onto him, gasping breaths heaving in my chest, as he presses kisses to my hair and my face. He rolls us again, his cock still settled deep inside, sending shockwaves of pleasure through me, and his arms wrap me in a crushing embrace.

His lips press into mine, the kiss full of all the emotion behind it. He pulls away, his chest still heaving with breaths as his forehead presses into mine.

"Thank you," he grumbles, before his head settles in the crook of my neck, his lips pressed into my skin as he holds me tightly.

I reach up and run my fingers through his hair, and feel his entire body relax over me, the weight of him grounding me.

"You don't have to thank me, Weston," I murmur and press a kiss into his hair when he sighs deeply. "I need you too."

CHAPTER FOUR

I wake to Weston's lips pressing into my temple and realize our bodies are no longer tangled together beneath the soft sheets.

"Go back to sleep, but come find me when you get up." His murmured words tickle my ear, and I manage a sleepy nod before I barely register that light has only just begun to shine through the windows.

I squirm into the space he occupied, curling into the warmth he left behind, and breathe in his scent. My limbs feel heavy and weak, brought on by more than just the emotional turmoil Dane left us with.

Weston barely moved last night, his breaths deep and his face relaxed after loosening the hold on his veil of unwavering strength. It's comforting knowing I could give him some kind of reprieve, even if it was only for a night, or only when we're shut in this room, alone. Already this morning, he's up before the suns rise, back to being the captain everyone needs.

I doze for a while longer until I feel like I have enough strength to crawl out of bed. Our meeting with Mara is in a few hours, and I don't want to miss it. I need to be alert and ready for anything, especially so we can figure out where we go from here. I won't sleep in and be left behind.

After dressing quickly, I fill my vest with all the blades I left on the desk, and secure my belt and dagger. The thought of this entire situation being a trap still lingers in the back of my mind, and I refuse to leave this ship unprepared. Today's meeting could be just as dangerous as last night, if not more.

Beneath the midday suns, there's no cover of darkness, no element of surprise. We should outnumber them if Mara actually follows Weston's orders, but if it is a trap, if Dane didn't actually leave, numbers might not matter. They'd be hiding, waiting for the moment we arrive. The Castaways are all older and stronger, bigger than most of the remaining Voyagers. More of us are trained; Weston and Sig make sure of that, but that doesn't account for Dane's desperation. The look in his eyes and the harsh severity of his words tell me he will stop at nothing to get what he wants, and that kind of action is dangerous.

I don't want to see anyone get hurt. No matter what, I have friends on both sides of all this. If someone is harmed, or worse, killed because of the lies Dane has been spewing for years, I don't know how I would live for eternity with the guilt knowing I started it all.

A crisp breeze ruffles my sleeves when I step out onto the deck. It's still early morning, and we have a few hours before we need to be out at the plateau. Taril is already off near the far rail mopping the deck, hard at work and wiping sweat from his brow while Stassia paces next to him, rambling about something. She throws her arms in the air every so often and stomps around him, tracking wet footprints over places he just mopped, but Taril doesn't waver. I can't make out her words, but she almost looks angry, and I wonder what set her off so early this morning.

Scanning the deck searching for Weston, my eyes snag on someone sitting on the quarterdeck, facing away from the ship. Trailing my gaze over his broad shoulders, the tense set of his back, and his rounded arms, there's no question at all that this is my captain, and I hurry across the deck to meet him like he asked me to.

When I crest the top of the stairs, I see he's alone, sitting quietly on a barrel and looking out toward the island. There's such a stark difference from last night, because right now, standing with my hip pressed into the railing, watching him, he actually looks peaceful. He doesn't turn, and I don't know if he heard me approach, or if he's too lost in whatever thoughts are troubling his mind as he surveys the place that in just a few hours we might be safe to return to. A place he's never really belonged. It wasn't safe for him. He was hunted, condemned, vilified, but now, all that might change.

My footfalls are quiet as I cross the quarterdeck and slide my arms around him, resting my hands on his chest and rising onto my toes so I can set my chin on his shoulder. He doesn't start, just subtly leans into me as I turn my head so my lips barely brush the curve of his ear.

"Do I still have to call you Captain in front of everyone?" I murmur, and he chuckles softly.

"I think we're a little past that, don't you?"

I shrug, my body sliding against his as I rest my cheek on his shoulder. "If we ever got back home, you'd have had to call me princess in front of anyone else. I feel like it's the same thing here."

"I still like calling you princess."

My lips fall into a frown, but I know he can't see it.

"I like when you call me Lennox."

Back when he first started using it, I thought it was only a nickname. He knew it wasn't, but without ever seeing the ring he never takes off, no one else could have known. Now, every time that word falls from his lips, all it does is remind me of why he erected sturdy walls between us. It reminds me of how he refused to tell me what he felt because of our titles. I know it has become almost meaningless now, because I won't ever be a princess again, but it still reminds me of how much space just that one word put between us, and how different our life here in Dawnlin could have been if he never got past it.

"I don't want to do anything that will cause an issue with the crew. No special treatment, remember?"

Strong fingers wrap firmly around my wrist and tug gently, guiding me around the barrel until he's pulling me onto his lap.

"I would say you already get special treatment." His voice lowers, but one corner of his lips tilts up in a smirk. "I didn't make anyone else in the crew come multiple times last night."

Cheeks heating and mouth open, my disbelieving laugh causes him to finally crack into a full grin.

"You know what I mean!" I say, shoving his shoulder, just as his laugh rings out over the quarterdeck. His grin turns devious, and he leans forward, closing the gap between us.

"Call me Weston," he grumbles against my lips, then presses our mouths together, the slow and teasing movements causing a flame to flicker to life inside me. After last night, after the past few days of being with him, able to touch him, my body's reaction to him is faster than I ever thought possible. He pulls away, and I inhale a deep breath, pushing down the desire to lean in again and instead focusing on his soft, content features.

"How did you sleep?"

"Fine, all things considered," I say. "You barely moved, so I assume you are well rested this morning."

He shifts me in his lap, wrapping his arm around my back so his hand rests on my hip.

"Honestly, it was the best sleep I've had in a long time. I don't know if it was exhaustion, or just the release from everything we'd been worried about for so long finally happening, but it was different."

Lifting my arm so it's no longer pinned between us, I settle it across his shoulders and toy with the seams of his vest, keeping my gaze focused on the task.

"Do you have nightmares often?" I sneak a glance at his face only to find his brows crinkled and his head slightly tilted.

"Not often. Why do you ask?"

My eyes dart back to the worn leather beneath my fingertips. "You were having one the night I left. It made it really hard to leave."

Bringing up leaving him and returning to the Voyagers is not something I like to do, but after seeing him sleep so soundly last night, I can't help but remember the pained look on his face that only smoothed away after the brush of my hand.

"How do you know I was having one?"

"You said something, and I thought you had caught me trying to sneak out of the room. When I turned around, your eyes were closed, and you looked like you were in pain."

"What did I say?"

"Don't leave." I pull my gaze back to him, watching, but he only looks back at me. His fingers flex on my hip, but his face stays emotionless, and my curiosity piques.

"I can see why you thought I caught you."

I huff a laugh. "I thought we were about to have the worst fight, even worse than when I first met you. I was prepared for you to rage at me."

"I did rage, you just weren't there to see it."

"Poor Sig," I say with a wince.

"Don't feel sorry for her. She knew what she was doing."

"It was for everyone. Including you, remember?"

"I know. But that doesn't mean I liked it."

"You should know a thing or two about doing what needs to be done to help everyone else." My fingers skate over the exposed skin on the back of his neck, and he leans into the touch ever so slightly.

"Right. I don't want you to have to do it."

A comfortable quiet falls between us, and his face relaxes as I slowly stroke his neck, and graze my fingers through the hair at his nape. I want to gather the courage to ask what I was really wondering, but part of me worries we aren't at the point where he would reveal that information to me. Sucking in a quick breath, I look away again, and let the question spill from my mouth.

"What were you dreaming about?"

A moment passes before he answers, and my chest swells knowing I was wrong, that he trusts me enough to know something that could make him seem vulnerable.

"I only ever have one nightmare. Clearly I don't remember every time I have it, because I didn't know you were aware, so I don't know how often it comes back. I don't make it a habit of sleeping beside anyone else, so there has been no one to tell me I talk in my sleep."

"What happens?" I ask.

The lump in his throat bobs with a harsh swallow, and his other hand settles on my thigh. His thumb moves in leisurely strokes, and I wonder if he's ever actually told anyone about the dream before.

"Remember when I told you I lost my mother when I was young?"

I nod, but stay quiet. I don't want him to stop talking now that he's started. I want to hear his story, to know more about his past and what made him the man he is, even the difficult times.

"She was sick, getting worse each day. One night, she took a steep turn. It was the worst she had ever been, and the healers had no more answers. My father had been by her side during every moment he was home, but on this night, he had to leave. He said he needed to travel to another kingdom for his work. I was young, and scared of losing my mother, and I didn't want him to leave."

He clears his throat and looks down at where his hand rests on my thigh.

"She died the next day," he murmurs. "And he was gone. He returned the day after, devastated he wasn't able to say goodbye. They were…" He trails off, as his head lifts, and he looks out over the ship, no doubt remembering his parents from so long ago. A soft smile graces his lips. "They were everything. They taught me what love was supposed to look like, and to see my father after she died…It makes me feel more guilty leaving him alone for the rest of his life."

I place my hand on top of his and twine our fingers together, squeezing them tightly. "It must have been a great thing to have witnessed."

"It was," he says with a soft nod. "Anyway, the dream is just reliving that night. The night he left and the night she died."

"I'm sorry," I say gently. "I can imagine that was really hard as a child."

His eyes meet mine again, and there's a hint of sadness despite the remnants of the memory-filled smile. "You shouldn't have to imagine. You know exactly what it is like."

I shake my head. "It isn't the same, at least I don't think it is. I never got to know her like you knew your mother. Instead, I had to mourn what I never had, and accept that I never would. I um…"

My voice trails off as I swallow down the lump forming in my throat. I haven't thought about the journal Edmond gave me in a while. Hearing Weston recount his nightmares of his mother's passing and the love he watched extinguish between his parents brings up a wave of memories of the entries tucked away between the leather covers. Now that healing my mother is impossible, the loss and grief are like a reopened wound, the pain even more than the first time I opened the worn leather cover.

It's my turn to clear my throat as I push through the pain to continue.

"Before I left, I came across an old journal. She wrote it when she was pregnant. Every entry was addressed to me. It brought up a lot of repressed feelings, especially after the healers were telling my father that it was time to let her go. I wasn't ready. It's actually the reason I started looking for Dawnlin. I tried to find other answers, but when I couldn't, I didn't want to give up hope. So I came here."

"I didn't know she did that," he murmurs. "I don't think Rem knew either."

A tear falls down my cheek, and I swipe it away quickly. "Maybe he didn't while she wrote it, but he knew about it after. He hid it from me. I didn't even know it existed."

His jaw tightens as he shakes his head. "I don't know what the fuck got into him after I left."

I consider it for a moment. If Weston remembers my father so differently, why did he change? Was it simply losing my mother? Was their love truly that strong? The father I know doesn't seem capable of a love like I fantasized about for years, or like Weston describes was between his parents. So what changed?

"I can imagine," I say, then pause, trying to swallow down the feelings of inadequacy that are threatening to bubble to the surface. "Maybe losing your wife and your best friend would be hard, and maybe that is why he changed so much. What I can't understand is that he may have lost a great deal, but he had me. Why wasn't I enough?"

My voice wavers with the question, and I barely have time to react before Weston's fingers wrap around my chin, pressing firmly and turning my face so I am forced to meet his gaze.

"Listen to me," he says firmly, his voice the low grumble that normally makes my stomach flutter, but this time I'm too wrapped up in years worth of hurt to feel it. "You *are* enough."

A half-hearted huff escapes me, and before I can speak he's turning my body in his lap, shifting me so I'm straddling him. His face is stern, and there's an edge to his voice when he speaks again.

"I'm tired of you talking down to yourself like that."

"I didn't say anyth—"

"I know you, Lennox. You were thinking it. The way his neglect affected you, and how the years of terrible decisions and isolation made you feel is inexcusable. He's going to have to live with how he hurt you for the rest of his life. A father should never do that to his daughter. I hope the man I knew is still in there somewhere and can see what he's done, and maybe because you never returned home, it will help him grasp the severity of it. But if he couldn't see what I see, what all the members of this crew saw when you became one of us, then he's a fucking fool."

My body feels like it is caving in on itself, and with every word I want to shrink away farther. For years I've wanted my father to see me, to think I was worth his time, his love. That I was fit to be queen. I'm used to being ignored, never praised, and for someone like Weston to say such things, to actually *see* me, my mind can't handle the way my body physically reacts to the words.

My eyes fall to his chin as I try to fight the war of emotions and feelings of inadequacy that always seem to overcome any desire and determination I have to prove myself, but he doesn't let me shy away.

"Eyes on me, Lennox."

I raise them slowly, and his stern face from moments ago has disappeared, replaced instead with an intense focus filled with kindness and understanding. Weston knows the basics of my relationship with my father, and while he may not have witnessed it, he knows how hard all of this is for me to hear.

He waits a moment, making sure he has my attention and I will not shy away again before speaking. His tone is warm and slow, letting me soak up each statement like the sunlight on my skin.

"You are smart. Methodical. Determined. You pay attention and learn so quickly, and you adjust to everything around you. You have listened to every person on this island, so much so that they know you care for them, and you know it too. Enough that you would physically sacrifice yourself for them, people you barely knew, at least in the scheme of all of us being here."

Tears well in my eyes as I stare into his, as all of his endearments tear me down and build me back up again a little stronger. I wish I had back in Blackwood, like the strength I only truly felt I had once I decided to leave.

Eyes bouncing between mine, he notes the tears, and his thumb gently strokes my skin, but he continues on.

"You put the feelings and wellbeing of others above your own, and do everything possible to make them feel encouraged and supported. You've taught them skills that you had, even if they had nothing to offer you in return."

A wet chuckle escapes my lips as I think about Fin and Roley grappling with the bows that are too big for them, the way their faces light up when they hit a target.

He catches my attention when he rolls his eyes obnoxiously and lets out a gruff breath.

"You're loyal, almost to a fucking fault because it took way too much effort to pull you out of his clutches, but now that you know the truth, I know that loyalty is just as strong for all of us." He lowers his voice, and a tear falls silently down my cheek. "If Remington can't see all of that, then *he's* the one who isn't enough. If who you are doesn't convince him you would be the best queen Blackwood has ever seen, then I don't know what does." The corner of his lips turns up in a smirk as his hands fall from my face to rest back on the tops of my thighs. "Plus, Jorn says you're the only one who can put up with my shit, and he's right."

A half sob, half laugh erupts from my chest, and I reach up to wipe the tears off my cheeks and take in his relaxed energy. It's almost as if he's waiting for me to argue, to tell him he's wrong, but I'm too stunned by everything he said, and the vortex of affection toward him it stirred inside me to do anything more than contradict his last statement.

"Sig can too," I sniff, "arguably she does better than me. You don't even have to say anything, and you understand each other. I just yell at you."

He shakes his head with a smile. "It's not the same. Sig had twenty years to get used to me. She watched me almost die. Our friendship was built on survival and a common purpose. You challenged me and refused to let me control you, even though I was the one in charge. You fought me, and called me out when I was being overbearing, even if I had reasons. It only took you about ten seconds of knowing me before you started fighting me."

"I see your point."

"You had my attention from the very beginning, anyway."

"Because I'm the princess," I say, a sinking feeling in the pit of my stomach reminding me why Weston even cared about me in the first place, why he followed me and protected me.

"You are, yes." He leans in a little closer, our faces drawing together until we're sharing a breath. "But you're also the most stunning woman I have ever laid eyes on, and the more I got to know you, the more I understood that beauty goes much deeper than you believe."

The pit that was there a moment ago flickers, the flame matching the one in his eyes.

"I don't know how you saw all of that," I say.

His lips turn up at the corners. "I watched you for a long time, remember? I didn't have to speak to you to see all of those things." He brushes a piece of my hair off my forehead, tucking it behind my ear. "You can't hide from me."

"You know," I say, clearing my throat and blinking away the rest of the moisture in my eyelashes. "If someone were following me around like that, watching my every move, my guard would have taken them out."

"Well, it's a good thing I'm your guard then." He leans in, his lips barely touching mine, before I pull back and drop my chin to my chest.

"There's nothing for you to guard me against anymore. Dane is gone, and I'll never be queen. My father will have to find a new heir when I never return."

He slides his hands up my back, stroking me softly.

"You'll always be my queen."

I let out a shuddering breath, and look up at him, finding only acceptance and affection in his eyes.

"There was something else you said." My voice trails off, and his brows dip in curiosity. "You know what? Never mind. I don't even want to ask." I try to retreat and slide off his lap, cursing myself and my overthinking mind as the question that dug its claws in fuels my embarrassment.

His hands clamp down on my thighs as I try to lift one over him, and he only pulls me closer, a devious grin twisting his mouth.

"You're not going anywhere until you tell me. Captain's orders."

I roll my eyes before they fall back onto his smug face. Biting my lip, I try to find the right words that won't make me sound naïve, or jealous, or inexperienced. Right now, deep down, I'm feeling every single one of those things, and nothing like the confident person he described moments ago.

His eyes fall down to my lip, and darken, before roaming over my face again.

"Tell me."

Weston has a habit of embarrassing me on this deck, and I refuse to let him see it this time. Setting my jaw and straightening my spine, I look him in the eye and speak as matter-of-factly as I can, just like the years of practicing with Edmond for the future court meetings.

"You said you didn't know you talked in your sleep because there had been no one to tell you. If that's true, how are you so good at what you do?"

I cringe inwardly the moment the words leave my mouth. My cheeks are probably inflamed, but I keep my face stoic, a task that grows increasingly difficult when his lips twitch, trying to hide a smile.

"I'm good at what I do, huh?" His eyes sparkle with humor, because I know he sees right through my falsely hardened exterior. He sees the same girl who was embarrassed as she read a love scene in front of him. He's licked or kissed or touched every surface of my body, yet talking about it is making me feel like I want to crawl into a hole and die.

"See, this is why I didn't want to ask." I push his chest and try to slide down his thighs, but he wraps his arms tightly around my hips, keeping me in place.

"You're cute when you try to hide it," he says, his smile finally breaking through the firm hold he had on it. "But you don't have to be ashamed with me.

I stare at his amused face, waiting for an explanation, and he doesn't make me suffer long before continuing as if there truly is no reason to feel uncomfortable.

"There were…other women, from before. You can attribute my skill set to them. But there were only a few, and all of them knew nothing would come of anything physical between us. You're the first woman I've ever wanted to sleep in my bed."

"So you just kick them out?" I gasp, a look of shock clearly written all over my face. I ignore the stirring in my abdomen that declaration gives me.

His head falls back as a hearty laugh rings across the quarterdeck.

"No, sweetheart, I didn't kick them out. My experience with each of them was usually only ever out of pent-up need, or if a woman had her sights set on fucking the First Guard. I wanted nothing from any of them beyond friendship."

"Did women try that often?" I ask. I can imagine if things were different, and Weston were the young, handsome First Guard in charge of running the kingdom's defense, he would catch the eye of all the eligible ladies in the kingdom. I ignore the spike of jealousy in me, knowing the same thing would probably happen again if we returned to Blackwood, and he took his place back behind my father.

"Honestly, more often than I liked. But I didn't fuck every woman who tried. Besides." His smile widens, and he leans forward slightly, dropping his voice lower. "I didn't have Tila's books to learn from."

I throw my head back with a groan. "I thought you would forget about that."

"Not a chance. And now I know why you were so flustered reading when I was taking my clothes off to bathe."

"You came in at the absolute worst time! I thought I was going to die of embarrassment. And then you started taking your clothes off, and—" I huff a breath, and he chuckles as his hands roam over the fabric of my pants, tracing patterns over my thighs.

"There's nothing to be embarrassed about. It was better that I didn't have to explain."

"Does it bother you that there's only been you?" I ask.

He tilts his head and presses a kiss to the side of my neck, his lips moving up the column as he speaks the words between kisses onto my skin.

"Does it bother me that only my cock has been inside you? That my tongue is the only one that's ever made you scream? That I'm the only one that's ever gotten to watch you come apart, and that I'm the only man that ever will?"

I squirm as memories of each of those things flash before my eyes, and my body heats, shuddering as his lips press a kiss into the corner of my jaw. They drag over my skin, and his breath tickles, sending shivers coursing through me.

"No, Lennox. It doesn't fucking bother me at all."

"Does it bother you I slept next to Dane?" I ask, breathless.

"No, it doesn't. I assumed you had, but I didn't know for sure."

"Only once. The night you took Fin."

"Ah," he says with a nod. "You don't hold any blame for how he manipulated you. None of that was your fault, nor was anything you did while under that coercion."

My chest swells, even though I knew he didn't look at me any differently because of how I had acted before. He's never seen the Dane-influenced version as my true self, but it doesn't hurt to actually hear him say it.

"I got nightmares around him," I admit, twining my fingers

together. "I never had them back home, but once I was here, after I almost fell through the bridge on my first real day, I had them every night. It was almost like..."

"Almost like what?"

I had thought little about the nightmares since they stopped, but now with all this talk about the past, especially after everything that happened, the memories are vivid, and something about them becomes even clearer.

"Almost like the magic was telling me not to trust him. A lot of them were about him attacking me."

A low grumble vibrates in his chest. "You had them in the brig."

I nod. "The day you came in was the last one I had until I was back at camp. They went away the first night I slept next to you, like deep down I knew you would keep me safe."

His shoulders sag, seemingly in relief.

"I told you," he says as his hands wind under my ass, squeezing the muscle there and making my stomach clench. "You belong in my bed."

CHAPTER FIVE

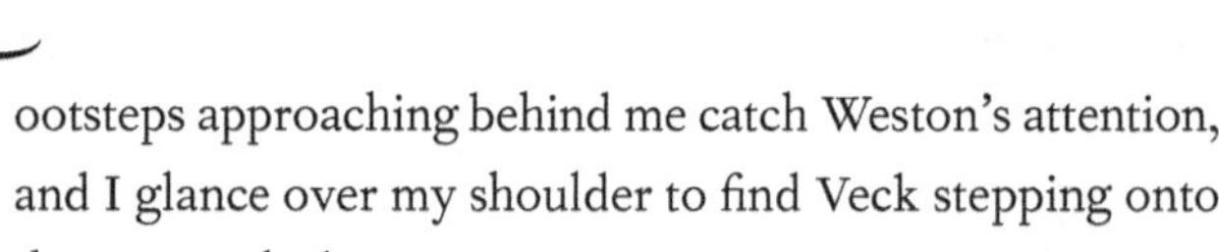

ootsteps approaching behind me catch Weston's attention, and I glance over my shoulder to find Veck stepping onto the quarterdeck.

"You wanted to see me, Captain?"

Weston nods, then looks down, eyes sliding over the weapons sheathed in my vest and his fingers flex on my thighs.

"Be ready. I'll be busy for a little while longer until we leave," he grumbles.

"Come find me when you're ready," I say, leaning forward and pressing a kiss into his cheek, my lips barely brushing the corner of his, then pat his chest twice. "Be the captain."

His chest rumbles, and I smile sweetly, sliding away from him until I can lift my leg over his and hop off the barrel. Sending Veck a quick wave, I shuffle down the steps back to the main deck and spot Stassia, still pacing wildly.

Very few of the crew are on deck, and Stassia is the only one who looks agitated. I glance around, looking for Sig, hoping she can enlighten me before I walk into a Stassia tirade, but there's no sign of her. Sig would never miss the collection crew meetup with Mara, but after breaking the news to her last night and all the change that comes with it, I can imagine she wants some time to herself.

My approach does nothing to slow Stass. It's as if she doesn't even see me until I lean against the rail, watching her boots tread soapy prints through everything Taril continues to mop.

"What's wrong, Stass?" I try to sound normal, but even I can hear the wary undertone to my question. She looks coiled and ready to strike at any moment, but does a double take when she finally notices me standing there.

"That fucking asshole!" she shrieks. Her hands stay planted on her hips as her steps pound into the wood beneath her. Taril looks over at me with what looks like sadness or disappointment in his eyes, and I glance between them, trying to figure out if it is Taril she's talking about, or someone else. I know Stass is direct, but if it was Taril that made her upset this early in the morning, would she really be pacing in front of him, calling him names?

Despite being completely unprepared and far too tired to be berated by one of Stassia's rants after such a late and emotional night, I set my shoulders and brace myself to ask.

"Who's a fucking asshole, Stass?"

Waves of fury ripple off her as she yells across the quiet deck, and I am surprised I didn't hear her before.

"Dane! That piece of shit just left us all here! He used it all, and just took off! Isn't he the one who is supposed to be guarding the island? But he just abandoned it! Abandoned us! Why the fuck did the island let him do it?"

My jaw slackens, and I grip the rail tightly, trying to squeeze out the uncomfortable feeling squirming inside me. How did she find out?

Stass can be unpredictable, but after the night on deck when Weston told everyone that the dust was running out, she was more…sad. This is a level of absolutely pissed that I've never seen on Stassia, and now I know why.

Taril's focus remains on the deck and dragging the wet mop over the wood. I watch him for a moment before looking back up at the quarterdeck. Veck still stands before Weston, looking just as serious as Stass does. With one arm crossed over his chest and the other holding his resting chin, he listens as Weston speaks soundlessly in the distance.

"How did you find out?" I ask. Stass spins on her heel and continues her pace toward me.

"Captain's been meeting with each of us individually since first light. He started with the collection crew, for obvious reasons." Her voice is calmer than a moment ago, but I can still sense she's holding it all back. "He wanted to be the one to tell us, so he's having us send the next person up once he answers every question we have."

My chest squeezes as I look back toward Weston to find the mask of the strong, unbothered Captain firmly back in place, shielding his crew and taking the brunt of the damage as he always does. He wants to give them the news gently and wants it to come directly from him.

I swallow hard and turn back to Stassia.

"For whatever it's worth, I'm sorry," I say, my voice breaking as I try to get the apology out. "If I hadn't tried to steal it, he might still be here."

She points a finger at me, wagging it back and forth. "You didn't force him to use it, Lennox. He did that on his own. Don't think this was your fault." She drops her hand and lets out an angry groan. "Guardian my ass!"

Last night, Weston assured me that no one in the crew would blame me for Dane's abandonment. While I heard what he said, the guilt still eats at me, and hearing Stassia fall in line with Weston's expectation despite her clear and potent fury, I have hope for everyone else.

"I swear to the gods," she grunts, "If this was all a trap and the Voyagers think they're going to get the upper hand in this meeting, they better be prepared to go to that clearing in camp, because we have nothing to lose anymore."

She's right. We have nothing to lose anymore. Dane took away our future, our hope, our purpose. But everyone who remains here is still people we know, we care about. They're our friends, all of whom are being manipulated by Dane. I don't want to hurt any of them. I want to help them see the truth.

A weight drops in my stomach as I remember wanting to fight them all on the beach the day they took me captive. I wanted to rage against Sig, and beg her to explain how someone who showed me such kindness could choose to help the enemy.

But now I understand exactly how Weston and Sig felt, exactly why they put themselves in danger to seize anyone who found the waters. They kept the new Castaways on this ship and helped them see the truth. All they wanted was for everyone to understand. Surely now, if we tell them what Dane has done and said to get what he wanted, they wouldn't hurt us.

"It's not their fault either, Stass. Dane's the one that should be punished."

"And Mara for going along with everything. She tried to kill you, Lennox! Don't even get me started on Storm trying to hunt every single one of us. Why? What did he want?"

I let out a sigh. "I don't know, and I can't figure Mara out, either. Last night, she looked...broken. Her face when she held out the empty pouch is the only thing giving me hope it isn't a trap. It doesn't change the way she attacked me and tried to kill Sig, but I don't want to give up on her. Not yet."

"Captain doesn't trust her."

"Weston doesn't trust anyone," I say. "Not when it comes to all of us."

"Ugh, I just want to get this over with," she says, turning on her heel again. "I don't know how we're going to work everything out."

"We'll figure out a way. It might take time."

She huffs a laugh. "We've got plenty of that."

If everything is as Mara says, and we can start to mend the relationships between the Voyagers and the Castaways today, would it actually take a long time? Would they truly believe what we have to say about Dane? Or would the same sort of war continue between us, keeping us isolated on the ship for fear of their retaliation?

I'm not able to think about it for long before tiny footsteps pound to my side. Fin sprints up the stairs and flies out onto the deck, spotting me immediately and running over with a wave.

"Hi Lennox!" he says with a cheerful smile. "You're up early today. What are you doing?"

Stassia's lips purse as she continues to pace, turning her face away from Fin so he hopefully won't notice how angry she is.

"Just talking with Stass. Why?"

"Do you want to climb with me? Please, please, please?" he begs, puffing out his bottom lip and letting his face droop.

I glance around the deck and back up to Weston, who now has Fern on deck with him. I don't want to miss the call for the collection crew, but keeping Fin occupied and away from everyone as they receive the news might be the best thing until we can officially tell him. Weston knows I am going to the meeting, and he won't leave without me.

"Sure," I say, "but not too high."

Jorn's lessons come back to me as we scramble up the mainmast and I follow Fin through the ropes and beams. Just as we reach halfway to the top, we stop and sit, looking out over the view, and Fin's chattering starts. He tells story after story, and I listen, trying to stifle my giggles at his enthusiasm and childish charm, and trying to determine what is embellished in the mind of a six-year-old, or what is actually true.

His mind runs wild, but when he finally gets bored with stories, we play games, spying things on the island and having staring contests. Anything to pass the time and keep him busy while I wait for the call from below.

A familiar low voice breaks our concentration, and I grip the beam beneath us as Fin looks around for its owner.

"Having fun up here?" Weston says as he pulls himself up onto the beam below us. My breath catches in my throat as he hops to his feet and walks across it without holding onto any ropes or hooks. I almost call out, begging him to be careful, but the way he moves with confidence and finesse makes me fall silent, reminding me he has lived on this ship for much longer than either Fin or myself. Scaling the mast and crossing these beams is probably second nature for him.

"Lot's of fun, mister Weston! Do you want to play a game, too?"

Weston looks at me before gripping the wood between Fin and I.

"Actually, Fin, I need to talk to you about something." The muscle in his jaw tightens, but his eyes soften as he looks up into the boy's face.

Fin waits eagerly, with no idea that the news Weston has to deliver isn't exciting, and I wonder if he will ever truly understand the weight of it all. Weston doesn't make him wait long.

"Do you remember when I told everyone the dust was almost gone? That we didn't know if we could get more?"

Fin's smile falters slightly, but he nods. "Uh-huh."

"Well, we found out that it is all gone, so we all have to stay here now. Together."

"Oh." Fin's voice drops along with the corners of his mouth as his brow furrows. "So I can't see my sister or my mom or my dad again? For real this time?"

Weston nods solemnly. "Yes. For real this time."

"That makes me sad," Fin murmurs, and my eyes snag on his chest as he takes in a shuddering breath.

"I thought it might," Weston says, and nods down toward the deck below. "But you have a big family here. Everyone cares about you, and we're not going anywhere."

Fin's eyes sparkle with the hint of tears, but he looks at Weston hopefully. "Are you going to be like my dad?"

Weston's throat bobs, but he doesn't look away from Fin. Tears prick at my own eyes and I blink them away, trying not to think about the lost vision we all had for our lives.

"How about more like a big brother?" he says, and my chest aches.

Fin looks at me, then back to Weston, and his nose scrunches. "But you're old."

Weston's laugh rings out around us, flowing on the wind, and I can't help but giggle with him.

"I'm not that old," he says with one of his rare, genuine smiles. Fin returns it.

"You're more like a dad old," Fin says, then turns to me. "Lennox, are you going to be my family, too?"

My chin quivers as I fight the quickly returning tears in my eyes. "Always, Fin."

This family may not be the one that any of us envisioned. Hell, who could envision meeting a group of strangers on a magical island and think you'd be willing to lay your life down for theirs? But it is who we have, for all of eternity. Even though it isn't the life that we pictured, that doesn't mean it isn't good.

He nods, his shoulders still slumped slightly. "I'm still sad, but I'm happy about you."

"We are too, kid," Weston says and pats his leg. "I also think Roley might come around soon."

Fin perks up at the news, his tiny body squirming on the dangerously high beam.

"Really? Can we play on the ship? Or maybe at camp? Can he have a bow too?"

Weston chuckles softly and taps the bottom of Fin's foot. "We'll figure all that out soon, alright?"

"Sure, mister Weston," he says, and there's a little brightness back in his voice.

"Let's head back down," Weston says, then his eyes find mine. "It's time to go."

CHAPTER SIX

ost of the collection crew stands already assembled and waiting on deck when the three of us descend the mainmast. Fin scurries to the steps, darting past Sig and Jorn, who step onto the wooden boards a moment later. Sig's stoic expression defines the entire tone of this afternoon, and I know she's prepared for whatever we are about to face.

Weston follows closely behind as I descend the stairs, and walk down the hallway to our room. I shoulder my full quiver and loop the bow over my torso, and Weston's sword sings as it slides into his scabbard. He finishes loading his vest with everything remaining on the desk, but when he turns back toward the door, I slide in front so he can't open it.

"As much as I would love to pin you up against that door, we don't have time for that right now, princess."

Use of the nickname prompts an involuntary glare that only causes him to smirk back at me. I raise an eyebrow and cross my arms over my chest.

"What is the plan for this meeting? We didn't discuss it last night or this morning. We have no strategy or contingencies. The First Guard should know it isn't smart to walk into something like this without a plan, especially if it's a trap."

He matches my stance, crossing his own arms over his chest, and glares back as if I insulted him by questioning his tactics.

"The collection crew knows how we handle these situations. Remember, we have been doing this a lot longer than you have."

"Not like this. Pulling someone off the beach isn't the same as negotiating the rest of our time here. Not to mention if Dane is actually there, and last night was a lie."

"Even if they show up with more than the two that Mara agreed to, our numbers and skills outmatch anyone left in the Voyagers. Dane, Storm, Mara. Sig could probably take all three of them by herself."

"So we're just going to fight them?" I say, throwing my hands up, but he doesn't move.

"Not unless they attack us first. That's always been the order."

"And what if it is a trap? What if telling us the dust is gone was just a ploy to get us to let our guards down?"

One corner of his lips turns up. "I'm glad to hear you're finally listening to me."

Rolling my eyes, I cross my arms again. "I'm being serious. If Dane wants only me, then that's my decision to make. I won't put the entire crew at risk just to protect me. Refusing to sacrifice one person for everyone else is absurd. It's not what a queen would do."

His face darkens as I speak, but I hold my ground, not letting my resolve waver for fear of pissing him off by being willing to protect my crew.

He takes a slow step forward, closing the distance between us. "I think you're forgetting one very important thing."

The space is gone in the next instant as his hands clamp onto my ass. He lifts me quickly, and my hands grip onto the firm muscles of his arms for support. My back presses into the door as he steps between my thighs, pinning me there with the strength of his body. He looks down his nose at me, and my chest heaves as I stare up at him, waiting for whatever has been brewing in his mind.

"My entire purpose is to stand between you and anyone who even dares try to harm you." The low gravel of his voice makes my stomach twirl, and my lips part when his eyes trace my face, landing on them.

"No one is going to touch you. As long as I am breathing, I will fight to keep you safe, and that includes you sacrificing yourself." His eyes flicker back up from my lips, and his teal pools land on mine, the severity in his gaze obvious as he lowers his voice even further. "Don't even fucking think about it."

"You still didn't answer my question." The words are breathy as I try to slow the heaving of my chest. "We can't kill Dane, so what is the plan?"

"If they attack us," he says, his tone much calmer than a moment ago, "there will be enough of us to get everyone contained and throw them all in the brig. We can discuss it and decide what to do after that. If they don't, and this isn't a hoax, then we give them our terms, and figure out if we can truly trust them. If we can, then everyone has a choice. Here or there."

"What if it's not that simple? After all this time and all the deception, do you really think it's going to be as easy as we just coexist?"

"We don't really have a choice. There's nowhere else to go. It has to be that simple."

Simple. My life has never been simple. Lonely, yes. Dull, absolutely. But simple? I thought this journey to Dawnlin would be simple, but it has never been, not from the moment I discovered that the man I had been trusting was lying to my face, and continued to do so every day after that. How can a life here that has been complex and twisted and built on magic and lies become simple?

Maybe Weston is right. Maybe now that our hope is gone, there's no other option but for it to become simple to change.

I nod, and our noses brush, but my eyes stay locked on his. "Let's go figure it out then."

His eyes fall to my mouth again, and it parts in anticipation as he leans forward. A barely there brush of his lips against mine makes my breath catch and heart race. Before I can chase after him, begging for more than such a simple touch, he pulls away. Mouth twisted into a knowing smile, he loosens his hold and lets the front of my body slide slowly down his, until my feet hit the floorboards, and I waver with the rush of the blood pounding through me.

Reaching around, he grabs the handle and turns, pulling the door open and gesturing down the hallway.

"After you."

"Asshole," I mutter. He chuckles softly as I turn on my heel, trying to ignore the desire coursing through my body. I stride down the hallway, feeling his presence behind me as always, which does nothing to tamp down the way I wanted him to do more than barely kiss me, leaving me flustered and distracted.

My boots pound on the steps and as I emerge onto deck, but when my eyes fall on the Castaways with their serious faces and bodies covered in weapons, everything we're about to do comes rushing back to me. All my nerves and worry that had been plaguing me since last night are gone, even if only for a few minutes.

He was trying *to distract me.*

I glance over my shoulder, but he's already put his Captain facade back on, and his long strides take him past me quickly to the front of the group, where Sig already waits near the gangway.

The energy in the collection crew is different from the last time we went to the beach, and even more different from when we left for the Oasis. Back then, we left the ship during daylight hours, and we are again today.

But this time, everyone knows why, and it isn't to relax and let loose.

"Listen up," Weston calls out, and the rumble of voices around me quiets. "We're meeting the Voyagers at the plateau. Surround the area but stay concealed while we wait for them to arrive. It should only be Mara and one other, but be prepared for anything. It's different this time. We don't have the night to protect us, so stay alert in case it is a trap. But remember, if he's there, no one touches Dane. He's mine."

The rumble in his voice with those final two words sends a shiver up my spine. Weston promised me he wouldn't kill Dane, but the vengeful look in his eye makes me feel that if that moment comes, I might need to remind him.

Or stop him. Again.

"Let's move." The gangway rumbles out behind him, and he steps to the side, letting Sig and Jorn lead the group down to the reef. The way he falls into step behind me has now become too familiar, but this time he's so close, I'm worried he is going to trip on my boots.

Still air settles around us, thick with anticipation that disappears the moment we're in the safety of the tunnels. We move swiftly, winding through the darkness toward the plateau, and my heart races the closer we get. The roar of the river overhead signals that we're close, and with it comes a flood of my nerves.

Despite all my animosity toward him for following me around like a guard, it is comforting knowing Weston is within reach in the face of all the uncertainty. I finally have someone who is by my side because they want to be, not because they are hired to be.

Reaching my arm back, I brush my fingers against his. When he hooks a finger around one of mine, and squeezes tightly before dropping it again, I'm able to breathe deep. I'm not going into this situation alone, not like last time. I won't be trapped away from the crew with Dane, with no one knowing where I am. I have them, and they have me.

Sig halts just before the exit, the same one we used when I returned to camp, and the crew stops, waiting as Weston weaves his way through until he's in the front beside her. He doles out groups and indicates where each is to hide themselves while we wait for the meeting time to arrive. He looks through the portal, scanning the area before waving us forward.

A small wave of relief washes over me that there wasn't an obvious threat. Maybe it isn't a trap.

It takes only a few minutes for everyone to get into position in the lush trees that surround the plateau. Sig and Jorn stop on the flat, open area, but just as I move to stand beside them, Weston's hand wraps around my elbow and he tugs me off to the side.

"Will you please hide in the trees?" he murmurs, his voice so low, only I can hear him.

"No," I say incredulously.

"Lennox, please, I'll be able to focus on whatever threats are coming if I know you're protected."

"Weston, I started all this. I'm not just going to hide."

He huffs a breath through his nose, his eyes pinning me to the spot, but I meet his stare just as seriously. I don't care if he wants me to hide away. I am not hiding from something that my actions caused. I will deal with the situation as it comes, the same way I would have as queen, and he'll be right there beside me.

"Stay close then," he grumbles, and his hand falls to the small of my back as he ushers me across the plateau, positioning me so I'm standing just behind him.

Beads of sweat drip down my back as the heat of the suns pounds on us. The damp still air is stifling, making it difficult to breathe. There's still no sign of the Voyagers. At least we have the upper hand, but I still shuffle my weight on my feet. Whether it is from nerves, impatience, or discomfort, I'm not sure.

The foliage conceals the crew so well that if I didn't know they were there, I would think it was only the four of us standing on this landing. Beside me, Sig and Jorn look as wound tight as I feel, and I can imagine all of us feel the same way. I'm sure Stassia, with all her earlier anger, is ready to pounce at any sign something is wrong.

Weston turns his chin to his shoulder and murmurs toward me. "Do you remember what I said last night?"

I don't take my eyes off the approaching paths and keep scanning for any sign of movement.

"I do, but I'm not listening this time."

"Lennox…" He shoots me a look, his voice a warning, and I break my focus to look over at him.

If something goes wrong, he wants me to get myself out, to keep myself safe and let him handle the threat, even though he has assured me repeatedly that he knows I can handle myself. But it isn't the same this time. There's no returning to Blackwood, no future queen to protect. I'd be saving myself for nothing, and I refuse to abandon people I care about for a kingdom that no longer matters. What's here is what matters.

"This is my family too," I say, keeping my voice low but loud enough that he can hear my determination. "And I'm not just going to leave any of them behind. It doesn't matter what I was, because I'm not a princess anymore. I have no kingdom, only everyone here, and I'm not leaving them. Or you. So you can stop with the grumbling and watch for Mara."

A muscle in his jaw ticks, but I see something else in his eyes.

Pride? Love?

Desire?

Not letting his eyes break away from mine, I reach up and pull my bow off my chest, nocking an arrow so I'm ready for whatever is coming our way. He turns back toward the overlook, but I notice the subtle shift in his body as he inches closer to me, and sets his hand on the hilt of his sword.

Despite Weston's overprotectiveness, I can still see enough to scan the area and search for movement of approaching Voyagers. But the island is still. Not even a breeze rustles the leaves, and the crash of the sea on the beaches seems farther away than normal.

"I don't like this, Cap," Sig mutters as she shifts nervously on her feet.

"It'll be fine, babe," Jorn says and wraps an arm around her shoulder. "What's the worst that can happen?"

"Someone dies," she says flatly, and Jorn tilts his head back and forth to the side.

"Alright, true, but besides that, it can't really get any worse than it already is."

I huff a laugh, and from the corner of my eye see Weston shaking his head quietly as Sig nudges Jorn with her shoulder until his arm falls back to his side.

A quick glance at the sky tells me it's almost time, and no one speaks as we watch the island before us. Weston lifts his hand to his brow, shading his eyes before he breaks the silence.

"They're coming. There's only two of them."

A pit forms in my stomach, and I peer in the direction Weston is looking, spotting the two figures walking toward us, moving as if they aren't in a hurry to get to this meeting at all.

This is it then. It's real. The dust is actually gone.

After all the talk amongst us that this meeting might be a trap, and the worry that Dane leaving with the dust a hoax, somewhere deep inside I considered that a possibility. I didn't realize how strongly I was holding onto that one last thread of hope, that we weren't truly trapped here, until it snapped.

The way Mara spoke of Dane's abandonment and betrayal felt so final, but after mentally and physically preparing all day for the possibility it was all a ruse, I'm now realizing I believed it. I convinced myself, even just a little, that this was all to give Dane what he wanted; to capture me, and force me to tell him the location of the waters.

I held on to the hope that this was all a sick and twisted plot, and that the dust wasn't gone. Dane wasn't gone. That we all still had a chance.

But we don't, and I have to force down the feeling—the same one I had in the tunnels last night as I cried in Weston's arms—that the world is crumbling again.

Because now, what deserves my focus is making sure all of us will be safe on this island again.

I keep my arrow nocked, pointed at the ground but ready to raise and shoot in the event of an attack. We watch as they get closer, only the two of them, just as Mara promised, until they come around the bend and through the jungle of trees, stopping at the base of the plateau and leaving a good distance between us.

Mara stands with her hand on the pommel of her sword, with Gauge beside her. His eyes widen as he takes in the four of us, one at a time, his gaze lingering on Weston and his towering and commanding form for a moment longer before moving on.

"You listened," Weston says, and Mara crosses her arms over her chest.

"You didn't really give me a choice," she snaps. The empty pouch hangs from the pocket of her pants, and my eyes drift away from it and lock back on her face.

"You were telling the truth," I say. "They're really gone."

She rolls her eyes and huffs. "Why the fuck would I lie about it, Lennox?"

"Careful," Weston growls, and Mara looks between the two of us before setting her attention back on me.

"I didn't lie. Dane left and took Storm with him. They used the rest of the dust, so it is still gone. It's over." Her tone is sullen, and her face is still puffy from whatever additional tears she shed after our meeting last night.

"Gauge?" I say, glancing at him. He still eyes Weston warily, and I can see every poisonous lie Dane planted in all of us reflected in the way he looks at us and holds his body, ready to defend himself against an attack.

"Yeah, um." He clears his throat before finally pulling his focus away long enough to answer, and turns to me. "The shit really fucking left us."

"So what now?" Mara asks, scanning the four of us. "Where do we go from here?"

Weston speaks first. "Nowhere unless you agree to stop hunting us."

"But you're the ones who—"

"Seriously, Mara?" I snap, refusing to listen to one more word of Dane's lies. "He lied to everyone for years. He left us all stranded here when he disappeared, taking all our hopes and lives with him, and you're still going to stand there and say we're the problem?" I gesture to my crew beside me, and glare at her.

She chews her lip for a minute before answering. "How can we trust you aren't tricking us?"

I let out a frustrated groan and mumble under my breath. "Now I understand how irritating I was. Remind me to apologize later."

Weston chuckles softly before mumbling so only I can hear, "I can think of a few ways."

I shake my head, ignoring the flicker of fire that ignites low in my abdomen, and yell back to her, "You'll have to try."

"We have done nothing to attack you after all this time, and you still think we're the problem. The trust isn't needed on your end!" Sig yells across the clearing, and Mara shifts her weight on her feet as the words settle between us.

Trust is more necessary on our end, especially after the way Mara attacked Sig and me, but it is amazing how damaging years of manipulation and coercion can be. You can know someone, be friends with them, put your life in their hands, and they still will turn against you because of what they've been told. It can negate everything you know, you've experienced, all because of someone else's words.

Weston lifts an arm, motioning with his fingers, and the entire collection crew steps out from their hiding places, weapons drawn but not poised to attack.

Gauge's head whips around, taking everyone in. "What the…" His eyes widen as they fall on faces he recognizes.

Mara's does too, and they both stand, mouths slack as they look around the group.

"Stassia?" Gauge says, his voice bewildered, but her hardened expression doesn't soften as anger still roils through her.

She dips her chin in his direction. "Hey Gauge."

Mara looks at each of the Castaways, but when she gets to Veck, her brow furrows. "Veck? Is that really you? You're alright?"

"I'm fine, Mara," he replies, and gestures to everyone around him. "We're all fine, and we're telling the truth."

Her mouth gapes as she looks around at all the familiar faces, and reality washes over her. She was wrong. We all were until we found the waters and learned the truth. Until we became Castaways.

"The choice is yours, Mara," Weston calls out, and her head snaps back toward him. "But if any of you hunt my crew, you'll be the one to answer for it."

"Alright," she says, her voice forlorn as she looks around one more time. "I'll tell everyone. We won't hunt you, but you can't hurt any of us either."

"We haven't yet," he says, "and we don't have any intention to. The only exception is if you attack first. From what I heard, Lennox still didn't hurt you, even though she should have."

"Yeah, well, *she* didn't have a problem punching me in the face." Mara points at Sig, and I have to stifle a chuckle at Mara's irritation.

"And I'd do it again, remember that," Sig yells, crossing her arms over her chest.

Mara's about to yell something back at Sig when Weston interrupts. "Can we get back to the negotiation?"

Her mouth slams shut, and she rolls her eyes. "Fine. Go on."

"Now that there's no choice but to coexist together," he says, "I expect there will be no issue with us being out on the island."

Her brows scrunch together as she processes what he says. "What do you mean, out on the island?"

"I mean, we will be free to be on the island." His voice is firm, but he gives nothing else up. All of us know he means we can actually step foot on land again, but to Mara, it must sound absurd.

She rubs her temples, and her eyes fall closed. "I have so many questions. I don't know what you are talking about."

"Until I can trust that you and the rest of the Voyagers stay true to your word, you won't have them answered. You weren't the ones hunted. We were. So until you hold up your end of this agreement and prove that you can be trustworthy, I won't be answering any of them."

Now it's Mara's turn to look irritated, but Gauge cuts in.

"We all have to live here now. There's no reason you can't be here too."

Weston nods once and continues. "Any of the Castaways who want to return to camp will be able to do so, agreed?"

"I'll have to escort them there," Mara says, and I hear Stass snort a laugh from where she stands across the plateau. Even with the revelations of Dane's lies, they are still just as ingrained in her as they were to me, so much so that she can't reason through one of the most obvious tells.

"We all know where it is, Mara," Veck says, and her eyebrows furrow.

"Right. I guess...yeah, right."

Watching someone else piece together the false narratives and lies makes Dane's deceptions so obvious now. It is still hard to fathom how I so blindly followed everything he said, and for what reason? Because he said he wanted to be with me? Because he gave me someone else to fear? At least watching her and Gauge understand means I wasn't the only one so deeply invested.

"What about any of us that want to see where you live?" Mara asks.

"That won't happen. Not yet anyway." Weston's declaration is firm, and unmoving, and Mara's mouth snaps shut.

"So to review," Weston says, crossing his arms and taking a step closer to them. "Dane is gone, and so is the dust, trapping us all here to live together, which we will do. The Voyagers will no longer hunt any of the Castaways, and we are all free to roam the island. *Safely*. Any of the Castaways who want to return to camp are free to do so, and we will live for the rest of our days peacefully."

"Yeah. Sure. Agreed. But why do we have to follow everything you say? Who put you in charge?" Mara snaps.

A chorus of Castaway voices rings out around us. "He's in charge."

Mara glances around at all of them, taking in the faces she knows and, I assume, some she doesn't, before turning back to Weston.

"Fine. Whatever," Mara says, rolling her eyes.

"Good," Weston says. "Fin wants to see Roley. We can meet him tomorrow."

"Sure, yeah, I'll tell him."

"We're done here. Head home, everyone." Weston turns and settles his hand on the small of my back, urging me forward as we walk past Mara and Gauge toward the path off the plateau. The crew shuffles out of the foliage, following closely behind, and weaves around Mara and Gauge, who still look shocked to see they are not the monsters they were made out to be.

Veck walks up to Mara, arms extended, and wraps her in a tight embrace, lifting her off the ground with a smile. He speaks to her quickly, his voice low, but I catch a few words of reassurance and another promise that Weston is telling the truth. Gauge waves to Stassia as she passes by, but the tension in her shoulders is still tight, and she only gives him a curt nod as she stomps down the path.

Once we are in the safety of the tunnels again, the relief of the crew is palpable, but even though I feel like we can breathe again, Weston's tense voice rings out over the crowd.

"No one is to say anything about the healing waters until I give the clear, understood?"

A chorus of ayes echoes off the walls, and Weston nods us forward.

"Do you really think we should keep it from them?" I ask once we've fallen into step at the back of the group.

He lets out a deep sigh, rubbing the back of his neck. "I honestly don't know. They can't go anywhere, whether or not they have it, but there are too many other possibilities to account for. We'll talk to Sig and see what she thinks."

I finally let the tension in my shoulders relax, my head drooping with the weight of the afternoon. "Is it wrong that somewhere deep down, I was holding onto hope that it actually was a trap, and that the dust wasn't gone?"

"Having hope is never wrong, sweetheart," he says, and weaves his fingers through mine. "Hard? Yes. But never wrong. Hope is the only thing that's gotten me through all this time."

There's a pang in my chest, because I did have hope. But now, it's lost, and I don't know how we'll get through the rest of time without it.

CHAPTER SEVEN

Fin's whoops and cries echo through the ship as he tears up and down the steps, his excitement evident after we told him he was going to see Roley today. It never became my official ship duty to occupy him, because everything happened shortly after Taril took over scrubbing the deck, but I know Weston is relieved that Fin can finally leave the ship and work off some energy. Being confined for so long with so little to do is hard on someone as young as he is, and if that is a silver lining we can find in this situation, I'll take it.

Despite the truce with the Voyagers yesterday, no one in the crew has ventured beyond the safety of the ship. It's as if everyone is still unsure if we can take Mara at her word, and no one wants to be the first to try. While I trusted her at one point, especially after saving my life, something in the back of my mind still tells me to be wary. The look in her eyes as she was trying to run me through with her sword is not an easy one to forget.

Sig sits on the railing of the quarterdeck, her feet dangling over the wooden boards beneath her, while Jorn balances along the beam at her side. Weston stands before her, arms crossed over his chest, with his stern look firmly in place. He glances over his shoulder as I approach, and the tension in his shoulders visibly relaxes slightly once I step beside him.

"What's on your mind, Cap?" Jorn says as he spins on one boot to walk in the other direction. "Not doing enough to keep your thoughts occupied?"

Jorn's mischievous grin is the perfect rival for Weston's scowl and glare, but it doesn't faze Jorn at all. He just shoots me a wink when Weston growls back.

"I'm trying to figure out how that is any of your concern, Jorn."

He snickers, and my tongue finds my cheek as I try to hide my smile. "Well, we are the ones who have to deal with you. It's in our best interest to make sure you're satisfied."

Sig rolls her eyes and smacks Jorn on the leg, instigating one of Jorn's full-belly laughs. "Ignore him, Cap. What's wrong?"

Weston shifts on his feet, still glaring at Jorn when he answers. "The Voyagers," he grunts, and a look of confusion crosses Sig's face.

"I thought after yesterday we would not have a problem. Not a significant one, at least," she says.

"Cap doesn't trust anyone, Sig," Jorn says as he hops down onto the deck with a thud. "I'm not surprised this isn't any different. What specifically, though? Enlighten us, Cap."

"We've kept the location of the healing waters secret for this long, but with Dane gone, I wonder if the rest of them can be trusted," Weston says.

"You think we should tell them?" Sig asks.

Weston lets out a deep sigh and rubs a hand over his face. "I don't know. If we were on the other side, we would want to know. But there are too many unknowns with Dane. Can we trust he's actually gone? He's still the Guardian. What if there is a way he can travel without the dust?"

"I don't think he can. On my first day here, he used it to leave the island," I say. "Also, when he was in Blackwood, it didn't seem like he was just coming and going. I think he was staying without using the dust."

Weston's head snaps toward me. "He was there?"

I had told no one that Dane and I had met prior to calling the Guardian. Mara had to know, because when we met on my first day searching, she mentioned he had disappeared for weeks, then came back with me. At the time, I thought nothing of it. I didn't know who he was, or the role he played in finding anyone seeking the healing waters.

Now I know why. He sought me out.

"For a few weeks, yeah. I had met him before I called him."

Weston's gaze hardens, and the muscles in his jaw clench as I'm sure he's figuring out what I already know: that I was Dane's target from the beginning.

Sig chimes in. "So we know he has to use it, but we don't know if it is actually all gone. But we can't confirm whether or not he was using the dust?" Sig asks, turning her attention to me.

"You think he still has dust?" I ask.

"He might. He might not," Weston says. "But can we trust that if he returns, Mara or anyone else won't run back to him? Just because Mara might be telling the truth that she believes, doesn't mean Dane isn't still pulling strings."

If Dane still has dust and only left the pouch here to deceive us and make us think he could never come back, that would completely change who or what I would trust, and it seems Weston feels the same.

"So we don't tell them," Sig says, "because we *do* know that we can't trust them. The island never showed them where the waters are, and that has been our best way of knowing someone could be trusted. It hasn't been wrong yet."

Weston nods. "Then we keep it to ourselves until the island tells us."

"We'll trust the island, just like it tells us to," I say.

"And if we're wrong," Weston mutters, "we handle it then."

"I'll make sure the rest of the crew knows it's still to be kept between us until they hear from you directly," Sig says.

"Good." Weston turns to me, wrapping his arm around my back and settling his hand on my hip. "Ready to bring Fin?"

"Oh yeah, he can't wait. Do we know where we're meeting—"

"EXCUSE ME?"

The call cuts me off and echoes over the deck, leaving the four of us to exchange confused glances.

It can't be.

I sprint across the deck, hitting the rail on the other side hard with my palms, only to be crowded by Weston, Sig, and Jorn, who peer over my head toward the voice.

Mara stomps across the jagged reef, eyes wide as she takes in the sight before her.

"When the *fuck* did this ship get here?" she yells. More members of the crew crowd along the railing of the main deck and at the opening of the gangway, leaning and peering out over the water. Murmurs rise as they look amongst themselves, and I glance up at Weston to find his calculating stare.

"Is anyone going to answer me?" Mara throws her hands in the air, waving them wildly. "I can see you all just standing there!"

"I think the island heard us," Jorn murmurs beside me, and Sig huffs a laugh.

"The island must trust her," I say, looking back up at Weston. "Maybe we can then, too. And maybe now we can just live."

"I think you might be right," he mumbles, and I feel him thread his fingers through mine.

"Hello? Anyone?" Mara calls before she turns toward us on the quarterdeck. "You! The one who punched me in the face. Answer me! Is this seriously where you have been this entire time?"

Sig laughs and cups her hands around her mouth. "The whole time!"

Her shoulders sag as a wave of shock washes over her face while she takes in the ship and the entire crew watching her, but Jorn's boisterous laugh pulls my attention to him.

"I forgot you punched her, babe! How come you didn't tell me before?" He jumps backward out of reach, and hops from foot to foot, throwing punches at the air. "To be honest, I don't think I would want to be on the other end of one of your right hooks."

A laugh erupts from my throat, and I rub my cheek at the memory. "Trust me, Jorn, you really don't. They hurt like a bitch."

The moment the words leave my mouth, I cringe and see Weston's head snap down to mine from the corner of my eye.

"What was that?" he says, now glancing between me and Sig.

"*Lennox*," Sig whines, and drops her head back, her arms falling limply at her sides. No one but Sig knew about the punch, well, other than the Voyagers who saw the bruise, but I had no intention of telling Weston. Sig already had enough to deal with the morning after I left, and I know how he feels about anyone laying their hands on me.

"Fuck," I curse under my breath and turn toward Weston. Outrage burns in his eyes, and I slam my palms into his chest as I hold his stare. "It was nothing. You weren't supposed to find out. Leave her alone."

"Signee," he grumbles, slowly turning to face her. "Explain. Now."

"Shit. Cap, don't hate me," Sig starts, but I cut her off, pressing my hands harder into his chest.

"Weston, stop," I say, and he looks down at me, raising one eyebrow. I know he won't be satisfied until we tell him, now that I accidentally divulged the secret. I roll my eyes and let out an exasperated sigh.

"The night I snuck back to camp, Sig sucker-punched me. We were trying to make everything look believable. You aren't allowed to be upset with her because it worked. They all believed it even more because I was hurt."

His chest rumbles under my palms, and my face heats as his eyes trail over my skin, caressing the exact spot on my cheek where Sig hit me.

"Oh shit, it was a sucker punch?" Jorn says with a laugh. "Even worse, babe. Poor little Lennox!"

"Sorry," Sig says with a wince, her shoulders rising to her ears as she throws her hands up in surrender at Weston. "I had a good reason. It was all to keep her safe, I promise."

The muscle in his jaw ticks, and he finally drags his eyes away from my face.

"I put salve on it. It's like it didn't happen. Just the memory," I say with a small laugh and a hopeful glance over at Sig.

"And her hard head really hurt my hand."

I snort, looking back at Weston, whose face is now stoic, completely void of the anger that was there moments ago.

"It's fine," he says, and Sig's shoulders sag in relief. "I understand why you didn't tell me. But Signee?" He wraps a possessive arm around my waist, tugging my body against him and gripping my hip tightly. "Keep your hands off my woman."

She starts to speak, but before she can even respond, he reaches out and shoves her shoulder. A high-pitched squeal escapes her as she stumbles backward, the rail hitting her waist as she topples over the side of the ship.

"Weston!" I scream, shoving away from him and rushing to the rail to lean over and peer down into the water. Sig's splash resonates from below, but moments later, she surfaces, a huge grin splitting her face, followed by a peal of laughter.

My jaw falls open, and I look back at him, only to catch him smirking with a playful glint in his eye.

Jorn crows from behind me, and before I know it, he's hopping onto the rail and jumping off the side, doing a full flip before hitting the water beside Sig.

I let out a disbelieving laugh before turning back to Weston. A small smile turns up his lips, and he lifts a shoulder in a shrug.

"What does it matter anymore? The island showed her the ship, so we have no reason to hide during the day." He steps beside me, leaning over the rail and beaming down at Sig and Jorn, who are floating in the water, splashing each other and giggling.

A crowd of expectant faces looks up at us from the main deck, well, more specifically at Weston. His arms are crossed over his chest when I turn back to him, waiting to see what he will do with everyone's unspoken questions.

Is it safe? Can we leave?

"Go on," he calls out, jerking his head toward the reef.

Rumbling vibrates the boards beneath our feet as the gangway extends out, thudding into the land on the other side. An eruption of emotional cries and cheers rises from the crew on the main deck, and my chest swells with everyone's excitement.

I can't imagine what everyone who has been isolated to this ship for so many years is feeling now that they're finally set free, now that the island has told them it is safe. As one of the newest Castaways, I'll never know the depth of their emotions, but I know even I am itching to come and go whenever I want.

Feet pound as the crew tears down the gangway, Stassia leading the pack and sprinting faster than I've ever seen her move. Mara stares after everyone, mouth agape as they barrel across the reef toward the shore. Stassia throws herself onto the beach, rolling around in the sand while others splash into the cove or run around in the sunlight, arms raised above their heads, laughing carelessly.

I spot Fin as he runs across the beach to find Roley standing near the bottom of the stone steps, watching everything unfold before him. Arms out wide, Fin runs up to him and wraps him in an embrace, then the two of them take off winding through bodies and splashing in the surf.

My cheeks hurt from smiling as I watch the pure joy emanating from these people I've grown to care so much about. While everything about our situation is tinged with sadness and loss, an entirely different world has been opened to everyone here, one that is safe and happy, and will be for eternity.

I look up to Weston, expecting to see him watching his crew, but he isn't. He's watching me, a soft smile playing on his lips. Stepping forward, I close the gap between us and raise my arms. His hands find my waist as he takes the cue, and leans forward, letting me wrap my arms around his neck and pull him closer.

"Come on, Captain," I say, unable to stop grinning as I take in the relief and happiness in his eyes. "Take me to shore."

CHAPTER EIGHT

Joy. Peace. Relief.

All of it explodes from the smile that breaks across Weston's face, and it's unlike anything I've ever seen. Pressure in my chest explodes as I stare into the playful eyes of this gruff and grumpy man who can finally just be, letting go of all the responsibilities and stresses that were settled on his shoulders for years.

The island gave us this gift, this light in the darkness, right when we needed it. The sunshine and freedom that accompany the trust of those we once called friends make the eternity that glimmers ahead of us seem so much brighter.

A peal of laughter rips from my throat as Weston drops down in front of me, his corded arms wrapping around my waist before he throws me over his shoulder.

"Weston!" I scream. "What are you doing?"

"Taking you to shore."

"I didn't mean that way!" I bounce up and down as he jogs down the steps then strides swiftly down the gangway.

"Hey!" I yell, my cry full of laughter as he hitches me up higher, making me feel like he is about to let me fall, so I have to wrap my arms around his torso and cling tightly.

"Stop complaining. Your captain is taking you to shore, as requested."

"I could have walked!"

His boots barely hit the reef before he's swinging me backward and sliding the front of my body down his until my feet are planted firmly on the ground.

"Where's the fun in that?" His eyes sparkle as he brushes my hair off my face before weaving his fingers through it at my nape. Tilting my head gently, he leans down, stilling me with the press of a scorching kiss. His lips part mine, and I match his movements, taking every deep stroke of his tongue. I can feel his smile, and the absolute bliss of the moment makes me forget about everything except the press of his body against mine and the taste of him on my lips. When his other hand finds the small of my back and pulls me in closer, I oblige, and fist his vest in both my hands.

The loud clearing of a throat nearby breaks my focus, and seemingly his as well, as both of us stop moving and he pulls away with a grumble. My eyes flutter open in time to watch him raise an eyebrow as his head turns only enough so he can speak just past my lips.

"Yes?"

"Is someone going to explain to me what the fuck is going on?" Mara says.

With all the excitement of watching the crew leave the ship and frolic on the beach, I completely forgot she was standing there, and I can only imagine what is running through her mind now.

"No," he growls, and turns back toward me, his lips pressing firmly into mine again before I break away. Flattening my palms on his chest, I push him back slightly, and shoot him a look.

"Yes," I say.

He sighs and straightens, then wraps his hand around mine before striding across the jagged reef. He pauses just before Mara, tugging me to his side as he looks her over. He looks more annoyed at her interruption than his typical captain glare, and I bite the inside of my lip to hide my smile.

She doesn't waver. Her head swivels between the two of us, then down at our joined hands before her gaze tracks up to Weston again. "Well?"

"The ship has been here as long as I have," Weston explains. "No, you couldn't see it. Yes, we all could. You can only see it now because the island must trust you." She opens her mouth to ask something new, but he doesn't let her get a word in. "Any other questions will be answered later. Right now, I'm going to spend the day with my crew. They've waited long enough to be on that beach. They deserve it."

Weston starts off toward the shore, leaving Mara staring after us.

"Wait!" she yells, and I hear her footsteps pound as she chases after us. "Why does it need to trust us?"

"Later," he commands over his shoulder as our boots hit the sand.

The beach is chaos as everyone revels in the freedom from the walls of the ship. Sig and Jorn must have swum to shore through the cove and now are traipsing through the waves, letting them crash over their bodies. You would never believe Roley feared the Castaways just days ago as he and Fin still run around the beach, weaving through everyone and laughing boisterously. Stassia still lies in the sand with Auralie beside her, smiling up at the sky.

Weston's grin hasn't faltered as we stand taking in the scene, witnessing the way everyone seems so carefree. It's the complete opposite of the palpable tension every time they left the ship during the daylight hours. The sight is gratifying, especially with as much suffering that I've had to endure over these past days. But instead of watching each of them, I turn and watch him. I don't want to miss seeing him realize he doesn't have to protect them anymore.

That he can just be.

A call rings out over the commotion, and both of our heads snap toward it.

"Hey Cap!"

Weston's smile fades as the captain's stern protectiveness is in control again, and his eyes move in the direction that Fern points.

Standing on the edge of the cliff, watching everything from above, are the rest of the Voyagers.

They peer over the edge, and the beach falls silent, until all that's left is the crash of the waves.

"Mara, you kept your word, correct?" Weston calls. My eyes stay locked on the cliff, despite the sound of what I assume is Mara shuffling through the sand.

"I wouldn't be standing here if I didn't," she says as she tromps toward the stone staircase. "It's alright! Everything is fine!"

It feels like I am back in the training ring, the standoff between the Voyagers and the Castaways so strained that each is waiting for the other to move first. I watch as some of them break, turning to the side and murmuring to each other. Gauge lifts his arm and points across the beach toward the cove, where the ship that they've now also spotted sits empty.

"The island trusts them too," I breathe, letting out a sigh of relief.

"He must really be gone," Weston says. "Now there's no doubt he was the one Dawnlin was protecting us from."

The sinking realization that Weston is right makes my stomach churn. The island *was* protecting us, and it was from the Guardian. The man manipulated and coerced every one of us, all to get what he wanted. He violated his position as the Guardian, the person who was supposed to protect the healing waters from someone like himself. But a flicker of hope lights in me knowing that despite all Dane did, every single person here was still trusted. He didn't destroy the good in us permanently.

The silence is thick as the Voyagers glance between us and the ship, piecing together that we were right under their noses the entire time.

Eirlick is the first to break the tension. "You coming down, or what?"

No one moves, as if they're still trying to reconcile how their beliefs don't match up with what is right before their eyes.

Veck calls out next. "Rylan, get your ass down here!"

It's as if a dam breaks the moment the Voyagers realize the beach is full of people they know, friends they haven't seen in years. People they were tricked into hating because of Dane's manipulations.

Rylan takes off down the steps, and watching one of their own decide to take a leap of faith was the only sign the rest needed. The other Voyagers take off behind him, jogging down the steps until they're all in the dark, wet sand below.

Tears prick my eyes as I watch everything unfold. My fears and worries about how the Voyagers and the Castaways would fare sharing the island all but disappear. Embraces, tears, laughter, playful pushing and shoving. It's as if no time has passed as friends and chosen family reunite. There's no need for bitterness, distrust, or fear. There's no need to be hunted or to do the hunting. We're all the same, trapped here through no choice of our own.

Stassia and Auralie walk up to Lilly, no doubt introducing themselves the same way they did with me. Veck has his arm slung around Mara's shoulders, and she looks relieved, and if I can believe it, comfortable. Echoes of 'Is that really where you lived?' and 'Can we see the ship' flitter through the air from some groups of younger boys, and I can imagine home will be quite crowded this evening.

Sig is beside us in the next moment, throwing her arms around Weston with a huge smile on her face.

"It's over, Cap," she says into his chest. "We made it."

"Couldn't have done it without you, Signee," he grumbles into her hair. His arms wrap around her, squeezing her in a tight hug as she swipes at her face with one hand.

"Thanks for not stabbing me and finishing the job in the last twenty years," he says with a smirk, and Sig barks out a laugh before pushing him away.

"Shut up, asshole. If you only knew how many times I thought about it."

"And I probably deserved all of them." His smile widens as his hands settle on his hips.

"You did!" she calls over her shoulder as she saunters back across the beach to Jorn.

No one could have predicted how everything turned out, but it would not have been this way if it weren't for Sig and Weston. If they hadn't held strong, if they hadn't done what needed to be done to protect the healing waters, Dane could have had them years ago. My life wouldn't be the same, untouched by every one of these people on the beach.

My crew. My family.

My loneliness would have been unchanged without them.

With Sig gone, Weston turns his attention back to me, and the playful happiness fades from his face, and my stomach flips with unease.

"What?" I ask warily as his eyes darken.

"You." He takes a predatory step toward me.

"Me?" I take a step backward to match his. "What did I do?"

"You started all of this," he says with another step, which I match again, when I see the gleam in his eye. The corner of his lips lifts as he prowls toward me, and I stumble backward through the sand. I have no clue what is running through his mind until his eyes flicker over my shoulder to the crashing waves behind me.

I throw my arms up in mock surrender. "You can't blame me! I did nothing wrong. I can't help it if I was a pawn in his plan!"

He chuckles and reaches over his head, pulling his shirt off and exposing the array of rippling muscles that I have become intimately familiar with.

"Weston…" My tone is a warning, but he ignores it, tossing his shirt to the ground before stepping out of his boots. His eyes stay locked on me, his predatory smirk in full force, no doubt trying to use his body to distract me from his plan.

I turn to run, but I'm not fast enough. He darts forward, and I shriek loudly as he scoops me into his arms, fully clothed and boots still on. He barrels down the beach and crashes into the waves, the water instantly soaking me through.

I gasp and splutter as we surface, wrapping my arms around his neck and pulling my body flush against his bare skin.

"You asshole!" I yell, swiping my hair away from my face, but the sound of his laughter makes my irritation melt away, accompanied by the grin spread across his face. We're past the breaking point of the waves, and he wraps my legs around his waist before wading farther into the cove.

He leans in, pressing a firm kiss to my lips, and I sink into him a little deeper, tightening my arms around his neck.

"Look at all of them," he murmurs against my lips, and we turn toward the beach where no one has stopped their celebration. I take them all in again, these people I care so much about and get to spend eternity with, and watch them enjoying their first real day of freedom since calling the Guardian. "This wouldn't have happened without you. If you hadn't left Blackwood to come here, if you hadn't put yourself at risk to get the dust, we'd all still be confined to that ship."

My chin wobbles, but his fingers still it, grasping it between his thumb and pointer and turning my face back toward him. Deep pools of teal scan between my eyes as his grip pulls me closer. "Even with the way it all turned out, knowing we're spending eternity here, you still gave them something they didn't have before. That's bravery and sacrifice befitting a queen."

I settle my forehead on his, and my eyes fall closed as the current of the water rocks us gently, clutching each other beneath the rays of the suns.

"They deserve it. You deserve it. I couldn't see it any other way."

The corded muscles of his arms tighten around me as he clutches me to him. We stand there unmoving as peals of laughter and shouts echo on the beach over the crash of the waves, and I can't help but feel content.

Completely content.

Despite all the heartache and subsequent joy at once again altered circumstances on Dawnlin, I am not alone. I'm in the arms of a man who would give up everything for me, who has seen me more than anyone in my life. I never thought I would have that, and if going through all of this was the only way to get it, then I would gladly deal with Dane and losing my future over and over again.

His lips find my skin, peppering it with kisses as he slowly moves along my jaw, nipping below my ear and causing my body to arch into his. His chest grumbles as I press into him. Even fully clothed and submerged in the cool water, I can already feel the heat building between my thighs.

"So," I say, lifting my chin to give him better access as his kisses continue down my neck and across my collarbone, his hand reaching up only to brush my wet hair aside. "We have all this newfound freedom. What do you want to do today?"

He pulls away, leaning back so he can look me in the eye, and smiles softly.

"Live."

CHAPTER NINE

Thunder rumbles in the distance, and I stir awake at the sound, stretching my body beneath the cool sheets. I reach across the bed, searching for Weston's warmth, only to find it empty. My eyes are still heavy with sleep when I sit up, clutching the sheet to my chest. I peer into the room, searching through the darkness and shadows for Weston, but there's no sign of him.

Worry coats my stomach as I throw the sheets back and slide out of bed, finding Weston's shirt quickly and slipping it over my head. I pad across the room, the door no longer locking me in when I turn the handle and step into the hallway, glancing down the steps and across the way toward the crew, only to find everything empty and silent with slumber.

By now, I've gotten used to him disappearing first thing in the morning to open the ship and make sure anyone who is on the island returns safely, but it isn't morning. The sky is still dark, and not just from the storm clouds I assume are overhead from the continued sound of thunder.

Where is he?

I take the steps to the main deck quickly, my bare feet hitting the wooden boards soundlessly. My worry drifts away the moment I peek over the threshold, and my eyes fall on him, sitting on the rail of the ship, feet dangling over the side as he looks out over the water toward land. Shadows settle in every groove of his muscular back and slumped shoulders. He hasn't heard me, probably from the sound of the churning water and the wind whistling through the sails, so I take the opportunity to just watch him. My eyes trace over his body, and all the tells it gives me.

For someone who was so alive and relaxed earlier today, he's feeling none of that now. I still can't believe that after living a life of never truly knowing another person, I have someone that I know well enough to tell how they are feeling just by looking.

And Weston is feeling.

Lightning flashes in the distance, followed by the rumble of thunder a few seconds later. I take advantage of the additional noise and pad across the deck. In times of his internal turmoil, he needs someone to be there beside him. I'm here, and I'm not going anywhere, and I want him to know that.

He turns his head over his shoulder just as I reach him, always in tune with my presence, even in the beginnings of a storm. My fingertips skim along his waist as I wrap my arms around him and press my cheek into his back, soaking up his heat. His hands grip my forearms, and my skin erupts in goosebumps as his thumbs gently stroke the sensitive skin under my wrists.

"Couldn't sleep?" My voice, hoarse with sleep, was made even worse from the time spent playing and yelling on the beach today.

My head rises and falls with his back as he lets out a deep sigh. "No."

"Nightmare?" I tilt my chin while still staying pressed into him, if only so I can try to see his face.

He shakes his head. "No."

I tug on my arms and he releases them, albeit reluctantly, so I can step to his side. Gripping the rail, I pull myself up and swing one leg after the other over before sitting, my legs dangling just as his are. The coarse palm of his hand finds my thigh, and he shifts his body closer to me so our legs are touching. I grip the rail harder and fight off a shiver as his hand gently slides up my skin, settling on my inner thigh. There's just enough pressure that I know he's not only steadying me so I don't fall but also reveling in my touch.

I'm still not used to how easily he touches me, not after we spent months avoiding any sort of physical contact. Now, I know he craves it just as much as I do.

We sit in silence for a few minutes, the night air punctuated only by the occasional bout of thunder and the familiar crash of waves.

"Do you want to talk about it?" I finally ask, but keep my gaze forward, not wanting to pressure him.

"Only with you."

Warmth blooms in my chest, and his fingers flex on my thigh as he lets out a harsh breath. "Am I making the right decision?"

"About what?" I pull my gaze away from the island to look up at him, and the tension I saw etched into his shoulders is written on his face too.

"Telling the Voyagers about the healing waters."

The rising wind whips at my hair, but I ignore it as I try to think through all the possibilities, just as Edmond would expect me to. "Have you already decided?"

His jaw ticks as he drops his chin, his focus drawn to where his hand still clutches my thigh. "I've protected it for this long. I've left it up to the island to decide who finds it. But now, it feels different. Does it still need to be protected now that Dane is gone? Does keeping it hidden even matter anymore?"

"Was the decision even up to the island?" I ask.

"What do you mean?"

"Did Dawnlin actually decide who finds the waters and who doesn't? I asked for a map to help me search, and so did Taril, and both of us found it. But as far as I know, no one else in the crew did. Everyone found it on their own."

Weston sits silently, mulling over my thoughts.

"It also doesn't explain how Fin found it. He's a child, and while he was out looking, he was mainly just exploring and playing. It seems like he stumbled upon it more than it was revealed to him."

"That's true," he murmurs, his eyes still trained on the island before us.

"All the dangers around the mountain seem like they were put there to keep people away and protect the waters, not to help lead people to them. There were signs and symbols, yes, but anyone could have seen those. They didn't magically appear. It's not controlling who gets there and who doesn't, and I don't think you should put that weight on yourself."

He lets out a deep sigh. "You're right, but I can't help it. And even if there isn't a concern over those left in the Voyagers and whether or not they should have found the waters, it doesn't make how I feel about the decision any easier."

Weston's hand moves as he thinks, his fingers tracing the length of my inner thigh, and I sigh, my shoulders sagging as my muscles relax.

I think about everything that has happened since I stepped foot on the island, and everything that led me to it.

My life in Blackwood. My father's isolation. My duty as the future queen.

I think about the future I thought I would take back by staying on Dawnlin. Being told I was unworthy. Having the chance of returning home ripped from my fingers.

The decision to let my mother go.

A lump forms in my throat, and I try to swallow it down.

"Maybe," I start, clearing my throat as years of feelings that always accompany the pit forming in my stomach come rushing back. "Maybe it's not our decision. Maybe it's theirs. They should have a choice."

It's all I've ever wanted. Now that I'm able to step outside of my world, one where I had no control over my life or future, it's easy to see the root cause of it all. So much of my pain and sorrow stems simply from not being able to choose for myself. I'm at the mercy of my father, of Brynne, of Edmond. Of tradition and expectations. Of duty. I don't think we should take that choice away from the Voyagers.

"In Blackwood, the most crushing part of my life was having every choice taken from me. The big ones, at least. I thought it was better here, but again and again I was proven wrong. With the island, with Dane, with the dust, with you."

His head snaps up, and his eyes find mine instantly. The stroke of his fingertips on my skin stills as the muscles in his face tighten.

"You feel like I didn't give you a choice?"

Thunder rumbles out over the sea, matching the turmoil I feel watching Weston fall so easily back into the man he was weeks ago, who built a wall of expectations and duty between us. It stings that he can so easily bring it back up again the moment he feels he did something wrong.

"No, no, that's not what I mean," I say and settle my hand on top of his, squeezing it tightly. His face relaxes slightly, but I know he's still battling the internal struggle of crossing boundaries with his princess, no matter how many times I've told him I didn't care about them.

"I'm not talking about being with you. I chose you, Weston, despite all your attempts to push me away. Besides the decision to find Dawnlin, it was the best decision I've made. It's probably the only actual decision I've made for myself, and I wouldn't have done it if I didn't want to. If I didn't want *you*." His shoulders sink slightly, and his thumb starts slowly stroking my skin again. I tilt my head and shoot him a look. "But you didn't exactly give me a choice to come to the ship, did you?"

"You know why I couldn't," he grumbles.

I nod. "I do now, but I didn't then. I just had the chance to save my mother ripped away from me, and then you appeared and tied me up."

"Technically, Sig did."

I fix him with a glare, and he smiles sheepishly.

"My point is, I felt like it was just another part of my life decided for me, and it was hard. Then, when I found out everything you hid from me, I was so angry that you took away yet another choice. You didn't let me decide whether to hate you or believe you. I was angry."

He opens his mouth to speak again, but I shake my head, cutting him off.

"Again, I know now why you did it. You thought I wouldn't believe you, and who knows, maybe I wouldn't have. But I was always taught to take in all information before I make a judgment, and you didn't let me do that. That is part of who I am, and with everything Dane was doing to manipulate me, I wanted to decide for myself. That's why I left, why I did what I did, because I wanted to choose how I could help. I finally had some freedom to belong and be me, and I don't ever want to go back to how I was before."

"All this is to say." I shift my hips on the rail, turning my body so I'm facing him. "I think we give them the choice. We tell them where the entrance is, and they can choose to go inside or not. They can decide if knowing matters more, even if they can't ever bring it home. Whatever decision they make, to go in or not, they will have to live with, and then the island will take it from there."

He leans forward and brushes his lips against mine in a tender but brief kiss.

"I hate hearing you talk about how hurt you were back home," he says, leaning back just enough so we still share a breath, "but you're right. I've protected it for this long, but ultimately the island showed the Voyagers where we are. It trusts them. They deserve the right to choose, so they don't have to spend eternity wondering."

"I wouldn't want to," I whisper.

His forehead presses into mine, but his eyes stay locked on me.

"I'm sorry I made you feel you didn't have a choice. You know my intention never was to hurt you."

"I know," I say, a soft smile playing on my lips. "Just don't do it again."

"I won't." One corner of his lips turns up in a playful smirk. "It's funny you think you had a choice with me, though."

I squeal as he grabs hold of my hips and hauls me over him, setting me onto his lap and wrapping my legs around his torso. I drape my arms around his neck and smile, impressed that he never so much as wavered on the edge of the ship.

"Even if I couldn't fully have you," he says, his thumb stroking the underside of my jaw reverently. "To the depths of my soul, you were always mine."

Warmth explodes in my body as I stare into his eyes that dance between mine, finding them filled with tender devotion and desire.

"I'm always yours, Weston. And you're mine. For eternity."

The grin that splits his face melts away any worry I had that his previous reservations about being with me were surfacing again, and I can't help but return it.

"For eternity," he repeats back.

The sky flashes above us, and this time the quick rumble of thunder that follows is much louder. Weston tears his gaze away from me and looks toward the coming storm before throwing his legs back over the rail and depositing my feet on deck.

"I want to take you somewhere. I want to get there before the storm hits." He looks me up and down, and I can only imagine how I look right now. I slipped only his shirt over my naked body before leaving the room to find him, and my waves are tangled from the wind. My cheeks heat as I glance down, finding my bare legs and at the way open buttons expose the curve of my breasts. Anyone could have woken and seen way more of me than I would be comfortable with, especially when we aren't swimming.

"While I love seeing you in my shirt," he says, his eyes gliding up and down my body, catching on the exposed skin of my chest and causing desire to throb between my thighs, "we need to get you some pants first."

CHAPTER TEN

hick storm clouds blanket the sky when we leave the ship, making it difficult to tell how late in the night it is. From the absence of any noise or movement in the ship, it can't be anywhere close to sunrise. Weston refuses to tell me where we are headed, but as we weave through the tunnels it becomes clear, especially with the cutout in the rock ahead of us.

Lightning fractures the sky, lighting up the dark fissure over the Oasis as the storm gets closer, although the winds don't seem to pierce the magic that keeps this place hidden. The tiny paradise is so different from the last time we were all here. There's no chaos or looming sadness following Jorn's incident. Instead, it's quiet and calm as Weston leads me across the soft beach toward the far rock wall. He grips my hand as we ascend a set of steps carved into the stone. They aren't hidden, but they aren't obvious either, unlike the ones I watched Fin climb repeatedly before jumping into the pool below.

"There's more to the Oasis?" I ask, trying to peer past his broad frame to see where the steps lead.

"Not much more. We mainly stay below. I don't know if anyone else has even discovered this yet, but I found it one day. Sometimes I come here when I can't sleep."

"So it's fine for you to put yourself at risk and leave the ship alone in the middle of the night, but no one else can?" I raise my eyebrows in a challenge, and he glances over his shoulder at me, smirking.

"I'm the captain."

I roll my eyes, and his chuckle echoes off the stone walls.

"You didn't have to come alone. I'm sure Jorn would have gladly come with you," I say as I take the last step before the stone flattens, the pathway curving around a bend and opening into a cavern. Jagged rock walls surround us, and stalactites drip from overhead into a pool below, but that isn't what makes me suck in a breath.

The far side of the cavern is open, and the pool flows over the wall, dropping off the cliff into the sea below. And the *view*. The sea expands before us, and the never-ending waves disappear off into the dark horizon. The storm brings a different feeling to it, an exhilarating power as the lightning cracks in the distance, but I can only imagine what it looks like from here with clear skies and the suns dipping below the skyline.

Weston scowls. "Jorn will not be accompanying me here. Ever."

"Never say never," I say with a giggle, and Weston's eyes darken in the dim light.

"Never. Only you."

My cheeks heat as I look down, finally taking in the pool that takes up most of the space. The dark depths are carved into the ground, with stone steps disappearing into it just before us. Rivulets of steam rise from the surface, and a soft trickling current flows toward the edge.

"A hot spring?" I ask, looking up at Weston.

"With one of the best views on the island." He releases my hand and toes off his boots at the same time as he finds his belt buckle. Seeing Weston with so few weapons feels strange. From the first moment I met him in the cave, he was always heavily armed. It's a testament to how much he believes we are safe from Dane, how much he trusts the island's view of the Voyagers.

The tendons in his forearms ripple as his fingers deftly undo his belt, dropping it and the single sword onto the stone floor with his boots. He tugs the hem of his shirt from his pants, his arms crossing over his body as he lifts it over his head before letting it fall to the ground. Eyes grazing over his abdomen, I follow the ripples of muscle, trailing across his scar and down to the deeply cut crease that dives into his low-slung waistband. My mouth goes dry, and I don't realize I'm biting my bottom lip until his sultry laugh rumbles over the trickle of the water.

My head snaps up to his, only to find a satisfied smirk planted there.

"Enjoying the view?" A single eyebrow raises, and his eyes sparkle in the darkness.

"Can you blame me?"

His smile widens, and he lifts his chin toward me as his hands grasp the button. "Are you going to take your clothes off or do I have to come do it for you?" His pants fall to the ground, and my lips part as my eyes devour Weston's beautiful, naked form. Heat surges through my body as my heart pounds steadily between my thighs, and flutters of anticipation pull my focus away from responding to his question.

Weston embodies every primal desire, his body so commanding and unyielding, it's no wonder he's the want of almost every woman who lays eyes on him. Despite every word he's said to me, his oath, his worshiping of my body, I still can't believe that this man wants me.

And he does.

I can see it in the way he watches me, waiting for an answer, holding himself back from taking what he wants. What is his.

You're mine.

"I don't know," I say, holding my arms out in front of me so the long sleeves of his shirt dangle off my frame. My lips tip into a smirk as I tilt my head to the side. "I might need some help."

He doesn't hesitate, accepting my invitation as he closes the distance between us. Heat warms me through the thin fabric as his hands find my body instantly, wrapping around my waist. His fingers work, gathering the hem of the shirt as his eyes drag over the swell of my breasts that peek through the deep neckline from where I lazily left it unbuttoned.

Rough knuckles graze my skin, goosebumps erupting in their wake as he fists the shirt and lifts the fabric over my head, dropping it down into the pile he's already created. My nipples pebble at the exposure, and I tilt my head back to watch him watching me. My breath catches, and they harden further when one hand wraps around my ribs, settling just beneath the curve, close enough that his thumb gently strokes the underside, causing them both to go heavy.

"Step out of your boots." The command is low and gentle, and our eyes stay locked together as I kick them off. His hands slide down my body, rough fingers grazing the sensitive skin, causing goosebumps to rise in their wake. With his thumbs tucked into the waistband, he gives a gentle tug, pulling me even closer toward him. My lips part on a breath as he sinks slowly to his knees, his hands deftly taking my pants with him, until they're sliding off my feet and I'm bared in front of him.

My hands find his hair, and I weave my fingers through it, trying to focus on anything other than the ache forming between my thighs. I squeeze them together, trying to get any relief, and the smirk that's directed up at me a moment later tells me he noticed.

"Come on, princess," he says, rising to his feet and stepping behind me. "Let me show you the view."

I tilt my neck back and glare at him. "Stop *calling* me that."

Ignoring my irritation completely, he wraps both hands around my waist and walks me forward, leading me to the steps that disappear into the dark pool. The moment my foot breaks the surface, warmth flows through me, accompanied by an instant calm.

Magic.

The spring must have magic.

No wonder Weston would come here on nights he couldn't sleep, when his mind was probably racing through all his worries and responsibilities for everyone on the ship. It's as if all of my worries have disappeared as I sink farther into the water, and all my muscles relax.

Every surface of my skin tingles, and I let out a contented sigh. Weston must know the exact feelings washing over me, because I feel his front press into my back, as he wraps a muscular arm around me, his forearm brushing the undersides of my breasts as he holds me upright. My head lolls back into him and my eyes flutter closed, basking in the absolute tranquility that is this hidden cavern.

Weston walks us through the pool, our bodies sinking farther into the water as we get closer to the far side. My toes barely touch the floor, but his hold on me doesn't let me go under, despite the laxity in my limbs. Years of flowing water cascading down the cliff below has smoothed the stone of the far wall. I rest my crossed arms on the surface and peer over the side.

"It's amazing up here," I say, as Weston wraps his arms around my waist and settles his chin on my shoulder. "I could stay up here all day."

The beauty of the sea is remarkable, and the storm only adds to it. The dark clouds move across the sky, and lightning flashes, illuminating the dark billows then crashing in the air around us.

"If you want to, we can stay," he says. "We have nothing stopping us anymore."

"We didn't leave anyone in charge of Fin," I say with a chuckle. "But now that he can play with Roley, I think he will be a lot happier. Or at least a lot more tired by the end of the day."

He lets out a sigh of relief. "Thank the gods."

Rain starts to drizzle just outside of the opening, and another clap of thunder feels like it shakes the island. Neither of us moves, the rise and fall of our chests in sync as we watch the roll of the ocean and building frenzy of the storm. There's nowhere to go, nothing to do, no dust or waters to search for.

Is this how every day is going to be? An endless cycle of doing anything and nothing at the same time for all eternity?

Fear and uncertainty wiggle their way into the depths of my mind. There are so many things in life I thought I would experience, even after everything I missed before. And now, I won't. We won't. They will all look different from the vision either of us had in our minds. The creeping fear builds, and I can feel the magic warring against the rising panic, trying to reduce it, to calm again.

Will we ever tire of each other? When all of my extremely limited life experiences have been recounted, all my stories told, will we grow bored? Will he grow tired of me? Or will we only learn to love each other deeper every day, creating new memories and having a life that we never thought we would in Blackwood?

Only time will tell.

"I can hear you thinking," Weston murmurs in my ear. "Tell me."

His arms loosen from where they are wrapped around me, and his hands splay across my stomach as they start to roam over the curves of my hips.

"It's nothing." The breathless words tell him just how much his touch is affecting me. He doesn't stop the torturous journey downward, getting even closer to where I want to feel him.

"The wrinkle in your forehead says otherwise." The rumble in his chest against my back makes the worries evaporate, especially as his hand slides down my thigh, fingers trailing up the inside and only making me ache even more. His legs nudge mine from behind, spreading them wider, but his hands never falter.

If it weren't for the feel of his hard cock pressing against my backside, I would think none of this affected him. Not the magic, not the touch. He just continues to watch the rain fall over my shoulder, without a hitch in his breathing or a change in his expression.

His fingertips trail up the inside of my thigh, breaking past whatever barrier he had been avoiding to slowly stroke me with the barest of touches. Throbbing pressure starts to build, and I squeeze my eyes shut as the warmth of the water and the tease of his fingers make everything else in the world dim.

"Tell me something from before." I bite my lip as his fingers part me, then slowly trace circles around my entrance. A soft whimper escapes me, and I feel his body shift behind me, pressing into my back just a little more as his movements continue to torture me.

"What do you want to know?" I manage to get out before sucking in a harsh breath, as he presses just the tip of a finger inside.

"Anything. Everything. I want to know everything about you." His voice drops lower as his lips brush the curve of my ear. "What would you tell me if I was a suitor?"

The thought of Weston courting me sends images flickering through my mind. Dancing at balls. Stealing looks across the room. Brushing up against each other when no one is looking.

Would he steal me away to one of the dark corners of the castle, as I'd seen and heard other castle staff do? Would he touch me like he is now? Would it be too forbidden?

Would he care?

The vision of Weston with his hand between my legs, hidden beneath layers of my skirts, away from the prying eyes of everyone at home, sends off a wave of flutters low in my abdomen. I can't stop myself. I need him closer. I reach up and wrap my hand around the back of his neck, gripping him firmly and pushing my body back into his.

"I don't really know," I say, my voice stuttering with the hitch of my breath as he starts slowly circling again. "I've never…never had one to talk to."

"I'm sure you can come up with something," he murmurs, pressing a kiss against my neck before settling his lips against my ear.

"You already know me better than any suitor would have." His smile widens against my skin at the same time as he slides a finger inside of me.

"Oh," I moan, and tighten my grip on the back of his neck. My head tilts back, eyes still closed as I soak up every sensation.

"I do, and more than just the feel of you clenching my hand," he says, his voice grumbling against my ear, setting off a wave of full-body shivers with the searing warmth of his skin and the spring around us.

"I can't think with you doing that," I pant as he unhurriedly slides it in and out.

"Do you want me to stop?"

"No."

He chuckles softly but removes his hand, settling it firmly on my hip.

I let out a low whimper. "That is the opposite of don't stop," I grumble.

"Trust me, sweetheart, I'm not stopping. Put your hands on the wall."

I follow his command and wrap my hands over the top of the smooth stone wall in front of us. He grips my hips firmly before lifting me so my toes barely scrape the floor of the pool, scooting my ass back so my arms are locked against the wall in front of me. The tip of his cock brushes against my already aching entrance just before he tilts my hips, arching my back to change the angle and pushes inside me.

My grip tightens, and my head falls back with a moan, feeling every inch of him as he slides in to the hilt, stretching and filling me at a dangerously slow pace.

I move my hips, begging for friction, but his hands squeeze, stilling the motion.

"Not yet. Just relax."

"Please."

"Trust me," he says, and I nod, sucking in a deep breath and letting our bodies fit together. The fullness turns the rising need into a steady throb, and I have to focus to keep my body from moving against his. The front of his thighs press into the back of mine as he shifts my legs, lining them up with his before gripping the wall on either side of my hands. He shifts, pulling himself forward, and nudging my body until I'm sitting in his lap. The change in angle pushes him deeper, the fullness almost too much as he touches something deep inside. One hand releases the wall and settles on my stomach, the light pressure making my head roll back onto his shoulder as I feel him so fully.

"Now tell me something," he mumbles, and the vibration of his voice resonates in my back.

"I like to read," I say as I try to slow my heaving breaths and get used to the pressure. If I stay perfectly still, the slow and steady pulse of excitement is manageable. He was right. I can focus a little more than I could before, as long as his fingers don't decide to play with me again.

"I already know that. What's your favorite book?"

"*The Maiden's Moonlight Venture.* It was the one the island gave me the night you went on your first shift back."

"Was that one of Tila's books?"

I nod and immediately regret it. The movement jars my body, shifting me and making my core flutter around him.

I suck in a breath. "Yes."

He chuckles in my ear. "When did you discover those?"

"When I was fifteen. It was around the time I learned about marriage alliances and needing heirs. Without a mother to have the more… intimate conversations with me, I think Tila made sure I found them."

And I'm glad she did. I'm grateful Edmond never went farther than to explain the expectations of a queen, and the possibilities for using a marriage to benefit the kingdom. The thought of him trying to describe the…logistics…makes me want to die.

"They were educational, I'm sure."

"They were enough. But you surprised me with some of the ways…" I trail off, feeling slightly embarrassed to even say it.

"I fucked you?" he fills in, and I can hear the smile in his voice.

"Yes," I say and feel my shoulders curl in slightly. "None of the books had some of the things you have done, so at first I thought I did something wrong."

A low grumble escapes his throat. "There will never be anything wrong with letting me put my tongue between your legs." The press of his hand on my abdomen firms a hint more, and I fight not to wriggle my hips over his.

"Noted," I say with a laugh, and he presses his lips into my hair.

"I distracted you from the books."

"Right. The books. While those parts of the stories were… appreciated, I kept going back for more than just that. I loved the romance, too. Reading about love was important to me."

"Why?"

I tilt my head back to look up at him. "Do you want the truth?"

"Always, princess."

I shoot him a glare, but he just presses a quick kiss to my lips, and my eyes flutter again as he sends a wave of pleasure coursing through me.

"I never thought I'd have that—the love in the stories. It always seems so pure and unconditional." My eyes break away from his and settle on my fingers gripping the wall. "I've never had someone love me unconditionally, and surely never expected anything more than a loveless marriage alliance after being hidden behind the castle walls for my entire life."

"I love you," he murmurs, and my head snaps up, finding his gaze searing into my face. His hand leaves my abdomen and strokes the curve of my jaw with a knuckle as his eyes shimmer with uncertainty. They scan mine, darting back and forth assessing, trying to read me like he's usually great at, but this time, he questions what he sees. "Even when you piss me off, and defy my orders, and put yourself in danger, and leave me." My breath hitches at the last one, but he doesn't stop; his voice just drops lower as his chin tilts to his chest. "I still love you."

The vulnerability and uncertainty on his face makes my chest ache. How could he question my feelings? How could he think I wouldn't return them? After everything that has happened, that he's done for me, and the future we have ahead of us, could he really believe I don't love him?

This declaration is different from before. When he swore his oath to me, he never explicitly said it. Not in this many words. Not in the way lovers do, not in the way all the stories I've read have.

The love I thought I'd never have is staring me in the face, waiting for me to say it back, and I realize that despite the overwhelming love that grew since I decided to keep him a secret, I never said it to him. I longed for him when I snuck away. I begged for him to see me differently than the princess he couldn't have, but I never told him. He admitted he was falling in love with me, that he had started to the moment he looked into my eyes, but the only words that left my lips were that he was mine, and I was his. That I chose him, but not that I loved him.

I won't make him wait any longer.

Reaching up, I cup his cheek in my hand, and pull him closer, hoping he sees in me every bit of sincerity I see in him.

"I love you too, Weston. More and more each day."

The muscles in his face sag in relief, and he leans in, pressing a bruising kiss to my lips, but I push him away, and a look of confusion comes over him.

"You're going to laugh," I say, but I'm only met with a smile lighting up his face.

"Tell me."

I reach out and grab his hand, my fingers finding the warm metal and stroking it softly and feeling the rough edges of the carved seal.

"When you told me you were here for a woman, and I saw the ring, it made me feel a lot of things I wasn't ready to admit to myself." Mischief sparkles in his eyes, but I don't let him interrupt. "I didn't like that there was another woman, no matter how many times I told myself I pitied anyone who had to put up with you."

His lips purse as he tries to keep himself from laughing, but I continue. "I didn't want to accept that I was jealous you were here for another woman, and clearly you loved her if you were willing to sacrifice everything for her. It just reminded me of the love I always wanted, that I never thought I would have. Especially if you still loved her after all this time, enough to know she was still alive."

"I only knew she was still alive because you were standing in front of me." His thumb strokes my cheek, and I lean into his touch. "And I did love her. Do. But never like that. Not the way I love you."

"I know that *now*, but back then I didn't like the way it made me feel."

He smirks and trails his hand down my neck, settling in the crook and holding me closely. "So you admit you were falling for me way back then, even though you hated me?"

I roll my eyes. "Clearly, I was out of my mind."

He laughs, a loud, boisterous laugh that rings out in the cavern, his shoulders shaking and jostling my body, reminding me of how deep-seated he still is inside me.

I suck in a gasp, and his hands find my hips, clamping down and shifting me again, enough that I feel him move deep within.

"Oh," I moan, and he leans down to nip my earlobe.

"Tell me more."

I swallow harshly, but my mind is blank of anything that might be interesting or entertaining to share with him, especially with his cock still filling me. The life I led back home was monotonous and empty, but here, here it's full of light and love, and people to spend it with.

I shake my head. "Story time is over. I need you." Reaching down, my fingers graze over my hips, diving between my thighs until I can feel where we are connected, where his hard length disappears inside of me, and I take advantage. I press my hand down, rubbing against his flesh and over mine, begging him to move.

"Fuck." The hiss of his voice followed by his cock firming even more inside me makes my blood pound through my entire body.

His fingers wrap around my wrists and lift my hands, setting them on the wall.

"Don't let go."

I do as he says, gripping the wall again as he stands straighter, gripping my hips and taking them with him. One hand settles on my low back, and the other on the front of my thigh.

"Weston," I plead, and he answers quickly, pulling his hips back so he's almost out, then slamming them back into place. I cry out, loving the delicious friction after having him tease me for so long. Water sloshes over the sides of the wall as he pulls out and slams in again.

"Oh gods," I cry, and his pace picks up, his motions rougher than before. I can't control myself as my arms lock into place, pressing my hips harder against him, begging for more.

"That's it, Lennox. Take what you want, sweetheart."

I feel every ridge of his cock as he slides in and out of me, but I can't control the groan that rips through my throat when he tilts my hips, changing the angle so my feet are no longer touching the floor of the pool. I'm completely at his mercy as he slams into me, and just when I think I can't handle any more, his fingers find the sensitive spot between my thighs, pressing firm before stroking circles in time with his thrusts.

"Weston!" The pressure builds, and fire licks up my inner thighs, pulsing through my flesh and burning me from the inside out as my core quivers around him.

"Good girl. Squeeze my cock, sweetheart," he grunts, and I can't hold it back any longer. My body explodes, a guttural cry that tangles with his fills the air around us as he pulses inside me. Heat blooms within as my walls quake, squeezing him with each of the last pumps of his hips that draws the pleasure out even more. His arms wrap around me, scooping me up and pulling my back flush against his chest just as my limbs go limp, unable to hold myself above the water.

He spins me around, cradling the back of my head and pulling me in close before pressing his forehead to mine. I can barely keep my eyes open, my body still humming from the exertion and consuming emotional confessions.

"You're perfect," he whispers, peppering my lips, my chin, my face with kisses. His chest heaves with exertion, and his breaths are hot and heavy on my skin as his hands cradle my head, brushing my damp waves off my face.

"I love you," he grumbles, and kisses me again, deeper this time, not needing to hear my reply, but I give it to him, anyway.

My eyes flutter open and meet his when he pulls back, just enough that I can see him, but still close enough that I tingle with his proximity.

"I love you too," I say between my breaths, and a soft smile forms on his lips.

A thumb moves to caress my cheek as his eyes dart between mine. "I don't know what I did to deserve you, but I'm thankful every fucking day that I don't have to spend eternity alone. Not anymore."

Tears prick my eyes, and a lump forms in my throat. "Me too."

He leans forward and kisses me again, this time, the softest brush makes my chest warm before he pulls back.

"I'm happy you brought me here," I say. I'm finally able to move my heavy limbs, and wrap my arms around him, grasping the nape of his neck.

He smirks. "I hope you're happy after how hard you just came." I roll my eyes and scoff, but he chuckles softly. "I'm glad you came with me. I wanted to show it to you. Although it feels different now, having you here."

"Why?"

"I came here a lot when I couldn't sleep, or when things felt hopeless. The magic always helped with that, but having you here, holding you in a place where I felt alone and hopeless so many times, just makes it feel…"

"Feel what?" I ask, swallowing the hard lump forming in my throat.

"Whole. It doesn't feel empty anymore."

My lips tip up slightly as we just watch each other, not needing to say anything, letting the feel of our bodies pressed together and our synced breaths do all the talking.

"You know," he says as he walks forward, pressing my back into the wall for support. His thumb moves from my cheek to my jaw, stroking and caressing as if I'm the most precious thing he's ever seen. "This place always reminds me of something my father used to tell me. Whenever I would feel hopeless, I would come here and look out over the sea, wondering if he was still out there somewhere and if I would ever get back to him. Then I'd hear his voice in my mind, repeating the same phrase over again." He chuckles to himself, his gaze breaking away as he remembers his father, whom he clearly cares about, before they rise to meet mine again. "He used to tell me that light always finds a way, even through the blackest woods."

My jaw falls open as a gasp rips from my throat.

Weston's face falls in an instant, his brows bunching together as his arm tightens around me. "What's wrong?"

My mind reels, and my breaths come in short and stuttered as what he just said rings in my ears.

No, it can't be.

His brows bunch together and his jaw tightens as he looks me over, waiting for me to say something, but I can't. His body straightens slightly, the sound of water splashing around us as he becomes more alert, ready to jump in and help me.

"Lennox, are you alright? Did I hurt you?"

I drag my gaze over every curve of his face, the same one I have looked at so many times. In hatred, in friendship, in love. I never saw it, but the moment he uttered those words, the pieces snapped into place, like the puzzles Edmond used to give me.

He has his eyes.

The curve of his jaw.

But other than that, he's completely different.

He must take after his mother.

I try to muster my voice, but it comes out barely a whisper. "Weston, what is your last name?"

His brow knits in confusion, and he stares at me for a moment, trying to figure out why I am asking before he answers.

"Rowe."

Sir Rowe's face flashes before my eyes, the man I called my friend. The man who, since the day he introduced himself to me as my tutor, would never let me use that formal name.

He crouched down to my level, smiled, and told me I was only ever to call him Edmond.

"You're Edmond's son," I whisper in complete disbelief.

Edmond's son.

Weston is Edmond's son.

The son I didn't know existed until the moment that changed the trajectory of my entire life; the moment Edmond told me about Dawnlin.

"What?" Hope fills his voice as his hand wraps around the side of my face.

"He knew I would find you," I breathe. My eyes dart between his, and I can't believe how much I overlooked now that I look at him. "How didn't I see it before?"

His eyes widen, and his mouth parts slightly. "You know my father?"

I nod, and my eyes fill with tears. "Besides my guard and Tila, Edmond was...*is* my only friend at home."

He shakes his head in disbelief. "How would you even know him? He was an advisor a long time ago."

"He wasn't an advisor. He was my tutor." His eyes widen in understanding. "I've spent every day since my childhood with him. He taught me everything I know."

His face hardens. "So he's the one who made you starve yourself on my ship."

A wet laugh bubbles from my chest. "Unfortunately, yes."

His hands settle on the top of his head as he looks down at me. "I never thought I'd ever see him again, but I at least wanted to know if he was all right. We didn't expect that I would never come home."

"He knew you were coming here?"

"He knew I was trying. He was the one who told me the story."

I nod slowly. "He's the one who told me the story too." I can't help smiling at the memory now. "That was the day I found out you existed."

A hint of sadness touches his features. "He didn't talk about me?"

My smile falls as I see how much that hurts Weston. I shake my head and soften my voice. "He never talked to me about his family, not until right before I left. He looked sad when he mentioned you, and I thought it was because you had died as a child. I thought it was too painful for him to talk about the family he lost. I just had no idea that he lost you this way."

His shoulders rise and fall with a heavy sigh. He lowers his hands from where they were wringing his hair, and sinks back into the water, wrapping his arms around my torso once again.

"Besides Rem, my father was all I had. He knew me better than anyone." His lips curve up at the corners. "Maybe that's why he sent me you."

"Do you think he really sent me? Did he really think I would bring you back?"

"If you spent your whole life with him, I think he knows you pretty well. I saw your determination and stubbornness right away, so I have no doubt he believed you would."

My lip quivers as the feeling of failure washes over me. "But I didn't. I didn't bring you home."

"That was through no fault of your own. Don't blame yourself for that." He smooths the pad of his thumb across my bottom lip, stilling it before holding me again. "I have no doubt that if he knew you well enough to believe you could find Dawnlin and bring me home..." He pauses, as if thinking to himself. "He probably also knew that you are the woman for me."

My chin quivers, but a slow, sad smile spreads over his face. "I'll never get to thank him for it."

A traitorous tear falls down my cheek as I whisper softly, "I miss him."

"I miss him too, sweetheart." Pressing my back more firmly into the wall, he wraps my legs around his body, then leans forward, resting his chin on my chest. His eyes sparkle as he looks up at me before he murmurs. "Will you tell me stories about him?"

"Of course." His lips curve at the corners, and he waits quietly, patiently, as memories come flooding back. Ones I hadn't thought about in years become so clear and vivid in my mind, so I recount them. With every story, Weston relaxes, the muscles in his shoulders and face loosening, but his smile stays in place. It's the happiest I've ever seen him.

It wasn't until the third story about a time I defied Edmond or skipped lessons that the realization hit me. With each story, I'm not only telling him about his father, I'm telling him about me.

I didn't want to tell him I was worried about us running out of life to reminisce on, or him becoming tired of me, but my fears aren't warranted. There are so many things I can tell him about, so many stories. There's more to me than just being the isolated princess of Blackwood.

Hours pass as we sit in the magic-imbued water, sharing stories of our childhood as the storm rages around us. We laugh, I cry, but we never let each other go as I tell him all about the time I got to spend with the father he will never see again.

CHAPTER ELEVEN

By the time the suns crest the horizon, the storm has run its course. The dark clouds overhead brighten, and we finally decide to pull ourselves from the spring and head back to the ship. Clothed and looking less disheveled than when we came, we make our way back through the tunnels, knowing there's a chance now that it is light that we will run into an early riser.

But Weston veers off, leading us in a different direction, and I glance back over my shoulder, questioning my memory. "Wasn't that the turn?" I ask.

"Yes."

"Then where are we going?" Torches light before us as we weave through, getting to a stretch where the ground ramps up before us.

"We're going to go give the Voyagers a choice."

Warmth blooms in my chest knowing Weston's worries are now at peace. After the morning we had, the talk about choice, the memories of Edmond and his lessons, and whatever influence from the calming water, I'm happy knowing the difficult decision is no longer weighing on Weston's shoulders.

The tunnel opens near the entrance to camp, and it feels strange being back here again, after the finality of the last time I left. Even though it was only days ago that I walked this same trail, my hand in Dane's as he led me away from the safe house where I planned to meet Sig, I never expected to be back so soon and so willingly.

"After you," Weston says, gesturing to the dense jungle we traipse through to get to the portal.

"Do you know the way?" I take the lead, and he follows closely behind.

"Yes, but I've never been inside. Jorn showed me one night, but we didn't risk going through the portal. I don't know if the island would have allowed us."

"I never thought about that before. Dane always perpetuated the fear of the Castaways sneaking into camp, and none of us ever considered the island closing the portal to you." I glance back just as he shrugs.

"It might have; it might not have. Maybe it knew if we were found we'd be attacked. That would negate all the work it did to keep us concealed. Who knows? I guess we never will."

Pushing aside the vines covering the portal, I gesture him forward. He grabs my hand as he steps through, and the overwhelming feeling of magic surrounds us until we are on the other side.

It didn't stop us.

The clearing is empty, and the sound of water dripping from the leaves of the soaked trees is the only noise in the entire space. Weston's expression is neutral as he looks around, taking everything in.

"So this is camp." His eyes trail over the wooden pathways, following them around the entire circle. The torches are dim in the early morning hours, and I assume, because of the storm, everyone is tucked away safely in the cabin.

"This is camp," I say, and take it in again myself.

It still doesn't feel like home. Bitterness coats my tongue as I think about all the lies I was told here, and the way I was convinced to see everything through Dane's eyes.

"I like my ship better," he grumbles, and I let out a laugh.

"I do too," I say, turning and walking backward toward the ladder. "Come on, this way."

I reach up and pull the ladder down from where it is hidden and climb, my loose and relaxed muscles straining with the sudden exertion. The ladder pulls taut as Weston ascends behind me, making it easier to push my tired body up onto the platform. He's on it just behind me, again looking around and getting his bearings, so I quickly point out the main features.

"The bunks are on either side. The tavern where we ate is back there. The armory is over there. It's all pretty simple. We didn't spend a lot of time here except in the evenings because we were all out searching."

"So where is everyone then?" he asks, looking around.

"In the cabin. It's just because of the storm. This way." I grab his hand and walk along the boards until I get to the door Taril led me to during the last storm. I don't want to barge in. While everything went well yesterday and the island seems to trust that the Voyagers won't harm us, I don't want to make any mistakes. I still want to tread cautiously, even if it is optimistic.

I raise my fist to knock on the door, but I don't, instead spinning around quickly to face Weston.

He raises one eyebrow. "Change your mind?"

"No, but…" My voice trails off. I don't know what came over me, or why I feel the deep need to do this, but I can't push it away, and if I don't follow through, I feel like I will regret it. "I want to be the one to tell them. When the island deemed me unworthy, I promised myself I would bring everyone back at camp to the waters, so at least they had a chance to be. I know they can't bring it home, but I still want to be the one to tell them. To help them find it. I feel like it is the least I can do, especially with how things turned out with Dane.”

“If that’s what you want, Lennox. You can tell them.”

My lips turn up at the corners as he catches my chin between his fingers, tilting upward and leaning in closer. “But don’t talk like you’re responsible for any of them not finding the entrance, or for what Dane did. I’m sure if they all knew the truth, they would understand.” He presses a soft kiss to my lips and pulls away with a nod to the door. “Now knock.”

I shoot him a playful glare, then spin back around, pounding my fist on the door three times, then wait. There’s no sound from behind the door, and it feels like minutes pass in silence. I start to fidget, impatiently waiting as if there are hot coals on my bare feet. They’re probably confused and not expecting us since everyone at camp is behind this door already, but I’m anxious. I want to tell them, so we can all move on from it.

“Mara, it’s me. Open up,” I call out, and a few more long seconds pass before the door swings open. Mara stands in the doorway, her gaze flicking between Weston and me.

“Hi,” she says cautiously. “What’s going on?”

“We just wanted to talk to everyone. We have some things to explain.”

“Are you finally going to give me answers?” She folds her arms over her chest, and I’m brought back to the first time we met. It seems like no time has passed, even though it has, and she’s gone from hating me to befriending me too many times in that span.

“Some at least,” I answer.

She pulls the door open, gesturing inside. Weston and I step through the threshold only to be met with a room full of blank but curious stares.

“Hey everyone,” I say with a wave.

“Hi Lennox!” Gauge calls and raises his arm high from where he sits in the back of the room. Movement catches my eye as Roley runs up to me, giving me a quick hug before running back and sitting on his sleeping mat.

I breathe a sigh of relief. The sentiment from the beach doesn't seem to have died overnight, and no one looks like they're ready to stand and pick a fight.

Mara shuts the door and steps past us, plopping down on her cushion before calling out, "So what do you need to tell us?"

Everyone stares at me expectantly, waiting for whatever is so important that it brought the first Castaways to camp. I don't know how Weston does it. He's stood in this position so many times and delivered tough news or made commands, and that's only since I've been around.

How would I have done it as queen?

I glance over at him, and he gives me a nod of encouragement, despite the stern Captain's expression firmly in place.

Turning back to the group, I take a breath and let the words tumble out.

"First, I wanted to say thank you to all of you, you know, for not throwing us in the cage the moment we stepped through the door."

"There's a cage?" Weston mutters, and I clear my throat, ignoring him.

"I guess that's a step up from my last first time in camp." Weston grumbles behind me, and a few snickers erupt around the room. I smile, already feeling looser; more in charge.

"I know Dane disappearing was a shock to us all. To be honest, I'm still processing and dealing with the betrayal, and I might be for a while. You all have been here longer than I have, except you, Lilly, so I can imagine you feel like I do. Dane told me he didn't know how to replenish the dust, and that's why I tried so hard to come up with an answer. I didn't want the choice of returning home taken from any of us. That didn't turn out the way I hoped."

I look down at my feet, trying to find the strength to say the next part and not feel like I betrayed my friends by keeping it from them. Even though it was the right decision because of what Dane was after, I still feel a thread of guilt knowing I hid from them exactly what I vowed I would help them find.

"Dane kept us all controlled, in fear, focused on finding what he wanted. We didn't have a choice in how he treated us and how it eventually took everything away. It is hard to come to terms with, and because of that, we…" I glance over at Weston, and he looks up at the group, his eyes falling on each of their attentive faces. "We decided to give you back the choice. Dane told all of us that the Castaways hunted the Voyagers, but that isn't exactly true. He was right about one thing. Each of us was taken against his or her will, at first at least, but it was for a good reason. You only become one of the crew after you find the healing waters."

Mara gasps. Her hands fly over her mouth as she stares at me in disbelief, and several other cries of surprise ring throughout the room.

"You found them? You all did?" Mara asks, her head swiveling between Weston and me.

"We did," he grumbles, then looks back at me to keep explaining.

"After I found the waters, I didn't have a choice but to go with him back to the ship, but I chose to stay there. I learned the truth about Dane's motives and everything he had done, and made my own decision. You all have been looking for so many years, and now that things are the way they are, we agreed to tell you the location."

Pure shock is apparent in all the expressions before me. Gauge jumps to his feet, his hands on top of his head as he paces back and forth. Roley looks around at everyone, then back at me, like he is still having trouble understanding. Lilly reaches up and swipes at her cheeks. I can't even fully comprehend what they are feeling, because this situation is so different from when we all found the mountain.

"It is going to be a hard decision. We can't leave Dawnlin now. Whether or not you get the waters is up to you and the island. I completely understand if you choose not to try. Being granted them and not being able to return is something I don't know if I could bear.

But I also understand not wanting to live for eternity wondering and questioning. If I were on your side, I would want the choice."

"What do you mean 'being granted?'" Lilly calls from the back. "Don't you all have them?"

I start to answer, wondering how I am going to explain the insides of the mountain to them, but Weston beats me to it.

"When you enter the chamber where the waters are held, the island decides if you are worthy of them," he says. He shifts on his feet and rests his hands on his hips. "None of us have received them. We don't know if it will be the same with any of you."

The silence in the room is palpable, as the weight of the news sinks into all of them. Going into the mountain with the expectation that you may leave empty-handed might actually be better than my experience. Recovering from having the hope ripped away, and walking out feeling unworthy only to be captured by the enemy wasn't easy to move past. It took time, and now we have that.

"Like I said, it's your choice. You should really think about it," I say.

"We can bring you all tomorrow," Weston says as the silent stares turn toward him. Gauge still paces in the back of the room, and Sawyer's head is now in his hands as he stares blankly at us. "You can sleep on it. Anyone who wants to try can meet us on the beach in the morning."

"Thank you for telling us," Mara says, her voice hoarse with unshed tears.

"You're welcome." I give her a soft smile, and she returns it, though slightly wavering as she holds back emotion. Despite everything that transpired between us, I truly don't think Mara hated me, even when she acted like she did. She was hurt that she had lost another friend to the Castaways and was dealing with facing the reality that she would most likely be alone if she returned. And it's hard to blame someone for their actions when they were blinded by manipulation.

"So you're really not mean?" Roley asks, staring wide-eyed at Weston.

He shakes his head with a chuckle. "No, Roley, I'm not mean."

"That's debatable," I mutter, and his low huff brings a smile to my face.

"Can I go see the ship?" Roley says and jumps to his feet.

"Sure," Weston agrees. "I bet Fin will be excited to show you everything."

Murmurs erupt in the room as everyone can't contain themselves any longer, and I take it as our cue to leave and let them do what they need to come to a decision.

"Does anyone have questions?" I ask, but everyone still looks too stunned to voice anything right now.

"If any come up, you know where to find us. Otherwise, we will see whoever wants to try in the morning." Weston's hand settles on my low back as he leads me toward the door. I give the Voyagers a final wave before stepping back out into the open air and loosing a deep breath. Weston closes the door behind us before his arms cross over his chest.

"That went better than I expected," he says.

"I agree," I sigh. "I feel relieved."

"You did great, Lennox."

"I don't know how you talk to the crew like that all the time. I feel like I could take a nap now."

He chuckles and then steps toward me, his hand finding my back again. "Lots of practice. You would have gotten the hang of it."

Because I would have had to do it my entire life once I was queen. *Not anymore.*

We start off down the walkway toward the platform, but I remember something I wanted to do, that I didn't have the chance to before. The last time I left camp, I couldn't do anything that might tip Dane off that I didn't plan to return, but now, I don't have to hide anything.

"Follow me. I want to grab something." I weave my fingers between his and lead him through camp until I get to our set of bunks.

"I'll be right back." I release his hand and grab the rungs of the ladder, climbing quickly to my platform. I hope it's all still there, and that Dane didn't destroy it after he discovered I was a traitor.

When I reach the top, I pull myself onto the platform, only to be startled that Weston didn't stay behind.

"This is where you slept?" His arms rest on the edge, his body still propped on the ladder as he looks over the space.

"This is it."

He nudges my boot, and I move to the side, giving him enough space to climb up. He sits beside me, his back leaning against the railing that ensured I didn't roll to my death, and crosses his ankles in front of him. I feel oddly self-conscious as he looks around, glancing at my lack of personal effects, before he takes in the trees and the skies above.

"It's nice up here."

"I thought so too," I say and press my shoulder into his.

"Why did you pick this one?"

My cheeks heat and I look down at my fingers, picking at a nail. It seems like so long ago that I was choosing my bunk the first night I arrived on the island with an abundance of hope and optimism. The reason may seem insignificant, but to me, it was everything. Dane never asked, even though he knew I went all the way to the top, but Weston cares enough to know about this tiny piece of me, a remnant of who I was when I stepped foot on the island.

"I hadn't ever seen the stars," I breathe. "I wanted to stay under the sky for as long as possible."

"I remember that feeling." He tilts his head back, resting it on the wooden beam behind us as he looks up at the blanket of thick clouds that is oddly reminiscent of home. "When Sig and I finally left the cave, I remember being amazed by how clear everything was. I appreciated it much more after almost dying, and it made me realize how much I took it for granted every time Rem and I traveled anywhere outside the kingdom. After surviving, I try not to do that. I try to appreciate the little pieces of beauty and be grateful for things that happen. I don't want to overlook even the little things. You never know how quickly your entire life can change. Recent days have proven that."

I nod solemnly then lift my chin, but he's no longer staring at the sky, taking in the beauty of nature. He's looking at me. His eyes caress every inch of my face before moving up to hold my gaze. My chest tightens and my throat thickens. I thought I'd only learned to have hope and trust here on the island, but Weston is right. Everything can change in a moment. What you thought you had could be ripped away, and if we don't take the time to live in the moment, to love what is in front of us, we forget that it can be fleeting, and could be gone in the next.

My lips curve into a soft smile, and I shift to my knees, clambering over his lap so I'm straddling him. His hands settle on my hips, and he watches me watching him; soaking up the moment that we have, because another isn't ever guaranteed.

"This bunk may have started out that way, but I don't have very good memories of it." I lean down and press a firm kiss to his mouth, pulling back only slightly before speaking against his lips. "I like your bed much better."

"You're fucking right about that," he grumbles and snakes his arms around my waist, squeezing me against his chest. "What did we come up here for anyway?"

"Well, I told you to stay down there, but you didn't listen." I wiggle out of his grasp, and he adjusts himself beneath me. I can't keep the smirk off my face. "I just came here for my stuff." I shift to the edge of my sleeping pad, looking for my last piece of home. The fabric peeks out from under the bed, where it must have gotten shoved the last time I was here. I reach under and pull out the balled-up clothing, the thick cloak wrapped around everything else, and tuck it under my arm.

"Alright. Let's go." I scoot toward the ladder, but Weston puts his hand out, stopping me.

"Nice try." He slides in front of me, descending the ladder first before I follow. His hands find my waist as I reach the bottom, and he lifts me off the ladder, setting me back firmly on the floor beside him. The lump of fabric disappears from under my arm, and I turn to find him grasping it all in one hand, and reaching out to weave his fingers through mine with the other.

"Lead the way. I'm not sure how to get out of this place."

I laugh and squeeze his head. "You would have been so lost if you had ever snuck in here."

"Jorn would have shown me."

Camp is still quiet as we follow the walkways, and I can only imagine what discussions started in the cabin after we left. When the platform hits the ground, we step off, and I take one more look around camp. I doubt this is the last time I will be here, but it feels so different walking out of it with no intention of ever returning, this time with Weston by my side.

Once we're back on deck, I take my clothes from his hand and head straight toward the stairs. The door clicks closed behind me, and I know he followed, probably curious about my hint of urgency.

Bending down, I lift the lid to his trunk and drop my balled-up clothes inside, slamming the lid shut right after. My chest heaves with a huge sigh as a weight lifts off my shoulders, and I turn to find him softly smiling at me.

"What was that for?"

"It's time to leave Blackwood and Dane behind." I cross the room and take his hands in mine. "It's time to let go of the worry about everything we can't control or the wonder about how things could have turned out. It's time to live, just like you said. Can you leave all that behind too?"

His smile is dazzling, and my chest squeezes.

"Anything you say, Lennox."

CHAPTER TWELVE

espite the storm and ongoing cloud cover yesterday, we woke to clear skies and warm suns, so the girls and I decide to move our breakfast to the deck. We pull together a makeshift table and chairs of crates and sit below the helm, soaking in the sunshine.

With everything that has happened in the past few days, along with our newfound freedoms, I haven't been able to spend much time with them. It feels odd to say that, especially since now we have nothing but time. I need this, though. With all the change, I've missed the companionship of my friends.

"Today's going to be a good day," Stassia says as she sits down on a crate on the other side of the table. "I can feel it."

"Who are we to discredit one of Stass' intuitions?" I say. "The last time you had one, you were right about the heat wave."

"Lennox, you've been here long enough to know I'm usually right," she jokes and snaps her teeth into a smile after popping a berry into her mouth.

Auralie shakes her head with a smirk. "Always the humble one."

"What?" Stass says, lifting one shoulder, her tone clearly mocking. "Why be afraid to say it if it's true?"

"I hope today is a good day. I don't know if I can handle another bad one so soon."

We still plan to bring the Voyagers to the mountain this morning, and despite the overwhelming excitement and shock from the Voyagers that should fuel the excursion, the memory of my unworthiness still slithers to the surface. Some, if not all, of the Voyagers are going to experience the same letdown today, and we will be there to console them, since we've had longer to process those feelings.

But what if the island grants someone the waters? How are they going to feel knowing they are trapped here with them?

Would the island even grant them, knowing no one can leave?

"It'll be fine," Sig says, scooting her crate in before picking up her fork. "If it isn't, we'll do what we always do and make the best of it."

"At least I'm happy to see that you're all still here," I say. "After everything settled, I didn't know if any of you were going to stay on the ship or go back to camp. Or one of the houses, I guess."

Stassia scoffs. "Why would we leave? This is our home."

"I saw you throw yourself on the sand, Stass. You were so happy to be on land. I figured you might want to go back. To feel more normal."

"This *is* normal. I don't have any plans to leave. Do you, Sig?"

"Nope. I'm staying put," Sig says, and takes another bite.

"I'm not going anywhere either," Auralie says.

"And we're all pretty positive that Captain won't let you go anywhere, so it looks like you're stuck with us," Stassia says.

"Besides, I doubt Stassia would want to leave if Taril wasn't." Auralie looks down at her plate, moving the food around on her fork while trying to hide a smile.

My eyebrows raise as I snap my head toward Stassia. "Have I really been *so* busy that I haven't heard anything about this?"

"Well, you and the captain have been quite scarce," Stassia says with a knowing look. "I'm sure you had far more pressing matters to attend to." She winks, and I feel my cheeks heat. "Maybe you should tell us more about that?"

I point my fork at her. "Stop trying to deflect the conversation. What's going on with Taril?"

"Ugh!" she groans, dropping her head back and throwing her hands in the air before slamming them back down on her thighs. "I have no clue! Probably nothing! He doesn't seem bothered by me. He doesn't seem to like me either. That's it. He's just unbothered."

"They've been spending lots of time together," Auralie fills in.

"It's not that he's the new guy," Stassia interjects, "I just…I don't know. I like spending time with him." Her shoulders slump slightly, and I never expected to see shy and self-conscious Stassia ever in my life.

"Have you made yourself clear?" I ask.

Stass chews on the inside of her cheek. "I mean, I don't stop talking to him. When I'm not with all of you, I'm usually with him. I don't know how much clearer I can get!"

"He's kind of quiet, Stass. Maybe he's just listening to you. Maybe that's his way."

She sets her elbows on the crate and rubs her temples. "I don't know. I just don't want to fuck this up and then have to spend eternity avoiding him. Maybe then I'd go live on the island."

We all laugh. "I don't think you're going to fuck it up, Stass. If he didn't like you, he wouldn't be around you," I say.

"You mean he wouldn't put up with me." she says.

A chorus of 'no's' and scowls mix together, along with Auralie's, "Don't talk down to yourself."

"Hey," Sig says, her lips tipped up in a smirk. "Lennox is the only one who can put up with Cap, and she wanted nothing to do with him at first. They couldn't even be near each other. Be happy Taril wants to be around you."

"Hey!" I cry and pick up a berry off my plate. I throw it, hoping to surprise her with the flying fruit, but she leans to the side and catches it in her mouth, chewing with a smile.

"How are things, by the way?" Auralie asks, turning to me. "Everyone seems happy. Much less growly."

"If you mean Cap isn't going to take anyone's head off anymore, then you're right about that." Sig's eyes widen and her head tilts, as I'm sure the memory of Weston's fury when I left is fresh in her mind.

"Yeah, well, regular fucking will do that to you. Had to get all that frustration out," Stass says with a wave of her hand.

"You know, Stass, I want Taril to get a little courage," I say, "because I can't wait to poke just as much fun at you."

Stass looks at me with a half shrug. "As long as someone is getting poked, that's what matters." I almost spit out my bite as laughter bursts from the four of us, and rings through the calm morning air. Slapping my hand over my mouth, my shoulders shake with laughter, and my cheeks hurt from smiling so much.

How did I go my entire life without having female friends like this?

The echo of familiar footsteps sounds from behind us, just before Weston's voice rings out in the ship's hull.

"Collection crew! Meet on the quarterdeck!" Weston steps out onto the main deck a moment later, and I look over my shoulder at him. He seems much more relaxed this morning. His hair is more tousled than it normally is, and I bite my lip as my eyes drag over the rest of his body. The buttons at the top of his shirt are undone, exposing the hard planes of his chest, and his hem is tucked unevenly into his pants. There's no vest today, probably because safety is no longer a concern. He doesn't have to be as heavily armed as he usually is.

As if he can sense it, his eyes catch mine and he smirks before turning toward the bow of the ship. His fingers flick at the group lounging at the far end of the deck, calling them over, before he steps up behind me.

"Good morning, ladies," he grumbles and leans forward, placing a brisk kiss on the top of my head.

Stassia shoots me a look, and I narrow my eyes at her playfully before Auralie responds cheerfully, "Morning, Captain."

"Let's go," he instructs, jerking his head toward the staircase leading to the quarterdeck. The girls slide their crates back and step away from the table as Weston extends his hand out toward me. I lay my palm on his, and he pulls me to stand before ushering me up the steps in front of him with a hand planted firmly on my waist.

The girls follow closely behind, and it is only minutes before the crew is gathered, standing in a semicircle and waiting for Weston's next direction.

"You're not going to tell us something went wrong again, are you, Cap?" Jorn jokes, and he's met with a few chuckles.

"No, nothing like that," Weston says with a smile, which is already so different from the energy that surrounds our normal collection crew gatherings.

"Good, because I'm getting a little tired of all the back and forth," Stassia says, tossing her hair over her shoulder. "There's too much commotion."

"I agree, Stass. Hopefully, there are no more surprises. Not now at least," he says and settles his hips on the railing behind him. "But you'll all be the first to know if there are. Some of you already know, but we told the Voyagers about the waters yesterday morning and gave them the night to decide if they want to go into the mountain. If anyone wants to help us guide them over, you are welcome to come."

There are a few nods and hand gestures, and Weston acknowledges them with a single nod. He crosses his arms over his chest before he continues.

"We don't know if anyone will be deemed worthy, especially with the change in the situation on the island. But since we're going to be out there, if anyone wants to go out on a shift during daylight hours, it might be different than looking at night."

"I'll go, Cap," Veck calls out, and Eirlick adds, "Me too."

Weston nods. "You can leave once we get them all inside. Report back if you find anything out of the ordinary. We're all settling into this new normal, but I promised I wouldn't stop trying to get you home. Even though I want us all to be safe and happy with how things are now, I don't want to give up hope."

"Aww, Cap, don't get soft on us," Jorn says. Weston shoots him a glare, but Jorn only laughs heartily.

"The same as we always do, I'll be waiting for them on the beach tonight. Anyone who wants to gather more of the crew and prep a bonfire, I figured we could all be there for them. Support them. We know what each of them might go through, and this could be the last time we'll see anyone come out of that mountain. I want to leave it on a good note."

"I'd be happy to gather some of the crew and get things set up, Captain," Auralie says.

"Good. Thank you everyone. Anyone who is coming to the mountain, we're leaving in a few minutes." Gripping the rail, he leans far over and looks toward the beach, then lets out a huff. "They're already ready, and from the looks of it, every single one of them is going to try."

Bodies clamor and footsteps shuffle as we all make our way to the railing beside Weston and peer toward the beach. My eyes fall on the group gathered there; all the Voyagers waiting patiently for us to come.

Weston straightens and gestures toward the stairs to the main deck, giving everyone the go-ahead to move.

"Let's go see what Dawnlin decides."

CHAPTER THIRTEEN

The dull murmur of conversations among the Voyagers quiets as the entire collection crew approaches the beach where they've gathered. I scan the faces to find that every single one had decided to try. There's no one waiting back at camp willing to let the chance at what they came here for slip away.

"Captain," Mara says with a curt nod, the corners of her lips turned down in a frown. She still hasn't warmed up to Weston being in charge, but with the way the entire crew and even some Voyagers continue to defer to him, she doesn't have much of a choice.

"Mara." His hands rest on his hips as he looks over the crowd, taking in the hopeful faces as they wait for the next step. "Is everyone ready?"

A collective of affirmations echoes through the crowd, and even though it sounds enthusiastic, I want to be sure. I know what being denied the waters did to my self-worth, and I don't want anyone to experience that pain if they don't want to. I have to know that everyone who is here is here willingly and is ready to face whatever Dawnlin decides.

"Are you all sure? Once you go in, there's no turning back. You can't decide you would rather live without knowing." I look specifically at Roley, but he just gives me a smile.

"We're all sure," Mara says. "We talked about it last night. We've all been here too long not to know."

"Then let's move," Weston calls. "We will lead you to the entrance. Once we arrive, follow my lead, and then we will see you on the other side." He nods toward Sig, and she starts out across the beach, waving her hand overhead. The crew falls into step behind her, chattering among themselves. Weston takes my hand and follows the last of the crew, and Mara motions the Voyagers forward.

We aren't bringing them through the tunnels. Before we left the ship, the crew all agreed that even though the island trusts the Voyagers enough to reveal us, we still want to have something to ourselves. Something to keep us safe in case the worst happens. After living in hiding for so long, it's hard to just change overnight.

The energy thrumming around us feels different. The excitement of the Voyagers is palpable, but it also feels like the island knows exactly what we're doing. Like it expects us.

Maybe it will finally tell someone yes.

Sig comes to a stop just before the stone bridge, the mist from the falls already coating us as we approach. The crew moves, forming a barrier between the bridge and the pathway so no one can cross, or worse, be called into the lagoon. Dropping Weston's hand, I step in line beside Sig and watch the faces of every Voyager as they take in the scene around us.

They've seen it thousands of times before, passed by it every day, and by the looks on their faces, they're stunned.

So obvious, yet so well hidden.

"We'll help lead you in, and stagger everyone by a few minutes," Weston yells so the group can hear him over the roar of the falling water. "Like Lennox said before, once you go in, you can only go forward, so if anyone has changed their mind, now is your last chance."

He pauses, waiting for a response, but the only sound is the crashing water behind us. "You will be inside all day, but it won't feel like it. We'll be waiting for you at the end. There's nothing to be afraid of." He looks directly at Roley before meeting the hopeful gazes of the other young members. "Just remember that we've all been through it, and you will make it, too, whatever Dawnlin decides."

My chest squeezes. Weston doesn't really know any of the remaining Voyagers, but is still treating them as if they are already part of his crew. Hope is written all over his face, and I know he wants someone to be granted the waters, even with no dust to return home. Maybe if someone is, the island will reveal how to replenish it.

"Line up!" Everyone shuffles at Weston's command, forming a long line at the base of the bridge. "Sig, you, Veck, and Stassia stand on the bridge and be ready to go in if anyone slips. Jorn, you're with me on the platform. Ryum, help them get started across." The crew jumps into action, moving to their assigned locations, with the rest surrounding the area and keeping watch for any dangers the island might throw at us.

Weston turns to me, leaning down and lowering his voice. "And you. Please keep your feet on solid ground. I've already jumped in after you once."

I push him away with a scowl, but I can't help but huff a laugh at his knowing smirk. "I'll space them out," I say, but before he can turn away, my fist clenches around the fabric of his shirt and I pull him closer to me. He doesn't pull away, simply quirks his head with a curious look on his face. "Please be careful."

He leans in and presses a firm kiss to my forehead before his thumb trails down the side of my face. "Always."

Jorn's crow echoes over the roar of the water, and when I turn to look, he's already gone, stealthily hidden in the portal behind the waterfall. I make my way over to the front of the line, where Mara stands beside Gauge, the first volunteer to brave the unknown, and I can't say I'm surprised.

My breath catches in my chest as I watch Weston step out onto the slippery ledge, but despite his graceful movements and sure-footed steps, I don't let it out until he safely disappears on the other side.

Turning back toward Gauge, I give him the most reassuring smile I can muster. "Are you ready?"

"No. Yes. I don't know." He shifts back and forth on his feet, eyeing the ledge and then glaring at the roaring falls.

"I don't think any of us were really ready." I reach out and give his arm a quick squeeze. "But you've been searching for this. You just have to trust the island, and take the first step."

He lets out a deep sigh and rolls his shoulders. "Alright. Let's do it."

Ryum reaches up from where he stands on the rocks, and Gauge steps forward, grasping his hand and planting his feet on the ledge. I watch his back as he slowly scales it, crossing until he's disappeared through the portal on the other side. When I turn back to see who is next, Mara has tears in her eyes.

"Are you all right?" I ask softly.

"This whole time," she says, her voice so small compared to how big it normally is. "All this time, it was right here, and I never found it."

I remember this feeling, this moment of realization that the waters were hiding almost in plain sight. The mountain—the crux of the island—held the secret. It felt so obvious, even though I knew it wasn't. I know the flurry of feelings she's having right now, but she has been here longer. No one knows how much more time it would have taken her, if she even ever found the entrance.

"A lot of us didn't find it, Mara. It wasn't just you."

She turns to face me. "But you did. You found it, and you had barely gotten here. Fin too. How did you both find it after so little time, but I walked by it every single day?"

"Do you want to know the truth?" I ask, and she nods. "I asked the island to help me make a map. I hid it from Dane. It was how I noticed a pattern in the dangers; how the island changed. Then I narrowed down. And after I remembered the symbols on the fountain, I just found it."

Her mouth falls open slightly. "I don't remember the fountain at all. I don't even know if I looked at it closely enough back home."

I shrug. "Then you shouldn't blame yourself for not finding it. The fountain was fresher in my mind than for you, and it helped me. The rest…" I trail off. It feels crazy to talk about the magic that lies in Dawnlin. None of us can explain it, or know anything about it more than we've experienced, but it gives me a feeling, and I don't understand why. No one else has expressed anything similar, and I don't want to come off as strange.

"What?" She tilts her head expectantly.

I wave the next person forward, and they start off along the ledge before I turn back to her.

"I don't know. Sometimes I felt like the island wanted me to find the entrance, even though I wasn't worthy. I just felt something when the pieces fell into place, and with the map…After everything Dane did, it just felt like it was meant to happen. Every step and setback and decision helped change this place, even though we are stuck here. It felt like I needed to set things in motion. It didn't end how I expected, but it still helped in a way."

Her eyebrows draw in, and she tilts her head. "What do you mean after everything he did?"

I let out a sigh. I've become close to everyone in the crew, and they don't even know the entire truth when it comes to the connection between Dane and me. I am sure Sig knows because of Weston, but I haven't shared everything with anyone else yet. Bringing it back to the Voyagers isn't something I've even considered until this moment. Can I trust Mara to know everything?

The island trusts her.

I wave Sawyer forward and weigh my options. If I don't tell her, she might question her trust in me, knowing I hid something important from her, which could eventually develop issues between the Voyagers and the Castaways. On the other side, the dust is gone. There's no way to get home, and because of that, Dane isn't coming back. Nothing will change if Mara knows the truth about his connection to me and my family. If anything, it will help explain Weston and my relationship, and hopefully keep Mara from shooting us pointed looks every time he touches me.

Fuck it, I've got nothing to lose.

Words spill from my mouth, the story flowing freely from the very beginning—at least the beginning as I experienced it. Dane is from home. He is connected to my mother. He manipulated me.

I tell her it was actually he who killed the last Guardian, and blamed it on Weston to control us. I tell her he almost killed Weston intentionally because of his friendship with my parents. I don't miss a single detail, recounting it all down to the moment in the cabin when he revealed everything, and as the words tumble out of me, I watch fury rise in her face.

"That asshole!" she yells when I am finally finished. "How did he get away with all of this? How are we stranded here, and he just left after holding us hostage? How did Dawnlin let this happen?"

I shrug, and I can't keep the sorrow out of my voice. "I don't know. But I have to trust that what was meant to happen, happened. We're all still alive. We're not hunting each other anymore. Hopefully, we can find happiness here, despite everything he took from us."

She shakes her head in disbelief. "So all this time, the Castaways were just searching for a way home?"

"Yes, that's all they wanted. They weren't trying to take anything or anyone. They were trying to protect the waters from him."

"I tried to kill you," she says, a look of horror on her face. "All because he lied to me."

I scrunch my nose in a playful wince. "It's probably not a good idea to remind Weston about that."

"Yeah, I gathered. By the way he looks at you, he'd probably have my head if I hurt you. Again."

"He was not thrilled the first time," I say with a laugh. My cheeks heat as I remember exactly what he did with all the emotions of finding me hurt, returning to the ship. I push it down and wave the next Voyager through.

"For what it's worth," she turns to me, her face laced with sincerity. "I really am sorry. I know Dane was controlling all of us, but I should have known. I should have seen it. When he disappeared for so long and then came back with you, I should have known something was wrong."

Sig's lesson comes crashing back to me, back from when I was having this same internal crisis, back when I found out Dane had lied to me, too. The betrayal cut deeply, and that was before I knew the extent of it. I feel like Mara needs to hear the words, if only to help her grieve the friendship she thought she had over so many years. "It isn't our fault how others treat us, especially if they try to harm or control us. What matters is that when our eyes are finally opened to it, we remember our value and don't let it happen any longer."

Her face hardens as if it's set in stone. "It won't. If he ever comes back, he'll have all of us to deal with."

"He will. And we're stronger together." I reach out and squeeze her hand, and she squeezes mine back.

Peering past Mara, I look at the front of the line to find Roley with a nervous look on his face. I smile down at him, ruffling his hair the same way I do with Fin.

"Are you ready, Roley?"

"I dunno," he says and kicks the ground beneath him with the toe of his boot.

"It's safe, I promise. There's nothing to be afraid of. The island will take care of you," I say, and he looks up at me with a sheepish smile.

"What if it says no?" he asks.

I crouch down and set my hand on his shoulder. "Then it says no. We can't control it, and we can't change it. You wouldn't be alone. It's the same answer the rest of us got. There's nothing to be ashamed of."

"Okay," he whispers. I smile, then glance over my shoulder toward the entrance, only to find Weston scaling the ledge back to our side. He steps back onto the solid ground and walks over to us, his clothing completely soaked through from the spray of the falls.

"Let's go, Roley. I'll carry you over," he says, extending his arms out.

Roley's shoulders touch his ears as he takes a hesitant step forward. He looks back between Mara and me as if asking for permission, or more likely reassurance.

"He won't hurt you, Roley. He's not the bad guy," I say, and watch as Roley's throat bobs with a gulp.

"I'm going to put you on my back, alright? You need to hold on tight," Weston says to him, and before Roley can utter any denial, he reaches down, hoisting Roley onto his back. The moment he's in the air, a grin breaks across his face before he's wrapping his arms around Weston's shoulders and wiggling with glee.

Weston scales the ledge again, Roley's tiny body dangling down his back the same way I've seen Fin do countless times, until he sure-footedly disappears through the portal on the other side.

"I can't believe we thought he was a monster," Mara murmurs, shaking her head in disbelief.

My chest squeezes, and even though I can't see him any longer, I know he's probably reassuring Roley again, making sure he's safe entering alone. He may think he's just doing his duty as the captain, but I know it's more than that. Weston cares, and he's a good man. One that deserves more than the life he's been dealt.

I swallow the lump forming in my throat. "We only saw what we were told to see, but that's not who he is. Not at all."

"He wouldn't have kept all of you safe for that long if he was a monster."

The morning moves along as the suns trail across the sky. The entire line of Voyagers disappears into the mountain, leaving only Mara standing beside me.

"This is it," I say, smiling at her. "Are you ready?"

"I'm terrified," she says with a deep sigh. "But I have to know, you know? I don't want to wonder. I've been wondering if my mom is still even alive for all these years, and I don't need something else to add to it." She steps to the edge of the land, where the boulders form beneath the ledge. "Maybe it's better this way." She stares at the waterfall, her face drawn with her own internal thoughts and preparations before walking into what she wanted the most. "I doubt there's anyone left for me at home, so at least here, I'm not alone."

"You wouldn't have to be alone, Mara. If we could go home, I'd find a place for you at the castle."

Her head snaps toward me. "Wait, did you just say castle?"

Shit.

I may have left out the future queen part of the story, only focusing on the fact that Dane previously knew my mother.

I gape at her, trying to come up with a quick explanation, but there's only the truth, and we don't have time for that right now. She has something to accomplish, and I will not stand in her way.

Mara laughs, her eyes wide as she stares at me. "Tell me, Lennox!"

I shake my head and shove her shoulder, causing her to stumble toward the mountain wall. "There's plenty of time for that. Right now, you have more important things to do. Get inside that mountain. We'll see you on the other side."

CHAPTER FOURTEEN

Auralie spent the afternoon prepping the beach with a few of the others, so by the time the suns set, the entire crew left the ship and made our way down to the collection beach. After we made sure all the Voyagers were through the entrance, the energy level of the crew was high with anticipation and constant chatter, wondering if anyone would be worthy.

And now it is time to find out.

Fin clutches my hand and swings my arm back and forth as we walk down the main path toward the beach. The edges of the sky are still pink, while the purples and blues deepen above us, and I find myself lost in thoughts about the finality of this night. As I look out over the landscape, and take in all the people around me, it is so easy to see that what I thought was a curse months ago, turned out to be a blessing. I only needed time to see it.

A breeze comes off the water, sending a chill through me despite the warm day. Weston follows behind, close enough that I can feel his presence but far enough away that Fin and I have our own space. I smile softly at the memory of the last time we walked on the island, toward the collection beach. His trailing was much different from today, especially after I yelled at him not to follow me like a guard.

"Do you think Roley will get it?" Fin asks with a skip then a hop as he drags me along behind him. "I think he should. He's nice. But so are you, and you didn't get it."

"We will see when he comes out. Either way, we will be there for him," I say.

"Can I show him the ship? What if he wants to stay there like me? Can he mister Weston?" Fin cranes his neck to look over his shoulder at Weston, his eyes wide and hopeful.

"Do you want to stay on the ship?" Weston asks. After telling Fin that we would be living on Dawnlin together forever, we hadn't discussed whether he wanted to stay or go back to camp. Even with the threat of Dane eliminated, I just assumed, and my stomach tumbles at the thought that he might want to leave.

"Course!" he says with a smile. "The ship is way more fun than camp. Besides, there's no one to tell me stories there."

Weston reaches out and ruffles Fin's hair. "Then sure, Roley can come if he wants. Even if it is only once in a while."

A cry of excitement explodes from Fin's tiny body as he jumps up and down. "We need to get him a bed! He can stay if he wants, right? Oh! And Jorn and I can teach him to climb! And, and, and," he stutters over his words, his elated thoughts going faster than his mouth can keep up with.

I can't hold back my giggle. "I'm sure the ship will give him somewhere to sleep. You two will have fun." If herding one energetic kid wasn't exhausting enough, I can only imagine playing hide and seek with two of them all day. I sneak a glance at Weston, only to find him smiling softly. His gaze is fixed on Fin, and I watch as his eyes slowly move to where our hands are clasped together.

The last time Weston and I spoke about him wanting a family, he avoided the question, instead explaining that he already has one. Here. This. All of us. But I can't tell if the look in his eye tells me there was more he wasn't saying.

Longing.

His eyes flicker to meet mine, and I turn away, my chest squeezing tightly. I can't handle thinking more about what we've lost, what we've sacrificed. Not tonight. Tonight is for the Voyagers.

The moment our feet hit the sand, Fin takes off running toward Auralie's setup on the opposite side of the beach. An enormous pile of dry sticks and logs is steepled high between the portal and the surf, circled by blankets and linens for if the night turns cold. Stacked crates form makeshift tables that I'm positive will fill with food and drinks as soon as everyone arrives.

Auralie waves enthusiastically beside Stassia from beside the bonfire, beckoning us all to join them. Just as I raise my hand to wave back, my foot sinks into an unusually large divot and I stumble, but before I can even put my hands out to brace my fall, Weston's hands are there, wrapping around my waist and keeping me upright.

His warm chest presses into my back, and I feel the tickle of his breath brushing the curve of my ear. "Already stumbling? Jorn hasn't even broken out the wine yet."

I twist in his arms, and wrinkle my nose at him. "*You* are actually the only one who has been drunk." He cocks an eyebrow and I smile innocently, knowing he's trying to piece together what he's missing. "It was juice. I was faking."

His face morphs as he finally figures it out. "Signee," he grumbles, and I can't hold back my laugh.

"Guilty."

The muscle in his jaw flutters as he stares down at me. "So you weren't drunkenly betting me to kiss you."

"Nope," I say, drawing out the sound, and watch his expression soften. "I did that with all my wits about me, but you said no. Even if you didn't think I was influenced by the drink, I don't know if you would have. I'm still mad about that by the way."

One corner of his lips turns up, and his eyes stay locked on mine. "My father would be proud to know you are such a skilled strategist and actor. You would have been great in negotiations. All those years of training clearly weren't wasted." He reaches up, his hand cupping my jaw as his thumb runs over my bottom lip. "But Lennox, if only you knew every single time I thought about kissing you, before that night and after it."

He steps closer, his head dropping toward mine, and I tip my chin up to hold his gaze. His eyes dart to the side, checking to see that there's no one within earshot, before his voice lowers impossibly deeper. "If only you knew about all the other thoughts, the things I pictured doing to you over and over again. Things I convinced myself I could never do. If you only knew all the ways I wanted to make you scream my name every time this perfect face scowled, or those beautiful eyes rolled."

My cheeks light on fire as my stomach bottoms out, and I squeeze my thighs together. His smirk deepens as his eyes flicker to my cheekbones, catching the blush I'm sure is there, before they fall to my mouth.

"Like what things?" I whisper.

A low chuckle grumbles in his throat. "You're already well acquainted with some of them." His tongue runs over the inside of his bottom lip, and I catch mine between my teeth as heat pools low in my belly. "Things with my hands. Things with my tongue. But it sounds like I have some making up to do. We wouldn't want my queen to be mad at me, would we?"

"No," I breathe, and his mouth widens into a grin, his eyes never leaving my lips.

His hand finds the column of my neck, and his thumb presses into my chin, tilting me back and pulling my face to his. Hungry lips crush mine as he kisses me with all the desire I knew he was holding back that night on deck. He shuttered it again, the moment I mentioned our titles, but it never went away. I've been reminded of it over and over again, but each time his lips touch mine or his fingers brush my skin, it feels like I've been waiting forever.

Now, there are no titles to hold us back.

His other hand slides over my hip, sinking to my low back and grazing the top of my ass as he pulls me into him, our chests pressed tightly together. My hands fist his clothes as lips part mine, and his tongue sinks deep, jaw working to devour me until my breaths become shallow. His fingers slide around the back of my neck, lacing through the hair at my nape and my knees threaten to buckle.

If he kissed me like this on the ship, the night I had to tear myself away from him and walk back toward the enemy, the *real* enemy, I wouldn't have wanted to leave. With every move, every stroke, every breath, I feel everything he wanted to tell me, even back then.

I want everything else to disappear. I don't want to leave this moment, this kiss.

A sharp whistle rings out next to us, followed by Jorn's telltale laughter, and Weston's chest vibrates with a growl beneath my hands.

He breaks the kiss, but doesn't pull away, as his hooded eyes stay fixed on my face. "Fuck off, Jorn," he snaps, capturing my lips again in another searing kiss before he straightens, leaving me reeling.

Blinking rapidly, I try to slow my breathing. My lips feel swollen, and it's hard to ignore the burning desire building deep in my abdomen.

"Still mad?" he asks with a smile. His fingers glide through my hair, tugging at the windblown knots before brushing against my scalp and doing it again. My eyes flutter closed, and he chuckles softly.

"If I say yes, will you kiss me like that again?"

His darkened eyes clearly say he was not finished with me yet, but he keeps stroking my hair and holding me close.

"I'll kiss you like that every day for the rest of your life if that is what you need to know how much I love you. How much I want you.

If I need to remind you every time you're mad, or every time you're happy, or sad, I will."

I swallow down the lump forming in my throat. "Next time, can we make sure Jorn isn't nearby?"

Weston's smile widens into a grin as he lets out a deep laugh. "I'll do my best."

He weaves his fingers through mine as we stride across the beach. The tension surrounding the last time we were all here is nowhere to be found tonight, as everyone in the crew saunters around, laughing and talking.

"I'm going to check in with Veck and Eirlick to see if they have any updates after today," Weston says before releasing my hand. He plants a kiss on the top of my head and mumbles, "I'll find you after."

Stassia and Auralie are bickering as I approach where they kneel at the the fire pit. Auralie strikes a flint, shooting sparks into the base, while Stassia flaps her hands at the sparks Auralie is creating.

"We need more air!" Stassia snaps as sparks fly once more.

"There's plenty of air, Stass. It won't catch if we don't have any kindling!"

"Let me try." Stass holds her hand out for the flint rock.

"You already did, so I can do it." Auralie strikes again, but still no flames catch.

I stand behind them, peering over as they are crouched at the base, still bickering, and stifle a giggle. "Who knew starting a fire was so difficult?"

Both of their heads swivel to look at me, frustrated looks plastered on their faces.

"Why don't you try then?" Stass says as she falls back onto her heels.

I throw up my hands and take a step back. "I wouldn't even know where to start."

"You've never started a fire before?" Auralie asks, confusion written all over her face.

I shake my head. "No. The staff always had it started for me."

"Staff?" Auralie's head tilts as the muscle between her brows wrinkles.

Stass pins me with a stare, then her eyes widen with understanding. "Oh, gods, you weren't kidding. When you said princess, you really meant it, didn't you?"

The last time we were on this beach was the only time I ever spoke of being a princess to anyone other than Weston and Sig. It was just after I fought with Weston in the tunnels, after he lied to me about who he was and used my title as a means to push me away. Stassia noticed, and I said it. I didn't try to hide it. I was past holding myself back from these friends, this family, by then. But she never brought it up again.

There's no point in hiding it anymore.

My shoulders touch my ears, and I wince slightly. "The princess of Blackwood isn't really the one going around and lighting the fires in the castle."

"No! You're lying," Stass says, her jaw falling open. "Your father is the *hot king*?"

I roll my eyes, and Auralie bursts into laughter. "It was so uncomfortable when you said that. Please don't ever say it again."

"Oh, I'm going to say it, because it is the truth." Stass takes in the look of disgust on my face, but her grin only widens. "Why did you keep this from us for all this time?"

I shrug. "No one needed to know. I didn't want to be treated differently because of who I was, although…" My eyes lift to find Weston, and I spot him still talking with Veck. His eyes find mine, and he smirks softly, but I turn back to the girls. "*Someone* didn't agree."

"Captain knew?" Auralie asks. "How?"

I let out a deep sigh. "It's a long story for another day, but yes, he knew."

"Wow," Stassia muses as she nods slowly. "So there was more to his grumpiness than just fighting feelings. Everything makes so much more sense now."

I nod. "But that's why I am probably the worst person to help you with a fire."

"Move. I can do it." Sig walks up from behind and nudges past me, squatting between the girls. "Not everyone here is an inexperienced princess." She turns over her shoulder and shoots me a sly look before reaching out to shuffle some of the kindling. Auralie stares blankly at Sig as she grabs the flint from her hand. Sparks fly with the first strike, and Sig crouches lower, blowing gently toward the base, and coaxing the flame to life before sitting back on her heels with a satisfied grin on her face.

"Wha—" Stass gapes as she looks between us. "What the hell is going on, and why is everyone keeping secrets?"

Sig laughs loudly and stands, her hands on her hips as she watches her work literally burst into flames and engulf the gigantic pile of wood. "There's no point in secrets anymore," she says. "It's not like we can go back to our kingdoms. There's no such thing as princesses for us."

"Tell that to Weston," I grumble, and Sig huffs a laugh.

"I need time to process this," Stass says, rubbing her temples as Auralie pushes to her feet, swiping the sand off her clothes.

"Well, while you process, I'm starving. I need food to focus. Let's eat."

Trays of food now cover the crate tables, and the suns have finally dropped below the horizon. We pile plates high and find an empty blanket, sitting to eat and watch the freedom and happiness around us. Fin pulls Weston into some sort of game, and Jorn is trying to convince everyone, including us, to get in the water despite the quickly cooling breeze.

About an hour after sunset, movement near the portal catches my eye, and it's as if the air is sucked out of all of us. Silence falls over the group and everyone stills, turning to watch Gauge step away from the rock face. All eyes are on him as he shuffles to the sand, the same dejected look on his face as was on Taril's; the one I know we all had.

He wasn't worthy.

My stomach sinks. Is this only the beginning of the torment, where we find out repeatedly for the rest of the night that none of us are worthy? And if so, is it actually the best outcome since we no longer have the choice to return home?

A broad frame crossing the beach pulls my gaze, and I watch Weston approach Gauge, clapping him on the shoulder and saying something none of us can hear over the crackle of the fire and the crash of the waves. Gauge nods solemnly, then mimics Weston's gesture, before they both release and walk back toward the surf.

The tension of the moment bursts, and no one needs confirmation of what they already knew was coming before returning to their evening, continuing the conversations that were abruptly cut off, and the games that paused. It's only a matter of time now before the rest of the Voyagers trickle from the mountain. I can't seem to focus on the conversation, and instead look over at the portal every few moments.

"Hey," Sig says, bumping my shoulder with hers. She must have noticed my inattentiveness or felt my anxiety. "It'll be fine. It's the same thing we've dealt with every time before."

I let out a deep sigh. "I know. I just can't help but have hope that at least *one* of us would be told yes. Even though I'd be heartbroken that they couldn't bring it home, I really want to know that at least one of us was deemed to have the purest intentions. I don't know why the island doesn't see that."

Her shoulders rise and fall as her chin settles on one of them, looking toward me. "I don't think we'll ever know. But we can't let it bother us for eternity. At some point we're going to have to accept our fate."

"Weston doesn't want to give up," I murmur. "I don't know if he ever will."

"Cap..." She pauses as she collects her thoughts. "He's always been adamant about holding onto hope. He didn't want to give up and have the promise of real life taken away from any of us. But I can imagine..." Her voice trails off as she chews on the inside of her cheek.

"What, Sig?"

Her chest heaves with a sigh. "I don't want to upset you."

"I'll be the judge of that. Just say it."

"Fine. But don't be mad at me, alright?"

"Promise."

"Cap always wanted to find a way home, but it was never about himself. Everything he did was for all of us. I don't think he saw much of a future for himself, especially after all this time. If we ever returned home, everyone he knew would have moved on. We had no way of knowing how much time had passed, and we didn't know if anyone we knew would even be alive. But things changed. He changed. I watched it happen. I think that maybe there was more to his decision to keep looking than just to get his princess back to her kingdom."

Tears prick at my eyes, but I hold her gaze, even as the image of his face as he watched Fin hold my hand flashes before me. Is Sig implying Weston wanted a future with me? That he didn't want to give up in the end, because he saw more?

I shake my head. "He kept saying we couldn't be together because of who we were back home. He wouldn't try harder to get back if he wanted more."

"I know that man very well. He doesn't talk a lot, but when he does, it isn't necessarily what he truly thinks. Or wants. Sometimes, he says things because he's trying to convince himself."

A single tear escapes as I look out across the beach, my eyes drawn to him instantly. As if he feels my stare, he looks over at me. His smile falters and his brow furrows as he scans my face, clearly seeing the tear. Jorn laughs beside him at something one of the boys in the group says, but Weston steps away, turning toward me and no longer hearing the conversation he was just in.

What's wrong? he mouths. His jaw tightens, and his gaze bores into me, looking like he's going to cross the beach toward me the moment I say I need him. I shake my head, giving him a slightly water smile.

Nothing, I mouth back, but he strides forward, halting only when I shake my head again. His head tilts to the side, and his eyebrows draw in closer.

I'm fine, I mouth again and flick my wrist to shoo him back to the group. He takes a reluctant step back and turns toward the group again, but not before sneaking another glance my way, his relaxed smile now a close-lipped line.

"See?" Sig says, and I turn back to her. "He's different."

"I just don't understand. Why would he push me away for so long if deep down that's how he truly felt? If he thought life back home would be better, why would he tell me we couldn't be together, when here we could be?"

I swear my loyalty to her, Lennox Holt, and vow to stay by her side in whatever way she will have me.

The words settle in the pit of my stomach.

Would it actually be better back home? We would have purpose, a life to live with real experiences that we'd be denied here, but be unable to have them together? Would we be cursed to constantly be near each other, but never able to act on the love that has grown between us? At least not while my father was still alive.

But that could be years. It is my duty to provide the kingdom with an heir. Would Weston stand by and watch that happen? Would I be able to court a prince, one that would provide Blackwood with opportunity or protection, knowing that the man standing behind my father is the one I truly want? Or could I ignore tradition, like my father did, and choose who I want?

Choose Weston?

Maybe it is better we are trapped here, so I don't have to make that choice.

The thought makes my chest ache. There's no right answer. There's no better choice. Each is different, but only one thing matters.

Right here, right now, we didn't get to choose.

"Because he's more stubborn than you are," Sig says, and looks up just as another Voyager steps through the portal, the same sullen look on his face.

I sneak a glance back at Weston and watch the shadows from the flames dance across his features.

This future may not be ideal. It may not be what we visualized or chose for ourselves, but we chose each other.

It's the best future we have.

CHAPTER FIFTEEN

One by one, the Voyagers leave the mountain, and with every fallen or defeated face, the crack in the hope I've held onto deepens. But it isn't until I see the small body with slumped shoulders step onto the beach that my heart truly breaks.

"Roley!" Fin calls from the other side of the now roaring fire. His tiny form leaps up, his legs pumping as he darts across the sand toward his friend.

"I'm going to go check on him," I tell the girls, and am met with nods and words of approval. I cross the beach behind Fin and almost run into him as he comes to a halt watching Roley swipe at his cheeks.

"Oh, you're sad," Fin says. "Did Dawnlin tell you no too?" His voice is sullen, and I stifle the emotions bubbling in my chest. Roley needs strength and encouragement, not disappointment that he wasn't successful either.

He sniffs before nodding, and Fin's shoulders sink too. I step past Fin and crouch down before Roley, reaching out and gently grasping his hand.

"Well, Roley, that means you're one of us now. None of us got it either," I say.

His chin lifts, and his watery eyes widen, his eyebrows scrunching on his forehead.

"You mean I'm a Castaway now?"

"Only if you want to be. But that's how we all became one. The island told us no too."

"Yeah, so now I'm a Castaway forever!" Fin cries, throwing his fists in the air. He tries to crow, the screeching noise making me flinch with a smile. Jorn calls out Fin's name from somewhere behind us, and Fin's eyes brighten as he looks back toward the beach where Jorn stands, a huge grin on his face and his thumbs up in the air. Fin holds his hand up, returning the gesture, before turning back to Roley, whose eyes bounce between us.

"It's okay, Roley! Now, you can see the ship and play hide and seek with mister Weston and me. He's really good and always finds me. Maybe now that there's two of us, he might lose and we win. And Jorn can teach you how to climb, and you can see my job. It's lots of fun being a Castaway," Fin rambles, and Roley's tears dry up quickly as he listens.

"I dunno," Roley mumbles, kicking his boot into the sand.

"You don't have to decide anything. How about we just have some fun tonight?" I say.

"Yeah! Let's do something fun!" Fin yells.

"Come on," I say, grabbing both their hands and leading them toward the water. Not long ago, I would have felt my breath seize and fear overtake me as we approached the surf, but now, I feel nothing but calm. I look down at the hands of these two boys, and listen to Fin continue to babble, telling Roley more about the Castaways, and Edmond's words flow through my mind.

Light always finds a way.

They may be children for the rest of their lives, and never see or truly understand the hopelessness of our situation, but they will always bring us all joy, and I along with everyone else here will make sure that despite the darkness that has loomed over our situation, for them, for all of us, we will always try to find the light.

We chase the waves, back and forth as they roll in and out, seeing who can get the closest without getting wet, or who can make the most laps before the next set comes in. Roley forgets his sadness quickly, and Fin's laughter rings out over the crashing water and chatter of everyone nearby. It doesn't take long before more of the crew join in our game, although some of the older boys make a point of ignoring the loose rules and instead start throwing others into the chilled water.

I lose complete track of time as we all play on the beach beneath the clear sky and blanket of stars, without a care for whatever comes next. Roley finally asks if there is any food, and he's probably starving after his long day in the mountain.

I take the boys back to the crates and get them each situated, rolling some blankets up into makeshift pillows for when their energy eventually crashes, and they fall asleep the same way Fin does on any late night with the crew. A quick glance around the beach tells me that most of the Voyagers have returned and have incorporated themselves as if there were never two sides.

The only one left is Mara.

As if I've summoned her, she walks through the portal barely a moment later, her arms wrapped around her middle, and her face stoic as she takes in the scene on the beach.

I watch as she looks around until her eyes fall on me. Even from this distance with only the light of the moon and the glow of the flames, I can see her chin quiver. My feet act on their own, bringing me across the beach and kicking up sand in my haste. Slowing just before I reach her, I approach cautiously, waiting to see how she will react, but it's as if my proximity opens up a dam, and she bursts into tears. I immediately close the gap and throw my arms around her shoulders, squeezing her tightly as she cries into my chest.

Mara was my very first friend, my first *real* one, even if she was reluctant in the beginning. If being on the island has taught me anything about friendship and love, it is that we are there for those we care about, when they need us, and even more when they don't think they do. Mara needs me, especially now that she is experiencing the same pain we all went through after losing our hope.

"Even if we could get home, I couldn't have helped her," she says through her sobs. "She's probably already gone, and I lost all the time I had left."

"I know, Mara. It isn't what any of us wanted," I say, squeezing her tight, showing her through my touch that she isn't alone.

"What the fuck are we supposed to do now?" Her back straightens, and she steps out of my grasp, swiping at her eyes. They're red-rimmed and already swollen as she looks at me, her face the most vulnerable I've ever seen it. "How do we keep going, day after day with no reason to be here? What's the point?"

"We have to find purpose in each other." I reach out and take her hands in mine. "We can't let him take away our happiness too. He doesn't deserve that. We have to live the best life we can for as long as the island lets us."

Footsteps approach in the sand from behind, and Mara glances over my shoulder as Veck stops beside us, a sympathetic and understanding smile on his lips.

"You alright, Mar?" he asks.

She nods and sniffs again. She drops my hands as he steps closer to her, throwing an arm across her shoulders and pulling her into his side. "Come on," he says, "let's get you something to eat."

Veck smiles at me before leading her away toward the crates, to the group of people she's now part of. They must have been good friends before Veck left, and I'm glad it's as if no time has passed between them at all. I think Mara needs that. She needs to remember she isn't alone here, and that there's no us against them any longer. We're all in this together, and we have no reason to be anything but united.

I scan the area for Weston as I make my way back toward the fire. The boys and then Mara returning pulled my attention away, and I lost track of him. Rounding the edge of the fire, I skim over the faces, trying to find the outline of his body, which normally stands out, especially to me, but in the darkness and shadows, everyone blends together.

A warm hand catches mine as I round the fire, gently tugging me to a stop.

"Looking for someone?"

Weston sits on a large blanket near the fire, an amused look on his face, I'm sure from watching me look right past him.

"Not anymore." He pulls me toward him, and I crouch down, turning to settle my back against his chest. A shiver courses through my body as I press into his warmth, and he wraps his arms around me.

"Cold?" Reaching down, he rubs his hands along my pants, and the wet fabric makes me shiver again. "You're soaked."

"I wasn't very good at the game. The boys are faster than I am. Hey!" I say, as his warmth disappears from behind me. A moment later, he drapes a blanket over my legs, wrapping it snugly around us and settling me firmly against his chest once again. His warmth combined with the heat from the flames in front of us is almost instant, and I sigh deeply, letting my head fall against his shoulder.

"Better?" he grumbles as his jaw presses into my temple.

"Mmhm," I hum with a nod.

"How were Roley and Mara?" he asks, and a smile tugs at my lips.

"Were you watching me?" I ask, tilting my head back to look up at him.

His eyes glitter in the moonlight as he looks down at me. "I'm always watching you."

"That doesn't sound obsessive at all," I joke.

His chest vibrates with a low chuckle. "I can't help it. Even if it wasn't my job, I still wouldn't be able to take my eyes off you."

Warmth blooms in my chest at his words, but it's tinged with sadness as I think of the answer to his question, the reason behind it.

"They'll be alright." My voice is almost a whisper as I drop my gaze back down to the fire. Silence falls between us as the heaviness of my answer settles. It's final, and while we were all eventually fine with the island's decision, this time feels like more.

His cheek presses into the side of my head, and his warm breath tickles my ear. After long moments of only the crackle of the flames and the distant jovial chatter of the rest of the crew, Weston finally breaks the silence.

"Are you going to tell me what upset you earlier?"

The conversation with Sig comes rushing back to me, along with my worries that Weston has stronger feelings of loss than he's led on. The guilt I feel for causing this fallout with Dane is like an overwhelming wave, especially knowing that somewhere deep down, he did actually see a future for us back home, no matter what he has said out loud.

I shake my head. "No."

"Alright," he murmurs, and presses a kiss just behind my ear. He doesn't pry or question; he just accepts my response. I take a deep breath and curve onto myself, sinking closer into him, and he clutches me tighter with one arm, reaching out with the other and resting it on his bent knee beside me.

We sit in companionable silence as I try not to think more about what Sig said, and instead focus on the sounds of the beach around us. Light glints in the corner of my eye, and glance to the side to find the fire reflecting off the golden metal of Weston's First Guard ring.

My eyes fixate on it as nerves tumble through my stomach. Before I can stop myself, the words spill from my mouth.

"Do you have any regrets?" My head stays straight, but my gaze is still stuck on his ring as I wait for his response.

He takes a moment before his voice rumbles in my ear.

"Is that why you were upset? You think I have regrets?"

"Just answer the question."

He chuckles softly. "So demanding. Yes. I do have regrets."

I tilt my head back to find him already looking down at me. "Really?"

"Mmhm," he hums, and his chest vibrates against my back, but he doesn't elaborate.

"Are you going to tell me what they are?" I ask, and the glint in his eyes is playful.

His hand runs up and down the side of my thigh, stroking my tight-fitting pants that are finally drying under the heat of the fire. "I regret never having had the chance to see you in a ballgown."

I huff a laugh. "You didn't miss much. I didn't wear them often because there wasn't any need to. Besides, it's just a dress."

"That's true." He presses a kiss onto the top of my shoulder, then slowly trails them up my neck until his lips brush my ear, sending a shiver down my spine. "But getting to watch you dance all night, knowing that I'll be the one taking it off you later is something I regret missing."

My breath catches in my throat, but my mind snags on one specific word.

"Watching? You would be the one dancing with me."

His sad laugh makes my heart sink. "We both know that's not how it would be." His voice drops even lower, and I can hear the sadness in it. "It was just a bedtime story, sweetheart."

"Well then, don't regret it," I say, dropping my chin down to face the flames. "That's not the life we were meant to live. You get to take my clothes off all you want here."

His growl rumbles in my ear. "The way it should be. I like it better when you're naked."

The golden glint of his ring catches my eye again, and I reach out from under the blanket, wrapping my fingers around his hand and bringing it to my lap. The seal stamped into the surface is rough on the pad of my thumb as I rub my finger over it.

If it weren't for this ring, everything would be different.

If it weren't for this ring, Weston wouldn't be in Dawnlin.

But if he had never come to Dawnlin, none of this would have happened. We wouldn't have happened. He never would have come looking for the healing waters to save my mother. He never would have been trapped in this time, in this age, and we would have passed by each other, only ever interacting with formalities and decorum.

But if it weren't for this ring, if we were back home like he secretly wanted, we might have a future.

"I could make you take it off, you know." My voice is barely a whisper, and I don't know if I'm even saying it to him or just to myself. He must hear me, and his fingers wrap around mine.

"If you did, I'd be just another citizen of Blackwood. Without it, I wouldn't be able to be anywhere near you." His voice quiets even more, and his fingertips slowly stroke mine. "Please don't take that away from me."

I lace my fingers through his, and squeeze his hand tightly. "It doesn't matter. There's no kingdom anymore."

"Even so, promise me you won't."

I swallow hard, hoping this will be the end of the guilt I feel. It's true. There is no kingdom anymore. His ring doesn't matter. Whether he wears it or not is up to him, despite everything it symbolizes.

"I won't. I promise."

Silence stretches between us again as I stare into the flames, clutching his hand as if he will disappear if I let go. The edge of his ring digs into my palm, a constant reminder of what would have happened to us, to this, if we had gone home.

"I have other regrets." His voice trails off and is almost too quiet to hear over the popping of the burning wood and the laughter of the others.

I stay quiet, hoping he'll tell me, and he doesn't make me wait long.

"Sometimes I regret letting Dane live for so long. I should have killed him a long time ago."

The breath is sucked from my chest. If he had, he would be tethered to Dawnlin forever. He'd be the Guardian, the one who brought me here instead of Dane, and then I'd never see him again. Neither of us would ever know what we were missing, because none of this would have ever happened.

He doesn't give me a chance to respond before he speaks again.

"If I had, every one of them would be home." He nods toward the crew and the Voyagers all around us. "I was selfish."

The blanket falls to my hips as I sit up abruptly, and turn until I'm facing him. "How could you say that? After everything you have done for everyone here? You are not selfish, Weston. Not at all. You kept them safe this entire time and kept Dane from finding the healing waters. Risking yourself, the sleepless nights, the worry, putting yourself in front of them? That was all sacrifice. Nothing you did was selfish."

"I selfishly chose my life instead of theirs. And when I had a chance again…" His eyes hold mine, and I know he's remembering that night, when he had the tip of his sword pressed into Dane's neck. How easily he could have ended it all. His jaw works, but his gaze stays strong. "I selfishly chose you."

I take his face in my hands, and he winces slightly at my touch, his guilt-ridden features causing agony to course through my body.

"It isn't selfish to do something for yourself, Weston, especially not when you've given your entire life to other people. You're allowed to choose yourself and have a life outside of your duty."

I bite back my shock at the statement. Am I telling him, or am I telling myself? Everything I have done or chosen has been for my duty, for my kingdom, for my future role. The first time I did something for myself was coming here to save my mother, but even then there was more to my decision.

But it isn't about me, not right now. This is about Weston, about the pain and guilt and regret I see in his eyes. He's been holding this in for years, and he needs to know he didn't make a mistake. He wasn't selfish. He didn't choose wrong, and he wasn't responsible for this either, just like he told me.

His eyes dart between mine, and I rise onto my knees and tilt his head back. I look into his eyes, hoping he sees the severity on my face, the urging for him to let it go and forgive himself. If the only way for him to do so is to take the burden off his shoulders, then that is what I have to do.

"I love you, Weston. If anything should make you feel less selfish, it's that. You didn't make that decision for nothing. You made it for you, but you made it for me too."

His jaw unclenches beneath my palms and the tension in his shoulders relaxes just slightly, as if I've taken a weight off. I can carry it for him. It's my duty to shoulder the burden for my people, and Weston is one of them. I lean in just a little closer and keep my eyes locked on his.

"You have nothing to regret or feel guilty about. It wasn't your choice. It was mine." His throat bobs with a swallow, and I stroke the pad of my thumb over his stubble-covered cheek. "I told you not to kill him. Consider that an order. You can't feel guilty or selfish about something that wasn't yours to decide."

His chest rises and falls with a harsh breath just before his hand finds the back of my head, his fingers weaving into my hair. He pulls me down, crushing my lips into his. My arms wrap around his neck as his lips move, opening them and sliding his tongue against mine to deepen the kiss.

He grabs my jaw, his grip gentle but commanding as he doesn't let me go, holding me and telling me everything he's feeling with his body instead of his words. Lifting my knees, I set them next to his hips and sink into his lap, so I can feel the rise and fall of each breath as our chests and hips mold together.

If there's anything I've learned about him in the short time we've been together, it's that touch calms him. Closeness slows him down. It's why he's constantly reaching out and taking hold of me in some way, and I can't help but wonder if, after all this time, it helps him feel like he's not alone.

I break away, my lips swollen and chest heaving. I used to be uncomfortable showing any affection to Dane in front of others, but with Weston, none of that matters. I don't care who sees, who looks, even if it's Jorn poking fun. Weston needs it, and there are no rules to follow here.

"Is that all?" I whisper, and he shakes his head slowly, his eyes still hooded from the kiss.

"Sometimes I think I should have told you earlier."

He doesn't have to say it for me to know exactly what he means. I was furious with him that he didn't tell me, and my words must have struck a chord. Told me who he was. Told me the truth about Dane. Told me that everything that caused me such hatred for him in the beginning wasn't true.

"I'm glad you didn't."

"Really?" he says, his head tilting slightly.

My lips tip up at the corners, and I glance away, trying to find the right words. "You were right. For my entire life, I've been told what I need to know or do, and had to accept it. Edmond taught me to learn everything I could before deciding, but that was for later, once I was queen. I never got to practice that. I had to fall in line and follow my father's orders. When I came here, I wanted to decide everything for myself. I needed to see it, and figure it out, and make my own judgment. I would have rejected it if you had just told me everything outright." I run my hands down his chest, feeling the firm muscles tighten as I graze over them. "I needed to get to know who you were in here." I press my palm over his heart, and lift my chin to meet his eyes. "If I hadn't, we never would have gotten this far."

"I'm never going to get tired of hearing you say that," he says with a sly smirk.

I narrow my eyes at him. "Say what?"

He leans forward, closing the distance until we are sharing a breath. "That I was right."

I roll my eyes and smack his chest. "Out of everything I said, *that's* what you focused on?" His boisterous laughter rings in my ears as he crushes me to his chest and plants a quick kiss to my lips.

"I heard the rest, too. If that was what you needed, then I'm glad I didn't do it."

"Good," I say and pinch his chin, dipping it low and forcing him to stay focused on my now serious face. "No more regrets."

His eyes drop to my mouth, and he leans in, but a voice from behind me calls out loudly.

"Yo, Cap!"

Weston drops his head back and groans. "What, Jorn?"

"Well, *excuse* me for interrupting, but does anyone care for a drink?" I glance over my shoulder and find him standing at the front of the blanket near the fire with both arms extended, the neck of a bottle clenched in each fist.

"Not for me," Weston says with a shake of his head.

"I'm good, thanks Jorn," I call with a shake of my head and a smile.

"You two are no fun when you're like this. More for me then!" He rounds the fire, going to the next group and passing the bottles to them.

Weston's hands find my hips, and his thumbs slowly stroke my hipbones. When I turn back to face him, I find one eyebrow raised. "You don't want to pretend you're drunk and try to seduce me?" His face widens in a glittering smile that makes my insides melt.

"I don't think I have to be drunk to do that anymore, Captain," I tease.

His chest grumbles, but just as he leans closer Jorn calls out, "Who wants to hear the story about when I stole the Captain's boots?"

"I do!" I shriek, throwing my hand in the air. I spin around and settle back into Weston's chest. Jorn stands off to the side on top of a crate so everyone that has made their way to the blankets around the fire can see and hear him. He points at me with one bottle then raises it in a salute, his normally goofy grin plastered onto his face.

"Trust me, you want to hear this one," Sig says as she plops down on the empty blanket beside us.

Weston groans loudly behind me. "I wish everyone would fucking forget this story."

"Not a chance," Sig says, her own wide smile matching Jorn's.

Jorn jumps into the story, his slightly inebriated behavior fueling the humor. Everyone slowly makes their way back and listens to Jorn recount the event. I can't help but throw my head back into Weston's shoulder, laughing as it goes on and on. Tears fill my eyes, and I can feel Weston shaking his head behind me, chuckling as I giggle uncontrollably.

Laughter and lightness floods the entire beach as everyone reminisces on happy times, or in my and the Voyager's cases, hears about them for the very first time.

"More!" I call out once Jorn finishes, and he launches right into another recounting of, shockingly, a time he played a joke on Weston. A cool burst of wind comes off the water, causing sparks to float through the air. I reach down and grab the blanket again, scooting back into Weston's chest and draping it over us, letting the heat from our bodies fight the chill in the air.

Weston's shifts his arm under the blanket, his hand sliding over my hip and resting on the top of my thigh. His thumb strokes slowly as we listen to Jorn's enthusiasm increase with every sentence, and I smile.

Happy.

This is what true happiness feels like.

Sitting on the beach with full bellies and a fire, surrounded by people I love, listening to stories of times that weren't shrouded in worry and hopelessness. When I first went to the Oasis, I thought I could live the rest of my time here content.

But this.

It's not at all how I expected tonight to feel after the Voyagers went into the mountain. But it's real, and if this is how the rest of our days will feel, then I can be nothing but grateful for it.

"Fucking gods," Weston mutters as I cackle when Jorn tells us about a time where he and a few of the guys lifted Weston's bathtub out of his room and hid it in the ship. "That was not funny," he grumbles as I wipe the tears from my eyes and try to breathe over the uncontrollable laughter. "They wouldn't let me in the showers either. It was awful."

"I'm sorry," I gasp, "but you have to admit it is a little funny." I tilt my head back and see the amused scowl on his face. "I know how much you like to soak in your tub."

"He was a very grumpy Captain that week, huh boys?" Jorn chides, and a chorus of yells breaks out from the other side of the fire.

"Pick on someone else, Jorn!" Weston yells, and Jorn points over to us.

"You got it, Cap," he says with a wink, then turns to find Eirlick, proceeding to dive into an entirely new story, one where Weston was not the center.

"Don't be grumpy," I say. "I like hearing the stories." I can feel the shake of his head in my hair and the low grumble of a laugh in response. His fingers stop tracing patterns on my thigh and his hand flattens, wrapping around the inside and sliding a little higher.

His breath brushes my ear, sending a shiver up my spine as his voice grumbles low against it.

"Let's go to bed."

"But I'm not tired," I say, and his responding chuckle has me curling my toes in my boots.

"Neither am I."

My stomach dips and flutters in anticipation, but I keep my breaths steady and try not to let him see. "Want to make another bet?" Jorn's story is barely a hum in the background as I wait for Weston's answer, and it feels like forever of my heart pounding in my ears before he mumbles.

"What do you have in mind?"

I purse my lips, trying to hide a smile, but I can't help how Weston's competitive side sparks a thrill inside me. "I bet you can't catch me, and I can make it back to the ship before you do."

"Why wouldn't I just leave with you?"

"Because you're going to do the captain thing and make sure everyone's all right, and leave someone in charge, and make sure there's a plan to bring Fin back."

He chuckles softly in my ear. "Am I that predictable?"

"Absolutely you are. Plus it gives my shorter legs a head start." His hand rubs up and down my leg before settling in the same spot, but I don't let it distract me. "So do we have a bet?"

"What do I get if I win?"

"Whatever you want."

His hand tightens around my thigh and my breath catches in my throat. "And what do you get if you win?"

"Whatever I want."

He presses a kiss to the back of my jaw, just in front of my ear before nipping it softly. "You better get moving. Your time starts now."

CHAPTER SIXTEEN

Scrambling to my feet, I fling the blanket to the side and start off toward the stone steps across the beach. Jorn is still animatedly telling a story, and everyone is watching intently, including the Voyagers, who seem to be recovering from the disappointment well. Sitting amongst everyone, they actually look like part of the crew, and it feels like a relief knowing that we could all get along peacefully here.

I peek past lounging bodies to check on Fin and Roley, both already fast asleep on a blanket, the late night and day full of excitement finally having caught up to them.

Just as I'm about to pass the last set of blankets, someone grabs my forearm and tugs me to a stop.

"Where are you going?" Stassia asks.

Shit. She's using up my time.

I try not to look like I'm eager to leave, but I want to win, and getting caught up with Stassia will not help that.

"Just tired. Gonna head back," I say vaguely.

She shoots me a knowing look. "Sure you are. Have fun. We'll wish Captain goodnight when he gets tired in a few minutes, too." She releases me, and I purse my lips, trying to hide my smile.

"You're a good friend, Stass."

"Yeah, yeah," she says, shooing me away with her fingers. "A jealous one. But a good one. Now go." Auralie giggles beside her as they both turn back toward Jorn, who has now pulled Taril up in front of the group and is using him to act something out.

Resting my chin on my shoulder, I flick my gaze back toward the blanket, hoping Weston is distracted by the story.

He's not.

He hasn't moved, hasn't started his Captain duties, and instead sits with his eyes fixed on me. My cheeks heat at the sly smile playing on his lips and the challenge in his gaze. He cocks his head to the side and lifts a single eyebrow, and I turn away quickly as a giddy flame flickers to life inside of me.

I want to win. I won the first bet, and purposely lost the second, but this time, there's nothing specific at stake, and I might need to save this prize for a time when I need it.

Now that I know he's watching me, I need him to think I'm taking the long way through the island, not through the tunnels. We still haven't shown them to the Voyagers yet, so I don't want to go through them anywhere I could be seen. Laughter echoes behind me as I climb the steps quickly. I need to move fast, because I don't know how much of a head start he's going to give me, especially after I already got stopped by Stassia. I can't risk looking back to see if he's following, so I keep my head down and hurry along the path. Hooking a right, I head toward the ship, and I've barely taken a few steps when I get an idea.

The mist from the falls is chilling on the already cool night as I cross over the bridge. Darkness makes crossing significantly more difficult than in daylight, and I don't have Weston holding my hand and leading me across the slick rock to make sure I don't fall. If I do plunge into the depths, this time, no one will know where I am.

You won't fall.

My heart pounds in my ears as I try to take it slow, but move fast enough that Weston doesn't catch me. I swing my leg over the side, lowering myself down boulder by boulder until I find the right one. Water splashes, soaking my clothes as I slide behind the cascading water and into the dark cave behind it. Hopefully now that I'm a Castaway, the island will let me open the door at the back that Weston snuck through both times we were in this cave. The tunnels will help me cut through the fast way and beat him back to the ship, and if I'm lucky, he takes my bait and tries to follow me the long way.

The moonlight barely touches the space through the thick wall of water that covers the entrance, and the darkness is overwhelming. I've been here before. I know where to go. But as I step further into the darkness, I hesitate.

I've never been afraid of the dark. Growing up in a kingdom without true sunlight will do that. I lived in a cold and dark castle my entire life, but this time the darkness gives me pause. It's not the darkness I'm afraid of. It's the island. Even though I found the healing waters once before, this is still a location where dangers lurk to keep it protected. The island could change at any time, and the thought causes a flicker of fear inside me.

Spinning back toward the waterfall, I focus on the bit of light that I can, contemplating whether I should go back through and abandon my plan.

There's nothing to be afraid of. The island won't hurt you now.

I take a tentative step backward, retreating from the crashing water, when my back presses into something, something that wasn't there in the darkness seconds ago. A scream rips through my throat. The sound resonates off the stone walls and rings in my ears, as a hand wraps around my mouth, stifling the noise. Panic rises in my chest as flashes of Dane's furious face from the night in the cabin flicker before my eyes. I immediately reach for my waistband, trying to grab my dagger, but a strong hand grips my wrist and holds firm. Our arms around my waist, tugging me backward until I am pressed into the hard planes of a body.

"Were you trying to let me win?"

The soothing voice grumbles in my ear, and relief floods through me. *Weston. Not Dane.*

I'm safe.

He releases my mouth and wrist, his arms instead circling my waist and pulling me into his warm embrace. I drop my head back onto his chest, settling against him, and let my tense limbs relax, then think better of it and jerk my elbow into his abdomen.

He lets out a huff followed by an amused laugh.

"You scared me, asshole! I almost pulled my dagger on you."

"You mean this dagger?" The blade glints in the scarce moonlight before me as his arm extends, and he flips it deftly between his fingers.

"How did you—" I reach out to grab it, but he pulls it away, holding it out of my reach. I hadn't even felt him take it off me, and now I'm questioning whether he even did it here, in the cave, or back on the beach. How did he disarm me without my noticing? Then, the thought pops into my head. He knew he was going to catch me.

"This is why I'm in charge, both here and in Blackwood." I can hear the smile in his voice, and I know he will not let me live it down. He'll probably force me to practice defending against it in the next training session. His lips brush the curve of my ear and cause goosebumps to erupt on my neck. "You don't need it right now, anyway."

I feel his arms move as he slides it away in his belt, and the memory of being disarmed here before is too familiar. This time though, I'm not itching to get it back. I know he won't keep it from me.

"Are you finally going to tell me how this door works?" I ask, stepping away from him and turning toward the complete darkness at the back of the cave. I'm barely a pace away before he reaches out, grasping my hand and spinning me around until I fall into him with a thud.

"Where do you think you are going?"

I can barely make out any of his features in the shadows, but the lilt in his voice is enough to give me an idea of the challenging look on his face.

"Home?" I say warily.

He steps forward, walking me backward until I'm pressed against the wall of the cave, and yet another memory of him in this cave surfaces, only this time, I'm not fighting him with every ounce of hatred I have. The dim glow silhouettes his shape before me, but his features remain dark. I feel before I can see his movement, as the pads of his fingers lift my chin and tilt my head up toward his.

"I believe I won the bet."

"You did," I say playfully. "What do you want?"

"I want a lot of things." His voice is dangerously low, bordering on the growl he usually reserves for when he's angry. But he's not, and I can tell his voice is laced with something besides anger.

"But I won, and I want you pressed up against this wall with my cock buried inside of you."

Heat blooms between my thighs in anticipation of Weston's prize, but more than being overcome with my own desire, I'm caught off guard.

"Here? Right now?" My eyes strain to see his face in the darkness, to see if he is serious or playing more games.

"Yes, sweetheart, right fucking now."

My pulse rises as his hips press into me, his desire already apparent as his hard length fits against me.

I suck in a quick breath as a pulse of pleasure surges. "I can't see you," I say, the words coming out breathy as I search for him in the darkness. My skin prickles as he leans closer, and his breath caresses my skin.

"You don't need to see me. Just feel me."

My lips part as his brush tenderly along my jaw. The fabric of my shirt tickles my stomach as he slowly bunches it into his fists, pulling the ends from where it is tucked into my waistband. His hands are on me then, hot and firm as they lie beneath my shirt, trailing up my skin. A low hum fills my throat as the backs of his knuckles brush the underside of my breasts. I swallow hard, the anticipation of his touch without the lace between us getting stronger with every second. The tip of his nose glides down the length of my neck, and his lips press into my collarbone.

"You smell fucking amazing," he grumbles, breathing deeply, and I turn my face away, giving him more access. "I never knew what I was missing until my sheets smelled like you. You're lucky I let you leave my bed."

He frees my breasts, tugging the lace over them and causing my nipples to peak. His fingers find them in the next instant, rolling the firm buds between his thumb and forefinger, at the same time as he sinks his hips further into me. My head falls back, and my eyes shutter closed as a low moan escapes me.

Hot breath against my skin and a low chuckle are his only responses. Need is already growing steadily, as the darkness makes it so I can only focus on everywhere he touches me. His lips meet my skin again, never kissing, just brushing along, leaving a trail of desire in their wake. They graze my throat, settling in the divot at the base of my neck, and I turn my head back to the center. I lower my chin and lean forward trying to capture his lips with mine, but he pulls back just out of reach as his palms cover my breasts, kneading and squeezing and pressing so I'm trapped against the wall.

I let out a frustrated groan.

"So impatient," he says, and I can hear the smile in his voice.

"I know what I want."

"So do I."

His hands slide out from under my shirt, releasing my breasts so the aching fullness is now even more apparent. My shirt lifts over my head, followed by my undergarments, and the sound of the damp fabric hitting the cave floor along with the cool air on my now exposed skin makes me shiver. There's a rustle of more fabric, followed by the clink of his belt buckle before more items fall to the floor.

The hot, bare skin of his chest presses into mine a moment later, followed by the grip of firm hands under my ass as he lifts me and wraps my legs around his waist. He lines his hips up with mine, fitting them against me and pressing me into the wall so his length rubs against my core.

"Oh, gods," I whimper. My breaths become shallow as I grind my hips into his, begging for more friction, but his grip tightens, holding me firmly and eliciting another frustrated groan.

"Patience, Lennox," he says, and I can tell he's enjoying feeling me want him. But I need him. After that kiss on the beach, after the confessions of regret, after the promise of tearing me out of my ballgowns, I need him to touch me, more than the way he's teasing me now.

I take his face in my hands and pull it toward me, needing him closer, his lips on mine, but it's as if he anticipated my movements. His hips still hold me off the ground as his hands wrap around my forearms, his strength overpowering me until my arms are pinned on either side of my head.

"Weston, kiss me," I pant, chest heaving as I try to fight against him, but I'm no match for his size and strength, not when he has me half naked and dripping with desire.

"You don't get to make demands, princess. This is my prize, not yours."

Anger sparks in my veins. "I swear to the gods, if you keep calling me that," I grind out, squeezing my eyes shut.

"You'll do what?" he growls, his body still and dominating as he towers over me.

"I don't know," I breathe, my mind completely blank of any threats I could impose on him in this moment when all I want is for him to be inside me, no matter what he calls me.

Pulling my wrists from the wall, he leans back slightly and lowers my hands to my breasts. My breath hitches when his fingers move with mine, pinching both my nipples before pressing my palms down firmly over the aching curves.

"I want you to play with yourself. Touch them like it is me."

I moan and nod quickly, even though I know he can't see me. I catch my bottom lip between my teeth, biting firmly as I feel his hands move lower. The throbbing in my core intensifies, all but distracting me from where he tugs at the waistband of my pants enough so he can slide his hand inside, leaving nothing between us.

His chest rumbles loudly as his fingers slide over me, and I suck in a quick breath. His forehead presses into mine as his fingers continue to stroke through my excitement. "You're so wet for me, Lennox. Have you been wanting me to fuck you tonight as much as I've been wanting to?"

"Yes," I gasp, and tilt my head again, trying to find him in the darkness as my hands still knead at my chest in the same way he likes to. He dodges me once again. "I always want you."

"I promise, I want you more."

"Weston," I say, my voice coming out as a low whine. "Please kiss me."

His parted lips hover over mine as I pant into them, our breaths mingling together as he still denies me what I'm begging him for. My core pulses, clenching around the emptiness as his fingers spread me apart, the tips playing with my entrance.

"There's no need to beg, my queen."

I cry out as his mouth crushes mine, his tongue diving deep at the same time as his fingers push inside me. White hot fire licks along my spine, the sensation overwhelming as pressure builds from my toes. I can't focus on anything but the feel of him consuming me from the inside out. His tongue strokes deep, the rhythm matching the thick push and pull of his fingers.

"Oh, gods," I scream, breaking away from his kiss, my body and emotions unable to handle the soaring pressure and pleasure ripping through me. His teeth snag on my lower lip, pulling it into his mouth just as his thumb finds the spot at the apex of my thighs, rolling languid circles over it, matching the pace of his fingers.

"You're so fucking beautiful," he says, "and you drive me fucking wild when you scream for me."

"Weston," I cry, begging him to bring me over the edge, for release.

His fingers slide out of me, and the empty feeling so close to release makes me call out in frustration.

"Ugh! No!" I groan, releasing my breasts so I can reach out to touch him, to pull him back in and finish what he started.

A soft chuckle meets my ears before his hands once again wrap around my wrists and push my arms against the wall. The brush of his breath on my ear makes me want to combust.

"I said don't move."

"Why did you stop?" I say, my voice wavering with emotion as my body still begs to be filled. His hands are back at my waistband, wrapping around the edge before they slide my pants down over my ass, pulling them farther down my thighs until I'm bared to him.

"Because this is my prize, and as much as I love you fucking my fingers, I said I wanted my cock buried inside you, not my hand."

I barely notice him tugging at the laces of his pants and pulling himself free before he's notching the tip of his cock at my entrance. With a flex of his hips, he's thrusting inside me, the wet heat of my core taking him to the hilt in one swift movement.

"Fuck!" I scream loudly as my head falls back farther, my back arching as I press my hips farther onto him, begging him silently to go deeper. My body is already sensitive and wound up from his hands before, but the narrow angle of my thighs from the tension of my pants makes it so I can feel every inch of his rigid cock with each movement. He rolls his hips, and all I can do is squeeze my eyes shut even tighter before he pulls out, thrusting firmly back into me again. My legs quake as I tighten them around his waist, pulling him in and begging for more.

"I need to touch you," I say, the words more of a plea than anything else.

He grabs my wrists, pulling them away from the wall and flattening my palms against his chest. His rhythmic thrusts still drive me higher, and I need to ground myself in him. I grip his muscles; my nails scrape across his nipples, down every ripple of his abdomen. His stomach clenches with every thrust, and I dig my fingers into his skin, holding onto him like my life depends on it.

Because it does. This man is my life now, and I never want to give him up.

I try to rock my hips into him, and he grips my hips harder, his bruising fingertips pressing into the muscle, and tilting me until I can feel the press of him right where I need it, as he pounds into me again and again.

A cry rips from my throat as my muscles begin to clench and quake around him, the pressure unable to be contained any longer.

"That's my good girl. Let go, Lennox." He grunts as he buries his face in the crook of my neck. He sucks the skin there and presses his chest into me again.

I don't know if it's his command, or the swell of his cock inside me, or the heat of his body pressing into mine, surrounding me and making me feel like I'll never be alone again, but I can't control it anymore. My mouth falls open in a silent scream, my chest heaving and hands gripping as intoxicating pleasure thrums through my core, my body, my limbs.

He sinks his teeth into the muscle in my shoulder, his own roar loud in my ear as he thrusts one last time. Heat blooms between my legs as he comes, and I can do nothing but pant, sucking in air and breathing him in. He stills, both of us breathing deeply, the only sound over the roaring of the waterfall.

My head lolls lazily to the side as my lips search for his. He kisses me gently, the barely there press of his lips so different from the rough and frenzied actions that consumed him moments ago. His tongue strokes mine, the movement barely a whisper as I come down from the high, my core still clenching around him as my chest heaves against his.

His forehead presses into mine, and we stay just like that for a few long moments before he breaks the silence.

"I know I'm not a man of many words," he murmurs. I wrap my hand around the back of his neck, steadying myself so I can focus on what he's telling me. "I don't like talking about how I feel. It's probably a product of watching my mother die, and seeing my father live with the regret of missing her."

There's a pang in my chest knowing now that it was Edmond who went through the pain, who missed the death of his wife, and who raised his young son alone.

"I regret leaving Blackwood without telling certain people how I felt about them, or telling them what I needed. I don't want to make the same mistake with you."

His chest rises and falls with a heavy breath, like he's trying to find the courage to say what he feels, instead of bottling it up inside and being the strong one; the one who never needs.

"I told you before that I don't know how I lived this long without you, and I don't want to do it again." His palm settles on my cheek, his thumb stroking my skin softly. "I was serious earlier. Please don't take that away from me."

I reach up and lace my fingers through his, feeling the warm metal of his ring press into my skin as I hold his hand against my face.

"There's nothing to worry about. No one it taking anything from anyone. You don't need to live without me." He lets out a sigh filled with relief as his shoulders curl in, cocooning us in our cave, whispering promises that only the island and we know.

"I'm yours forever, Weston."

His hand slides down my cheek and under my chin, lifting it and giving me a soft kiss, sealing his promise.

"And I will spend every second of forever making sure it stays that way."

CHAPTER SEVENTEEN

"Reset."

My training blades clatter to the deck as I fold over, resting my hands on my knees. Sweat drips down my face, and my chest heaves as I try to catch the breath that Weston is doing his best to make sure I never do. This afternoon, he and Sig pulled out the training weapons to work out some more restless energy in the crew. I spent most of the day helping Fin and Roley, who stayed on the ship after last night. Roley was excited to have his own child-sized bow, just like Fin's, which made their target practice much more effective, and fun for them.

Weston came over to watch while on a break from the lessons he was giving Gauge. He had stopped by the ship this morning and ended up staying the entire day, and was quite excited when he saw the swords.

Standing beside me with his arms crossed over his chest, Weston called some advice out to Roley and Fin, which was met with a chorus of very serious 'Aye, Captains', followed by intense concentration etched on their faces. Before heading back to the rest of the crew, he leaned toward me, his voice low and filled with challenge. "Come over once I'm finished with them. You're mine for the rest of the evening." I tried to keep the blush from my cheeks as he walked away, doing my best to avoid watching him saunter across the deck, back to the eager group waiting for his next instruction.

Keeping a straight face for the rest of the day and trying to hide my anticipation of finding out what he meant by the challenge was difficult. But as the crowd slowly dispersed, and the boys Weston had been working with all day sat off to the side, it was clear he actually meant training. He sauntered across the deck toward me, a set of swords in each hand, and a wicked smirk on his face.

We've been here ever since, in our own training ring, because Weston decided today was the best day to teach me how to use two swords at once. Hours have passed, and despite the complete exhaustion and aching muscles, I'm more invigorated than I've ever been in a training session with Brynne.

Now that our relationship is no longer the antagonistic captain and the defiant captive, Weston's lessons are completely different, even more than the day he taught me to disarm him with my dagger. He isn't afraid to touch me, to let his hands or gaze linger, or push me harder than he would have. Where he was patient and understanding before, he's now firm but playful. If training had been like this my entire life, I can't imagine how skilled I would be with a sword.

"I need a break," I gasp, still sucking air in deeply. I lift my head from where it had fallen between my shoulders and look at him across the deck. The colors of the sunset behind him are vibrant pinks and oranges, and the last light of the day makes the sweat on his skin glisten.

"Your attackers won't stop to give you a break," he says, fists resting on his hips, still holding both swords he has been fighting me with.

"Who's going to attack me? Them?" I throw a hand out toward the crew sitting off to the side, watching our training.

"I'll fight you if you need me to, Lennox," Veck calls out, and Weston scowls, leveling his sword at him.

"No."

Veck laughs and holds his hands up in a mock surrender. "Whatever you say, Captain." The group mutters and laughs, and taunts about who would beat each other in a real spar make me smile, especially once they place bets on it.

"Let's go, princess," Weston yells, and I groan loudly, snatching my swords off the boards below and getting my feet back into position.

The weight of the swords feels heavy on my overworked muscles, and my clothes are damp and sticking to my skin. I can only imagine how wild my sweat-soaked and windblown waves are after spending hours on deck, but the way Weston still looks at me with heat in his gaze tells me he doesn't mind.

Raising my blades, I watch him, waiting for his first move. He hasn't used the same one since we started sparring, and constantly varies his approach so I can't pick up on any patterns or slack off.

When our eyes lock, his lips curl into a smirk. He straightens, his shoulders relaxing, and his arms falling out of his fighting stance. I eye him warily. I can't trust that he's taking a break, not after he just scolded me for wanting one. No, he's up to something.

I track his movements, watching as he takes both hilts into one hand, as if he's changed his mind about the attack. His free hand drifts to the hem of his shirt, which already sticks to his taut muscles beneath despite being halfway unbuttoned and exposing his glistening chest. My eyes follow his movements as he reaches the hem and tugs it from his waistband. He lifts it slowly, exposing every curve of his abdomen, his raised scar, all the way up to his chest, and uses the fabric to wipe the sweat off his brow.

My mouth parts slightly, and I can't pull my eyes away. A bead of sweat rolls between the muscles, and I catch my lip between my teeth. My muscles are tense from holding this position, but all I can think about is stripping that shirt the rest of the way off him.

I don't catch his attack until the last second, and barely have enough time to react. He darts across the deck, swords back in each hand, and swings both of them at me in a downward blow. I throw my arms in the air with all my strength, just quick enough for our blades to crash together. My muscles quake from the amount of strength that it takes to hold him off, but he just grins at me in the space below the intersection.

"See something you like, sweetheart?"

I glare at him. "You did that on purpose."

"I'm not sure what you mean," he says, a devious glint in his eye.

"Asshole," I mutter and continue to stare him down between our raised arms.

He lowers his head, the grin still irritating as ever, yet it still makes my stomach flutter.

"We've already covered never letting your guard down, so here's the next lesson. Never let the enemy distract you. They'll use anything they can against you, and you can't let it affect your goal: to stay alive."

He presses a quick kiss to my lips then steps away, the metal of the blades singing as they slice down each other and separate.

"Again."

"That wasn't fair," I say, narrowing my eyes and pointing the tip of my blade at his chest.

"Enemies don't play fair."

I look around the main deck, which has remained empty except for the boys still watching us train.

"I still don't see any enemies," I say. "But I guess if we're playing games…" I reach up to the top button of my shirt and pull it open, watching as his eyes are now the ones tracking my movements. "I am getting mighty overheated." Tugging the fabric away from my chest, I fan myself with it, letting the air cool me down as I tilt my head and raise an eyebrow at him. I slide my fingers down the fabric to the next button, ready to tug it open, when the flat of his sword slaps the top of my hand.

"Don't you dare, princess." He jerks his head to the side, toward the rest of the crew. "They don't get to lay eyes on you. You're mine."

"Well then don't play dirty," I say, leaving that top button undone, knowing that the curve of my breasts peeking out from the top of my shirt is going to be enough of a distraction for him, and may even end this training session early.

"I'll save that for later." He swats the curve of my ass, and I yelp, my head snapping to his only to find a deep smirk and playful eyes as he steps back and raises his swords again.

"Will you two stop flirting and get back to the fighting? I've got a lot riding on this next spar," Ryum yells, and Weston smiles widely, his gaze falling to the floor as if he's trying to hide his moment of happiness, and my chest swells.

"Again," he commands, raising his eyes to fix on mine once more, and I lift my blades. He doesn't try to distract me this time. I'm ready for his attack as he steps toward my side, circling around me and forcing me to use the footwork he's been correcting and adjusting all afternoon.

"Are you ever going to tell me?" I ask over the clash of metal. The movements feel natural, more natural to me than when I only have one sword, but I don't know if that is just because I'm better using both hands, or the superiority of Weston's teaching.

"Remind me what I'm supposed to tell you?"

"About Dane. You promised you would explain what I don't know."

He steps back, avoiding a swipe I thought would hit home, before barreling forward at me again, forcing me to back up quickly and defend.

"I'm not sure I want to do that with weapons in your hands."

"What? Are you scared I'll beat you if I'm fueled with rage?"

"I have no doubt you can do that already, princess. Rage or not." I swipe again, this time at his throat, so close that if he hadn't arched out of the way in time, I might have won.

I level the blade at his chest, my jaw clenching as I stare him down. "Talk, Captain."

A series of chortles and whoops echo from the group watching as Weston spins the hilt of the sword in his hand.

"I do love when you get like this," he says, his grin threatening to break my resolve. "Makes me want to throw you over my shoulder and fuck all that aggression out of you."

I step forward, striking at him with each arm in sequence, just as he taught me. He easily blocks every one, his sultry smile not wavering a bit.

"Save it for after. Right now, I want to hear all of it."

It's only now that his features soften, but his movements don't. He still challenges me, forcing me back striking, pushing, turning, trying anything to throw me off balance, but I hold firm. The only sound is the clink of our swords with each movement, before Weston finally speaks.

"What do you know about your family?"

"Only that my father and I are the last two alive in the royal succession, and the names in our ancestral line. I know nothing about my mother."

His jaw works as he blocks my strike, the slice and pressure of his sword spinning me around and making me dizzy.

"Your mother was orphaned when she was very young. She grew up in the city, in a home that took in lost children. That's where she met Dane. They were friends throughout her entire childhood. They were still close when I met her."

My steps falter as I finally hear someone tell me about my mother. No one ever spoke to me about her. The pain was too much for my father, and it was as if he forbade everyone else from bringing her up as well. Edmond was the only one who defied that order, and it wasn't until he handed me her diary. Hearing all of this for the first time almost brings me to a halt. It's as if something I've been missing and yearning for is finally snapping into place.

Weston must see my reaction, and he keeps pushing, keeping me focused on his moves, and only letting up enough so I can still process what he's telling me.

"Rem met Lyla one day when we were out in the city. The moment he saw her, I knew he was done. He was never the kind who cared about love. He knew what was required to produce a legitimate heir, but the moment he saw her, it was like love finally mattered to him."

I clench my jaw. Weston's story feels made up. I know this is the man he knew, but this is not the father I knew. This man doesn't exist anymore.

"I saw it in her eyes too, the way she looked at him. It was more than just someone in awe of the king, or wanting a place of wealth and power and security. No one could fault her for that after living the life she had. But that wasn't Lyla. She was pure and kind and happy. She made him more of those things too."

Tears prick my eyes, and I step back to catch my breath. My swords fall to my sides as I take a minute to collect myself. Weston watches me, and understanding flickers over his face.

"It's alright, I can take it."

He knows how hard this is for me, how hard it is to reconcile the life I knew with the one he describes. How hard it is to hear about the woman I so desperately wanted to know that I came here to save her, only to have that ripped away from me. And despite his constant reminders that I fight with too many emotions, he's letting me use them to take it all out on him.

Because he is there to catch me as I fall.

I charge at him, my movements fueled by bitterness and longing for the life I never had. He blocks every strike, every jab, but he doesn't stop telling me exactly what I asked for.

"They were inseparable, or as inseparable as they could be with his position. After that first meeting, we left the castle to see her every day, and of course during that time, we met the only *family* she had. Dane."

My breaths shorten, and I focus on slowing them, knowing that if I don't, I won't be able to make it through this fight.

"We found out quickly he wasn't her actual family, even though she regarded him as such. Rem and I both could see he was in love with her, even though she never looked at him the same way. She was clearly as much in love with your father as he was with her. When Rem proposed, Dane was…unhappy. Unsupportive. She came to the castle crying one night, telling Rem about how Dane tried to change her mind and talk her out of it, giving her every reason she shouldn't be with him."

"Because *he* wanted to be with her," I grind out, as my blade slams into his.

He nods. "Yes."

I shove him off before striking out again. "Keep going."

"She tried to remain friends with him after the wedding, but Dane pulled away. When he found out she was pregnant, he all but disappeared. She was upset, despite how happy she was about you and for their new family. Dane was the only family she ever knew, and he abandoned her. But she had Rem, and you, and she decided that was all she needed."

Now it's his turn to step back and lower his weapons. I follow suit, chest heaving and jaw aching, as I look up at him, steeling myself for whatever he's preparing to tell me.

His throat bobs as he holds my gaze. "The night you were born, Dane snuck into the castle. We don't know how he got in, and I—" He looks away, somewhere over the rail of the ship and off into the distance for a moment before turning back to me. His voice is thick when he starts again. "I take responsibility for that. My guards didn't see him, didn't find him in time."

His eyes fall to the deck between us. "I don't know exactly what happened. All I know is we heard shouting. Rem took off running, faster than he ever had before. Even I couldn't catch him. By the time I got there, he was crouched on the floor at the bottom of the stone steps, holding her. There was blood everywhere, covering her, covering him. He yelled at me to find Dane, so I knew it was him. He was responsible. I tore through the halls, calling all the guards and setting everyone on a search. I could hear Rem calling for the healers, and it was like the entire castle exploded in movement.

"I couldn't focus on them, even though that was my entire purpose. All I could do was try to find the man who harmed the queen. By the time the entire castle had been searched and the guards were pouring out into the city, you had arrived. It wasn't the day that either of them wanted or talked about. Her body couldn't sustain the injury, and it put her into labor. When I came to the throne room to update Rem on the search, he was holding you in his arms. It was the only time I'd ever seen you until I watched you walk through the paths on the island on the first day."

A sob erupts from my chest, and I try to cover it with my wrist. My fingers ache from where I grip the hilts so tightly as Weston's words sink in. I refuse to drop these swords. They're the only things keeping my hands from wringing my hair, or keeping me off the ground.

Weston's brow softens. "We never thought he would hurt her, not after how much we saw he loved her. We were clearly wrong. I had the entire guard out looking for him, and the last thing I expected was to be the one who found him, especially not the next day as he was tackling me to the ground as I landed in Dawnlin. I'll never forget the look in his eyes when he stabbed me, like he'd been waiting for a while to do it. Maybe he was seeing Rem, or saw it as a way to get back at him. Maybe he partly blamed me for her disappearance in his life. But it was all his fault. She wasn't his to control, and he couldn't handle that."

There's a roaring in my ears as I try to keep everything I'm feeling firmly behind the wall I've constructed to get me through these few days, but this isn't just about Dane and what he did. An entire lifetime of feeling roars to the surface, breaking the dam so I can't hold it back any longer.

My face breaks, and Weston is on me in an instant. His swords clatter to the deck, and his hands find my face, his fingers weaving into my hair as he tilts my head back to look into my tear-filled eyes.

"He's the one who took her away from me," I cry through gritted teeth. I can feel the sobs bubbling up in my throat. "This whole time, my whole life, I thought it was me. I thought my birth caused this. It was my fault she was gone, that I grew up with no one. That's why my father hated me, because I took her from him."

"No, sweetheart, it wasn't." He bends down and presses a firm kiss to my lips before pulling back, his gaze boring into mine. "It wasn't your fault. You didn't cause any of this. You were a victim, just like Rem was, like Lyla was. Rem should have fucking told you."

I didn't hurt my mother.

Waves of grief crash over me, and my knees almost buckle under the weight of it. Weston clutches me tighter, pulling me against him, and supporting me as everything I told myself comes back to the surface.

I took my mother away from my father, from my kingdom, from me. I was responsible for her death, whether it happened when I was born, or when we finally let her go. I'm the reason my father can't stand to look at me, or be in the same room as me, because I caused him the most pain I could, and I wasn't enough to soothe it.

I wasn't enough.

But it wasn't me. It was Dane.

As if Weston hasn't done enough for me, given me enough, he gives me this gift. His truth has broken the shackles I've kept myself in, and all the blame and guilt and despair can finally fall from my body. But as they do, as I let go of everything I've settled on my shoulders, the entire reason I came here, it's replaced by something even stronger.

White hot fury.

My teeth clench together in a grimace, and I squeeze my eyes shut until color flashes in the darkness. Sobs wrack my body and slowly turn to animalistic grunts. I wrap my hands around Weston's wrists and squeeze, trying to ground myself to him, because I can't handle the pain and anger coursing through me. Not alone.

"I hate him," I growl. "I hate him so much."

"I know."

"He got away with it. He ruined her life, my childhood. And he just got away with it."

"I know," he says, sadder this time, but still strong.

For me.

Hot tears stream down my cheeks, and I let out a feral cry. It's one I've had pent up inside me for years, that I could trust no one else to see or hear.

But I'm not alone anymore, and I don't have to hide from him.

It explodes from my body, completely out of my control. My nails dig into Weston's wrists, my forehead presses into his chest, but he doesn't waver. He just holds me, and lets me feel.

I heave in air, my throat burning as I try to get hold of my breath again. I feel Weston pulling away, and the movement jars me, forcing me to snap my eyes open and find him. His hands fall from my face, pulling out of my sharp grip, but his eyes stay locked on mine, as if to say, "I'm not going anywhere."

He bends and picks my swords up off the deck, extending them out toward me. My fingers wrap around the hilts, squeezing until my knuckles turn white. He steps back and retrieves his own before straightening into position, our gaze still unbreakable.

His jaw ticks, and he gives me a firm nod.

"Let me have it, Lennox. Let it all out."

So I do.

There's no correcting or chiding; there's no commenting on my form or focus. He lets me channel my rage into every strike, every slash. He meets me blow for blow, our synchronized steps moving us around the deck, and nothing else in the world exists.

The tears stop as I focus on the rage, pretending every blow isn't one to the man that I love, but instead to the man that I loathe. Weston doesn't falter. He pushes me harder, the fierce look on his face comforting. He understands. He holds hatred for Dane too, because Dane also took away his life, almost in the most literal and final sense.

But even with everything he did, every way he hurt me, my family, my friends, there's a tiny sliver deep inside me that is grateful. If Dane hadn't done it, I wouldn't be here with Weston. There would be no us. I might never know what it feels like to be loved unconditionally.

The gratitude feels like a betrayal, but feeling it all is the only way I'll ever be able to heal.

I grunt loudly as the sword I slam into Weston's sends vibrations into my hand. The moves feel as if they are happening on their own, like my body knows what to do, what it needs, to let this all go. I swipe again, catching his blade at just the right angle. I flick my wrist, winding my blade around his, the same way he'd done to me earlier today, and yank my weapon back. The sword pulls out of his hand, and the metal clatters to the boards beneath us.

There's a flash in Weston's eyes, and I barely have time to register the emotion behind it before he's reaching to his side and pulling a dagger. He swipes it out in front of him, and my body reacts faster than my mind. I let go of my swords and grab his hand, wrenching his wrist and sliding the hilt from his grasp before rapidly flipping it and stepping into him.

The exact way he taught me.

The dull training blade presses against his throat while my other hand fists his damp shirt and pulls my body flush against his.

And that's when I see it again, the emotion in his gaze.

Pride.

Distant cheers ring out over the deck as we stand pressed into each other, our breaths heaving in rhythm. A grin breaks out on his face, and it snaps me back into my thoughts.

Holy shit. I just won.

"Yes!"

"She's a fucking warrior!"

"Cap, you're never gonna live this down!"

Their cheers and jeers finally resonate in my ears, and as I look up into Weston's proud face, I can't help but let myself smile.

"Yield, my queen," Weston grumbles, and I lower the dagger from his neck. His other sword hits the deck, and then I'm in his arms, his lips crashing into mine as the toes of my boots drag across the floor.

Catcalls and whistles worse than anything Jorn has ever done erupt from the group as Weston kisses me unashamedly. He doesn't let up for even a moment as the chatter and footsteps of the crew disappear down the stairs, leaving us alone on deck.

I pull my face back, my arms still firmly wrapped around his neck, and try to catch my breath.

"Did you let me win?"

He strokes his nose along the length of mine, his eyes lifting from where they are fixed on my mouth to catch my gaze.

"No, Lennox. That was all you."

My face splits into a smile so large that my cheeks twinge in pain. Weston matches it, and despite how difficult it was to hear everything tonight, I feel lighter. Happier. Ready to move forward, and it's all thanks to him.

He kisses me again, his tongue invading my mouth as his hand fists in my hair before he pulls away. His eyes darken, and one corner of his lips tips up in a smirk.

"Now it's time to teach you a lesson for beating me in front of my crew."

I squeal loudly as he flips me over his shoulder. His palm swats at my ass, and my yelp is only met by a deep laugh before he spins us around and heads toward the steps. Torches blaze around the deck, and it's the first time I realize how late it is. Time stopped while Weston and I battled, but now the suns have disappeared, and the dark purple sky is already deepening to a star-studded black.

"Shouldn't we go to the mess? Aren't you hungry?" I cry. I press my hands into his back, propping myself up so I can turn toward him. A low growl emanates from his chest as he looks back at me, his eyes trailing up my body until they land on my face.

"Starving."

My cheeks heat and my thighs clench together as he takes the final strides toward the steps.

"If you really are hungry, I—"

A yell echoes from above us, and Weston jerks to a halt. My body tenses, because it isn't just the sound that has me snapping my head back up toward the main deck.

"WESTON!"

No one ever calls him by his name.

He lowers me quickly to the floor, and my feet hit the deck with a loud thud as tension pulls at his shoulders.

"WESTON!" It's louder this time, more urgent, and I know that voice.

Something's wrong.

"Jorn," I whisper, looking up at Weston, the same look of confusion mixed with panic I'm sure I have on my face reflected in his.

Weston's head snaps to the mast, his neck craning back as far as it can as he peers into the darkness.

"WESTON, GET UP HERE NOW!"

We barely look at each other before we both take off, running straight for the mainmast.

What could have Jorn so out of sorts that he's calling Weston by his name? I've never heard him use anything but Cap or the captain. But the sound of his voice, the repeated cries. This isn't the Jorn I know.

We need to find out right fucking now.

Weston's long legs carry him across the deck faster than mine. He stops at the base of the mast, spinning and planting his feet. The moment I'm in front of him, he wraps his hands around my waist, hoisting me over his head high enough that I can grab hold of the ropes and pull myself up. He's next to me in an instant, climbing faster than I've even seen Jorn move. I follow behind, the ache from exertion all afternoon completely gone as worry and nerves take over. I climb, keeping my focus trained on Weston's back and my handholds so I don't fall to my death.

"What the fuck is going on, Jorn?" Weston yells as we near the top.

Jorn's face appears hanging over the edge of the crow's nest. His skin is ashen, his eyes wide as he splutters. "I-I-I don't know. I've never seen it before. I'm here all the time, you know that. *All* the time. It's never...I never..."

I plant my feet on the last crossbeam next to where Weston balances and grab hold of his belt, stabilizing myself before I look up at them.

"What?" Weston snaps, and Jorn lifts his arm, pointing past us, toward the island.

Our heads turn almost in unison, and as I stare through the darkness out over the land, my breath stills in my chest. My knees threaten to give out from under me, and I grip Weston's belt harder, my mouth falling open in complete disbelief.

I snap my head back to his, and his lips are parted, his eyes as wide as Jorn's. The wind whips at us, threatening to knock us off the mast, but there's no fear. His hand settles on the small of my back, holding me firmly against him, and his eyes finally break away from the sight.

That's when I see it.

What I thought he lost is now shining brightly.

Shining as brightly as the golden glow settled deep in the pitch-black forest on the far side of the island.

Hope.

"Light always finds a way," I mutter over the whistle of the wind around us.

"Even through the blackest woods," Weston finishes.

"Edmond..." I say, my voice barely a whisper, and a breath huffs in Weston's chest.

"He was trying to tell us how to get home," he grumbles. "This whole fucking time, he was telling us how to get home."

CHAPTER EIGHTEEN

"Find Sig. NOW!" Weston yells as I leap off the bottom rung of the mast into his arms. The climb down was a blur. My arms and legs moved so quickly, it felt like I was flying. He catches me easily and launches me toward the steps. I descend them quickly, my boots pounding into the wood as he and Jorn run behind me, but instead of following down the second set of steps, they peel off down the hallway.

"Weapons!" Weston commands, and I hear his footsteps pound toward our room and Jorn's toward Sig's. He'll get mine; I know he will. Right now, my sole focus is finding Sig.

"Sig!" My voice cracks with my scream. Leaping from the last few steps, my knees threaten to buckle as I pound into the floor, startling a few of the crew who sit in the lounge. I scan their faces, hoping one of them is hers, but they all just stare blankly back at me.

I race down the hall and throw the door to the showers open, and barely even register the startled looks of the Castaways inside.

"Sig!" I call, but there's no response. "Shit," I mutter and spin, the door slamming behind me as I sprint down the hall, past the infirmary, straight to the mess. Calls of my name sound garbled as I block out all other sounds. I know I look frantic, because I am. But I can't stop. I need to find her.

"Signee!" I scream as I burst into the mess, still full of crew eating a late dinner. The noise feels deafening as I scan the room frantically, but my shriek must have cut through it.

There.

Sig's head snaps toward the door from where she sits across the room. The muscles in her face turn to stone as she takes in my panic, and she shoots out of her chair.

"What's wrong?" she says. "Is it Jorn?"

I sprint toward her, skidding to a halt in front of the table, before I grip her arm and yank her firmly.

"We need to go. Now."

The crew sitting around her stare at us, but I ignore them. I can't explain in front of them. I can't take up any more time than it took to find her. I sprint back to the door, dragging her along with me, but I can feel her hesitation.

"Lennox, what is going on?"

My chest heaves as we fly up the first set of stairs, but I need to give her something and get to the deck as fast as possible.

"We found it, Sig. We found the dust, or, we think we did."

I can feel the change in her the moment my words sink in. Her arm yanks from my grip as she runs faster, no longer needing me to drag her and urge her to move.

"You better not be fucking with me!"

"I'm not, I swear!"

We hit the first floor and bound up the last set of steps. Sig's long legs take two at a time, and she pulls in front of me before we burst out onto the deck. Jorn and Weston wait at the gangway, tension filling their already armed bodies and hands laden with Sig and my waiting weapons.

The moment I'm close enough, Weston grabs my waist and shoves my dagger into my waistband before his palm is hot and urgent on my back.

"Go!" he yells, urging me forward, and the four of us take off running.

My boots pound into the dark rock, the steps so quick that my feet barely hit the floor before pushing off again. Sig and Jorn pull ahead, but Weston stays beside me, even though I know he could be running past all of us in a moment. He won't leave me behind.

"Through the tunnels!" he barks, and we don't slow down. The four of us barrel straight through the portal, the magic barely a flash around us before we're inside.

"Will someone tell me what the fuck is going on?" Sig yells.

The torches flare to life, barely able to keep up with our speed as we sprint into the darkness. Legs pumping as hard as I can, it's as if my body has completely forgotten the intensive training Weston just put me through with the anticipation of finding the dust. My chest heaves with breaths, but I barely feel any of it. My only thoughts are of what could be waiting for us on the other side of the island.

"I saw a glow," Jorn says. "A glow I've never seen before. It was in the forest."

"Do you really think—" Sig starts, and Weston doesn't even let her finish.

"Yes."

The certainty in his tone makes my chest swell. It's as if he knows without any doubt that this is what Edmond had been telling us. He doesn't need confirmation to believe it; it just feels right. And after seeing the glow, there can be no other explanation.

"Shit," she curses, and focuses back on the dark tunnel ahead.

We take the same path Weston and I used only days ago, the one to meet Roley near the edge of the forest. This time, we don't bother stopping to check our surroundings for threats as we follow each other through the portal.

Jorn takes the lead, and Sig follows closely behind as he cuts straight through the trees.

"Where is it?" she asks, her voice laden with heavy breaths.

"Straight back!" Jorn yells, gesturing off into the distance.

We weave through the trees, leaping over felled logs and jutting rocks. The terrain is just as treacherous as the last time I ran through this forest, but with every stumble, Weston steadies me, his hands wrapping around my waist and urging me to keep going. Trees whir past, and from the corner of my eye I see the cabin from that night. I pull my focus from it, and back onto the darkness before us that gets deeper the farther we go.

I breathe in, trying to shutter the rise in emotions from being reminded of that night so abruptly, and then it hits me.

The scent in the air.

It's the same scent I noticed when Dane brought me to the cabin days ago. I couldn't place it before, but it seemed…familiar, and felt like a small bit of magic washed over me, making me feel content and happy. Hopeful.

It was the dust.

It is the same scent I inhaled every time Dane opened the pouch. The fragrant floral notes washed over me in Blackwood, back when the Guardian showed up to whisk me away to this magical land.

This is it. We really found it.

The revelation fuels me, and I push impossibly harder, despite barely being able to see Sig and Jorn in front of us. I'm trusting the island, trusting it will bring us right to it, and that it will end this involuntary fate.

Then I see it.

Just ahead, the barest hint of light breaks through the darkness, glowing like a beacon and drawing us straight toward it, the same glow we saw from the mast.

I can barely breathe. My chest feels like it might explode as my legs fly beneath me, and the glow gets closer and closer. I'm so focused on it, fixated, that I almost slam into Sig's back as she comes to a stop in front of me. I step up beside her, and tears spring into my eyes as they fall onto the pocket of forest that no longer is coated by darkness.

Everything shimmers. The colors and glitter are like I've never seen before. No gold or jewels back in the castle match the magic that is before us, coating the trees. Blooming, sparkling golden flowers unlike anything you would ever expect to grow in a dark forest cover every branch, from the trunks to the peaks. The smell is intoxicating, and waves of happiness roll through me as I crane my neck, jaw slackened, and stare up at the branches. It's the only light in the otherwise complete darkness.

Edmond knew.

I don't know how, but he did.

Light always finds a way, even through the blackest woods.

I always thought it was only a lesson, something that was passed through our kingdom because of the descriptive words chosen to mimic the kingdom's name. It was always a lesson about having hope, finding the light in the darkness, the good in the bad, the happiness in the despair. But it was more than that. It was a way to let us know we could return, that we weren't hopeless.

It was our way home.

A peal of laughter cuts through the quiet, the only other sound being the collective heaving of our strained breaths. I glance over at Sig and find the brightest smile I've ever seen on her splitting face. She jumps up and down, her eyes on the trees above as another wave of laughter overtakes her.

I whirl around, my eyes searching for Weston, and they find him, hands resting on top of his head, and a complete look of disbelief and wonder painting his features as he takes in the glowing grove behind me.

His eyes are wide as they meet mine, and huffs a small laugh.

"We found it. We fucking found it," he murmurs. The grin that pulls at his lips glows brighter than the dust around us and makes my chest clench. After all this time, this was the moment he had been waiting for, the moment where all his sacrifice finally mattered, and I get to witness it.

His strides are long as he closes the distance between us. He sweeps me into his arms, and crushes me against his chest as his face falls into the crook of my neck. I can feel his smile against my skin, and I can't stop mine as I wrap my arms around his neck and hold him tight.

Laughter bubbles from my chest as he spins us around in circles, his bulging arms flexing and trembling as if I can't possibly get any closer. Pure joy emanates from him, as we spin around, and his laughter mixes with mine. My head spins when he stops abruptly, pulling back just enough that I can see his emotions all over his face as he presses his forehead to mine.

"We can go home," he says, his voice a low rumble. "We didn't lose hope, and now we can leave."

"*You* didn't lose hope, Weston. You never wanted to stop trying. You're the one who kept everyone safe and happy so that they got to go home. You did this."

His eyes soften as they dart between mine, just before he's kissing me, his lips bruising as his arms tighten again, further caging me against his body. I can't control my smile through the kiss when I hear Jorn's crow and Sig's screams of excitement coming from behind me, and use the distraction to push against Weston's chest.

"We need to get the pouch right now. We have to go to camp."

He nods and lowers me to the ground as the commanding captain takes over once again, figuring out the strategy and taking the next steps.

It's as if the time that no longer mattered merely an hour ago now flies by. When you have an unlimited amount, haste means nothing, but the moment that disappears, it is everything. We can't waste another minute.

We can go home. We can leave *tonight* if we want to.

We were given our choice back, and the buzz of energy in the air makes me feel like the island is watching, waiting to see what we do with it.

CHAPTER NINETEEN

"Stay here," Weston says firmly to Sig and Jorn as he grabs my hand and starts walking through the trees, back in the direction we came. "We'll be right back."

"Cap, I'm not going anywhere," Sig says. Her head is still tipped back as she smiles up at the glowing trees, unable to take her eyes off them.

The glow disappears behind us, and the darkness returns as we hurry through the forest. Neither of us speaks. The weight of everything that is about to happen as well as the urgency to get where we are going is too much to focus on words. My mind whirls. The exact thing we've been searching for, and everything we thought was taken from us, is within our grasp.

The reality of our restored futures settles in my stomach like a stone in a pond. I'd been learning to accept the way life would be here in the days since Dane disappeared, but now, in this moment, *tonight*, it could all change.

Again.

We make it to camp quickly and don't hesitate for a breath before barging through the portal. The night is dark, but it isn't late enough that everyone would already be in the bunks, especially with no reason to wake up early to search for the healing waters. When I see a large group still settled in the clearing, I feel a small twinge of relief, accompanied by even more anticipation.

"Mara!" I scan the clearing, trying to find her among the faces shadowed by their fire's glow. A figure stands on the other side of the pit, and I see right away that it's Mara, with a look of confusion etched on her face.

"Lennox? What's wrong?"

I dart toward the fire, closing the distance before calling out, "We need the pouch. Now!"

Her eyes flick between us as she hastily approaches. "Why? What's going on?"

"We'll explain everything later," Weston says, stepping beside me. "We need it. Now. Then you need to gather everyone and meet us at the ship."

Eyes widening, as if she's already guessed what has happened, her jaw falls open and her head snaps to me.

"You found it?"

"We found it," I say, tears filling my eyes at the hope that shines back at me in hers.

Without another word, she sprints across the clearing to the ladder, flying up the rungs before charging through camp toward the bunks. I can feel the anxious energy pouring off Weston as he watches her race through the walkway. He's trying to keep it contained and in control, but I know it is killing him to stand here and wait on someone else.

I wrap my arm around his and lace our fingers together, squeezing tightly. He squeezes back and doesn't let go, doesn't lighten up as we wait for Mara to return.

The Voyagers in the clearing have barely noticed we are here. Rylan raises an arm at us in a wave, as if seeing us walk into camp is completely normal. I wave back weakly before sneaking a glance at Weston, watching as the muscle in his jaw works.

"Hey," I say, trying to sound reassuring as my heart pounds in my chest from both the run here, and the longing to get back to that glowing patch of trees. "Everything will be alright. We found it. It's not going anywhere."

"What if it does?" he grumbles back. His eyes stay focused on the wooden pathway above us, waiting to see Mara start on her way back to us.

"You think it's going to disappear?"

He tears his gaze away and looks down at me. "What if it does? We don't know how long those flowers will bloom. Do we want to risk missing it?"

Pressure fills my chest as my fingers tingle. The dust disappearing wasn't something I had considered in the moments since we found it, but Weston is right. I don't want to take the chance that we'll miss it and lose our hope once again.

We need to get the pouch and get back there as soon as possible. Mara needs to hurry.

She appears seconds later, sprinting until she hits the platform and kicks the latch so it falls to the ground. When she reaches us, she's out of breath, panting heavily as she holds her hand out to Weston.

"Here," she breathes. "Go get it."

Weston grabs it with his free hand, and gestures to the Voyagers sitting in the clearing. "Get everyone back to the ship. Wait for us there. Tell Veck to gather everyone on deck. We'll be back as soon as we can."

She nods rapidly, no longer questioning Weston's authority in the slightest before she turns to me. "Lennox, is this real?"

"Yes, Mara. It's very real."

Her composure threatens to fall, but she holds it together before spinning back toward the Voyagers.

"Put the fire out! Everyone, get your stuff from your bunk and get to the ship!"

I don't have time to see anyone's reactions before Weston is pulling me back through the portal, and we're running, racing against an uncertain amount of time and hoping that the island doesn't take away the hope it just gave us.

I breathe a sigh of relief when the glow comes into view, and the tension in Weston's hand loosens. It didn't disappear. Our chance isn't gone.

We can all get home.

This is real.

"Did you get it?" Sig yells when she sees us approaching.

"Yes," Weston grunts, coming to a stop in front of them. "Any idea how to get it?"

"I tried to climb," Jorn says. "But the bark is so slick and the trunks are too wide, I couldn't get a grip. I thought you could hoist me up, but there are no holds low enough."

Weston scrubs a hand over his mouth as he looks up at the trees, still glowing brightly above us.

"It wouldn't finally appear just to keep it from us, would it?" Sig asks.

"I hope not," Weston says.

We can't have gotten this far, been this close to having a way home, and can't collect it. There has got to be something we are missing, something that we need to do to make it more accessible.

Unless this is just another way the island is protecting the magic.

The thought makes my stomach sink.

"It doesn't make sense," I say, as my mind tumbles over everything we know from all the searching and through all our theories. "Jorn can climb anything, but can't get up there." I turn to Sig. "You said the Guardian was a kind old man, the one who brought you here. How could the island expect him to get the dust all the way up there if none of us can?"

Sig starts to answer, but stops, her mouth closing slowly as she tries to think it through.

"We're missing something," Weston mumbles, and continues to look around. He raises his hand, his gaze lowering to the pouch he has clenched in it, before looking back at the grove. Taking slow steps toward the nearest glowing tree, he holds the pouch out toward the trunk, placing his hand on the bark.

Splitting and crunching and cracking meet my ears, and a stunned gasp tears from my throat. The tree comes to life. The bark ripples, and Weston startles back as chunks of the wood burst from the trunk, creating...steps.

My jaw falls open as a staircase forms before our eyes, winding around the trunk and weaving through the branches above. Weston doesn't hesitate. He dashes up the steps, and I crane my neck to watch as he reaches the first glowing branch. Steadying himself on the trunk, he reaches out and plucks the nearest glowing bloom. The light illuminates his face as he looks inside the petals, and immediately wrestles the pouch open with his other hand, turning the flower over in the opening.

The glimmering petals fade before our eyes, the only glow present now deep inside the pouch, the same as when Dane opened it to bring me to the fountain.

"Holy shit," Sig breathes next to me, and Jorn lets out a loud crow.

The cheer snaps Weston out of the trance he was in, staring down into the pouch that is begging to be filled. It's as if a fire is lit inside him. He reaches for the next flower, dumping the contents into the opening, and repeats his steps until there isn't a single flower left on the branch and he can move on to the next one. He works quickly, following the winding steps up to the very top until it is no longer glowing and gallops down the steps to move to the next one.

"Here, give it. I want to help," Jorn says, extending his hand toward Weston.

He hands Jorn the pouch without hesitation, and Jorn approaches the next tree. Steps appear just as they had with Weston, and Jorn runs, crowing again as he reaches the first branch.

Tears prick at my eyes just as I feel Weston press firmly into my back. His arms wrap around my shoulders, crossing over my chest as he squeezes me into him, the rough stubble on his cheek settling into my hair.

"How was it this simple?" he murmurs, and I can hear the awe and disbelief. "How did we never see it before?"

I stand in silence for a moment, watching Jorn scamper up the steps to the next branch and start plucking flowers. Sig stands below the tree, hands on her hips and her neck craned to watch him, no doubt making sure he doesn't do something stupid or risky in the excitement. I wouldn't put it past Jorn.

"Maybe it wasn't simple," I say hesitantly. "Maybe we never saw it because it wasn't ever there before, at least not until the other night. We were too busy trying to figure out how to deal with Dane's betrayal and with telling the Voyagers that we didn't notice."

"What are you thinking?"

I reach up and wrap my hands around his forearms. What *am* I thinking? Weston was right, this feels too easy. But what if it wasn't meant to be difficult? What if it wasn't that we didn't notice or weren't worthy? What if what happened just was the way it was supposed to be?

"I'm thinking that maybe…maybe we couldn't get it, no matter how hard we looked or how much we begged the island, because the trees didn't bloom until the dust was gone."

He stays quiet, but I can feel him considering what I'm saying.

"Besides the Guardian abandoning the island, the only other thing that changed was that the dust is completely gone. That's never happened before, not since you and Dane have been here, so there was no reason for the trees to bloom. That's why no one ever saw it, and Dane didn't know how to replenish it, because the Guardian didn't tell him. But somehow Edmond knew. How did he know?"

"I don't know," he mutters, his head shaking slightly where he rests it against mine. "The good news is, we'll finally be able to ask him." His arms squeeze me even tighter, and he plants a firm kiss on the top of my head before his chest rumbles against my back. "Because we're going home."

CHAPTER TWENTY

Home.

It's not a word I associate with Blackwood. Not anymore. It belongs to Dawnlin, with these people, my new family, but more than that, it belongs to Weston. Wherever he goes is my home, and when all the rest of them spread out across the kingdoms, I will have places I can go, places I can visit and live and love when I finally get out of the confines of the castle.

I'm not ready to think about that yet. It's what we've all been waiting for, but it means I won't get to wake up and see all these people I've grown so used to seeing every day. Some I may never see again. I don't know if Jorn or Sig or even Weston has thought through it yet, and I can't blame them. We finally found what they've spent years searching for, and they're reveling in the joy of it finally being over.

The life I have to return to is nothing compared to everything I've gained here, and while I am grateful to be given back the chance at a future, at actual experiences, I still feel grief for everyone I am about to lose and for the freedoms that are about to be taken from me, again.

My stomach turns at the thought of how my father will react the moment I step back into those dark, cold halls. How furious will he be about my unexplained and sudden absence, or my relationship with Weston? How will I be able to live with my failure, especially in the moment we let my mother go?

If he hasn't already done that.

Focus on this moment, right now, Lennox.

I squeeze my eyes shut, and instead revel in the brazen way Weston wraps his arms around me, in the heartwarming sound of Jorn laughing while Sig playfully scolds him and hurries him along. I soak up the warmth of the humid air on my skin, breathe in the dust's fragrance, and try to memorize this moment, because it could be one of my last with these people.

The last time we're all this happy. The last time we're together.

It takes us longer than expected to clear the trees of dust. Jorn, Sig, and Weston did most of the collecting. I tried once, but it took about a minute to realize my reach would not get as far as fast as they could, and I got a warning and a stern look from down below when I tried to shimmy across one branch to reach.

Cracking and popping followed by a thud ring through the air the moment Weston's boot lands back on the ground after harvesting from the final glowing tree. The stairs are gone, the bark returned, and you would never know that this dark grove held so much magic only moments ago. The pouch is plump and full in his hands, the golden tie straining to keep the dust contained as he ties it to his belt.

It's almost impossible to see anything through the darkness of the forest, especially with the way the dense treetops block out any light from the moon. A torch appears a moment later, extending from the trunk of the tree Weston just stepped off, and giving off enough light that I can at least see the others.

"Back to the ship," Weston says as he reaches out and plucks the torch from the bark. "I need to tell the crew." He takes my hand, walking briskly toward the ship, and the excitement from moments ago disappears as if the reality of what finding the dust means is finally setting in. This life we've grown to love and these people we cherish will be gone in an instant.

Now that we have a choice, it is going to be hard to choose to give it all up.

No one utters a word as Weston leads us past the portal and instead winds along the pathway, across the island. Our pace isn't slow, but it isn't fast either, as if he's giving us the chance to see it all one final time.

The torches on deck are bright against the darkness of the night, and it's clear that Mara must have followed Weston's instructions. Energy hums in the air as we traipse over the sand and toward the reef, the same way it always does when something big happens, and I know the island is watching.

Everyone waits on deck — the entire crew, all the Voyagers. My chest aches as we crest the top of the gangway and my eyes graze across them. Happiness, excitement, speculation, and anticipation. It's written across all their faces as they wait and wonder what their captain has to tell them.

The chatter and laughter quiet the moment they see us step onto the deck, and the silence is deafening. Weston sets the torch in a holder and pulls the pouch from his belt. Sig and Jorn form a line on the other side of him, looking out over the crowd, their expressions a mixture of hope and sorrow.

Weston clears his throat, breaking the silence, and holds the pouch out in front of him.

"We found it."

An explosion of cheers and cries erupts in the night as every single person reacts to the declaration, knowing that their fate is no longer sealed, and their life is no longer confined to this ship, to this island.

Tears of joy, whoops, and laughter echo all around us, and I can't stop the tears that prick at my eyes and the giggles that shake my shoulders as I watch them all.

After watching their hopes crushed when Weston told them the dust was almost gone, and knowing he spoke to every one of them, telling them Dane stranded us here, this reaction makes my knees weak. It all but erases the memory of the heartache and loss, because now, in this moment, we have what each one of them worked hard to find. Even when hope seemed lost, a kernel of light still lived inside each of us and kept us going. We had hoped for a happy life here, together, and now our hope of finding our lives at home has been restored.

The roar of excitement calms, and all but diminishes when someone calls out, "What do we do now, Captain?"

His throat bobs and his eyes soften. I know he's realized it too. We're leaving. All of us.

And it's time to say goodbye.

His lips turn up in a soft smile. "We go home."

Murmurs start up but fall silent again as he raises his hand, quieting everyone quickly.

"But first, I want to tell you all how honored I am to have been your captain for all this time. Even those of you who haven't been here that long"—his hand squeezes mine as his eyes drift to Taril, then to Fin— "and those of you who didn't get the chance to be with us." He nods toward the Voyagers who all sat in the same general vicinity, except Gauge who threw himself right into the middle of the Castaway mix.

"Everything I did, every decision I made, whether they were easy or extremely difficult, was to get to this moment, so all of us could return where we belong. The island kept us safe, but we were never meant to stay. I can't tell you how grateful I am that it gave us a sanctuary and made the life we shared here one that will stay with me forever. I will never forget any of you, and I have hope that you will take everything we learned here, and all our experiences, and live the best life of your choosing back home."

My throat tightens, and a tear falls down my cheek. Weston doesn't show his emotions very often. He stays strong for his crew and the people he cares about, but now in front of his family that he is about to let go, I can hear the thickness in his voice as he bears his heart to them.

He releases my hand and cradles the pouch between his palms, and the gaze of everyone on deck shifts to it.

"I don't know if it will work, or if the Guardian is the only one who can use it, or if we need to be back at the plateau—"

"We don't," I say with a shake of my head. "He left from other places on the island."

Weston nods, then looks back at the group. "Well then, I'll be right here for anyone who wants to go tonight. If you need to take some time, that's fine too. But know I won't leave until everyone gets back home."

The air is still as Weston's words settle. Right now. Everyone could be home in the next few minutes and find out what happened to their loved ones they left behind.

But no one moves.

It's as if no one knows *what* to do. How can we leave everyone we care about here, behind? How can we not? No one was prepared for this to happen, in this moment. We'd hoped, and with every shift, every search, the anticipation was there. But it wasn't tonight, and the stunned looks on everyone's faces as they stare back at Weston, processing his offer, prove that.

"I'll go, Captain."

Something in my chest breaks when I hear her voice, and I look over to see Stassia rising from where she sits with her arm slung around Auralie.

"Are you sure?" he asks as she weaves through the bodies, making her way across the deck toward us.

"I'm sure. Someone has to be the first. I'm not afraid. Gotta make sure it works, right?" Her tone is light, in her usual Stassia way, but I can hear the sadness she's trying to hide.

Weston nods, then gestures to everyone behind her. "Do you want a minute?"

"Uh, of course. Just because I volunteered, doesn't mean you can get rid of me that easily."

Everyone stands as she turns her back on us, and heads into the crowd, walking around, giving hugs, and laughing with each person. Even the Voyagers she didn't really know, who came after she found the waters, all say their heartfelt goodbyes.

When she gets to Auralie, who has been sobbing the entire time Stassia moved through the group, I no longer can keep it together. Despite being from the same kingdom, life will never be the same back home as it is here. I cry silently as I watch the embrace of two women whose friendship held them together when the loneliness of this life and the possibilities that were left behind were too much.

A chasm opens in my chest as I watch the evidence of their friendship, of my friendship, and know that I have nothing like that to return to. They're all here. And now they'll be gone. Every woman should have a friend like that, who supports her and is there for her, and I am so glad I got to have them, even if it was for so short a time. Now I'll never question what friendship feels like, because I discovered it in Dawnlin.

Stassia breaks away, leaving Auralie swiping at her eyes, before walking to Jorn, giving him a shove followed by a warm hug, as smiles and laughter exchange between them. I can't watch as she hugs Sig just as fiercely as she hugged Auralie, but when she steps in front of Weston and offers him an exaggerated salute, a watery giggle bubbles through my tears.

"Aye, Captain. Thank you for this crazy ride, and all you did for us. Don't forget to smile every so often."

"You're welcome, Stass," he says with a smirk, then opens his arms. "I'll miss you."

Stepping into his embrace, she wraps her arms around him. Her head rests on his chest facing me, and her mouth falls open, an exaggeratedly excited look on her face as her eyes playfully roll to the back of her head. I giggle again, holding my fist over my mouth, knowing she has been coveting that hug for a very long time.

Her head tilts, and a closed-lip warm smile spreads on her face as she steps in front of me.

"Lennox."

"Stass."

She throws her arms around me, pulling me tight, and I squeeze her back, my shoulders shaking as we cry into each other. All the thoughts escape my mind as I say my first goodbye to someone who showed me I belonged here, who wasn't afraid to tell me what she thought, and urged me to trust all of them. I've told Stass how I've felt about her before, and how much I would miss her. *Will* miss her. But I almost startle when she mumbles in my ear so that only I can hear.

"Whatever you do, don't let that go." I squeeze my eyes shut as another round of tears pours down my cheeks. "Most people only dream about what you have, and they never find it. Trust me. I know. Don't let fear or duty or anyone else's opinions take it away from you."

I nod fiercely into her shoulder and hold her tight until she pulls away, leaving me to swipe at my face.

"I'm going to miss you, Stass."

"Of course you are." She winks as she steps back in front of Weston, but before she stops, a startled look passes over her face. "Oh! I almost forgot."

Her shoulders pull back as she stands a little taller and strides across the deck, right to Taril. He was quiet the entire time she said goodbye, even when it was his turn, only giving her a shy hug and a wave. The look on Stass' face says she's up to something. Whistles break out, followed by Jorn's crow as her hands fist in his shirt and she pulls him down toward her, pressing a firm kiss to his lips. She breaks away, leaving him looking stunned as he stares down at her, but she only pats his chest gently.

"If you're ever in Akarion, come find me." She spins on her heel, her hair whipping over her shoulder and a smile on her face as she crosses the deck again and stands in front of Weston.

"Alright, Captain. I'm ready." He holds the pouch out toward her, loosening the string enough so she can reach inside. A bright yellow glow seeps through her fingers as her fist clenches around the dust, and a single tear falls down her cheek as her chin trembles slightly.

"I love you all," she says, lifting her hand just over the crown of her head. Granules drift down over her face, lodging in her eyelashes, and falling onto her shoulders. Then before our eyes, her body starts to shimmer…and fade, and Stassia disappears.

CHAPTER TWENTY-ONE

"I'm ready too, Captain," Auralie calls out as she stands and swipes at her tears.

"Me too," Eirlick grunts from the other side of the deck. Noise erupts from the crowd as more of us agree they are ready to leave. Goodbyes start as crew and Voyagers turn to those beside them, wrapping their arms around each other, gripping shoulders and patting backs. It's as if time slows as I watch tears get wiped away, and others unable to suppress giant smiles. Ryum claps Veck on the back in a firm hug, then turns to do the same with Eirlick. Auralie flits around saying her sweet goodbyes, and all at once, the moment I wasn't ready for has arrived.

This is it.

This is the end of Dawnlin.

The Castaways, who I once feared and hated, have become my home; the Voyagers my friends. And now I have to tell each of them goodbye.

Laughter rumbles through the air as a group of the boys approach Jorn and proceed to fight and wrestle each other to the ground one last time, shoving each other away with playful grins. Once they've had their fun, they form a line and walk right to Weston, each of them taking their turn to shake his hand and pull him into a hug.

He was the captain, for so many years. They respected him, trusted him, but they also loved him just as much as he loved them. They are letting him go the same as he is to them.

My body feels numb as it tries to protect itself from the pain of every goodbye. The moment the next person steps in front of me, a new wave of grief consumes my thoughts. Every hug and tear shed is a hope that they know how much I will miss them, and how much they have impacted my life, for the better.

The line wraps around the deck, slowly moving as each person grabs their share of dust and drops it over themselves, disappearing just before the next takes their place to do the same. When Gauge makes his way in front of Weston, his smile contagious, even with the blanket of sadness surrounding us.

"Just when I find out I actually like you all," he says, beaming as his head swivels between the four of us, before focusing back on Weston. "I wish I had longer with you."

Weston raises an eyebrow. "No, you don't."

"You're right," Gauge says with a laugh. "No, I don't. But you're pretty bad ass, Captain. I wish I could have learned a thing or two from you."

The corner of Weston's mouth turns up as he claps Gauge on the shoulder. "If you're ever in Blackwood and want to train with the guards, just come to the castle and ask for me. I'll take care of the rest."

"I won't forget it, Captain." His smile brightens further before he reaches into the pouch and grabs a handful of dust. He waves one final goodbye before he drops it into his hair and disappears.

Sawyer takes his place, but when something squeezes my leg, my breath falters as I pull my attention away.

Oh no.

The inevitability of the goodbye I've been avoiding hits me like a firm blow to the gut. I squeeze my eyes shut, the tears falling steadily now as I tilt my chin and open them slowly, only to look down into Fin's smiling face.

"Lennox! You found it! You found what mister Weston was looking for!"

"We did." My voice quivers, and his face blurs even more as a fresh wave of tears pools.

"And now we all can go home!" He squeezes my leg tighter as his feet patter happily on the floor.

A sob escapes my chest as I fight to keep smiling. "Yes, we can."

He halts, and his face falls slightly. "Then why are you so sad?" His eyes drag over mine, tracking my tears as they trail down my cheeks, leaving dark blots on the fabric of my shirt.

I swipe at them and sniff before crouching down onto his level. "Because I'm going to miss everyone.

"Oh." His mouth forms the shape of the sound, and his eyebrows raise as he begins to understand what this means. "So I won't see you anymore?"

I shake my head. "No, Fin. Not anymore."

His eyes turn glassy, and his lower lip quivers. "But I don't want to say goodbye. I don't want to never see you again."

"I don't either, Fin," I say, reaching out to stroke his hair softly. "But you'll be home with your family, and hopefully with your sister."

"Who will tell me if I'm using the bow right?" he asks, ignoring what I said about his family. "And…and…who will play hide and seek with me? Will I get to see mister Weston?"

I bite my lip and shake my head, sniffing hard to hold everything back so he doesn't see my heart breaking as I wrap him up in my arms.

"No, Fin. Mister Weston won't be there either."

He pulls just out of my embrace so he can look me in the eye, the tears gathering in his finally threatening to spill over.

"I don't want to go if I can never see you again."

My lips pull into a gentle smile. "Just a day ago you were sad about having to stay and never seeing your family again. I'm sorry, Fin. I'm so sorry. I know it hurts, but we weren't meant to stay here forever. You were meant to grow up, and learn how to do fun things. You were meant to get big and strong. You aren't supposed to stay little forever."

His eyes widen as a flash of excitement crosses his face. "And tall like mister Weston?"

I let out a watery laugh. "Maybe. You'll probably be taller than me."

Shoulders rising to his ears, he kicks his toe at the wood of the deck shyly. "Will you come visit?"

I nod fiercely and hold back a sob. "I'll try. Maybe you can come visit me too. Because guess what?"

"What?" A new brightness shines in his eyes, and he's all but forgotten about his sadness from a moment ago.

I lean in and lower my voice to a conspiratorial whisper. "I live in a castle."

Fin gasps. "You do?"

I nod. "I do. Just like the one we built. And maybe one day, you can come see me."

"And meet the king and queen?"

My smile falters, but I don't think he notices. "We only have a king, but yes, you can meet him."

"Do you have a princess too? Just like your story?"

"We do." I gulp. "You can meet her too."

He jumps at me, throwing his arms around my neck, and squeezes me in a hug. "Maybe it's okay to go home then. As long as I can still see you."

"One day, Fin." I swipe the tears off my cheeks and pull back from him again. "We don't have to go just yet. There's still a little time."

I stand, my hand brushing the back of Fin's shoulders as he continues to hug my leg tightly, and realize the group has dwindled.

There are only a few of us left, and my eyes travel down the line, falling on Mara with Roley at her side.

His brows furrow, and his lips turn into a frown, as if he's already realized what all of this means. I give the last few final goodbyes to everyone as they step in front of us, leaving Roley and Mara to be the last. My head throbs, and my face feels swollen. I don't know if I have it left in me to let go of everyone left standing on this ship.

"When I woke up this morning, I didn't expect it to be my last day here. I don't think any of us did," Mara says quietly as her gaze trails over the four of us. "I just wanted to say thank you for never giving up, and for forgiving me. The last days here were hard, and I can't imagine how much worse they would be if I were alone."

"You're welcome, Mara," Weston says, and she gives him a shy smile before gesturing to Roley standing beside her.

"I'm going to take him home. We live near each other, and I don't want to send him back by himself."

"I appreciate it," Weston says with a nod, just as Roley steps in front of me.

"Goodbye, Lennox. I'm going to miss you." His gaze falls to the deck at his feet, and his hands stay clasped behind his back.

"I'm going to miss you too, Roley. Keep working with that bow, alright?"

Head snapping up, and eyes brightening, the words rush out of his mouth. "Can I bring it with me?" He looks to Weston expectantly.

"As long as you make good choices when you use it. Target practice only," he grumbles, and is met with excited nods from both Fin and Roley. He juts his chin toward the entrance to below. "Go get it."

Fin releases my leg, and the boys race across the deck, and disappear down the steps. The quiet is thick around us; even the crash of the waves sound more faint than normal. I turn to Mara, and my chest tightens.

She was my first *real* friend here on the island, even though we had a rough start. Bonded over the hope to save our mothers, further solidified when she helped me instead of letting jealousy overcome her. After years of searching and leaving empty-handed, she could be returning to nothing, her mother long gone and no one else waiting for her. Nowhere to call home.

I smile weakly. "Thanks for saving my life, but then trying to kill me again."

She laughs, the sound brittle and sad. "Any time. Thanks for being a traitor. If you hadn't been, we never would have gotten home."

"Anytime," I say through even more tears.

I step forward and wrap my arms around her shoulders, squeezing her in a tight hug, before stepping back again. "If you're alone, come to the castle in Blackwood. Ask for me. You won't be alone anymore."

She quirks her head. "What, do you work there or something and can get me a job?"

After our conversation in front of the mountain, we were too distracted by the unworthy decision that we never talked about who I was again. There's nothing to hide anymore, and I don't want her to leave without knowing.

"I'm the princess, Mara. It's my kingdom."

She narrows her eyes playfully, with no trace of the same shock that Stassia and Auralie had on learning the same news. "So you *can* get me a job."

I let out a feeble laugh. "Sure, if you want one."

The boys bound up the stairs, their tiny feet pounding across the empty and quiet deck, holding their bows and full quivers above their heads.

"We got them!" Roley yells, and comes to a halt in front of me. Fin sidles up beside him, and I crouch down, wrapping Roley in a tight hug.

"Be good, Roley. Remember to keep your back elbow up."

He pulls away, nodding fiercely with a look of determination on his face like he's trying to commit that to memory.

He turns to Fin then, both of their faces etched in sadness, and once again my heart shatters into pieces.

"Bye, Fin," Roley says.

Fin gulps, his tiny face falling as he looks at his friend. "Bye Roley. Thanks for being my friend."

They come together, wrapping their arms around each other in a hesitant hug, before backing away, each with tears in their eyes.

"Voyagers forever," Roley mumbles.

"Castaways forever," Fin replies.

Mara extends her hand to Roley, and he takes it. Without hesitation, she reaches into the outstretched pouch and grabs enough dust for the two of them, sprinkling it over their heads before they disappear.

A tiny sniffle meets my ears, and I can't bear to look down and see Fin crying. Each goodbye has been harder than the last, but this…

This feels like I'm losing the brother I never had.

"Come here, little guy," Jorn says as he walks toward us. He scoops Fin into his arms and tosses him into the air. Peals of laughter break the silence, halting Fin's crying instantly. "Want to climb the mast one last time with me?"

"Yeah!" Fin cheers, and Jorn sets off, lifting Fin onto the first beam and following closely behind him.

Sig steps in front of Weston and me, and it's the first time I've actually seen her face since we walked back through the portal. She's just as much of a mess as I feel, with her eyes puffy and her cheeks tear stained.

She holds her hand up to us, her eyes averted. "I'm not leaving tonight. I—I—can't. Not yet. If that's okay, Cap."

"It's alright, Signee," Weston murmurs. He moves to step toward her, but she steps back.

"Don't." She shakes her head and squeezes her eyes shut. "I can't take any more tonight."

Weston nods, and she turns away, her shoulders shaking as she wraps her arms around herself and disappears below.

Weston's arms wrap around my shoulders, and he pulls me into his chest. If I thought I wasn't holding back earlier, I was wrong. Sobs wrack my body as I bury my face in his hard chest. He holds me tightly and lets me cry, one hand wrapped around the back of my head as he gently strokes my hair.

After a few moments, I feel the rumble of his voice against my cheek. "I'll bring Fin home, then I'll be back."

I can only nod and cry harder, the reminder that this is final, too overwhelming to utter any words. I told Fin I would try to visit him, but I have no idea when that could be. I have no idea what is going to meet us back in Blackwood, if my father's wrath will have effects that last years, or if he will be too caught up in both of our return that he will forget.

I don't ask Weston to leave some dust here when he goes. He knows I trust him to come back for us. He wouldn't ever leave Sig or Jorn or me behind. But this is his one final act as the captain, and I know he wants to see it through.

I barely hear when they approach from behind. Fin's sadness is gone, his excitement from racing Jorn up the mast overshadowing it all.

Weston's arms loosen around me and I pull away, pressing the heels of my hands into my eyes and sucking in air, trying to steady my breaths before crouching down to talk to Fin.

"Is it time to go?" he asks softly.

"It is."

His chin quivers as he throws his arms around my neck and squeezes tight. I hold him, and let the tears fall silently now, shocked that I even have this many left in me.

"I love you, Lennox," he says, the sound muffled against my shoulder. "I wish you were my sister, too."

"I love you, Fin. I may not be your sister, but I'm so glad I get to be your friend."

I lean back and hold him at arm's length.

"Weston is going to bring you home safe, alright? He'll know where you live, so maybe one day we can visit."

"Will you practice your stories so you can tell me more?"

"I will do that." My voice cracks on the last word, and I pull him into another hug before letting him go.

For how long, I do not know.

I now know how overwhelmed Sig felt because it feels like the world is crashing down on me.

The deck is too empty. The island is too quiet.

I can't watch two more people I love disappear, even if I know one of them is coming back.

My head drops between my shoulders, and I feel the urge to wrap myself in my arms, just like Sig did, but the moment I step away, a hand clasps mine, tugging me back.

"Hey," Weston grumbles, lifting my chin with his thumb. I force myself to meet his gaze, even though it makes my eyes well again. "I don't know how long I'll be gone, but get some rest." He leans in, pressing a firm kiss to my lips. "I *will* be back."

I nod and roll my lips together, trying to keep from falling apart, but his eyes don't break away. They won't until he's satisfied that I know he's serious, that he won't leave me behind.

I spin around and stride quickly across the deck, my only focus is getting to our room. I barely make it to the opening before I have to slam my palm over my mouth when I hear Fin's voice carry on the breeze.

"Eew. You kissed her. Do you love her, mister Weston?"

"Yes, I do, kid."

My breath catches, because even though he's told me himself, hearing him say it to someone else is more love and devotion than I've ever had.

"I do too, but not like that. Blech."

Weston chuckles. "Give it a few years and you'll probably think differently."

"But I already love Lennox. Will I find someone like her?"

"One day you will, Fin. Even if you have to wait a really long time."

I almost break when I take the first step down into the ship as I hear Weston's last words.

"She was worth the wait."

CHAPTER TWENTY-TWO

The silence in the dim Captain's quarters is heavy, filled with loss and grief, and loneliness. There have only been two other times in my life I felt this way. The first was when we were told to let go of my mother, the second when I was unworthy. Both will remain etched in my memory, with their newest companion, the moment I walked alone into Weston's room after saying goodbye to my entire new life.

My gaze stays trained on the floorboards as I shuffle inside, shutting the door firmly behind me. I can't bring myself to look up, to take in the details of a place that has become so familiar to me, so comforting. This will be one of the last times I see it.

I float through the room, feeling as if I'm no longer in my body. It's like I'm watching every step I take from somewhere else, the numbness from too much emotion finally overtaking me.

Sig and Jorn are just down the hall, having left before I hurried away to avoid watching two people I love disappear. I know if I truly needed them, they would be there for me, but I refuse to bother them, not for a loneliness that I used to live with every day. Tonight is their last night in Dawnlin too, and possibly their last night together, before duty and tradition rip them apart.

Like it might take Weston away from me.

I can barely process the thought before it slips from my mind again, pushed out by the suffocating loneliness that is punctuated by the absence of noise from the crew. The first night I spent on this ship, when I was locked in the brig, I felt alone. I was ripped away from the Voyagers, from a man I thought I loved and who I thought loved me. But I was never alone. From the moment I stepped onto this island, Weston has been there, making sure I was never harmed, but not interfering with any of my decisions. He traipsed through the jungle, followed me into the deadly lagoon, breathed life back into me, broke the door down after hearing me scream from nightmares.

But he's not here now, and even though I know he is coming back, it doesn't feel that way. The crew is gone. The Voyagers are gone. Fin is gone. The island is empty, and our hopes of the healing waters are dashed.

It's too much to bear.

I pad over to the bathtub, my feet and hands moving as if on their own as I reach out and turn the knob, making the water as hot as it will go. I strip my clothes off and wait for it to fill before easing myself over the side and lowering my body into the steaming water. Knees bent, I rest my cheek on them, my eyes falling closed as I let the burn from the heat distract me from the aching pit in my chest.

Every time my mind tries to wander, cycling through the possibilities, the worries, the conversations and arguments that might befall me the moment I step back onto the castle grounds, I push them away. I have no idea what will meet us when we return home, but my training and nerves want to take control and prepare me for the worst possibilities, despite each new scenario winding me tighter and tighter.

The heat does nothing to relax my tense muscles as I sit in the water, my gaze fixed on the wall. I don't move, barely breathing the shallow breaths this position will allow me, until the water turns cold and I fill it up again. This time, I force myself to move, washing the day away before sliding into Weston's shirt and crossing the room to the bed.

Climbing in, my body curls into itself, surrounded by the sheets and the scent of Weston. I inhale deeply, hoping to find comfort, but it only brings a prick of tears to my eyes. I don't know how long he will be gone. The way time passes in our world compared to here is unknown, so it could be hours, or it could be days. Fin never talked about where he lived in relation to the fountain, or if it would take a while to travel. I don't want to be alone for that long.

Actual tears come then, and I can't hold them back any longer. I close my eyes, letting them leak from the corners, dampening the pillow beneath my head as I pull the bedding tightly around me. I never thought being able to return home would feel like this. I don't know how something that I wanted so badly can hurt this much.

I must have fallen asleep because the press of a kiss to my temple wakes me. I startle from where I lie completely wrapped in blankets, and blink my eyes open to find Weston, hands pressed down into the mattress as he hovers over the edge of the bed. His smile is filled with sorrow, and his damp hair falls over his forehead as he leans in, watching me sleep.

The room is still dim, but early morning light peeks through the windows. Without a word, I lift the blankets, and he slides in beside me, leaning back against the pillows and shifting me so I'm tucked into his side. Pulling them back over my shoulder, I wrap my arm around his torso and squeeze him tight against me.

"Fin is home safe," he whispers, and the ache in my chest I thought would disappear with sleep is back in an instant. "He's in Grebar, and lives very close to the fountain, so it didn't take long to find his family. His parents were relieved and thankful to see him. They thought he was dead."

A sob escapes my throat, and I press my face into his skin, letting the heat comfort me. He wraps his arm around me tighter, and his fingertips brush my scalp, running through my waves and back again.

"I'll remember where it is if you ever want to go."

I nod quickly but say nothing. I don't have to. He already knows.

"I'm glad you got some sleep."

"Barely," I croak, and his chest rises and falls under my cheek with a sigh.

"Today was…a lot. It's alright to feel this way."

"But tomorrow is going to be worse."

He pauses. "Why would tomorrow be worse?" I can hear the confusion in his voice, and I realize he hasn't had the time like I have to lie here, thinking about every single way tomorrow could go wrong, about every possibility that would break me more than today did.

I push myself up so I can look at him to find he's already watching me, his brows drawn together.

"Because we have nothing figured out. We didn't think this was ever going to happen, not after the dust was gone. We have talked nothing through."

His brow smoothes out, and his quiet composure returns. "Then let's talk now."

"How can you be so calm about this?"

He shrugs slightly. "Because I'm not worried."

"How can you say that, Weston?" I say, my voice rising to reflect the panic churning inside me. His arm falls away from my back as I sit on my heels. "How are you not worried about what will happen when we go home? What are we going to tell my father? What are we going to tell *your* father? How are we going to explain to everyone who you are, or where you've been, or why you still look like you do?"

"Lennox, the people who need to know, already know. And the rest don't need an explanation."

"Sure. Fine. Alright. Ignore that part. Because no one is going to notice that the First Guard hasn't aged a day in twenty years. What about the rest? My father doesn't even speak to me, and I'm just supposed to walk back into the castle and say, 'Guess what? I'm fucking your best friend?'"

"I'd prefer if you didn't say it that way. It probably wouldn't go over well," he says flatly, and I let out a frustrated groan.

"Weston, we have no plan!"

My chest heaves, and my fists clench as I can't hide the panic any longer. More tears form a lump in my throat as I try to hold them back. I can only imagine how I look after hours of crying, now to be panic-stricken and raving on my knees before him.

But if he sees it, he doesn't acknowledge it. He just shifts to his knees, walking forward until they press into either side of mine, caging me in and grounding me with his touch. His hands find my face, and he leans forward, pressing his forehead to mine.

"Breathe." His thumbs stroke my cheeks as he breathes in deeply, then lets the air out slowly, urging me to follow his command. But I can't. My chest stutters with shallow breaths, and my fingertips tingle with numbness. The edges of the room blur and darken, and I squeeze my eyes shut, trying to hold everything back as this overwhelming sense of helplessness and dread threatens to control me.

"Lennox, look at me."

I pry my eyes open and meet his, finding only love, and no judgment for my inability to control everything I am feeling. It makes the tears want to fall harder.

"Breathe."

I inhale through pursed lips, and my chest quakes as I do.

"Again." He pulls back slightly, his eyes never leaving mine as I do as he says. The tingling in my fingers subsides, but it still feels like my chest is in knots.

"It will all be fine," he says, nodding as I take another deep breath. "I have a plan."

I blink at him rapidly. "But you didn't talk to me about it," I squeak.

He shakes his head. "I didn't need to because you aren't part of it."

I pull back slightly, my jaw falling open as his lips tip up at the corners when he registers my surprise.

"Let me explain. Once we are back in the castle, and once my father and your father know we are home, I'm going to be honest with my best friend." He pauses, and I wait with bated breath, not knowing how this would be any different from my crude example of how to admit our relationship to my father.

His hand slides across my cheek and down the column of my neck, and his thumb gently strokes the skin where my pulse threads the surface. "I'm going to tell him I cannot live without you, and that I've done that for far too long." My chin wobbles, and his eyes flicker down to it. His smile deepens as he leans forward and presses a soft kiss to my lips before leaning back and continuing.

"I'm going to tell him I've sworn an oath to you, and that I would do anything for you, more than just within the confines of a devoted castle guard."

I sniff loudly, and he closes the distance, kissing me again, and pulling back once more.

"And I'm going to tell him,"—he pauses, just long enough for me to see the determination in his face—"that, effective immediately, I no longer want to be the First Guard."

My jaw falls open. "What? But you...you made me promise not to take it from you—"

His fingers brush over my lips, stilling them and stopping my knee-jerk response that threatened to send me into another wave of panic.

"I am going to ask him to make me the second."

A gasp rips from my throat, even past where his fingertips lightly press into my lips.

"But he won't," I say, shaking my head. "He left it unfilled for so long. If he wanted someone else, he would have given it to them."

His gaze falls down as he chuckles softly. His fingers find my fists clenched on my thighs, and they unwind the tension as he laces them through mine.

"I think he will." His thumbs stroke my palm, sending shivers up my arms, and he watches the movement intently. "I saw the way he looked at your mother the first time he saw her, and almost every time after that. If the man I know is still somewhere inside him—" His eyes meet mine, and my breath catches with what I find there. "He'll see it when he looks at me, too."

"What if he doesn't?" I whisper. "What if he forbids it, or releases you, or worse?"

He chuckles, and there's a playful gleam in his eye. "I have a way of bypassing the whole 'he's the king' thing. I'd make him see it."

Tears stream down my cheeks, and I push up onto my knees, throwing my arms around his neck and pulling him close until our chests are flush together.

"I already lost everyone else. I can't lose you too."

His arms cage me against him, his muscles flexing with the crushing force.

"You will not lose me."

"I had nothing, Weston," I sob. "Nothing. I'm so scared to go back to that life."

His hands slide over my back and grip my ribs, pushing me back onto my heels so he can look at me again. "It won't be the same as before. I will be there with you. You won't be alone. And you won't be stuck inside the castle. I won't let that happen, and I'm pretty sure after being here, you won't let that happen either."

I huff a laugh and drop my chin to my chest, my eyes drawing to the ripple of raised skin slashing across his abdomen.

"After constantly being surrounded by people, being in such close quarters with everyone, after finally having friends…I just don't want to be alone again."

He reaches up and brushes my hair off my face. "You won't be alone. I'll be standing right behind you."

"Beside me."

"Whatever you want, my queen," he grumbles. "Although." He tilts my head back so I meet his eyes again. The smirk and sparkle in his eye make my stomach flutter and remind me of the Weston who couldn't help but joke and coerce me into becoming his friend. "The Lennox I know doesn't just submit and take what is handed to her. If you fight your father half as much as you fight me, then I have no doubt you'd have me as your guard." He leans forward and presses a slow kiss to my lips. "I can't wait to watch you go toe to toe with someone that isn't me."

I feel the tug of a smile and try to suppress it. "Maybe I just have a thing for fighting assholes."

He laughs deeply, his head falling back, and bearing the strong column of his throat.

I shrug. "It's just everything, I guess. I wasn't prepared for any of this to happen today, and to deal with it all over again tomorrow, and possibly even worse. I feel like I lost myself a little tonight."

"It's alright to feel lost, as long as you never forget, I will always find you." His eyes dance between mine, and his face blurs as tears well in my vision. I close the space between us, kissing him slowly and gently, and he returns each motion without pressure, without expectation, his lips a gentle caress over mine.

"Let's sleep," he murmurs, and I frown, my body wanting to be lost in him, to forget everything except the sweet words he just said. He presses a kiss to each side of my mouth, kissing away the emotion before sliding back down into the mattress. He reaches out and pulls me toward him, and I snuggle back into his warmth, so grateful that he sees everything I need before even I do.

"I love you," he grumbles into the top of my head, just as my eyes flutter shut.

"I'm not ready," I say, my voice barely a whisper.

His voice is so low, I almost don't hear it as sleep creeps in. "I am." There are only the sounds of his deep, steady breaths for minutes before he speaks again. "We'll figure it all out together."

My nod is small, the exhaustion, both physical and emotional, overtaking me as I drift to sleep, pressed into his warm skin, listening to the steady and calming beat of his heart.

CHAPTER TWENTY-THREE

*L*ifting the lid of the trunk at the foot of the bed and pulling out the clothes that I had only just stashed there, feels wrong. I thought I would never need to see them again, but Dawnlin had other plans. I dress quickly, stealing a few glances at the bed where Weston still lies sprawled across the surface. The sheets pool around his hips, exposing the muscles of his back and the steady rise and fall of his breath. My throat tightens with a fresh wave of tears that accompany flashes of memories that this room holds. I need to leave it, now, before it is too hard to walk away. I'm already prepared for my uncontrollable emotions to set Sig's off the moment I see her.

There's nothing in this room I need other than my dagger and the man lying soundly asleep in that bed. The familiar blade is already tucked safely into the waistband of the thick pants I wore when I snuck into the city, not expecting to actually leave my kingdom that night.

The suns are high in the sky when I step onto the deck, the heat already causing sweat to dampen my back beneath the thick tunic and cloak. It's clear that after the emotional day and late night, we slept well past midday. The quiet is still too eerie, and being out here alone, knowing no one is going to come bounding up the steps, laughing or rushing to do their task, makes my heart sink.

I need to say goodbye. To the island. To the sky. To the waves and the water. To the heat.

Weston promised he wouldn't let me stay trapped inside the cold, dark walls of the castle any longer, that he would help make sure I got out like I always wanted. But it won't be like this.

It won't be like here.

How could visiting another kingdom feel as free and alive as Dawnlin? I want to remember every second.

Resting my elbows against the railing, I lean forward, looking out over the water toward the beach and watching as the waves crash into the sand.

If the girl who stepped foot on this island months ago stood in front of me today, I don't think I'd recognize her. When I came here, I was so full of anger and resentment, and the desire to prove everyone wrong. I was too trusting and eager, but it was mostly because I was missing so much. Love, companionship, friendship, the hope for a future. While some of those feelings have changed, or I understand them better, they aren't gone; rather, the experiences I have lived here have helped fill in pieces of myself that I didn't know were empty. I've bandaged up some of those wounds.

I now know what it's like to love, and be loved in more than just a romantic sense. I know how it feels to care for others, and have them care for you in return, enough to put their lives on the line for each other. I know what it is like to hope, and to have those hopes fulfilled, but also crushed. And I know what it is to want, not only to want a person, but to want more from life.

Sig said that an eternal life trapped on Dawnlin lacked purpose, and the real chance at being human was back home in our world. When I look back at who I was when I arrived compared to who I am now, I agree with her sentiment, but also disagree. Dawnlin gave me so many more life experiences than I ever had back home, and in a way, took them away from me too.

Now that we are going home, and I can truly appreciate what I missed before, and what I would have missed if we stayed here, I can't return home to a life that is the same. I can't continue to live without everything I had here. Friends, independence, love. I refuse to settle back into the life I had before, starting with Weston.

I don't know how my father will react when he hears of our return, and the more my mind has tried to come up with every outcome, the less I care. He can't use Weston's position or their previous relationship as any sort of reason to keep us apart. It's been twenty years since my father last saw or spoke to his friend, and his life went on. Weston's didn't.

How could my father refuse him happiness, solely because of who I am? Or who I'm related to? If he truly cares about his friend, he won't deny him the same hope for life he had when he found my mother.

Then again, I have only ever known a father who has denied me that life. Maybe he really would do it to Weston too.

We are about to find out.

I don't know how long I stand at the rail, looking out over the island and reliving the moments that might fade away after years of new experiences replace them. I might never remember exactly how the breeze feels, the smells and the sounds. This place will only ever live in my memory.

The sound of footsteps on the wooden steps makes me turn over my shoulder only to find Sig and Jorn slowly stepping onto deck. Sig's eyes are swollen, her shoulders slumped slightly as she clings to Jorn's hand, and looks up at me with a sad smile. Her eyes trail up and down my clothes, and my eyes water as she takes in a shuddering breath.

"You look better in the clothes from here," she says, and a watery chuckle escapes me.

"I agree, but I'd be freezing the moment we landed. Plus, it might draw too much attention."

They cross the deck and stop beside me at the rail, and I look between them. A sad smile plagues Jorn's normally joyful face as he opens his arms to me.

"Hey, little Lennox."

A harsh breath escapes my chest as I step into his arms, wrapping mine around him tightly. He squeezes me back, rocking me playfully from side to side.

"I had fun with you," he murmurs, his voice the most forlorn I have ever heard it, even after he almost died before my eyes. "I'm glad you were around, even if it wasn't for that long."

"You always kept things interesting, Jorn. You know I'll never forget you."

He lets out a sad chuckle. "You better not. Keep the captain in check for me, alright? He needs to smile every so often."

I laugh into Jorn's stomach. The sound is muffled, but I can hear Sig's soft giggle too.

"I'll do my best." I step away, and he winks down at me.

"If all else fails, just find some way to make him jealous."

I can't help the smile that pulls at my lips. "Apparently you're lucky you still have arms after all of that."

Jorn barks a laugh, his head falling back before he looks back at me, grinning. "Desperate times. He needed a push."

"Thank you, Jorn. For everything."

"No need to thank me, little Lennox. We take care of each other." He ruffles my hair and then drapes his arm around Sig's shoulder.

"Cap awake yet?" she asks, and I shake my head.

"He wasn't when I got up. I've been out here for a while though."

I barely finish my sentence when I hear his boots on the stairs. The three of us turn toward him, and a lump forms in my throat, threatening to choke me.

It's not Weston, the captain I've come to know and love, stepping out onto the deck for the final time.

It's Weston, the First Guard.

Gone are the loose shirt and leather vest, replaced by the thick, form-fitting fabrics of the guard uniform as his heavy cloak billows behind him in the breeze. The hilt of his sword sparkles at his side, securely sheathed in the belt he took back from me, because he needs it. I don't. Light glints off his ring, the flat face now turned to the proper position with the seal of Blackwood prominent and visible.

His eyes hold mine as he slowly crosses the deck, and I have to remind myself to breathe. The moment he reaches us, he presses a kiss to the top of my hair, and it's clear he understands the internal struggle in my mind, equating the man I know with this new one that stands before me.

"Everyone ready?" he grumbles as he turns to face Sig and Jorn, his head swiveling between them.

Sig's brows rise and meet in the middle as her face crumbles, but she presses a hand to her mouth, and nods silently.

Jorn doesn't hesitate and closes the distance between him and Weston, each of them wrapping the other in a firm hug.

"Til we meet again, brother," Jorn says, and Weston pats him on the back.

"Won't be soon enough," Weston says right before they step apart. Weston's jaw works, and my heart breaks. All the goodbyes yesterday were hard on him, but Sig has been there from the beginning, and Jorn has been like a true brother. The weight of this goodbye can't be lighter than all the rest combined.

Sig moves to me then, and we both burst into tears. Her arms crush me, and I crush her back, our sobs out of sync and loud as we cling to each other. I try to control my breathing, try to stop the stuttering sounds that escape me at the thought of no longer seeing my friend every day, and she only squeezes me tighter.

"Look after him, alright?" She mumbles so that only I can hear. "He'll never admit it, but he needs you just as much as we all needed him. Don't let him hide everything away. Fight him if you need to." I nod into her, and she pulls back, her arms resting on my shoulders until she can look me in the eye.

"And you, don't forget to live. Don't waste this second chance we were given. Grab hold of it, and make it everything you've always dreamed of."

"I could say the same to you." Steady streams of tears fall down my cheeks, forcing me to blink them away to see her clearly again. I clear my throat and sniffle as my chest hollows out. I can't leave without her knowing how much she meant to me, because despite her urging, and my plans to do exactly what she insisted, I don't know how soon those things will happen, how soon I could ever see any of them again. I don't want to walk away from her without her knowing what she means to me.

"Thank you for everything, Sig. For listening to me, for being there for me even when I lied and pushed you away, for fighting for me and believing in me. I finally know what true friendship feels like, and if I never have another again, at least I had you. I wouldn't have made it through any of this without you."

Her lip quivers as her hands slide down my arms until they clasp my fingers tight. I squeeze back, then let her go, because as hard as that moment was, I know I'm not the one she needs to let go of the most.

"Signee," Weston says softly.

Hesitantly, she turns to him, the tears in her eyes welling again before she throws herself at him. She digs her face into his chest, her harsh cries still audible despite how smothered she is into him, and he wraps his arms around her shoulders, holding her gently. Weston doesn't move, letting her cry in his arms the same way he lets me, and after a few moments, he leans down, and says something in her ear, quiet enough that neither Jorn nor I can hear. His words only make her cry harder, her sobs echoing around us until she leans back and punches him in the arm, before turning away and running her palm across her face. He smiles softly, but I can still see the sadness in his eyes as he pulls the pouch from his belt.

"Don't be a stranger," I say, smiling through my now quiet tears.

"Do you really think either of you could get rid of me?" Sig says with a sniff. "Maybe you'll finally leave that castle and come visit."

"Count on it," I say. "I'll be expecting an invitation."

Weston holds the pouch out to them, and both reach out, their hands disappearing into the fabric, only to reappear a moment later, the space between their fingers glowing brightly despite the light of the day.

It's as if the rest of the island falls away as they turn toward each other. Nothing else exists—not Weston, not me, not the crash of the waves or the heat of the suns. Sig and Jorn stare into each other's eyes, unspoken words passing between them. Jorn leans down and gives her one last brush of a kiss, then, their movements mirroring each other, they each lift an arm, and let the dust fall over their heads.

The gold sparkles and the air starts to shimmer as my friends slowly disappear, leaving Weston and me alone.

The only two left in Dawnlin.

I stare at the empty space Sig and Jorn occupied just moments ago, my eyes aching from all the crying, and my jaw clenching so hard my teeth feel like they are going to crack. My eyes sweep over the normally bustling deck, the emptiness making the pit in my stomach feel even deeper.

When my gaze finally settles on Weston, I swallow hard.

"It's our turn, princess."

Hot anger bubbles up inside me, completely overshadowing the sorrow and emptiness I felt only a moment ago, and I finally snap.

"How many times do I have to tell you to stop fucking calling me that!"

After all the history between us, everything he had to get past to see me as me, not the princess he had to protect, it frustrates me knowing he won't stop, even though I have asked. It became a joke after he finally uttered my name for the first time, but now, after all of this, I don't want to be reminded of every time I felt rejected by him because of his duty and oath to my father.

Especially not now, not in one of the hardest moments of my life, after I've said goodbye to everyone I care for.

I spin around and grip the rail, staring hard into the rolling water below. The quick anger is probably a result of the onslaught of emotions I've had to deal with in the last day, but now, as I stare into the waves, my outburst having settled between us, I feel a twinge of guilt. He's had to deal with just as much as I have, if not more. But he's the only one I can show my true self to, the only one who can see the real me, not the version of me where everything I feel hides beneath the surface. He's the easiest person to unleash my anger on. The safest. The one who won't hate me or fault me for any of my feelings, and tries to take them and bear the pain himself to save me from it.

"Lennox."

I try to hide my wince as his hand settles on my waist, softly nudging me to turn back toward him, but I resist his pressure.

"Lennox, look at me."

Letting out a breath, I reluctantly turn back around and stare up at him, but just as I expected, his sorrow and acceptance of my verbal lashing is written all over his face, and it all but extinguishes the fire beneath my skin.

"I can't."

"What are you talking about, Weston? You can't understand that I don't want you to call me that anymore?" I say, crossing my arms over my chest.

"I understand you want me to stop, but the moment we step back into your kingdom, you are the princess. I can't."

My arms untangle and slowly fall to my sides as his sad gaze holds mine.

He can't.

Because we're going home.

There is no more forgetting who we are, no more pretending I am just Lennox. I am the princess, and will be to him, despite everything that has happened between us.

No matter how much he loves me.

No matter how much I love him.

Our titles will always separate us. Our duties will pull us apart unless we're alone, hidden away behind closed doors.

I spent months trying to get him to see past that title, to see only me, Lennox, not the princess. To live in the moment, here on Dawnlin, where we didn't have to answer to anyone but ourselves. To suppress his deep devotion to his duty as the First Guard, only for all of it to return the moment we can go home.

And for me to have to do the same, and become the princess and future queen I am meant to be.

My chin quivers as I look into his eyes, and see everything I'm feeling reflected at me.

I push up on my toes, wrapping my arms around his neck.

"I'm sorry," I whisper.

Without hesitation, he closes the distance between us, his lips finding mine. The slow caress is everything I need. Dawnlin fades away as he kisses me, his movements gentle as he coaxes my mouth open, brushing his tongue against mine.

The first time he kissed me on this deck, only steps away from where we stand now, was raw, filled with fear and worry and passion, but this…this is different. This feels like love, and certainty, and stability. His mouth claims mine, claims me as his, reassuring me that despite my fears and the inevitability of my role, he isn't going anywhere. He will be beside me, just as he swore to me

Heat blooms in my belly as I kiss him back, my thumbs brushing the underside of his jaw as his arms wrap around me, his hands almost bruising through my thick clothes as he holds me close.

I'm stunned and breathless when he breaks away, but his lips don't leave my skin, only move to press firm kisses up the curve of my jaw.

"Remember my words," he grumbles before pressing a firm kiss. "My sword." Kiss. "My body." Kiss. "My life." Kiss. "My heart." I drop my head back, giving him more space as his lips brush the space just below my ear. Shivers course through me when his teeth graze the sensitive skin, followed by the heat of his lips.

"My queen."

The deep rumble makes my knees tremble, threatening to collapse beneath me. I'm overwhelmed with everything this man feels for me, and I feel for him. It was only ever something I imagined in my dreams, but he's real. I can feel him beneath my fingertips, against my neck, wrapped around my body, pulling me even closer to ensure I don't fall.

"Not another soul can change that oath," he grumbles. "Those words are for you, and you alone. I don't give a fuck if anyone doesn't like it. Until the breath stills in my lungs, I'm yours."

His words reverberate through me, warming every cold and lonely corner and giving me hope that despite everything we've been through, it will all turn out exactly how we want it. I didn't realize my eyes were closed until they flutter open as I lower my chin, to find his teal eyes sparkling.

Digging my fingers into his hair, I pull his face to mine, the movements not soft like before. I crush our lips together, and he follows my lead, walking me backward until my body hits the railing. Without a hitch in the lavishing movement of his tongue, he lifts me onto the railing, quickly stepping between my thighs. Eager hands slide up the sides of my legs, over my hips and settle on my low back, pressing the heat of my core against the firm planes of his body.

I groan impatiently when he breaks away and settles his forehead against mine.

"It's taking everything I have not to take you back to our room and fuck you in my bed one last time."

"I have a bed back at the castle." I lean forward, pressing another slow kiss to his lips.

"Technically, I do too," he says. "Or at least I did."

I pull away just enough so my lips barely brush his as I lower my voice to a playful murmur. "But I have a closet full of ball gowns."

His grin widens against my lips, and I lean back so my eyes can scan his, finding them filled with playful excitement.

"That's a much better idea, my queen." It only lasts for a moment though, before his smile falters and his expression turns serious. "Are you ready?"

I nod slowly, my lips pursed together.

Standing to his full height, his arm encircles my waist, supporting me so there is no chance I'll fall back into the water. His hand finds the wooden railing next to me, his fingers wrapping around it as he looks out over the sea toward the island.

"Thank you," he murmurs, not to me, but to whatever magic is listening. His gaze falls to where his hand rests on the rail, then up to the helm on the quarterdeck, no doubt saying goodbye to his ship, his place of refuge.

He finds the pouch at his belt, slipping his hand inside before pulling out a fistful of glowing dust. I circle his body, clasping my hands firmly behind him, and settle into his chest, sending my own silent thank you to the island for letting us have this moment, just the two of us, before life and time return.

A single tear slides from the corner of my eye, dampening his uniform where my face presses into him.

"Let's go home, Weston."

CHAPTER TWENTY-FOUR

y fingers ache as I unclench my hands from behind Weston's back. The hum of the magic surrounding us dissipates moments after my boots hit the firm ground, and a deep sigh escapes my chest.

Cold.

It's the first thing I notice before I see the cloud of my breath in the air. A full-body shudder overcomes me, my skin already begging to be engulfed by the warmth of Dawnlin once more. Weston's arms cinch tighter, pulling me in so I can soak up his heat, and giving me a moment to let the truth of our reality settle.

We are back in Blackwood.

We made it.

The thought feels surreal, but also expected. After everything we fought through, all the doubt, the hope, the despair, the betrayal, the acceptance of our stolen future, it feels like this moment is a dream, and that I'll open my eyes and be back in the captain's quarters, ready to search for the dust on another day.

But it's real. The cold confirms it.

"Do you want my cloak?" Weston murmurs, and I shake my head.

"No, I'll be fine." I clench my jaw as it starts to chatter. "I guess it's just been a while. I'm not used to the cold anymore."

My arms fall to my sides as he steps back, bursting our bubble and shattering my grip on hoping for more time with only the two of us. He reaches up and grabs my hood, pulling it over my head, before pulling the cloak tight around me and deftly clasping the front all the way to my waist.

"We'll be inside soon." His eyes stay focused on his task.

"We don't have to hurry." I let out a reluctant breath. "I don't want this to be over yet."

His eyes meet mine, and he smiles softly. "You're nervous."

"What was your first clue?" I say sarcastically.

He brushes off my jab, and instead intently focuses on my face.

"This right here." His thumb hooks my lower lip, pulling it out from where it is clenched between my teeth. "Then this." He runs the pad of his finger between my eyes and across one eyebrow, forcing me to release the tension I'm holding there. "And you keep shifting your weight back and forth."

I tilt my head, being the one to assess him now. "Do you really notice all that about me?"

"I notice everything about you." His eyes darken as he leans forward and gives me a soft kiss. "But you don't have to be nervous. Nothing is over. It's just…going to be different."

I huff a laugh. "It will be my turn to say I'm always right when you get a nice glimpse of what my life is like here."

"And we'll change it. You'll change it. I have no doubt."

My shoulders sag slightly, and my lip juts out in a small pout. "Can we at least take the long way?"

He smirks, then nods. "Yes, we can take the long way."

Looking to the side, he takes in our surroundings, a look of understanding adjusting his features. I hadn't considered that we'd be back in the same alleyway that started this entire journey, the same one he was in when he came to Dawnlin. Where Dane hid in the shadows, waiting to brutally attack him from behind, and where I stood as Dane looked around for anyone that might try to cheat the magic the same way he did.

"That's different." I follow his gaze to the dirty and still fountain beside us.

"What do you mean? It looks the same."

He shakes his head. "It wasn't like this when I left. It was…clean… and beautiful. The water flowed and trickled. It was inspiring. This is… disheartening."

I look at it, taking in all the places I had rubbed the dirt away only to find that it has already been replaced with a new layer of grime. "This is how it looked when I left. It hasn't changed at all."

"Interesting." He steps away and walks around it, taking in the fountain from top to bottom.

"It was one thing I wondered when I found it. I wondered if the magic in Dawnlin was gone, because the fountain didn't look the way it did in the story."

"But it wasn't. You still got through."

"Yeah, it still called the Guardian."

We stand in silence, both of us looking at the fountain that started it all and brought us to the land that deemed us unworthy of helping who we loved back home. It's only a few moments when I hear myself speak, my thoughts too important to hold them in.

"I wonder what happens if someone calls him now? He's somewhere without the dust. What would happen then?"

"We may never know."

He takes my hand and rests the other on the pommel of his sword. Tension roils through his shoulders as he assesses the alley, determining it is safe enough for us to proceed through.

Light still brightens the thick grey clouds that blanket the sky, but I can tell night is coming. We step out onto a main road, and the walkways are bustling with people, who are no doubt heading home to prepare for their evening meal. Weston's hand stays tightly wrapped around mine as we walk in pace with the crowd, my body firmly tucked to his side.

Despite how conspicuous I feel walking through the streets among my people, no one spares me a glance. They are probably used to seeing staff from the castle walking home or to a tavern in the evening, but it still feels foreign to me, especially after being gone. Unsurprisingly, Weston draws the eyes of people passing by. If it weren't for his towering frame and clenched jaw, his gaze darting everywhere, assessing everything, he might not look out of place compared to the casual calm of everyone around us.

"It all looks the same. It feels like I never left," Weston murmurs as his eyes scan the road before we turn onto it and continue our winding walk through the city.

The buildings and roads are familiar from back when I took some time to wander and try to see more of the city on my own. The square where I spent most of my time is ahead, and a small part of me wishes I could go inside the library, even if it is only for a few minutes.

"The first time I ever saw it was only a few weeks before I came to Dawnlin. I barely know my own city, let alone my kingdom."

"You will," he says, glancing down at me briefly before continuing his watch of our surroundings. "In the meantime, I can tell you stories."

I make a face. "I much prefer Jorn's stories. I am not particularly interested in hearing about your nights out in the city and all the women vying for your attention." I catch the smirk on his lips as my eyes trail up and down his body, my mind still trying to get used to this First Guard version of Weston. I've never had reason to take a second glance at the guard uniforms before, but now that I see him in one, I can imagine how he feels about ballgowns, and why he had so many women seeking his attention. The way the fabric molds across his shoulders and strains over chest is enough to make clear the strength of the man beneath. It would intimidate any man, and entice any woman, and my mind flashes with images of what it would be like to take it off him.

Now is not the time for that. We have bigger issues to confront first.

He chuckles softly. "Those were not the stories that came to mind, but jealously looks good on you." I scowl up at him as we round a corner, but he ignores it, his smirk unrelenting. We halt, stepping to the side off the walkway so others can continue to pass by.

"See that archway over there?" he says, pointing across the street.

"Yes?" I've passed that archway before, but noticed nothing particularly interesting about it. It's just a stone structure marking the entrance to a different part of the city.

"Your mother was walking through that archway when your father first saw her. He couldn't get across the square fast enough." His body turns until he's pointing to the side of it. "I stood just over there while they talked. When she left, he wanted to follow her, but he was afraid of scaring her off."

My throat constricts. I'd been so absorbed in my lack of experience in my own kingdom that I never considered a truth that Weston just made so obviously apparent. My mother lived here. Pieces of her are all over this city, and Weston knows many of them. More than that, he didn't hesitate to tell me the story, unlike everyone else who hid all knowledge and memory of her from me until the moment Edmond handed me her diary.

I gulp down the large lump in my throat, my voice hoarse when I speak again. "What else?"

"Over there—"

"Excuse me, Addy?"

A familiar voice interrupts Weston, and my head swivels toward it in the same moment that he shifts, his body angling in front of me as he assesses this stranger who has stopped in front of us.

Though she's not a stranger. Not to me.

"Estelle," I say with a breath of relief, but despite my familiarity, Weston doesn't relax at all. I'm surprised to see her, especially since I've never interacted with her outside of the library. I was not expecting to see anyone I knew beyond the castle grounds, and, surprisingly, even with my hood drawn low over my face, she still recognized me.

Her gaze slides to Weston beside me, taking in his uniform and his protective stance, and no doubt realizing he isn't Dane, before she turns her attention to me once more.

"Is your apprenticeship going well?" she asks kindly.

My brows furrow, trying to think back to whether I had ever lied directly to her about working on the castle grounds. "Apprenticeship?"

Confusion taints her expression. "It had been so long. I thought you must be working as a healer now, or at least in the middle of your training."

"Oh," I stammer. "Yes, I mean, no. I'm not in an apprenticeship yet. Maybe someday soon."

"Ah." She nods, and a knowing smile turns her lips as she looks between Weston and me. "I see. Well, I thought an apprenticeship was the most likely culprit keeping you occupied and away from the library over the past year, but…" Her smile widens at Weston. "I'm sure there are many good reasons for you to be away."

I balk at her.

The past year.

I shake my head slightly, my eyes clinching shut before opening to meet hers again. "I'm sorry, how long did you say it has been?"

"Oh, it's probably closer to two at this point. This old head has too much about books in it to remember specific dates. There may have been days I missed you as well, but I haven't seen you or the other gentleman friend of yours in quite some time."

Almost two years.

I've been gone for almost two years.

My breath is almost a gasp as my mind reels with this new information, and suddenly I cannot fathom how Weston felt the moment he found out he had been gone for twenty-one years. Now, twenty-three. Weston's warm hand settles firmly on my low back, steadying me as my knees feel weak and lending me his strength while I stumble looking for words.

"I apologize," he says, breaking the silence while Estelle watches me with concern, "for keeping her away for so long. We will be sure to come see you more often, Miss Estelle."

Pink flashes in the tops of her cheeks as she regards him, then turns back to address me. "As always, I am available if anyone from the castle should need anything at all. It would be lovely to see you again, Addy. But I must be off. Mouths to feed."

I clear my throat, trying to hide the shock that is still coursing through my body. "Thank you, Estelle. I will see you soon."

She smiles warmly and hurries down the road, disappearing into the crowd as I still flounder with this new information.

"Addy?" Weston grumbles, the lilt of a question in his voice.

"I used the name of my handmaid and changed my hair when I snuck out of the castle. I didn't want anyone to know who I was."

I feel the press of his lips on the top of my head through the cloak, then the grumble of his voice in my ear. "Good girl."

"It didn't matter though," I say, ignoring the shiver that runs up my spine. "Dane still saw right through it."

"He did, but with all that happened, we still made it here. I found you, and we're back home. Maybe it all ended exactly as it was intended."

"Maybe it did," I mumble. "I just can't believe it's been almost two years." I look up at him then, and the sad look on his face takes me back. "I'm sorry. That was really inconsiderate."

"You don't need to worry about hurting me, Lennox. If anyone knows how you're feeling right now, it's me." His fingers flex against my low back, and I lean into him, quirking my eyebrow as I tilt my head back.

"Why are you being sweet? What happened to the snarky captain that would have snapped back at me for being a pain in the ass?"

He laughs, and the sound makes me smile despite the churning in my stomach.

"He's still here. He's just readjusting to everything too. Same as you."

I let out a sigh and drop my forehead onto his chest. "Alright, let's just get this over with. Let's go deal with my father."

"And mine," he agrees. "Although I doubt he will even flinch after basically sending you to come find me. Rem might have some words with him about that, actually."

I roll my eyes. "He can get over it. I brought you back, didn't I?"

Sliding his hand over my waist, he releases me, lacing our fingers together once again, and starts down the road toward the castle. The light is fading; the grey turning deeper as time wears on. Business owners begin to light the torches near their doors, preparing for a bustling night despite the wet cold in the air. It looks so much like the last time I walked back to the castle gates, only then, it was Dane walking me home, not Weston.

I push the thought from my mind, not wanting to ever think about Dane again, especially remembering how kind and sweet he was to me when we first met. Being back here, walking the same streets, brings back those memories, and I want to erase them with new ones made with the man by my side.

The gate comes into view as we round a corner, with the guards stationed in front and just inside, the same as they always are. Their crisp uniforms match the one beside me, and I take a deep breath, wondering if we will be able to walk through unobstructed, or if this is how my father learns of my return.

But when I look at each of them, what I find makes my steps falter. "Lennox?"

My feet come to an abrupt stop, barely hearing him over the pounding in my ears. I pull his hand, tugging him closer to me to keep him from getting any closer to the gate.

"What's wrong." It's not a question. He knows me well enough to know something has made me uneasy, and he needs to know what it is.

"I—I don't know," I stammer, my eyes darting between all the guards stationed at the gate a mere block ahead of us. Weston glances between them and me, his jaw tight, as he assesses the situation. His hand settles back on his sword, and I can feel the tension building in his body, matching mine.

"We just need to get inside," I force out, trying to squash down the rising panic. "I know it's been a long time, but I don't know." I look at each of their faces, recognizing them all, but they aren't the same men stationed there when I left, when I snuck out even with the disapproval of my guard. The air feels heavy, and the laughs and jeers between them are jarring to my ears.

"Weston, something feels very wrong."

CHAPTER TWENTY-FIVE

A sinking pit deepens in my stomach as I stare at the gate, trying to make sense of one particular detail. The moment I noticed it, I knew something was not right.

Or more specifically, noticed *him*.

One guard stands behind the rest, his shoulders pulled back, his chin jutted high with a sneer across his face. I'd recognize him anywhere, because the last time I saw him, he was on his knees before me, reciting his oath to the kingdom, after calling me a piss-poor excuse of a princess.

Brynne sent him away, so what is he doing back at the castle?

It's clear from the way he holds himself that he is the highest-ranking guard at the gate, or at least he assumes he is in charge. He's not. Brynne is. I watch as he saunters back and forth, his scowl and shrewd glare at anyone passing too closely making me uneasy about how this encounter will be.

"Do you see that man, the guard in charge? He isn't supposed to be here. At the castle."

He glances over his shoulder, eyeing the group warily, and his eyes narrow the moment he zeroes in on him.

"Tell me why." The concern is gone in an instant, the sweetness from moments ago replaced by a fierce calm as he analyzes a potential threat.

"Before Edmond told me about Dawnlin and I left, my guard and I were training. He was watching our spar and made some comments about me. My guard took them as borderline treasonous and forced him to kneel and re-swear his oath. Then she sent him away to the border. I don't know why he's back. He shouldn't be back."

"What did he say to you?" The growl in his voice would frighten anyone who didn't know Weston the way I do. There's no leniency in his demand as his eyes bore into me, but I still shake my head.

"What he said isn't important. What *is* important is that his loyalty to the crown was in question. He should not be guarding the castle. Something isn't right. We need to find Brynne."

"Has he done anything else? Anything you can remember? Are there any other guards close to him?"

I shake my head again. "No, not that I remember, anyway. I never noticed anything else, and there were only a few snickers in the rest of the guards. They all stopped though the moment Brynne beat him."

"Will he be a problem when you walk through that gate?" His expression is deadly and makes the back of my neck prickle with worry.

"He obviously knows who I am. I…I don't know," I stammer, and look past Weston, back at the group of guards still talking amongst themselves. "I don't know the rest of them, but the last time I came in and out, they didn't question me at all. Barely even gave me a second glance."

He lets out a huff, and mumbles under his breath. He sneaks another glance back at them before reaching out and taking hold of both my wrists, his gaze intense.

"Stay behind me. Let me do the talking. If you need to, interject, but otherwise, stay with me and let me lead. If something happens, do not put yourself in harm's way, do you hear me? We will sort it out once we're inside."

"Don't do anything that will make me want to." I raise my eyebrow and shoot him a look.

His eyes darken and his voice lowers. "You know I can't promise that. Behind me."

Turning on his heel, he stalks toward the gate, his shoulders pulled back and head held high in the commanding way he does. My heart pounds in my chest as I walk quickly to stay up with him, and even though his focus is on the threat before us, I can still feel the way he's aware of me and stays shielding me with his body.

I shift enough so I can just see past him, and watch as we catch the closest guard's eye. When we are within steps, he bumps another guard's chest, then gestures in our direction, muttering something I can't hear from this far away. The others turn, and the banished guard moves, standing behind the group, watching us approach. The lower-ranking guards move then, squaring their bodies to us and forming a barrier in front of the opening.

"Who are you?" the guard who noticed our approach calls out, glaring at us. He eyes Weston's uniform, and his brows bunch in confusion.

"Weston Rowe, First Guard." The chill in Weston's voice makes it easy to imagine the look on his face. One guard shifts uneasily on his feet, while the others break out into a chorus of laughter.

"Did you hear that, Guthrie?" the man on the far left sneers.

"He can't think we're going to take him seriously," another says with a disbelieving laugh.

The man Brynne banished, Guthrie, shoulders his way through the line.

"I'm not sure what you take us for, or if you're just a fucking idiot," he spits at Weston, "but if that uniform were truly yours, you would know what we all do. There is no First Guard."

Weston doesn't hesitate, taking the name-calling and accusations in stride. His voice stays even, but I can hear the force behind it. "It is mine, and I'm sorry to tell you men that you are mistaken. I know there is one, because I am he, and I am escorting the princess home."

"Escorting the princess?" Guthrie bursts into coarse laughter. Spittle flies from his lips as he looks over his shoulders, seeing which of the guards are following along with his game. "Nice try, son, but just because you're pretty and I'm sure can get along well convincing any whore of anything you say, doesn't mean we're going to bow down to it."

Rage simmers beneath my skin at his clear insult to Weston. This man shouldn't be here, shouldn't be anywhere near this gate, or this castle. I don't even want him in the kingdom. *My* kingdom. And I refuse to let him bring such a disgrace to the guards of Blackwood any longer.

"Is there a problem here?" I lean farther to the side so I can see past Weston, and cross my arms over my chest. Guthrie's eyes slide to me, and I catch the barely there widening and the flash of recognition, before his jaw clenches and his gaze hardens. It's gone a moment later, as a sneer plays at his lips, his attention turning back to Weston. He looks him up and down and takes a step closer, shifting his hand to the hilt of his sword.

"You know, it's a crime to impersonate a member of the guard. The same goes for impersonating the royal family. Both of you have committed crimes against the crown and are to be arrested immediately." He nods over his shoulder at the guards behind him, who don't say another word before they advance.

Weston's hands fist at his sides, his knuckles white and his arms tense as if he's ready for a fight. But he doesn't move. Each guard takes hold of one of his arms, yanking them roughly behind his back and holding him in place, and I feel the simmering rage explode inside of me.

"Bullshit!" I yell, stepping up beside where the guard holds Weston back. "You know exactly who I am!" I point to my feet, grinding out the next words. "The last time I saw you, you were on your knees reciting your oath after insulting me before you were sent away for your piss-poor personality. If you want to threaten the princess of Blackwood, then you're the fucking idiot. As soon as Brynne—"

"Oho, she's got a mouth on her," he interrupts with a cruel laugh. He saunters forward, stopping right in front of Weston, but his eyes are fixed on me as he raises a hand, pointing in my face. "Keep talking like that and I'll give you something to do with that mou—"

There's a thud followed by a groan of pain as Weston's head slams into Guthrie's, knocking him to the ground as he clutches his face. Blood oozes from between his fingers, and in a flash Weston is free, and both guards that held him in place a moment ago now lie on the ground. A sing of metal cuts through the air as the point of Weston's sword settles in the dip of Guthrie's throat.

Fear coats the man's face as he looks into Weston's eyes.

"If you dare to finish that sentence and insult the princess, I will personally cut out your tongue before having you extracted from the guard and shipped off to the labor yards for treason."

Guthrie's eyes narrow, but his throat bobs, giving away his displeasure at Weston taking the upper hand. He scrambles backward just as motion catches my eye.

A shriek pierces my ears, and I realize it came from my throat as one guard swings the hilt of his dagger at the back of Weston's head. He lets out a grunt and stumbles forward, doing everything he can to keep from falling to his knees.

I start toward him, but he holds up a hand, halting me, as the guards use the opportunity to secure him again, the rest of them standing in the entrance jumping to aid the two in holding him back as he thrashes against them.

Guthrie stands, swiping his thumb at the blood dripping down his face and smearing it crudely over his cheek. "Bring him to the fucking dungeon. Both of them."

The guard who swayed warily on his feet steps away from the struggle of the others and moves toward me, but his steps falter the moment Weston steps closer, dragging the guards with him.

"Don't you fucking touch her," he snaps. The guard halts and looks between Weston and Guthrie, but Weston doesn't give anyone a chance to speak. "The moment any of you lays a finger on her is the moment you put your lives in your hands."

The young guard that moved toward me looks between us before stepping next to me, leaving his hands by his sides.

"Dungeon! Now!" Guthrie screams, his face reddening as he gestures to the castle.

"Walk, lady," he says sternly, but he can't hide the slight tremor in his voice. I'm sure after witnessing how easily Weston got the upper hand over all the other guards, he is taking the threat seriously.

The gate slams behind us as they lead us through the grounds, following the winding path toward the back of the castle, completely ignoring the staff entrance to the kitchens that I came and went through before. I keep quiet, and after his last outburst, so does Weston, but when we stop at a wooden door, I can see the thoughts churning behind his distant gaze.

The guard at my side pulls a set of keys off his belt and unlocks a large bolt, followed by a series of others that must keep the dungeon's secured from the outside. He huffs loudly as he pulls the thick wooden slab open and stands to the side. The guards surrounding Weston push him through the entrance first, and there's a twinge of pain in my chest as I watch them disappear into the dark corridor ahead.

We can't be separated. Not here. Not when we were so close.

I still can't wrap my head around what is happening, why Guthrie is back and why he is pretending like he does not know who I am. Dread fills the pit in my stomach as I wonder what is going on inside these walls, and what Weston and I are actually walking into.

My guard stands next to the opening and gestures for me to go through, but I hesitate for a moment as a lesson from Edmond pops into my mind.

Edmond. Where is Edmond?

He would get us out of this mess, but they won't go get him, no matter how much I ask. They will, however, need to get the highest-ranking guard, especially if they are locking prisoners away. I need to connect with him, make him see me on an even playing field, and once he does, convince him to bring me to her.

"What's your name, sir?" My voice is soft as I try a different tactic than the authoritative one Weston already had. Even after my brief outburst toward Guthrie, hopefully he can see that I respect our guards enough to talk to me.

He hesitates for a moment before deciding that it is impolite not to answer.

"Park, my lady," he mutters.

"Nice to meet you, Park. I'm Lennox." I step through the doorway, doing as he asked, as yet another way to show I'm not trying to fight.

His mouth forms a line as he turns away, pulling the door closed behind us, and quickly turning the key to bolt the locks. The light in the corridor is snuffed out the moment he shuts the door, leaving me barely able to see, if it were not for the dim lanterns that line the hall. I peer down as far as I can, but I can see no doorways or splits in the corridor through the darkness.

"You really don't recognize me?"

He extends his arm, and I take the hint to walk, but I keep my pace slow. After a few moments with only the sound of our footsteps on the stone floor, he finally answers.

"I'm just following orders, lady."

Following orders? Why would there be orders to detain me in *my* castle? Who the fuck is giving these orders, because Brynne never would. My skin prickles with goosebumps as I continue walking, but try to keep my voice even so he doesn't hear my nervous impatience.

"Who gave the orders, Park? Why would you lock me in my own dungeon?"

His face stays stoic, but there's something in his eyes that he's trying to fight. It's obvious he takes his duty seriously. "The commander doesn't believe you're who you say, so I have to listen. Besides, the princess hasn't been seen for years. Why would anyone believe you?"

"Because *you* know I'm telling the truth," I plead with him. "I need you to bring me to Brynne. Now."

"The Second Guard isn't available to speak to prisoners," he mumbles.

Frustration threatens to break through my calm facade. "She will speak to me. Bring me to her."

He shakes his head. "I can't do that, lady."

My chest rises and falls in a deep inhale. This isn't working. No matter how much practice I have at convincing people I am on their side, like I did in the beginning with the Castaways, clearly the guards' devotion to duty outweighs all personal feelings. It's a noble quality to have in those protecting your kingdom, unless they're throwing you in the dungeon.

Glancing down the dark corridor again, I consider making a run for it, but I refuse to leave Weston alone. With how Guthrie looked at him and the obvious indication that Weston could overpower even the entire group of guards, I don't want to risk them hurting him more than they already have. I also hate to admit to him and to myself that I've never seen this part of the castle. I don't have any idea where I am going, because I had no reason to ever be down here to begin with. Why hadn't I ever had Edmond bring me here in all the years of our lessons? Clearly it was a mistake, although I never thought I would need to know.

"Turn right, and step down," Park says, and I follow obediently, descending the stone steps into further darkness.

The room that surrounds us when the floor flattens is simple, a box of stone walls with a single wooden door on the far wall. An empty guard's station sits off to the side, probably at the request of those guarding Weston, to ensure they had all the help they could get. Park strides past me, opening the door and ushering me through, his hand clamping around my upper arm as he leads me deeper into the dungeon.

Cells with iron bars line the walls, each small room separated by a thick stone wall. No prisoners are locked inside any as we pass deeper into the dark, cold space. Park tugs me down the hall, his shoulders pulling back the closer we get to the mass of bodies illuminated by a single torch just ahead. I steel myself against the worry of what I will walk up to, as I take in the guards leering into the cage.

Dread fills me when I realize this will be the first time I've been separated from Weston since he saved me from Dane. With all the uncertainty surrounding our return home, I am trying not to let it affect me. I need to keep my mind clear, to think through everything the way I've been taught, and to get out of this as soon as I can.

I try to hide my shock when Park walks me past Weston's cell, in front of the group of guards, and right to the open iron door. A quick glance at Weston inside tells me he isn't harmed, but the look of fury on his face as his eyes trail down to where Park has his hand wrapped around my arm tells me it will not bode well for this young guard.

I step inside, and the door clangs closed behind me. Before Park can even step away, Weston is stalking to the bars, until he towers over the man. The look on Park's face would make anyone think there wasn't iron separating them, and his throat bobs with a gulp.

"I thought I said hands off." Weston's voice is a deathly growl, and Park startles away from the bars, causing the group of guards behind him to snicker.

"Eh, ignore him," one says. "He can't do anything to you now." The guard raises his folded arms, laden with Weston's belt and weapons, his sword laid across the top, and my breath catches when I see what else they took.

The pouch.

It sits on top of the pile, the value completely lost on the men before us.

I don't acknowledge it. I don't want to draw attention to it. When all of this is settled, we will get it back, because it can't fall into the hands of people who don't know what it is, or worse, would exploit it.

"Blackwood law states that prisoners can have an audience with the First Guard," Weston barks, finally pulling his glare away from Park and directing it to the group. "Since that is me, I demand to see the king."

"Right," a man scoffs. "We'll just bring him right down to talk to you."

"I've never even met the king," another says. "He wouldn't listen to me anyway, even if I had."

"Nice try, imposter," the man with Weston's things snaps. "Maybe next time, come up with a better plan than just trying to waltz into the castle."

I step toward the bars, wrapping my hands around them and softening my voice once again.

"Park, please. Please, just go get Brynne. Tell her Lennox needs her."

The other guards laugh, and Park's face stays unmoving, except for his eyes that look between us.

"Still going to stick with the 'I'm the princess' story?" the first man chortles.

"Maybe a night on the cold stone will get them rethinking whatever plan they thought they would get away with." They all laugh again, the noise of their chatter quieting as they walk back in the way we came. The slam of the wooden door leaves the dungeon in silence, and my shoulders sag with a heavy breath.

Weston is on me in the next second, turning me to him as his hands find my face.

"Are you alright?" His eyes scan mine, and I nod.

"What the fuck is going on?" I say, my voice hushed despite knowing we're alone again.

"I don't know, but those guards know exactly who you are. I saw it."

"I saw it too. Park said something odd when he brought me inside. He said he was just following orders."

Anger twists Weston's face. "You knew his name, and he didn't speak up that he knew you?"

I shake my head. "No, I asked him what it was. It was something Edmond always told me to do. When you are trying to influence someone, or get something you want, try to make it feel personal. If he feels like he can relate to me, or knows me, he's more apt to listen."

"But he didn't."

"No. Not yet, at least. But maybe he will bring Brynne here, even though he wouldn't bring me to her."

He looks down the dark corridor, toward the entrance of the dungeon. "Maybe. But who is giving these orders? It can't be the piece of shit at the gate. I swear to you, the second we get out of here, he's fucking gone."

"Weston," I start, then pause, trying to find the right question as my mind floods with every unexpected thing that happened in such a short amount of time. He waits patiently, and I try not to look too confused. "It was obvious you could overpower them. You're clearly better than any of them. Stronger. More trained. Why didn't you?"

He lets out a sigh and scrubs his face, looking away from me like he's embarrassed to meet my eyes.

"Because I made a mistake," he murmurs, and I can see the storm of guilt and disappointment building behind his eyes. "It's my sworn duty to protect you, but we both know that it's more than that. You know I will do anything to keep you from being harmed. My actions back there gave up that I would fight for you, and that asshole Guthrie could see that it was in more ways than just as your guard. In trying to protect you I put you at more risk. I let him know he could use you against me, and even though I'd fucking kill him if he tried, I shouldn't have reacted in a way that might cause you more harm. I knew Park wouldn't try after I gave him a warning. He's too inexperienced, yet his clear want for acceptance influenced him."

"He didn't touch me. Not until leading me in here, and even then he only held my arm."

"Good," he growls, but I can still see the turmoil in his expression and the tension in his jaw.

Reaching up, I grab hold of his chin, tilting it back toward me so he can't avoid my gaze any longer. "I know your oath is important to you, but I need you to figure out how to be the First Guard without letting what's between us get in the way. I know you can handle yourself, but I don't want to see a hoard of guards take you down again. I can't watch anyone hurt you either."

The muscle in his jaw clenches and releases again. "You know what I told you when we went to get Roley. Your safety is what is important."

"Stop with that bullshit, Weston. You know I won't care about mine if yours is at risk. This goes both ways."

He settles his hands on his head, his fingers wringing at his hair. "I'm sorry. I'll figure it out. It's my first day back too."

I soften at his words. "I know. We knew it was going to be different from Dawnlin, and there's an entirely new set of stakes now. I don't know how to act around everyone else yet, and we didn't even get time to figure it out before all of this was thrust at us. We need to get through this first."

A chill courses through my body, not from anything that happened, but from the actual wet cold seeping through the stone walls. Weston's arms drop to his sides, and he extends a hand out to me.

"We might as well try to get some rest. I doubt they'll be coming back in here at any point tonight."

I slide my fingers between his and he leads me to the back wall, far from the reach of the bars. He pulls off his cloak and slides his back down, settling onto the hard floor before tugging on my hand, urging me to follow. I cuddle into his side, soaking up his warmth. His deft fingers find the clasps on the front of my cloak, and he unbuttons them quickly, shifting the fabric so it lays over us both, before draping his heavy cloak on top.

I nuzzle into his chest, and the feeling of instant security washes over me as I breathe him in. I sigh, and his arm slides around me, weaving beneath my cloak until his hand settles on my low back.

His chest grumbles as he murmurs, "He didn't take this?"

His fingers flutter over my dagger, still secured in the waistband of my pants. When it was given to me, almost two years ago at my ceremony, I knew its purpose. Every king or queen of Blackwood was presented one to protect them, to give them the ability to defend themselves if the need arose. As isolated as I was, I never considered a time where I would ever need it, until Dawnlin. It became my security, my reminder of home, my knowledge that I could defend myself. I never thought I would need it back in the confines of my castle, but now, as I'm being held captive by the very guards who swore to protect me, I am grateful that I have it, and even more grateful that they didn't know about it.

I shake my head into his chest. "No. No one even asked me if I had any weapons."

"Good," he grumbles. "Fucking imbeciles. Rem should be appalled about the aptitude of these guards, but it's good for us. Use it if you have to."

His cheek settles on the top of my head and his other hand finds my face, the pad of his thumb brushing softly against my skin, and the heat of his palm warding off the bite of the cold.

"Go to sleep. Hopefully we'll figure out the rest of this chaos first thing in the morning."

CHAPTER TWENTY-SIX

"Why didn't anyone find me the second you brought her down here?"

The distant sound of Brynne's voice echoing off the dungeon walls nudges me awake. I bolt upright, the cloaks pooling at my hips, and the instant chill from the air brings on a full-body quiver.

"Weston, wake up!" I hiss. Pressing my hand into his chest, I jostle him slightly, my eyes straining to see through the dim light down the corridor. When he doesn't respond, I glance back, and icy fear slides up my spine as I take him in.

Shoulders hunched, body turned toward me, serene and unmoving. My eyes fall to his body, lying completely uncovered by the cloaks that had been draped over me only a moment ago.

"Weston?" Worry coats my voice as I spin until I'm on my knees in front of him. I'm too afraid to check for the rise and fall of his chest. "Weston?" I say more urgently now, my hands finding his face. Bile rises in my throat at the chill that meets my fingertips.

No.

"Weston!" I grab his shoulders and shake him again, more forcefully this time as tears well in my eyes. Panic claws at my chest, and my stomach threatens to empty, despite not remembering the last time I ate anything.

No. This wasn't supposed to happen. This can't *be happening.*

We were supposed to confront my father, to figure out how to be together despite the futures already destined for us. He can't leave me now.

"Wake up, please," I plead, my hands running up the column of his neck, feeling for the beat of his heart. All the air leaves my chest when his body twitches, his head slowly turning to the side as his eyes flutter open.

"Gods, you're alright!" I fall into him, pressing my forehead to his and taking his face in my hands.

"I'm fine," he grumbles as he reaches up to rub at his eyes.

I lean back slightly, scanning his face, trying to convince myself that he's alive, that he didn't just freeze to death in the depths of my castle.

"You're freezing." I pull his hand to my face and blow my warm breath on his fingertips before rubbing my hands over them, trying to force warmth back into his body. "Why weren't you under the cloak?" I reach down, grabbing it from where it lies on the ground behind me.

"You were cold," he mumbles, and I fight the urge to scowl at him. Gripping his shoulders, I lean him forward and wrap his cloak around his shoulders, clasping it tightly across his chest.

"Get this door open now!" Brynne yells, and my head snaps toward the sound of her voice.

"Is that her?"

"Yes, thank the gods. You need to get up and move." I grasp his hands, his fingers still like ice despite my effort, and he lets me help him to his feet. His movements are rough as he stretches his arms slowly.

Hopping up and down, he tries to warm his muscles again as the clang of a full ring of keys sounds from down the hall.

"Hurry up, idiots!" Brynne yells, and it's followed by the click of a lock and the loud creak of hinges from the thick wooden door.

I run to the bars, my hands wrapping tightly around the freezing metal, as I press my face into the open space between them, trying to get a glimpse of her. Multiple sets of footsteps pound on the stone floor, and I hope whoever she brought with her is ready to deal with the guards who threw us in here.

"Brynne!" Relief floods my body as the footsteps get louder. "I tried to tell them they were making a mistake, but no one would listen to me."

She will sort all of this out, and part of me doesn't feel sorry for those who are about to incur her wrath.

She steps into the dim glow of the lantern, and the moment my eyes fall on her, the relief I felt falls away into a sinking pit of dread. Guthrie stands behind her, sneering over her shoulder, but that isn't what makes my throat dry.

Brynne looks the same as the day I left, the subtle changes of the time that has passed hidden away behind the way her hair is pulled back, out of the way of her armor. It's the cold look on her face and her eyes zeroed in on me that makes her unrecognizable as the Brynne who told me she was proud of me almost two years ago. Confusion rocks me, and I gape at her until she stops in front of the cell.

"Brynne?" I barely get the word out before powerful arms cinch tightly around my waist and yank me away from the bars. Weston drags me away from the front of the cell and pins me against his body.

"Weston, wha—"

"Her name isn't Brynne," he grumbles in my ear. Ice coats my skin as I look up at her in horror, the answering smirk all the confirmation I need.

"And who might you be?" she says, her voice different than I've ever heard it before. Cold. Malicious. Seething.

"He's calling himself the First Guard," Guthrie says behind her. "Goes by Weston."

"Ah, so *you're* Weston."

My head snaps between the two of them as I try to piece everything together. Weston left Blackwood before Brynne had ever stepped foot into the castle. There's no way he could know her. And the way she just said his name sounded like she knew exactly who she was meeting.

That could only mean one thing…

My stomach falls as the pieces fit together, the stories and details all working into one big picture, where I somehow became the center.

"Weston, how do you know her?" I whisper. My hands clench around his forearms as they still crush me to him, and I wait with bated breath for the answer I know is coming.

"This is who has been guarding you the entire time?" he growls, his volume rising as he shifts me to his side and steps in front of me, protecting me with his body despite his movements still being stilted from the cold.

"This is Brynne, the Second Guard. *My* guard."

I catch his head shaking out of the corner of my eye as he stares her down through the bars. "Her name isn't Brynne, princess. It's Briony."

I choke on the breath in my throat. My jaw falls open as I stare past Weston at Brynne. *Briony*.

"How do you know?" I say. My voice is barely a whisper as she continues to smirk at me, armor clinking as she crosses her arms over her chest.

"She was…there," he says, his voice is strained, as if he is trying to say something about Dawnlin, but couldn't. "We saw her, and then one day, a long time ago, she was gone. We didn't know if something had happened to her or if she had decided to go home, but we never saw her again."

"Is that true?" I gasp at her, but all she does is smile.

"You know," she says with a tilt of her head, "when time is on your side, you can do whatever you want. There's nothing stopping you. Basking in the sunlight, making friends, getting fantastic at handling a sword."

The memory of Brynne showing up at the castle comes racing back to me. A young woman walking through the gates, demanding to compete in the tournament where the winner is named the Second Guard to the princess. The fury she caused in the other guards as she bested them, one after the other, despite them seemingly having years of training compared to her. She appeared out of nowhere, claimed no kingdom, and immediately took to me, even in my young age.

"I don't understand," I say, shaking my head, but Weston doesn't let me flounder.

"She's with him, Lennox," he murmurs, and the world I've known for years shatters around me.

There's only one him Weston is referring to, and there's only one way Brynne would have been able to leave Dawnlin.

Dane.

"This whole time?" The shock turns to rage as once again I feel like everything I've ever known has been a lie, but this time not one kept from me to protect me. "From the moment I saw you, you were working with Dane? For what, Brynne? Tell me why!" My voice rises with each word until I'm yelling, my despair connected directly to the increasing tension in Weston's shoulders.

"Why doesn't concern you," she snaps.

"Doesn't concern me? You don't think I deserve the truth? To know why you were lying to my face for most of my life? Why you were faking it all? What is the reason?"

"Because without me, there would be no plan, and you were too young and naïve to realize it. I started it all. Someone had to be here to watch you, to make sure you were where you needed to be. It took time, but there wasn't a single person in this castle who didn't trust me, who didn't listen to everything I said. It was too easy to adjust your training schedule so you couldn't protect yourself as well as you should have. Do you really think I just forgot to teach you how to use a dagger? That I let you focus on the bow instead of the sword? It was all so easy, and you were just so needy.

"And then when I overheard the old man talking to you about Dawnlin, I knew it was time. You thought you were so sly, sneaking out of the castle like I didn't notice. You got out because I *let* you get out. All because I knew who was there to meet you all along."

Her words land like a blow to the gut, and I can do nothing but stare. Brynne planned this, or at least my actions made me fall right into the palm of her hand. Memories come flooding back to me. The way the halls were clear. The way the kitchen staff didn't bat an eye. The way the guards never questioned who I was. The way she just let me say I was going to find Dawnlin, and didn't try harder to stop me.

She wanted all of this to happen.

"Half my work was done for me when the idiot king decided to isolate you. You were starving for attention. It was so easy to make you think somebody could be attracted to you, could love you—"

Brynne staggers back when Weston springs toward the bars. His arm shoots out of the cell and swipes at her, but she is just out of reach. Once she realizes she's safe from his attack, she regains her composure quickly.

"Careful, Weston," she says silkily, before the sound of her slapping the top of his wrist echoes through the dungeon. "That's a good way to lose a hand."

Weston takes advantage of her careless mistake to get close to him, and grabs hold of her wrist, yanking her firmly into the bars. A strangled cry erupts as her face slams into the iron, and he reaches for her belt and the weapons stored there. The other guards are there in an instant, grabbing her by the arms and dragging her out of his reach as she lets out a string of curses.

"Open the fucking cell!" she screams, but I barely register that the guards don't jump into action. I'm too busy still reeling over one part of her confession, the part that was the last piece of the puzzle, that final piece of information that makes sense of the worry that started coiling within me from the moment I saw the guards at the gate.

A plan. There's something bigger happening.

The murmur of a guard in the corridor pulls me from my reverie. "He threatened us if we touched her."

Brynne's face twists with rage and disgust. "And none of you can take an unarmed man? There's one of him and ten of you!"

"Do you want to try?" Weston growls, his shoulders tensing and emphasizing his commanding height.

Brynne looks from him to the group of guards, and there's a flash of hesitation in her eyes before she yells, "Open it! Now!" Park scrambles forward, pulling the ring of keys off his belt, but Brynne rolls her eyes in frustration. "Ugh, give me the fucking keys!" She snatches them out of his hand, and fumbles through them, looking for the one that must fit into the lock of the cells.

"Weston," I plead, using the distraction to sink my fists into his clothes and pull him to face me. "He's here. Dane's here."

It's the only explanation. The first step in their plan was to infiltrate the castle to get close to me; the second was for me to get the healing waters. Dane always planned to return for my mother. Even after all this time, he couldn't let her go.

Back on Dawnlin, we wondered where Dane could have gone, where he had disappeared to, and why.

But now, it all clicks, the pieces all fitting together for this plan that has been in place for most of my life.

He came here. For her. And that is why we are locked in the dungeon.

The understanding lights in Weston's eyes, followed by the hardening of his jaw. The iron lock clangs behind me, and Weston's hands grip my shoulders, spinning us so he's between me and the entrance.

"Remember what I told you." His voice is firm, but his face is pleading, and I blink up at him, my head shaking in disbelief as everything unfolds around us. How could this be happening? Where is my father, Edmond, Tila? How could Brynne do this to me?

"Weston," I breathe, my breaths starting to rise and fall more rapidly, and his hands wrap around my face.

"Who's fucking idea was it to put them together? Get him in chains now!" Brynne barks.

"Lennox, tell me you remember." His voice booms around me as I stare into his eyes, trying to block out the flashes of horrifying possibilities of what the guards might do to him if we're separated. My mouth falls open, but no words come out as the guards spill into the cell, led by Guthrie, who stands to the side, barking orders.

We're outnumbered. He's unarmed. No one knows we're here. My dagger will do nothing against all of them.

My limbs won't move, my body frozen in time as Weston is pulled away from me, his arms wrenched behind his back. Everyone is shouting, their lips moving rapidly, but I hear none of it, just a distant hum as Weston thrashes against their hold, throwing his arms wildly as he strikes at the guards.

A scream pierces my ears when one of them wraps an arm around his throat, squeezing tightly, and the sound comes back in an instant. Weston reaches up to the guard's arm, grabbing it with both hands and wrenching it away from his windpipe, but another guard acts too quickly.

Metal clangs as manacles snap around his wrists, bound together by a single loop, preventing him from using his arms. His eyes stay locked on me, his jaw clenched tightly, as the guard finally releases his hold, and Weston sucks in a deep breath. The group drags him backward, and someone reaches out to rip off his cloak before they push him stumbling through the cell door and into the dungeon corridor.

"Her turn," Brynne says, nodding at me, and another smaller set of guards files through the doorway. My first instinct is to grab my dagger. I can hear Weston's voice in my mind, telling me exactly that.

Use it if you have to.

But if I reach for it, if I show them I have it, I have this one chance. There are too many of them, and only one blade. It's better that they don't know about it.

The guards grip my arms roughly, and yank them out in front of me, shackling them in the same way they did Weston.

"Lennox!" he yells, the warning in his voice clear as the guards next to me stiffen, and I see Park in front of me, clearly nervous despite Weston's confinement.

"I'm fine," I call back, even though I feel anything but fine.

I need to snap out of this. I need to find my strength, my training that has been drilled into me, even if my confidence in it wavered the moment Brynne admitted to ensuring I wasn't as skilled as I should be. Weston has more than made up for it in the short time I've known him, but after watching him be choked, subdued, and shackled in front of me, I don't feel like the fierce warrior the crew thought I was just last night.

I need to find her.

They pull me through the door, and I stumble and trip on the stones trying to keep up with them. The guards at my sides yank me upright and continue to shove me along between them as we walk through the dim dungeon toward Brynne. There are sounds of a scuffle ahead, grunts and scraping of shoes against the stone. I wrench myself to the side, trying to see past her, only to find Weston struggling against the guards as the group closes in tighter on him.

"Stop her right there." Brynne steps toward me, closing the distance and towering over me like she always has. Never before have I felt uncomfortable when she did it, but now, after all of her revelations, after the sneer on her face and the hatred in her voice, I don't want her this close to me.

Their hands fall away from my arms as Brynne narrows her eyes. "Where is it?" she snaps.

My jaw works as I glare at her. "Where is what?" There is only one thing she can be talking about, but I won't give it up freely. I won't let her know I still have it. The guards took Weston's weapons, so there's a chance she will think I'm unarmed too.

"Don't play stupid with me. You aren't in charge here anymore. Tell me where the fuck it is."

I hold her glare. "I don't know what you're talking about."

My head snaps to the side as her palm strikes my cheek. The sting of the slap bites into my skin, but the shock and pain was exactly what I needed.

This woman lied to me. She manipulated me, just as Dane did. She was one of the few I trusted, who I thought cared about me, more than just in her role as my guard.

But I was wrong.

And now she is taking over my castle, my kingdom. She's hurting the man I love, and helping the one I hate, the one who stole my mother and my life from me. I will not let her get away with this. I will fight back, because I know that no matter her skills and training, or her belief that she ruined me, I'm smarter than her, and now, I have more to lose.

Dawnlin gave me that.

"Don't fucking touch her!" Weston thunders, his yell followed by more commotion behind Brynne. Bodies crash together, followed by the sounds of fabric ripping and blows landing. It only adds to my anger, knowing they are hurting him all at her command.

"Get him under control!" Brynne screams. She looks over her shoulder at the group of guards, and I shift just enough to see past her, the sight making bile burn the back of my throat.

Blood drips from a gash on Weston's forehead, the skin on his face red and swollen from the blows of the guards. I take in the ripped seams of his uniform, the fabric hanging open with the rest disheveled, and his hands still bound before him as he shoves the men that try to hold him. I swallow down my emotions when my eyes rise again and land on his, unflinching and only focused on me, as if the beating he's been taking hasn't bothered him at all.

I shake my head subtly, and he stills. His jaw remains clenched, his muscles still bulging against the restraint of the guards and the cold iron manacles, but he stops fighting. This isn't the place to fight. We can't get away from them bound and outnumbered as we are, not until the right time, and the more of a beating he takes, the harder it will be for him to fight when he needs to.

"Fucking finally," Brynne groans before spinning back toward me, her face pinching in frustration. "Trust me, Lennox, you don't want to do this the hard way." Without warning, she reaches out, her movements rough as she searches my body for weapons. While Sig treated me, a complete stranger, with respect and dignity as she searched me all that time ago, Brynne shows absolutely no familiarity as she wrenches my body around, tugging at my clothes and searching for my dagger.

My eyes flutter closed the moment she finds it, and regret surges through me. I should have hidden it in my boot. I should have given it to Weston, although he probably wouldn't have taken it. I should have done anything to keep her from finding it, but instead, I was too relieved to see the guard I thought would help us, not the one who would further harm us.

Opening my eyes once again, I find fury lacing her features. She rips my dagger from the back of my waistband, holding it in front of me, and the gold and jewels glitter in the dim light.

"Which one of you idiots didn't search them? *Both* of them?" Brynne yells. The guards fall silent, and the ones beside me awkwardly shift their weight on their feet.

"You thought you could hide this from me?" Brynne says, her eyebrow rising over the steely glare. She points the tip of the blade at me, and I set my jaw, glaring back at her, trying not to give away the plan forming in my mind. "Did you really think I wouldn't remember you have it? I was the one who told you to keep it, to bring it with you. I guess you really did listen to anything I said. Always the little girl that can't think for herself, aren't you?"

If I do nothing, I might lose our only opportunity to keep a weapon. I once questioned if I could kill someone in cold blood, back when I thought Weston was the one threatening my life. But now I know I will fight for him, kill for him if I have to, because I know he would do the same for me.

Without taking my eyes off her, I shove my bound hands forward and grab her wrist, wrenching it down and stealing the dagger from her grasp. The manacles make it difficult, but the element of surprise is on my side. I flip the blade in my hand, turning it back on her, and step forward to strike at the break in her armor that I know is there from years of training.

All before my legs are swept out from under me, and my back slams into the ground, forcing every breath from my chest.

The commotion down the hall is barely a hum, overpowered by the wheezing from my throat as I suck air into my burning chest. Spots mar my vision, peppering Brynne's face as she stands over me, a smug look spreading over her face.

She reaches down and plucks the dagger from my tense grip before sheathing it at her side.

"Well that was a neat new trick," she says, her voice dripping with disdain. "I guess I wasn't the only one who learned some things during the time away." She glances back to Weston, before turning back to me, her lips pulling into a snide grin. "Did your little lover teach you that move? Too bad it still isn't enough. You're outnumbered here, princess." She spits the last word at me, then gestures to the guards at my sides. "Get her up. Let's move."

Park and another man I don't know hook their arms under mine and haul me to my feet. Guthrie hovers near the group, a maniacal grin on his face as he watches the guards shove their shoulders into Weston, the points of their swords trained on him as they force him forward, back toward the door to the rest of the castle.

I work to keep up with them, my breath still not fully recovered, but my anger and worry for Weston keeps me on my feet. Brynne charges forward before us, storming through the dungeon and snapping more orders at the guards controlling Weston.

A hint of fear settles in my stomach, as I watch Weston walk ahead of me, but it slowly dissipates as I realize we are following the same path. They aren't separating us. Wherever we are headed, we are going together.

We climb the steps, slinking farther into the castle and winding through dim corridors. An enormous set of stone stairs lies ahead, and a guard opens a thick wooden door at the top, letting light pours into the space.

Weston disappears through the doorway, along with the horde of guards around him, and the rest of us trail closely behind. I recognize where we are the moment I step into the main hall, and scan the area quickly, hoping someone, anyone, will walk through the halls and can get help.

But it's empty.

"Move!" Brynne snaps, and strides down the hall. The guards shove Weston forward until we're standing side by side, our bound hands in front of us. We fall into step behind her, and the footfalls from the group of guards echo in our wake.

"Don't do anything stupid," I grumble to Weston, and he only grunts in response. After admitting to me last night that he made a mistake showing his devotion to me, it's clear he didn't learn from it, or make any changes, and we can't make anything worse. We need to figure out how to get the upper hand.

"What do you expect me to do, nothing?" he growls.

"Stop talking!" Guthrie yells, and shoves Weston's back from behind.

The silence is thick, marred only by our footsteps echoing off the cold stone walls as we walk deeper into the castle. Movement catches my eye, and I glance at the wall to find two of the older guards, ones I don't know well, but I've seen around for years. Ones that would surely recognize me.

Their eyes widen as their gazes jump from me to Weston and back again, their lips forming a line as they take in the manacles at our wrists and the guards following us closely. Their expressions betray nothing of what is going on in their minds, not an ounce of recognition of me, or him, or the scene unfolding before them. The already deep pit in my stomach sinks even further.

Was no one truly ever sincere when they swore their oaths? Was Weston the only one who cared so deeply about his duty? How could we have never noticed? Everyone in the castle seemed happy, taken care of. There were never complaints, fair wages, offered housing and accommodations. The staff and guards chose to be here. No one was ever forced, and despite my father treating me poorly and unfairly, he never seemed to do the same with his people.

Why would they all turn on us?

"At least the sky is clear today," Weston says suddenly, breaking me from my worries as his voice carries through the silent hallway.

I glance up at him, confused, when one guard behind us scoffs.

"How hard did you hit him?" he says with a laugh. "Sounds like you knocked some sense out of him, instead of into him." There's a chorus of snickers, and concern pushes my anger out of the way.

"Are you all right?" I whisper, trying to keep everything I'm feeling out of my voice. I know if he hears it, he will do even more to keep all the wrath of Brynne and the guards away from me, and directed at him. I can't let that happen. I can't watch them harm him, just for me.

My head swivels toward the wall of windows to our right, the overcast grey skies that blanket the kingdom the same as they are every day, then back to his stoic face. He doesn't answer, only keeps his eyes fixed straight ahead, as trails of blood continue to flow down his face, drawing my attention to his clenched jaw.

Weston would never ignore me. What is going on?

Brynne leads us around a corner, and the back of my neck prickles. I know exactly where we are going, but I have no idea what is in store for us.

Just ahead are the thick, black, wooden doors I last stormed out of after my ceremony, and I haven't been behind them since. For a time, I didn't think I ever would again. It's clear now, that worry did not come true.

Because now, we're headed straight for the throne room.

CHAPTER TWENTY-SEVEN

The last time I walked into this throne room, I was alone, as the future queen of Blackwood, with no hope for the life that was already planned and decided for me.

Now, I'm a prisoner, standing beside the man I love, with no idea of what is going to meet us on the other side of that door.

The carved black wood looms over us, parting down the middle as Brynne flattens her hands on the surface and pushes them open. One guard shoves me from behind, and I catch myself before I stumble over the threshold and into the empty room. Brynne strides down the aisle, her head held high, as Weston and I make our way across the black carpet behind her.

My focus stays locked on her back as I try to figure out not only what her plan is but also scramble to come up with one of my own. With both of our hands bound, and my one and only means of protection already in her possession, I'm failing miserably. There's no lesson I can recall that prepared me for this.

Looking back, it seems so similar to how I was taken by the Castaways, hands bound and thrown in a cell, but back then, I was locked up in a cage of my own making. They never intended to harm me. Their only goal was to get me to be comfortable enough that I would eventually understand their side.

Dane has already proven he will harm me, and Weston never looked at me with the malice that Brynne now does. Deep in my gut, I don't feel that anything I tried before will help me now, and beneath my anger there's a new sinking sense of dread forming that we may not escape this.

"Halt at the foot of the steps," Brynne commands over her shoulder, just before she steps to the side, in the same place she stood for my ceremony so long ago.

I suck in a ragged breath when the dais comes into view, and I realize I was wrong.

The room isn't empty.

Dane sits on my father's throne, *my* throne, his body slouched, his ankle crossed over his knee with a bored look on his face as his chin rests in his propped up hand.

"Well, well, well." One corner of his lips turns up in a sly smirk as we stop before him, and his eyes flicker to the guards before falling back to us. "When they said a man and a woman arrived claiming to be the princess and the First Guard, I didn't believe them. They had to be mistaken. The princess and the First Guard had no way of being here. I made sure of it. That is, until they brought me this."

He tosses something into the air and catches it, and I blink slowly as I realize what he now holds in his hands.

The dust.

So many emotions, so much time, so much effort went into finding that dust, and to keeping the healing waters away from Dane, but now, he has them again. The Guardian of Dawnlin once again has all his power and control back.

"You know," he says, tilting his head as his eyes drag to the pouch. "This has now caused me more irritation than it has helped me. I thought it would be the answer to all my problems, but all it has done is create more. You see…" He pushes to stand and hooks the pouch to his belt, then saunters across the dais. Glaring at us with a predatory focus, his eyes fall to me, and his lips pull up in a sneer.

"It gave me the exact advantage I hoped for when it brought you to me. But, it was also supposed to ensure that you were stuck *there* forever. You weren't supposed to come back, not after you were an absolute failure and couldn't give me what I wanted."

My jaw aches, my teeth threatening to crack from the force of clenching as I narrow my my eyes at him.

"Why are you doing this?" I grind out, refusing to look away.

"Don't you listen? Did you not hear me? Or were you so focused on *him* showing up to rescue you that you forgot everything the instant he opened his mouth?" He glares at Weston before turning his haughty stare back to me. "It's all for her. Every bit of it was for her."

"You can't save her, Dane," I say with a shake of my head. "None of us can."

"I could have, but your failure destroyed that part of the plan. I prepared for something like this to happen. I hoped it wouldn't go this way, but now that it has, I know what needs to be done." His head snaps toward Brynne and barks at her, "Bring him in and bolt the doors."

Brynne nods to the group behind us, and I look over my shoulder, watching as Guthrie steps away from the rest of the men and strides back down the aisle. When he reaches the end, he bends and hauls something off the ground. I swallow the lump in my throat as he wraps thick chains around the handles, winding the metal through layer after layer.

Ice-cold fear courses through my veins.

We're trapped. Again. Dane already threatened to harm everyone I care about, back in Dawnlin when he was going to hunt the Castaways and force them to tell him where the waters are. He knows where every single one of them lives, because he brought them all to Dawnlin. He could go back after them and hunt each person down just as he promised. But the chains on the doors tell me something more is coming, something worse, at least for those of us standing in this throne room.

I steal a glance at Weston, but he's barely moved. His eyes are locked on Dane, his body coiled with tension so tight, it looks like he's ready to snap. The harsh clang of a lock snapping into place behind us makes me jolt.

Fuck. How are we going to get out of here?

Immediately I look to the door on the side of the dais, the only other entrance into the throne room, just as it opens, and a figure slides through. Brynne strides in, a smug look on her face as she takes the steps back to her position. Storm saunters in behind her, and my mind reels. What could Dane need with Storm? How is he even part of all this? He barely interacted with me, and never did with Weston during my time on Dawnlin. What could he have against my kingdom?

Storm steps to the side of the doorway and gestures to someone just beyond it, and it isn't until the person steps through, that I realize *he* isn't the man Dane is referring to.

It is my father.

I barely recognize the man who steps out of the shadows and into the throne room. His face is sallow. His cheeks are sunken. Large dark circles beneath his eyes make him look tired and sad.

Was I the cause of this? Of his decline? Has my absence affected him this much, or was it something else? Something that Dane did? Was it actually out of concern for me, or simply because his heir was missing?

I stifle a gasp as an actual possibility makes goosebumps break out across my skin.

Was it caused by the death of my mother?

Unlike ours, my father's hands are not bound, but he walks stiffly, as if he is trying to hide pain. The moment he spots us standing before the throne, he pauses, his eyes widening as his head hinges from me to

Weston. His mouth falls open, and his legs seem to weaken as he staggers to the throne beside his. My mother's throne. Grasping the wooden arm for support, he gapes at us in disbelief before turning to Dane.

"What is the meaning of this?" This isn't the commanding and indifferent voice of the father I have known my whole life. This voice is weak, and pleading, and the vast difference startles me.

Guthrie crosses the room in front of Brynne, straight toward the door, and chains it closed, trapping us all inside.

"Well you see, Remington," Dane starts, and despite my feelings toward my father, I can't help the anger that flickers at hearing his name be used, not his title, especially from this man whose unnecessary hatred has stolen so much from me. "When I arrived, you were the only one left standing in my way, but your offspring decided to grace us with her presence after I had already dealt with her. So now we're all here together."

My father straightens, rising to his full height. He glances over at me before returning to meet Dane's gaze. "Tell me what you want, and I'll give it to you."

Dane barges toward him, his youthful strength no match for my father's weakened state as he fists my father's shirt and yanks forward, pulling their faces together.

"No, you won't! You've already proven that!"

My father's face pales even further at the blow of Dane's yell. "You can't have her. She was never yours."

"No, she was never *yours*. She was *always* mine." Dane shoves him away, and my father staggers on his feet, catching himself at the last moment without falling to the floor.

"If you cared about her, then you wouldn't have hurt her."

Dane's eyes widen, and his expression turns wild. "It never would have happened if you hadn't taken her! If you hadn't tricked her into loving you and wanting this life!" He gestures to the room around us, moving to stand in front of the throne again.

"Her thoughts and actions were her own. I didn't convince her of anything more than my love and devotion."

"You barely knew her! You could never love her like I did, like I do! Even after all this time, everything I did was for her. I will spend the rest of my life with her, and none of you can stop me!" He throws his arm out, gesturing to all of us in the throne room. A sharp intake of breath comes from Weston's other side, but I refuse to look. I can't take my eyes off Dane and my father.

"Dane, she's gone. She's never woken up. You need to let her go." I've never heard my father sound this desperate, never have I thought he was even capable of it, not as the king.

"She has held on for this long, and so have I. It was meant to be. *We* were meant to be, even if it's not the way I planned."

"Please," my father says, taking a hesitant step toward Dane as if trying to ward off a reaction. "If you love her, let her daughter go."

Sharp pain lances through my chest as I suck in a quick breath.

My father is…trying to protect me?

For my entire life, he's barely looked at me, only speaking to me when absolutely necessary, but now, he's trying to ensure I get away from this monster.

He continues. "Let them both go. They did nothing to you. It is me you want."

A maniacal laugh erupts from Dane's chest. "Oh, Remington. That's where you're wrong." He throws an arm out, pointing directly at Weston. "*He* is just as much at fault. *He* enabled your time with her. *He* helped coerce her into this world. *He* helped trap her in your snare. And then *he* took away my only chance of finding a cure when he took *her*." His eyes are dangerous as he turns on me, and if I had any doubts before, I know now that the Dane I knew is nowhere to be found.

I don't know this man who stands before me, but I fear him.

"Besides," he says, as he takes a step toward me, "I can't have any loose ends showing up and trying to lay claim to the kingdom. If she'd just stayed put, we wouldn't be in this predicament. But she couldn't, could she? Now, she's done it once, and I won't let her do it again."

I can barely breathe as my father darts across the dais, his eyes widening as he looks to me, before reaching his arm out to grab Dane's shoulder.

"No, please," my father begs, but Dane whips around, turning on him in a flash.

A shrill scream pierces my ears, and the pain that lances my throat tells me that it is coming from me.

I watch in terror as their bodies collide, my chest heaving with a sob as Dane pulls away, ripping a blood-soaked knife out of my father's abdomen.

And he falls motionless to the floor.

CHAPTER TWENTY-EIGHT

My father's blood seeps across the dark stone, pooling near the tip of Dane's boots, and all I can do is stare.

"Rem!" Weston's cry sounds distant beneath the ringing in my ears. In the corner of my eye, I see him lunge forward toward the dais, only to be hauled backward by a slew of guards as he fights to reach his king.

Dane lowers himself, crouching down until he can reach my father. Roughly grasping his cheeks, he jerks my father's pained face upward and sneers down at him.

"You took her away from me. All these years, I've suffered, waiting and wanting her back. But now, I am happy knowing that in your last moments, you'll die knowing she's finally mine, and there isn't a thing you can do about it."

My father's eyes fall closed, and the breath leaves my chest.

"Hold him back!" Brynne barks, and I tear my eyes away from my dying father to find Weston. I watch in horror as he thrashes against the guards with pure anguish engulfing his face, as they land blow after blow.

But I can't move. I can't do anything.

My body is numb.

My mind is blank.

My father is gone.

The moment that I've simultaneously dreaded and waited for has finally arrived.

I am the queen.

This is my kingdom.

But only if we survive.

Dane rises and turns slowly, his attention no longer on the fallen king. I push through the horror that I feel seeping into my bones, and find my voice, no matter how shaky it is. Filled with rage, filled with fear, I don't know. But I can't stay silent any longer.

"So you mean to kill me too?" I ask, hardening my gaze at Dane through the tears pooling in my eyes.

He scoffs. "Did you finally just figure it out? Took you long enough."

"Why? If all you want is my mother, why kill him? Why kill me?"

He gestures to the ceiling, and his obsessive expression returns instantly. "It's not as if she can just walk out of here with me."

Pain erupts in my tongue as I bite down on it.

He knows where she's kept.

But does he know just because Brynne passed that information to him? Or is she actually still alive? Still holding on?

"If I'm going to have her," he continues, "I have to have it all. This castle will be mine. This kingdom will be mine, all because she will be."

"It won't be yours. No one will believe you just took over the kingdom. No one will trust you!" I spit at him, but his lips just turn up into a slow smirk, and he shakes his head.

"Oh, Lennox. Sometimes I forget how naïve you were. You still are. You think you can see beneath the surface. Plans, motivations, the person hiding in plain sight, but you don't. You only see what you want to see, you stupid, selfish, useless girl."

"Don't listen to him, Lennox," Weston yells before there's a thud, followed by Weston's deep grunt.

"You're wrong," I say, trying to keep my voice firm, trying to block out the spite and cruelty in Dane's words, as well as the sound of Weston being beaten next to me. But it's too much. The feelings all of it evokes are too much to squash, and I can't stop the quivering from the lump forming in my throat.

"I am not wrong. All that time spent in the library, you were too focused on the useless information in front of you, and distracted by your little crush on the first man that paid you any attention. You never once looked at what I was reading."

My face burns as he descends from the dais, taking each step one at a time, his vile grin widening as he speaks.

"While you were searching for an answer in the books that I had already poured through and found nothing, I was reading other things. The laws of Blackwood, for instance. Did you know that if the king dies, and there is no heir, the throne passes to the closest living relative?"

I set my jaw, glaring at him as he takes another step, but don't answer. Of course I know the law. Edmond made sure I knew every law in my kingdom. How else am I to be queen and know how to govern the people? But I never gave this one a second thought. I exist. I'm living and breathing and standing in the throne room, *my* throne room, so the crown would go to me. There would be no need to enact the law.

Unless I didn't exist any longer.

Dane has made it clear since the moment the doors to this room were chained shut that this is his ultimate goal.

Eliminate anything or anyone standing in his way.

"So you want the throne?"

He ignores my question and continues his rant. "I tried to take the easy way, trapping you there, removing one of the two people standing in my way. But you had to come back. That stupid place had to give you a way, didn't it? Well, there's no magic here, and it can't help you any longer."

"Even if you kill me," I grind out, "you still don't get what you want. You can't just take the kingdom because you want it."

He chuckles softly. "Oh, but I do. I get *everything*. Even though she doesn't wake, she's still *alive*. The last living relative."

I suck in a gasp.

This kingdom will be mine, all because she will be.

"When you die, Lyla becomes the queen, and has no one left but me. Now, in her state, she obviously cannot be acting queen, so the role would fall to me. As king."

Chaos whirls in my chest as I try to fight my way through Dane's plan. There has to be something he hasn't thought of, some logic that would stop him from getting what he wants, and subsequently would keep me alive. If I can just keep him talking, I'll have more time to figure something out.

"You aren't together. You never were. The kingdom will never accept you as king!" I yell.

His face turns feral as he all but snarls at me. "If we weren't together, then why would I have this?" Reaching into his pocket, he pulls out a fist before extending it toward me, opening his hand so I can see what sits in the middle of his palm. A golden ring, fit with a deep red stone, glitters in the flickering light, and my eyes snap to his when I realize what it is.

My mother's missing wedding ring.

The one that disappeared the night I was born, the ring that was never seen again, after Dane tried to take her away from her home.

He has had it the entire time.

"Where did you get that?" I say as fury bubbles within me, seeping into my voice.

"As far as the kingdom needs to know, Lyla gave it to me. Trapped in a forced and loveless marriage, she gave me what was supposed to be a symbol of devotion, promising herself to me. I'll tell them all about her dreams for a life she wished we had together. They'll hear about how she was a hostage to the king, burdened with a child he forced her to bear."

My chest heaves with shortened breaths as every word Dane speaks makes my blood boil. I read my mother's words. I know she and my father were overjoyed with the opportunity to have a child. He is spewing lies, and I have evidence that would refute every claim.

"I'll tell them of the vows she spoke to me," he says, his face turning down in a mock frown, "and I to her, pledging our love and devotion in sickness and in health. It's why I waited all these years, despite her condition, for Remington to finally be gone and fulfill my promise to her. With this ring, there will be no doubt in anyone's mind she is mine, and I am hers, the one she truly chose before her fateful accident. And when both of you are gone, and the title falls to her, it thus falls to me." He steps off the final stair, stopping so close that I can reach out and touch him with my manacled wrists, before bending down, and lowering his face to mine until we share a breath.

"I will spend the rest of my days at her side, never giving up. I will find a way to heal her." He points behind him at my father's lifeless body, and grits his teeth, grinding out his words. "I won't ever let her go, not like he was going to. Never!"

"No one will believe you! A piece of jewelry proves nothing!"

His responding chuckle sends chills down my spine. "Oh, I know they will, because there won't be anyone around to tell them any different. No heir, no First Guard, no king. And every single person in this castle and this kingdom will follow my orders."

"But Dane, I thought—" Brynne staggers forward, her voice shaky as she stammers. Our heads pivot toward her, and I take in the hardened guard, the commander of Blackwood who betrayed me this morning. The fallen look on her face says she is finally realizing that I am not the only one who has been betrayed.

Dane laughs a cold, soulless laugh. "Did you really think I was going to let you be queen, Briony? I just needed you. You would never sit on that throne. There is only one woman for me, and if you couldn't grasp that, you are just as naïve as she is."

Her mouth falls open as her eyes turn glassy, the realization striking her that everything she thought she would get from betraying me, from betraying my father, was all a lie. Dane gestures to Storm, who moves across the room to stand next to Brynne, his hand on a sword in his belt in an obvious threat.

"Now, where were we?" Dane says, turning back to me before his gaze slides over to Weston, who is still behind me, held down by at least six guards. My stomach falls as Dane saunters in front of him, towering over Weston as the guards force him to his knees.

"I thought I got rid of you once, but it turns out you aren't easy to kill. I won't make the same mistake this time." Dane reaches for the hilt of the knife covered in my father's blood that is secured at his side, the same one that almost killed Weston before, that he threw into the fire when I tried to pry it from his hands.

The rage I felt moments ago instantly turns into debilitating terror, knowing that this monster has no qualms about brutality and no care for a life other than his own. I don't think, I just act, doing anything I can to stop him from taking Weston away from me.

"Dane! No! Please!" I scream, my voice cracking as I throw myself toward Weston, only to be stopped by a guard's arm wrapping firmly around my waist. Sobs wrench my chest as now I'm the one thrashing against his hold, kicking and throwing my bound hands anywhere I can harm them, trying to get loose. To get to Weston. "Please let him go! I'll do whatever you want! I'll sign anything, I'll give you everything! Just please don't kill him!"

"Lennox, no!" Weston commands, his jaw tight and his brows drawn as he stares Dane down above him. Dane's hand halts, the tip of the knife hovering over Weston's chest as it heaves up and down with ragged breaths.

I don't stop, don't listen to him telling me not to try anything to save his life. I can't live anymore without him, can't watch Dane kill him like I watched him kill my father. I throw myself to the ground, trying to use my weight to break the guard's grip, but it is no use.

So instead, I beg.

"Please Dane! I'll do anything! Anything! Just let him go!"

"Lennox!" Weston yells again, in warning, before his voice lowers to a deadly grumble. "Listen to me. She will disappear. I will make sure of it. You can have it all, and you'll never hear from us again. Just let her go. Please, Dane. Lyla wouldn't want it."

"You know nothing about what Lyla wants," Dane snaps, and Weston shakes his head, unwavering.

"That's not true. Lyla wanted her."

Dane doesn't move, as if he's actually considering Weston's offer. I can barely breathe as time stills, and it feels like an eternity before Dane's head swivels between the two of us.

His face twists into a terrifying smile. "You know what? I actually like this idea better."

Weston's shoulders sink almost imperceptibly, and I know exactly what he is feeling, but he doesn't want to show it.

Relief.

He doesn't want Dane to see how his change of heart has affected us both, because it would only prove to him how much control he has over us. Weston doesn't want to give him that power.

"Where are the keys?" Dane asks, glancing between the faces of the surrounding guards. Park steps forward and produces the keyring, placing it over Dane's outstretched fingers. Turning his back on Weston, Dane steps in front of me, reaching down to grab my manacles and proceeds to shove the key in the small hole. The iron clanks as it falls open, and Dane tosses it to the ground at my feet.

"Yes, this will definitely be better." Dane grabs my arm, his grip crushing as he jerks me forward and leads me up the steps to the dais until we are standing just before my throne.

Dane's voice softens to a dangerous coo. "He never got any punishment for the role he played in all of this. I accept your offer, Lennox. I'll let him live."

My knees threaten to give out beneath me as his words sink in. Gratitude isn't a feeling I ever thought I would feel toward this man, not after everything he's done. But at this moment, I do. He's agreed to spare Weston's life, and the cost means nothing to me. I would gladly give up my title and my throne if it means he can live.

We will do exactly as Weston said, and disappear forever, and I can only hope that the gods will give this evil man everything he deserves for as many people that he has harmed. Maybe our actions, giving him exactly what he wants, will put an end to his immoral behavior. Even if I can never see my mother again, I know after reading her words and hearing Weston's stories, she would never want me to succumb to Dane's wrath.

"I think it's a perfect punishment," Dane continues, his voice louder this time so not only I can hear it. "Fitting, for all the havoc he's caused for me and all the opportunities he took away." He reaches up and gently swipes a lock of hair off my face, and I try not to cringe beneath his touch. His head tilts to the side as his face breaks into a joyous grin. "The only punishment worse than dying is to watch you die."

"No!" Weston roars from somewhere behind me in the same moment that Dane's hands wrap around my throat.

CHAPTER TWENTY-NINE

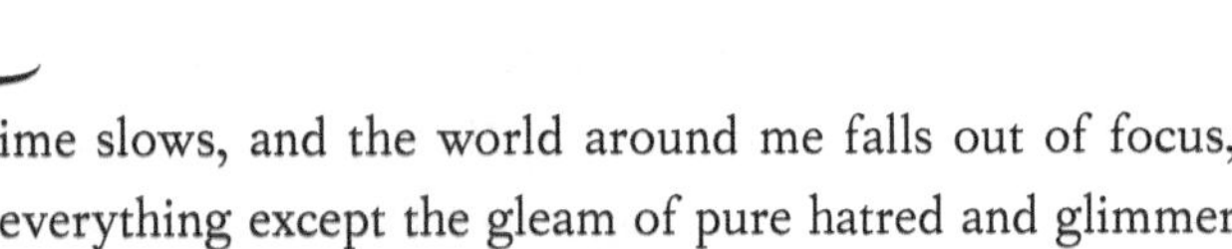

Time slows, and the world around me falls out of focus, everything except the gleam of pure hatred and glimmer of success in Dane's cold, amber eyes.

While my father could hardly ever look at me because all he saw was the face of my mother, it's obvious now that Dane does not. He looks at me and sees something entirely different: my father, or simply the person who was supposed to give him what he wanted, but now is standing in his way.

Dane has done nothing but take from me. My mother and father, my childhood, my chance at saving her, and now he's trying to take my life. I will not let him take any more. I will not let him win.

I am going to stop him, or die trying.

His grip tightens around my throat, his thumbs pressing in, and crushing my windpipe. He lifts me off the ground, and my eyes widen, the weight of my body worsening the pressure and making my mind scream for air.

I grip his hands, clawing at his fingers, trying to pry them from my skin.

Air. I need air.

I kick my legs wildly, trying to land a blow, anything that will get him to drop me, but his reach is too long, and my boots barely brush his body. Tears stream down my cheeks, and my mouth opens with noiseless gasps. Nails digging into his skin, I scratch and scrape, but he only squeezes harder, his sneer widening as he watches my panic set in.

"Lennox!"

Weston's roar sounds muffled, from somewhere far behind me. His cry is so feral, it's unlike any sound I've ever heard him make. He yells, again and again, but the noise in my ears dulls, covered only by the slowing beat of my heart.

My vision blurs, my view narrowing as darkness bleeds into the sides.

I need to breathe.

I *can't* breathe.

Booms. Thuds. Grunts. Screams. There's no indication of anything happening in the throne room around me, except for Weston's roars.

Focus on him. He is the only one I want to hear in the end.

Because this is it. This is the end.

This is how I die.

At the hands of someone who once convinced me he loved me, and I loved him. At the hands of someone whose hatred of my family precipitated this lifelong plot to tear us down, and steal what he claimed was his. At the hands of someone whose evil has ruined the lives and hopes of the people I call my family.

My limbs turn leaden as I still fight to break free, but with every breathless moment I'm losing the will. My thrashing slows, my grip slackens, and my head spins.

Resounding thuds continue to rumble, chains rattle, wood splinters. Swords clang together, and I search through the sounds for Weston, begging the gods that he's far enough away that he won't be able to see the light leave my eyes.

I hope he knows how much I love him.

I regret not having said it more.

After all the years of being alone, I hope the short time I was able to love him was enough to give him hope he will find it once again.

Maybe my father and I will have another chance together in whatever afterlife greets us, and I will wait for everyone else to one day be by my side again. I hope it takes a while; that they will get to live the long and full lives that were stolen from them. And one day, maybe soon, I'll finally meet my mother.

My eyelids droop as weakness overcomes me. Dane's face blurs, and my body falls limp, my hands dropping to my sides, finally giving up on the futile fight.

I love you, Weston.

My head lolls to the side, the world blackening around me, and I'm in a void. I've been here once before. The darkness is all-encompassing.

Then, there's light.

Burning erupts in my chest as my body heaves in air. Pain lances through my throat, my neck, my chest, my head. But the pressure lessens, and the hands wrapped so tightly just a moment ago slacken enough for one breath. My eyes are slits. The darkness barely dissipates as bright lights flash over my vision. My chest begs for air, and my body uncontrollably seeks it, coughing and gasping as tears stream from the corners of my eyes.

My eyes focus just enough to find Dane staring at me, with blood pouring from his mouth.

Pain resonates through my body as I slam into the floor, the already minuscule breath knocked from me once again. Dane crumbles beside me, his lifeless stare boring through me as blood pools around his body, and standing in his place is my father.

Blood drips onto the stone dais from both the tip of his king's dagger and the wound oozing in his abdomen. He stares down at

Dane for only a moment before his gaze slides to me. A sigh of relief huffs from his mouth before his knees give out and he collapses to the floor.

"Lennox!"

I hear him again. His voice cracks with strain and fear, and I know that this cry is even worse than all the rest. But I can't think. I can't move. I can't look around and my eyes flutter shut, freeing me of the throne room's complete and utter unrest.

Everything is limp. Heavy. Impossible.

Warm hands press into my cheeks, and relief floods my body.

He's here. I don't have to die alone. The monster who killed me won't be the last person I touched in this world. I will die knowing the last caress of my skin came from someone who truly loved me.

"Lennox, sweetheart, open your eyes."

His voice is urgent and filled with the strength I have found so much solace in, but I hear it waver, and my already almost still heart threatens to shatter. I can't be the one who defeats him, this powerful man who, even in moments when he needs it, is still being strong for me.

"Lennox, open your eyes!" He's pleading with me, and tears and panic fill his voice. "Breathe. Breathe! Come on, Lennox, you have to fight. Fight for me."

My mind screams at me to listen to him, to follow his command, to open my eyes and reach out and pull myself into him, but I can't.

"Where are the keys?" The boom of his yell would startle anyone, but not me. I soak up every detail of him I can, but it's interrupted by the scuffle of nearby footsteps, followed by the clank of iron hitting stone.

Then I'm in his arms. He crushes me to his chest, one hand weaving through my hair as he clutches the back of my head. His lips brush the shell of my ear, and pain coats his voice.

"Please, sweetheart, don't leave me. Just open your eyes."

My head falls back, supported by his steady hand, and I try. Try to answer him, to do what he asks, what he needs, but everything is too weak. I feel the whisper of something dampening my face, and my mind screams at me.

No, Weston cannot cry over me. I can't leave him. Not like this, not because of Dane.

I am locked inside the cage of my own body and mind, and no one else can hear me screaming and thrashing against it, all to get back to him.

My breaths are short and shallow, my chest barely rising and falling as another tear hits my cheek just above where the pad of his thumb softly caresses my skin. A flurry of heat burns inside me, and I want to rage against the walls closing me in.

I have to fight. I will not let Dane win.

A choked gurgle barely escapes my lips as I try to force out a sound, any sound. His body freezes, his hand on the back of my head clutching me tighter as I plead with my body to move, to say something, anything that will tell him I'm still here, and I'm trying.

Open your eyes.

It's a command to myself, because the desire to live can't just come from him. I have to want it just as badly. I cannot give up, despite my body begging me to.

Weston watched me die once before. He brought me back to life, and I watched the relief etched on his face when I took that first breath. But that was before; before everything happened between us.

The friendship, the trust, the oath, the love.

The promise of a future.

His forehead presses to mine so that the tips of our noses brush, and I feel his body shudder as he cradles me tighter.

"Don't let go. Not yet. I love you."

Broken.

Weston. My Weston. The captain, the First Guard, the protector, the one who holds strong so no one else has to, is broken. The voice that falls on my ears is filled with despair, but worse, failure. No matter how hard he fought, how hard he tried to get to me, to protect me, to save me, he couldn't. His oath, not only to the future queen, but to me, breaks with my final breath.

I will not let him endure that pain. I will not let him live the rest of his life knowing that he failed me, because he didn't. He never could. There's nothing Weston could have done that would have altered Dane's plan, that would have changed the trajectory of this night, not without risking him being in my place, and leaving me to endure the rest of my life without him.

He needs to hear it from me. I need to do exactly what he commanded me.

Fight with all my years of pent-up anger, and strength, and determination.

It's now or never.

My mind screams. My soul rages against the dark prison trying to overtake me, but I only focus on getting back to him.

It takes everything I have left inside to will my eyelids to slowly flutter open, and if I had the strength to wince against the light of the throne room, I would. My sight focuses on him, still pressed against my forehead. Eyes screwed shut and tears moistening his lashes, his brow is furrowed so deeply, his jaw clenched so tightly, he looks like he might implode.

But he's there. I can see him. I came back to him.

For how long, I don't know, but I'm going to soak up every second that I can, even if he doesn't know I'm there.

A grief-stricken scream erupts from him, the agonizing bellow coming from deep in his chest. The sound vibrates through me, echoing off the walls and ringing in my ears as he shakes violently, still clutching me like he never wants to let me go. I try to will myself to speak, but my throat won't function as pain slices through, the muscles unable to move after being the victim of Dane's hatred.

Weston's face falls, defeat sinking into his features. Opening his eyes, he slowly trails them up my face, wincing the closer he gets to my eyes as if he can't bear seeing me lifeless.

But I'm not. Barely. And I just want to see his eyes again.

When the darkened teal meets mine, they widen as he sucks in a sharp breath.

"You're alive." His words are barely a whisper as his eyes dart between mine, the defeat morphing into complete and utter shock. Tears escape the corners of my eyes as I blink gently, refusing to look away from him, and unable to escape the swell in my chest at the sight. It's the only answer he needs before he's crushing me to his chest again, cradling my head against him as if I will disappear if I'm not near.

"I need the healers now!" he screams, and there's more commotion as bodies shuffle around us.

I try to say his name, but there's no sound as my lips barely form the word with what little energy I have left. Fire laces my throat with every move, and all I can do is whimper from the pain.

"I'm here, sweetheart. Breathe for me, please." He scoops me into his arms and stands, turning his back on the room and shielding me from the brutal scene surrounding us. Kneeling on the plush black carpet, he lowers me down into the aisle and leans my back against the end of a pew. He may have set me down, but his hands never leave my body. They course over me, the same way he did back on the ship time and time again, searching for any injury, anything that could be causing me pain.

I want to close my eyes, and savor the feel of his hands on me, but I'm afraid of returning to the darkness. My breaths are still shallow, and pain accompanies each one, but I try to push it away, and focus on him. Not the chaos in the room, not the fear of what might happen, not the questionable future. I want to think only about the pressure of his warm hand resting on my hip, and the other wrapped around my nape.

"Where are the fucking healers?" he barks again, only tearing his eyes away from me for a moment before they're fixed back on my face, constantly assessing.

A man in a guard's uniform standing behind Weston answers succinctly. "They're with the king, sir."

"The future queen needs them now!" he snaps, and the guard turns on his heel and hurries across the room. Weston's entire focus is back on me in an instant, and there's fear in his eyes as they trail over my face and down my neck. With the way he's looking at me, I can only imagine how badly he wishes we were still back in the infirmary, using the magic that was so generously offered to us, despite never wanting to use it for himself.

There's a pang in my chest as I think back to him refusing to use the magic to heal the cut I so ignorantly gave him, but remember vividly how he didn't question using anything within his reach to heal me when I needed it.

His love was so obvious, and I ignored it for so long. It was almost ripped away from me tonight. My chest starts rising and falling rapidly as a swell of sorrow builds up.

"Slow, steady breaths," he croons, his thumb stroking my skin. "Everything is all right."

"No," I rasp. My eyes fill with tears, and I try to shake my head, but pain erupts in my neck, and I wince. Weston's expression is fierce as he looks over his shoulder, back toward where my father lay on the dais surrounded by the group of healers.

"Sir, everyone involved in the insurrection has been detained," a man says from my other side, but I don't turn to see who it is. It hurts too much, and I'm too afraid to let him out of my sight.

"Good. Shut the entrances down. I don't want anyone on or off the grounds until every person has been questioned. Get all the traitors locked in the dungeon. Separately. Make sure they've all been searched thoroughly."

"And the Second Guard?"

Weston's glare turns deadly. "She's no longer the Second Guard. Strip her of her sword and armor and lock her away. Alone. I will question her myself."

"Yes, sir," the man says, and I hear his footsteps grow quiet as he leaves, barking out the orders he was just given.

Weston turns back toward me, his face falling, and it is only then that I notice the uncontrollable tears still streaming down my cheeks.

"Lennox, baby, you're safe. It's over. Please don't cry." He leans forward to press a kiss to my forehead, but before he gets close enough, his body jolts to a stop, and a look of anguish fills his face.

All I want is to feel his lips on me, even just the barest brush against my skin, but he can't. We can't. Not here, in the midst of the chaos, so soon after I almost didn't live to ever feel his lips again. The pain on his face looks like it is eating him alive, not being able to touch me like he wants to, especially in this moment, and I know exactly what he is feeling.

I was so close to losing him, losing everything, and I can't even tell him all that I wanted to say. But more than that, it's clear things are going to be different than they were in Dawnlin, although still eerily similar. The way he commands everything around him, and the way everyone defers to his direction, even after all this time. They respect him.

A woman kneels beside Weston, and I recognize her immediately. Roxyana has been a healer in the castle for a long time and has tended to more than one of my scrapes or wounds over the years. But she's never seen me like this.

"What happened?" she asks firmly as her eyes rake over my body, assessing before she lays a hand on me.

"He strangled her." Weston's throat bobs, and the muscle in his cheek flickers before he speaks again. "She lost consciousness for a few minutes. She wouldn't respond, and then she did. Her breathing has been shallow since. She can't speak."

Roxyana gives him a brief nod, but she stays focused on me. "Please step back," she says and raises her arm to make room for her to get closer to me.

The threatening growl from Weston's chest is audible.

"No."

She shoots him an exasperated look, her mouth in a tight line. "I need space to examine the princess if I am to make sure there's no permanent damage."

Weston looks pained, as if it's taking him extra effort to step away, but he doesn't. His hands immediately find his head, wringing his hair as he watches the healer shift in front of me. Her hands are gentle as she begins, starting at the top of my head and working her way down. When she brushes the column of my neck, I can't stop the whimper that escapes my throat or the rapid breathing accompanied by a cower. Weston starts toward me, but stops himself as she pulls her hands away quickly.

"I won't harm you, princess," she says. "I just need to examine you to see what harm was done."

My eyes flick back up to Weston, and I can see the tension rippling through his body. I look back at her and try to mutter the only word I can manage in this moment. Sound barely comes out, and the movement is still laced with pain, but I give her my consent.

"Yes."

She moves slowly so as not to startle me, reaching up and gently pressing into the muscles of my neck, feeling the structures, and checking my face for any sign of pain at her touch. Fingertips press into the back of my neck, sliding down my spine and into my shoulders, pressing every bone, muscle, and ligament. Her face stays locked in a firm look of concentration that doesn't change even when she releases me.

"How badly did he hurt her?" Weston says impatiently.

Roxyana sits back on her heels and folds her hands onto her lap.

"The princess is very lucky. Things could have been much worse. Everything seems to be intact, but she will be in a bit of pain for a while. She will need rest."

"I'll make sure of it," he grumbles, and she moves again.

She looks into each of my eyes and instructs me to follow her commands. Moving my eyes and face, blinking at her, wiggling my toes and fingers. I follow each as best I can, but my body is weak. Even though I can do them, it feels too difficult, like I'm having to push my body too hard to accomplish something so simple.

"It might be difficult to speak for a while," she says once she seems satisfied that my body didn't lose any function, "but other than the pain and the voice, I do not believe you will have lasting damage."

Weston's hands fall to his knees as he lets out a gust of breath. My chest squeezes as I take him in, back hunched and head hanging between his shoulders. I would feel just as relieved as he looks if our roles were reversed, but I can imagine it's affecting him even more knowing the guilt he feels for Dane hurting me once again.

Roxyana stands and smoothes her skirts. "I will still continue to monitor you closely, just to be sure. We will give you a tonic to help with the pain. Strict bed rest for at least a week while the muscles heal."

"Thank you," Weston breathes, straightening to his full height again, just as the healer drops into a deep curtsey.

"Sir?" Another guard strides toward us as Roxyana turns away. His voice is breathless as he rushes to Weston, and it's only then that I recognize him. He was one of the older guards who stood in the hall, who watched Brynne lead us to the throne room.

And he called Weston, sir.

Did he recognize him? Does he remember him? Is that how this nightmare ended?

"What?" Weston says, turning to face the guard.

"The king is asking for her," he says, looking down toward me, his face solemn and respectful. He drops to a knee in a quick bow, dipping his head, before rising up once again. "Princess. The healers say he doesn't have much time."

"Thank you," Weston mutters, then sinks down beside me again. "Do you want to see him?"

His brow is soft as he scans my face, waiting for my answer.

Do I? It feels odd having the choice, but I have been honest with Weston about the relationship I had with my father. He must know how difficult it could be for me, and how much of our history might prevent me from wanting to speak to him, but just like back in Dawnlin, he's giving me the ability to choose, like I told him I always wanted.

His hand finds mine, and he squeezes reassuringly. "I know things between the two of you were not great when you left, and I would understand if you don't."

Staring blankly at him, I try to push through the fog in my mind that is still recovering from being deprived of air for so long, that is still reeling from everything that has happened tonight.

I didn't get to say goodbye to one parent, and despite my father and my history, I don't want to regret choosing to ignore him now. The gods kept him alive long enough to save my life, and there must have been a reason. Maybe it was only to give me the chance to let him go, to have closure, to walk into my reign with a logical mind and not worry about who I am trying to impress.

My voice is scratchy and barely audible when I force out my answer. "Yes."

CHAPTER THIRTY

Weston lifts me carefully and cradles my body to his chest. Despite the healer's reassurance that I did not sustain any lasting damage, he still moves with caution so as not to harm me himself. His hands grip me with the strength and comfort I have become used to when he carries me to safety, and I turn my face into his chest, trying to prepare myself for what is about to come, and avoiding the remnants of the violence around me.

Even after everything Dane did to me—the ways he hurt me mentally, physically, emotionally—I still don't want to see him lying in a pool of his own blood. I cared about him, and though those feelings have disappeared and morphed into hatred, I don't want to remember him this way. And I don't want to see my father's blood smeared across the stones and mixing with that of his murderer.

Whenever I entered this room, I was surrounded by order and structure, and tradition. I can't look around now and see the chaos that mars its perfection. I have to focus on the feeling of security Weston is giving me, because I don't know what I will feel the moment I look into my father's dying eyes.

Careful not to jostle me as he climbs the steps, Weston crosses the dais and kneels before the throne, setting me down gently and turning me so I am face to face with my father. I want to grab hold of him, to stay sheltered in his arms, so I'm not alone, but before I can even try, he rises again, standing just far enough from me to be considered appropriate, but close enough that I can still feel his presence.

A pit forms in my stomach as I take in the man before me. Sitting slumped against the throne, his face already ashen and sagging as his chest rises and falls in short, shuddering breaths. He clutches tightly to a clump of soiled fabric, pressing it firmly into his abdomen. His once fine clothes are bloodstained and torn, and my mind is brought back to a similar stain I found on Weston's clothing, back from when Dane committed the same act, leaving them both for dead.

I barely recognize the man before me, but the moment his eyes meet mine, I startle. I can recall exactly how many times my father has looked me in the eye, and his unwavering gaze is another time to add to the already very short list. The man I know is still in there somewhere, but in these last moments, he's finally able to look at me one last time.

"You're back," he says, his voice just above a whisper.

I barely manage a nod, and hear Weston behind me shift the weight on his feet when I wince from the pain.

"Did you find what you were looking for?" Father's brows rise, his eyes growing hopeful as his gaze swivels between Weston and me.

"Yes," Weston says tightly, and my father's eyes widen slightly. Weston clears his throat, and his voice lowers. "But we were unsuccessful in obtaining it."

Father's face and shoulders fall as the same acceptance we've had months and years to come to terms with washes over him. A heavy silence fills the space between us, but no one moves, not until my father nods slowly, as if to himself, before his eyes lift to mine.

"They say I have little time." His shoulders shake as a fit of coughs overcomes his body. He takes a short, choked breath, and pain morphs his features. "I needed to speak to you before the end. My words may not mean much, but they still needed to be said."

His voice trails off, and I wait, unsure of what is so important that after years of barely speaking to me, he wants to spend his last moments with me, and not the friend he has not seen in over twenty years.

"I'm sorry, Lennox. The last thing I ever wanted was for your life to end up this way. I know—" he winces, and presses his hand more firmly to his belly before starting again. "I know Edmond gave you your mother's letters. He has been pressuring me for many years to finally let you read them, but it was too hard for me to think about them, let alone look at them again. I wasn't ready for the inevitable questions you had about your mother, but you need to know that her words were true. *Are* true. You are the most important thing to her. To us."

A lump forms in my already constricted throat, and I try to swallow it down, but the pain and the swelling make it near impossible.

"But whenever I looked at you, all I could see was her. Her beauty, her warmth, her smile, her ferocity. Every single thing I loved about her is in you, and it made me hurt so much I couldn't bear it. It was the worst thing I could do as a father, I know that, but I'm a weak man. You were a constant reminder of the pain I felt the day we lost her, and when I looked at you, I relived that loss over and over again. Losing the person you thought you would spend your life with, and grow old together, is an unimaginable pain." His head tilts up, and he looks at Weston. His gaze lingers there for a moment as his face softens. "I believe you may finally understand what that feels like."

My already shallow breath hitches as my father smiles softly at his friend, then directs the same look at me. Was Weston right? Did my father see the way he looks at me and recognize the same feelings in himself? Did he watch Weston hold me, begging me to open my eyes and know that it was for more than just an oath to his kingdom?

Weston's weight shifts again, the movement a clear response to the assumption.

Father continues, and his face falls again, the softness from a moment ago gone. "No one knows the reason for my strict decisions. What I uttered was law. No one dared question the king except you. You were the only one who tried and pushed back, and each time I saw the disappointment in your face when I squashed your suggestions or ideas, it felt like a knife to the gut."

His eyes flick up to Weston quickly before falling back to me once again, and his voice is somber. "I didn't even have enough strength to tell the person besides your mother who I cared for the most. I'm running out of time. I need to tell you now. I need you to know, not so it will change anything, but so you don't spend your life wondering why all of this happened." He winces and shifts his body against the base of the throne, but gives up with a heavy sigh. "Do you know what happened that night? The night you were born?"

"I told her everything," Weston mutters, and Father lets out a sigh with a slight shake of his head.

"You didn't know everything. I got to her before you did. I knew from Lyla's cries that something was terribly wrong. When I ran to her, Dane's voice carried. He was shouting, and even over my own thoughts about getting to her, I could hear what he said. He didn't know I heard every word."

Tears fill my father's eyes as he looks directly into mine, and I can't stop the way mine fill at the sight. Not just of him crying, but of him finally looking at me, seeing me, and giving me the truth I've longed for.

"He was trying to take her away, to convince her to leave with him. He found someone who was willing to keep you, someone who wanted a child and would gladly welcome a newborn babe." He coughs again, and my chest clenches as I wait with bated breath for him to continue, silently begging him to hold on long enough to tell me everything.

"He wanted to punish me, to take you both away and destroy my family, the only true thing that brought me happiness, all because he thought I destroyed his. Your mother adamantly refused. I could hear her crying 'no', and trying to get him to listen to her. Everything she explained, her happiness, her love, he tried to tell her she was tricked. No amount of her yelling that he was wrong and that if he cared for her, he would see, changed anything.

"He tried to take her then by force, and when she fought him off, she fell. I watched as my wife, the mother of my unborn child, pushed her attacker away, clutching her swollen belly and attempting in every way she could to keep you safe. I watched as he grabbed her, and wrenched her down the steps, but she lost her balance as she fought. My scream mixed with hers frightened him, and he stared down after her, panicked and taking in what he had done. The woman he wanted to love, who didn't love him back lay crumpled at the foot of the steps, and it was all his fault. He saw me running toward her, and ran away himself. Once I saw the blood, I no longer cared about him, only about her and you.

"That night, when her body could no longer keep you safe, and I held you in my arms, I vowed I would protect you. He threatened to take you, and had already gotten into the castle once, undetected. I couldn't risk it happening again. I couldn't let him know you had survived. The only ones who knew were the staff, and the guards, and they were sworn to protect. He proved he would stop at nothing to pay me back for everything he thought I did to him. It is why I never let you leave. But even after that night, the years of stifling your spark, the guilt I felt, the internal turmoil knowing how disappointed in me Lyla would be for not letting you live, I couldn't change my mind. I couldn't let him take you away from me too, not after he already took her."

Tears stream down his cheeks, and his voice drops so I can barely hear it.

"Years of pain, an entire lifetime missed with my only daughter, and it was all for nothing. He took you anyway. I destroyed the life full of memories we could have had, simply by trying to protect you, and he took you anyway."

I reach out hesitantly for his hand, unable to stop myself from giving him the same comfort I would have wanted. His eyes fall to my hand as my fingers wrap gently around his, and his features morph before my eyes.

Longing, pain, regret, but also something different. Something new.

My father finally looks happy, even if it is only just a little.

"I made a lot of selfish decisions," he continues, "and I regret them immensely. But my regret does not change how they affected you, how they shaped you and made you doubt the love I held for you in my heart." He squeezes my hand and his brows draw in. "I don't expect your forgiveness, and I am not asking for it. I just cannot leave this world without you knowing that I do truly love you, Lennox, despite being a terrible father, and incapable of showing it. I never wanted to leave you to be a young queen ruling a kingdom, yet here we are. I did exactly that."

I lean forward slightly, wincing as I try to push past the pain and say what I need him to hear.

"You said I wasn't ready," I rasp, and his face falls.

"You heard me." The sadness in his voice is unmistakable, and I wait silently for him to explain, hoping he understands.

"I was not referring to you becoming queen, and knowing that was your first thought just shows how much I failed, not only as your father, but as your king. No, Lennox, I was talking about what I told you tonight, the truth of what happened. It was less that you weren't ready to hear it, and more that I was not ready to tell you. I was not ready to relive that night, and cause you more pain than I already had. But today I had no choice. I couldn't leave this world, leave you, without you knowing."

My body shudders with quiet cries at his words. I was wrong, like I had been before, but this time, it was not my fault. How could I assume anything different after years of him halting my attempts to advance in my position, to act the way the heir to the throne would? He admitted as much tonight, but knowing I was wrong, that it was out of his fear of being honest with me, not his doubt of my abilities, makes the deep hole of inadequacy in my chest a little shallower.

"You will be the best queen Blackwood has ever seen, Lennox. You will be even more loved than your mother was, I am sure of it. Your intelligence, your wit, your stubbornness, but most of all, your compassion. Your heart. Every bit of it is from her, and this kingdom needs it. We were locked away for far too long, and your people need you. I'm sorry I will not be here to see it."

But isn't that always the way it has to be? The parent will never see the regent their son or daughter will be come, they just have to know that they did what they could to shape them into a leader. My father had the chance to see me grow into the princess, the heir to the throne and all that I could be, but his selfish actions took that chance from him. Now, he will never have the opportunity to see who I will become, because while his heart still beats, there is no queen.

"West," he says, finally turning away from me, and beckoning Weston closer from where he still hovers behind me. Dropping to a knee at my side, he's as close as he can be without touching me, and I long to lean into him, to have him hold me as my father's words alter the axis of my world.

"I tried, Rem." Weston's throat bobs as his chin dips in grief, but my father shakes his head as coughs wrack his chest again, followed by a shrill, deep breath.

"No. Do not blame yourself," he wheezes. "It was just not meant to be. What is it your father always told us?"

"Light always finds a way, even through the blackest woods."

"That was it," he whispers, his lips tipping up in the hint of a smile as he glances between us. "I think there may be some light that has come from this darkness."

Weston's head raises, and he looks at my father directly, silently conversing with him, as maybe they had all that time ago. But as I take in the two of them, it is so obvious to see the magic of Dawnlin. Weston, still a young man, the friend and guard to the king, who now looks as if he's aged a lifetime. No one would look at the two of them and believe they grew up together, and once again, I'm thankful for everything the magic brought into my life.

Father releases my hand and reaches toward Weston's, taking it and placing it over mine, in the space where his just occupied. Without hesitation, Weston weaves his fingers through mine, squeezing tightly, and my father watches the movement.

"Keep her safe, West," Father says softly. "Do what I couldn't do. Give her life. Love her. Like she deserves."

My chest aches and I squeeze Weston's hand back. I thought we would have to fight to be together, especially among those who wouldn't understand Dawnlin and what happened there. I thought my father would be the first to forbid us, to remind us of Weston's oath and do anything to keep us apart.

I was wrong.

Weston clears his throat. "I will, Rem. I swear to you I will. And I do. I love her." He raises my hand to his lips and presses a firm kiss to my knuckles. "More than I ever thought possible."

"Then I can leave, knowing you won't be alone." He smiles at me, tears still shining in his eyes, and I can't hold back my emotions any longer.

I've now lost both my parents, and my guard. I've lost everyone I grew to love on Dawnlin, except for one. The one who is by my side as I say goodbye to the only true family I have left, and usher in a new era of my life, one that I was not expecting today of all days. If it hadn't been for Dawnlin, I would be sitting on this floor, truly alone.

My father's eyes slowly close, the soft gasps loud in my ears, until the rise and fall of his chest stops.

I don't know what I expected, whether I expected it to be different, or more ornate; whether I expected there to be some sort of physical passing of the title, to make it feel more real than it does.

But whatever I expected, it wasn't this.

Because the moment finally happens, the moment no one could ever be prepared for. The moment I *wasn't* prepared for, despite knowing it was coming my entire life.

As I look at my father's lifeless body and still clutch the hand of the man I love, I know my life will never be the same.

I am the queen of Blackwood.

CHAPTER THIRTY-ONE

All the air is sucked from the room as I stare at my father's blank face. I've gone my entire life without seeing death, and now, tonight, I've witnessed it twice.

Gone.

Father is gone, and now the entire kingdom is in my hands.

The room spins, and bile burns the back of my throat. I barely register my body swaying before I'm surrounded by warmth and strength, as Weston finally breaks his unspoken rule and wraps his arms around my shoulders. His voice is low as he murmurs into my ear, and even though I know the room is filled with guards and gods know who else, after what we just endured, it feels like it is only him and me.

"Sweetheart, I need you to stand for me. Can you do that?"

"Yes," I whisper, not knowing if any sound even left my lips. He may have posed it as a question, but I know I don't have a choice. I have to tell them all that their king is gone.

"Hold on to me." His strong fingers sink into my waist, steadying me. With trembling hands, I grip his forearms as he lifts me to my feet. My legs wobble beneath me, and my knees threaten to buckle, but the muscles in Weston's arms tighten, holding me securely. "I won't let you fall."

Pain shoots through the muscles of my neck as I tilt my head back to look at him. His eyes scan my face, and I don't know what he sees there. There are too many things circling through my mind to even know how I look, but in him I only find reassurance.

We turn in a slow circle until I am facing the room, but his hands don't leave my waist until he's sure I will not fall.

I am going to stay strong, even if it is only to get through these next few minutes.

Warily releasing me, he faces the throne room and the chaos that still fills it. Healers bustle around. Guards stand above shackled prisoners. Staff shuffle in and out of the doors, but it all feels like a blur. All I can focus on is Weston, and his voice echoing against the stone walls.

"The king is dead," he shouts, and everyone stills, their attention snapping to the First Guard standing on the dais. Sorrow, shock, disbelief, anger. Each face has a unique response to the news. My stomach churns in the next moment as all their gazes rise to me. Hands fisting on my pants, I wait for Weston's next direction.

"Kneel before your queen."

My nose burns as I watch everyone before me follow his command and drop to their knees. Weston scans the room, ensuring complies with the tradition, especially in the wake of the treason today. When he is satisfied, he turns toward me and drops to a knee, the same way he did in his room, before linking our lives together with his oath.

The muscles in his face relax as he looks up at me, his severe authority softening for my eyes only. His voice betrays nothing as he calls out into the room, the resonance causing me to startle.

"Long live Lennox Holt! Long live the queen!"

A loud echo erupts from the group kneeling behind him, but I can't take my eyes off of his.

"Long live the queen!"

He gives me a slow nod, and I don't know if it is permission or reassurance, but I pull my gaze away and look out across the room at all the people, my people. This moment is anything but easy. It is a double-edged sword, and only other regents will know the immense pressure and sadness that comes with it. I want to remember, to try to soak up the hint of pride I feel as I look out among so many faces I have known for so long, but it's too much. All of it.

I need time, space. I need to think straight before I have to be the queen I was trained to be.

I don't know what to do now.

Flicking my wrist, I urge him to stand and reach out for him. He doesn't need an explanation or a command; he knows, like he always does, what I need. Once he stands, so does everyone else, and the flurry immediately starts again. This time, I ignore it, keeping my focus on him.

"I'm taking you to your room," Weston grumbles, closing the space between us but not getting too close, as close as I am used to him being. "The healer said to rest. Everything else will be dealt with."

"Alright," I rasp, and gulp down the fire that singes my throat.

Motion catches my eye, and I turn my head slowly to find a familiar figure crossing the dais, stepping past the covered, lifeless body of the Guardian of Dawnlin.

"Hello, son."

Edmond's voice feels like a warm blanket wrapping tightly around me, and I blink back tears as my chest swells. Neither of us ever thought we would see him again, but here he is, still alive, and completely unchanged from the night I walked away from him and left for another world.

"Pop," Weston breathes, the relief in his voice palpable.

"My boy, it has been too long, but things like this always have a way of working out for the best." Edmond smiles, his eyes squinting in the way I have become so familiar with. "I had hope."

"How did you know?" I force out, and he shakes his head.

"That is a story for another day. Right now, Your Majesty, you need to heal. I am sure my son wants to take you away from all of this." He gestures to the surrounding room, a knowing look on his face.

Weston moves quickly, crossing the dais and wrapping his arms around his father.

"I missed you," I hear him mumble, and my chin quivers as I remember the look on his face back in the spring when I told him story after story of my time with his father.

Edmond's reply is harder to catch as it is muffled in Weston's shoulder, but I've been listening to his voice for far too long not to pick up on it. "I knew you both would come home."

Weston releases him and steps back. "Later," he promises.

Edmond smiles and nods. "Of course. Attend to the queen."

Weston looks out over the room, his eyes scanning until he finds who he is looking for.

"ONeal," he barks, and the man stops and stands at attention, waiting for his command. "Find Tila and tell her she's needed in the queen's chambers. Charles, clear everyone from this room except for the healers to shroud the king, then meet me upstairs at her door."

I barely have time to process the commands before Weston is striding back across the dais and scooping me into his arms. He cradles me close, as if he doesn't care who sees or that this is a completely acceptable action of the First Guard for a queen who has had her life threatened.

The men spring to action, but we aren't in the throne room long enough to see anything else. Weston blazes through the empty halls, his pace never slowing, even as he carries me up the long flight of stairs.

"Where are your rooms?" he murmurs, and I point to the right as we approach the top of the steps.

"That way."

We crest the top, and the tapestry-lined hallway I have walked down countless times feels different now. Weston starts down it fiercely, and the door I once saw as symbolizing my captivity, but I now see as a sign of safety, finally comes into view. But before we get close, I grab his torn uniform and tug, urging him to stop.

"Wait."

"What's wrong?" His arms tighten as he looks down at me, and I can see with the clench of his jaw that he's trying very hard not to look around, and be on alert, instead focusing on me and what I need.

"Open that door. I need to see." I point to the door I sped past for my entire life, that I avoided out of guilt and pain, but now that I know the truth of what happened, I don't want to avoid it anymore.

His hand lifts from where he's clutching me and grasps the handle. Turning it, he pushes open the large door, and I can't help but hold my breath.

Was this entire journey, with all the highs and lows, lessons and friendships, worth it? Or did my mother let go before I even had a chance to try to save her?

Light pours into the room from the windows, and as I look toward the bed, I let out that held breath.

She's still here; still lying in a perpetual sleep. Nothing has changed since the night I left, the night of my ceremony. The night I told her I would not give up on her.

My father didn't let her go.

"Lyla…" Weston mutters, and his voice trails off into the thick silence of the room.

"She held on," I say, the hoarseness of my already damaged voice now worsened with the swell of emotion. "He didn't give up on her."

"I'm sorry," he mumbles into my hair, and all I can do is squeeze my eyes shut, forcing tears to escape from the corners.

"Take me out," I whisper. He doesn't question it. He turns on his heel and tugs the door firmly closed behind us. It takes him only a few strides before he's in front of my door, turning to face it and tipping his head forward.

"This one?"

"Yes," I whisper, and he pushes it open, slipping us through the narrow opening before kicking it shut, and throwing the bolt into place. He sets me down gently on my feet, making sure I am steady before he takes his hands off of me.

"Don't move."

My skin prickles at the determination in his eyes, and the hardening of his jaw. He turns his back on me and begins searching the room, looking in every space, closet, opening; anywhere someone might be hiding. He checks behind curtains and underneath the bed before disappearing into the adjoining bathing chamber.

Moments later he reappears, and a bit of the tension has lessened, though not much. He wordlessly strides over to me, this time lifting me with tenderness and concern. Where I normally would snap at him and tell him I can walk, especially now that we are alone without pressure and observations of everyone around us, I don't. I want him to hold me, to take care of me, like only he knows how, and like he always feels compelled to do.

I once told him I wasn't fragile, but right now, I feel like if he lets me go, I will shatter.

He brings me into the bathing chamber and sets me on the wooden bench that sits alongside my tub. Dropping into a crouch before me, his forehead presses into mine and his hands cradle my jaw.

"Fucking gods," he growls. "I thought I lost you." His voice is harsh, but the crack filled with emotion sends a dagger through my heart. I've only seen him let his walls down like this once before, and even back then, when we thought we had experienced the worst, it was nothing compared to how he is now.

His shoulders shake with shuddering breaths, and he squeezes his eyes shut. I know he wants to be closer, to touch me, to show me his love in the way he feels it the most, but he won't, not after the way my body was abused. He would never inflict pain when he does everything in his power to keep me from feeling it.

"I thought so too." I speak through the pain, through the lump forming in my throat, grateful that I can make any noise at all. He lifts his chin, and my vision blurs as I watch his glassy eyes search mine. His thumbs stroke my cheeks, and his eyes blaze a trail down my face, falling on my lips, then gliding lower to my throat. His jaw clenches at whatever he sees.

"I'm all right. I think," I add.

He leans forward slowly, giving me every chance to tell him to stop, but I don't. I may feel fragile, but that doesn't apply to him. I need him. I need to feel his strength, to know that he is going to catch me if I fall. I need to feel his love.

His lips are soft as they press into mine ever so slightly, just enough to create a chasm in my chest. I don't know what the pain behind his eyes would have looked like if I had succumbed to Dane's attack. Thank the gods we will never find out.

"I tried to get to you." His throat bobs as he swallows harshly. Shame and guilt wash over his features, and his shoulders slump in defeat. "Gods, I fucking tried, Lennox. I thought he had agreed. I thought he was going to let us disappear and take everything he wanted, but when he grabbed you, I couldn't stop myself. I wanted to kill every single one of them for keeping me from getting to you."

"I know," I whisper. "I could hear you, but I knew it was too late. I didn't want you to see it."

It isn't until then that I notice how much Weston's body took the brunt of his attempt to get to me. Trails of dried blood run down his face from gashes that have since clotted. Others still bleed a dark red into his hair, the deep bruises beneath them matching the ones on his eye and along the length of his jaw. And this is only what I can see on the surface.

Yet he never stopped. He never hesitated for even a moment to think about his own injuries or his own well-being.

He only wanted to get to me.

He wouldn't stop until he got to me.

"If he took you away from me, he would have had to kill me because I would not have stopped until it was his throat being crushed beneath my fingers."

Fear tightens my chest as I think about Weston meeting the same fate, and I can't imagine a world without him and all the good he does for anyone he meets.

"Thank the gods my father didn't let either of us have to endure that."

He nods solemnly. "I should have thanked him for it." He presses another soft kiss to my lips, and I know it is still taking everything he has to hold himself back. He meets my eyes again when he pulls away, and the sadness has been pushed aside, as the First Guard slips back into place.

"I need to go take care of things downstairs. Do you give me permission to do that?"

My fingertips begin to tingle, and my breaths shorten.

"You're leaving?" My voice comes out as a squeak, and I wince at the pain from exertion. "No, don't leave."

"Breathe," he coos as his thumbs stroke my skin again, trying to soothe and calm me, but it doesn't work. I can barely think. Every possible scenario depicting reasons he wouldn't return to me runs through my mind, and the loneliness that accompanies them threatens to swallow me whole.

"Don't go," I sob, and wrap my hands around his wrists, squeezing so tight that my fingernails dig into his skin. "Please. Don't leave me."

"I'm not leaving you, my queen. I have to make sure the castle is safe, and that everyone who was involved is in the dungeon. I need it to be safe for you to be here. But I need your permission to do that."

He needs my permission, because it isn't just a term of endearment anymore. It's a name and title that would one day come to fruition, and that day is today.

I am the queen.

This isn't Captain Weston. This is First Guard Weston, and I am his queen.

While he acted without orders when I was in immediate danger, he still requires my command when there is no threat to my life, and I have to be strong enough to give it.

I have to be strong enough to watch him walk away and know he will come back, that I have nothing to fear, despite everything in my body and mind screaming at me that I do.

I shudder and force my hands to release his wrists to settle in my lap. Dipping my chin, I say the only thing I can.

"Yes."

"Thank you," he says, and presses a kiss to my forehead before finding my eyes again. His gaze is fierce as he puts all of his sincerity behind his next words. "I will come back, my queen. I'm not going anywhere."

I give him a tentative nod, and the muscles in my neck spasm as I do. I taste blood on my tongue when I bite down, doing anything to try to hide the fact that the simple movement caused so much pain.

A loud knock reverberates through my rooms, and Weston glances over his shoulder. The door is bolted, so no one can enter, but I don't want him to walk away. Not yet.

"You need a healer," I say, trying to stall him as the knock pounds loudly again.

"I will see a healer." He rises and runs his fingers through my hair, pushing it back away from my face before his hand settles gently at the nape of my neck. "I'll make sure you are safe, and I will be back as soon as I can."

I feel the absence of his touch the moment he disappears back into my chambers, but I don't move. The high-pitched creak of the bolt being removed from the door, followed by the turn of the handle, pulls all of my attention away from everything else.

"Someone needs to explain to me what is going on because I went to the queen's room—" The sentence is interrupted by a loud gasp, followed by the rustle of a dress brushing the floors and the click of the latch falling back into place.

Tila. Weston told the guard to send her, but the memory vanished under all the rest until I heard her voice. And the gasp. I'd almost forgotten. Tila *knows* Weston, and she was nowhere near the throne room this morning. Seeing him again for the first time in so long clearly took her by surprise.

"Tila," he says, his voice urgent. "You're the only one I can trust with her. I need you to take care of her while I figure things out."

"Weston? My...how did you...what—" She stumbles over her words, likely trying to process what her mind knows but what her eyes are seeing.

"I can't explain, but the king is dead. The princess is the queen now, and I need to make sure there is no further threat. Can I trust you?" There isn't even a beat of silence before she's spitting her answer back at him.

"Yes, of course. Don't insult me, young man, by ever questioning my loyalty. That girl is like my own."

I can hear the fondness and gratefulness in his voice when he responds. "Thank you, Tila. Thank you."

The hinges squeak as the door opens and then clicks closed again, and the rustle of Tila's dress gets closer until she appears in the doorway.

"My gods," she mutters as her hand settles on her chest. "My dear girl, what in the heavens has happened to you?"

"Hi Tila," I say weakly, and watch as her gaze flickers to my neck then back to my face.

She pivots on her heel, leaving me alone in the bathing chamber once more. Her footsteps stomp along the stone floors before she's yanking the door open again and barks commands outside.

"I need hot water drawn for the queen immediately. You go yourself and pull some food from the kitchen. No one enters this room unless it is the First Guard himself allowing it. Understood?"

There's a mumbled response before the door slams closed, the bolt secured once again. Her footsteps pound again, faster this time, until she appears in the doorway, her mouth a thin line.

"Let's get you cleaned up. Everything will be fine, Your Majesty."

CHAPTER THIRTY-TWO

The exhaustion from the emotional and physical abuse I endured today is overwhelming, and I fall in and out of consciousness for most of the day. Weston still hasn't returned by the time the light darkens in my windows, and worry stirs in my chest the longer the night goes on with no word. It feels like I startle awake every few seconds, anxiously checking to see if he's back, but am only met with the steady crackle of the hearth and the slow turning of pages as Tila reads across the room.

When the murmuring of voices wakes me some time later, there's no way of knowing how late it is. Fighting against the weight of my eyelids, I open my eyes, just barely enough to see the shadows of two people standing near the door.

"She has been resting all day, but only finally fell asleep," Tila whispers. "She's in a great deal of pain. I propped her pillows beneath her so she would not move, but she has been restless."

Relief washes over me at the answering rumble, and my body instantly relaxes. "The healers sent me with something that will help as soon as she wakes. Did she eat?"

"Barely a thing. It was too difficult. I've already instructed those you've already cleared in the kitchens to prepare soups and broth for her tomorrow. She needs strength to get through all of this."

Weston's voice lowers even more, and my ears strain to hear. "Thank you, Tila, for looking after her. I couldn't leave her with someone I didn't trust."

"You know there is no reason for you to be thanking me." Soft footsteps click as she walks closer to the door, and his follow behind.

"The crown isn't thanking you, Tila. I am."

There's a pause as Tila's skirts swish around, and her voice is hushed when she responds. "You care for her, don't you?"

Weston doesn't answer, not with words I can hear, and Tila starts again.

"Well, it is not my place to ask questions. I'm much too old to care about such things as propriety. As long as the First Guard puts the queen above all else, I'm sure that is all her father wanted."

"I do," he grumbles.

"Good. And the king? Are you at liberty to say?"

"There was an assassin. He was someone from the king's past. He tried to harm her too."

She lets out a huff. "Then we are lucky she is still with us."

"We are."

"I'm sorry for your loss, mister Rowe. It is a loss for us all, but I'm sure it is a great deal harder for you. I remember how close you were to the king."

"Thank you, Tila. It was not an easy day."

"You are correct. So, it is high time this day was over for us all. I am going to retire. I will check in on her in the morning. Goodnight, mister Rowe."

A strip of light expands across the room as Tila slips out the door, but it is extinguished quickly as Weston closes and locks it softly behind her. His footsteps cross the room, followed by the sound of a log being added to the hearth. The orange glow flashes brighter, followed by more crackling and popping as the flame catches the bark. He's rounding the corner of my bed in the next moment, and there's a clink of glass as he sets something on the bedside table. His fingers trail over the curve of my head, and I feel his lips press into my hair.

"Hmmph," I grumble, trying to will my eyes open, but everything feels heavy and difficult to move. When I finally force them open, the burning makes me want to shut them again, but I don't. I want to see him. I need to see him.

"Go back to sleep," he murmurs as his lips hover just above my skin, and I grunt again.

"No." My voice is a barely there rasp, and it feels like the cut of blades as the air from my breathing and speaking slices through the space, but I do it anyway. He leans back, hovering just above me, but the shadows cast over his features make him barely visible. I place my hand on his cheek, feeling for any bandages or stitches, and he leans softly into my touch.

"Did you see a healer?" I mutter.

"I told you I would. They said I'll be fine."

"Mmm," I hum, happy that he took care of himself and didn't just ignore his needs to take care of mine. I take a deep breath through my nose and inhale his fresh scent that tells me he must have cleaned up before coming back here.

"Are you in pain?" he asks gently, and I decide not to lie. What's the point? I don't want him to worry about me, but I also want him to know everything I'm feeling. There's no hiding anything between us anymore.

"Yes."

He straightens and turns toward the table, picking up the bottle he set there before.

"Drink this. Roxyana said it will lessen the pain and help you sleep." His hand cups my jaw while the other guides the bottle to my lips. He tilts it back, helping me take small swallows until the entire dose is gone. I was always grateful for the healing magic on Dawnlin, but I haven't missed it more than I do now. The injuries I endured there never seemed that bad, because the pain was so short-lived. The island wouldn't let us suffer long.

Not here.

Here the pain is prolonged and masked, and the healing takes away from everything else this new life demands of me.

"Thank you," I murmur. He doesn't respond, only sets the bottle down again, then kneels next to the bed with his elbows resting on the mattress at my side.

"Were there any more threats?" I sink into the propped pillows and turn my head slightly so I can face him, but it's still too difficult to see.

"No. It seems like everyone who knew about it was in the throne room with us. Everyone else was kept in the dark."

"How long were they all here?"

"Only a few days. They locked Rem in his room, so he knew something was wrong, but everyone else just thought the king needed solitude."

"Bastard," I grumble, and Weston huffs a laugh.

His hand reaches up and brushes my hair off my forehead before falling down to the bed again. "We'll learn more when we question the ones who were in charge."

"I want to be there. At least for Brynne and Storm."

"Of course," he agrees.

There's something I still don't understand, something that has been hovering in the back of my mind since I heard the guard in the throne room refer to Weston as 'sir'.

"If they were all kept in the dark, how did it all end? How did anyone know to come get us?"

"Remember when you thought something was wrong as they led us to the throne room?"

It seems like that happened so long ago now, but I remember. I remember Guthrie making comments about Weston being beaten too hard, and worrying that he needed help from all the blows they landed on him.

"Yes."

"The guards in the corridor, ONeal and Charles, have been guards for a long time. They started as young men, and while they may not look it now, that is how I remember them. I commanded them. I trusted them. So when I saw who was stationed as I walked by, I used a phrase that signaled a mutiny to them. They didn't forget."

"And they broke in," I breathe. The booming sounds, the splintering of wood, the rattling of chains. Those two guards gathered other trusted men and broke into the throne room.

They saved our lives.

If it had been any other men stationed there today, we might not be sitting here, whispering in the dark. I will never fail to be impressed by all the ways Weston is the best at what he does, and the quick and decisive way his mind works.

"I was so scared," I admit to the darkness, and my voice quivers with the coming onslaught of tears.

"I was too," he grumbles, his warm fingers wrapping around mine. "But Dane is finally gone, and you are safe, with me. No one who wants to harm you will be allowed to. They will be removed."

"What will happen now?" I whisper. "There's no Guardian. He and my father killed each other, and now there is no one to take his place."

"I don't know. But maybe it is better this way. The myth will become just that, a myth. No one will have to endure the pain of being unworthy and having their hope ripped away."

He's right. Without a new Guardian, no one will get to the mountain only to leave empty-handed. But without a new Guardian, all that hope will also be lost.

I'm not sure which is better.

Weston's thumb strokes the back of my hand, sending tingles up my arm as we sit in comfortable silence, but the lack of conversation only makes my mind reel. When I can't take it any longer, the worries slip from my lips.

"How am I going to be queen?"

The question settles between us, but before he can answer, my doubts and worries take over. "Getting to this point was what I always wanted. What I *thought* I always wanted. I'd finally be in control of my life. I wouldn't just be subjected to someone else's choices. I'd get to make my own. I got a taste of what life could be like, and I couldn't let it go. When I wasn't worthy, I wanted to stay on Dawnlin, just so I didn't have to give up that freedom. But now that it's here, I don't know if I can."

My throat screams when I fall silent, but I don't care. I had to get all of it out. His thumb halts, and I watch his shadowed face in the darkness, waiting for his response.

"Lennox, there is no question of going to be. You aren't going to be anything. You *are*. It is who you always have been, and who you always would become. It's only a title, nothing more. You are still Lennox Holt, whether 'queen' comes before your name, or not."

Lifting my hand, his lips press firmly onto my knuckles. "And you will always be my queen, even before you were officially."

Tears prick at my eyes, and I'm thankful for the darkness so he can't see them. I've cried so much recently, and I don't want him to see the mess I have become in the last few days. I want him to see the strong, fierce Lennox.

"Thank you for not letting me do this alone."

"I will never let you do anything else alone. Until the breath stills in my lungs, remember?" His voice is strong and insistent in the dark, and I know the exact look I would see in his eyes if I could.

"I remember."

"Good." He sets my hand on the mattress and rises before leaning over and brushing his lips over mine with another barely there touch. "Go back to sleep, my queen."

He steps away from the bed and crosses the room back toward the hearth, and the panicked feeling from before he returned comes back in full force.

"Where are you going?"

"I'm not leaving, sweetheart."

"Then where are you going? You said there isn't another threat, so you need to sleep too."

"I will." He lowers himself onto the chaise lounge and crosses his ankles in front of him. The glow from the fire outlines his body as he sinks back into the cushions and faces the door.

I stare at him across the room, and it's as if the weight of the entire day and the reality of what the future could be crush me where I lie. Weston has never intentionally harmed me. Instead he has done everything possible to ensure my well being and keep me safe, even back when I thought it was all an act.

But this hurts.

Watching him sleep across the room, after losing so many people I care about, feels like rejection. It feels like losing him too. Could my title or finally being back in Blackwood really change the way things are between us so drastically from what they were mere days ago?

My chest feels hollow as tears stream down my cheeks, but I hold my breath, trying to keep him from hearing my cries. I can't turn away. Between the pillows propped beneath me and the pain tonic that hasn't fully taken effect yet, all I can do is close my eyes and try not to let my thoughts spiral. The burning in my lungs from trying to hide the sound makes it impossible to do it any longer, and the swollen sniffling catches his attention. His boots pound across the room, and he's at my side again in barely a moment.

"Hey, I'm here. What's wrong? Where does it hurt?" He wipes the tears from my cheeks, though his touch is gentle, as if he's trying not to jostle me.

"What happened? Did I…did I do something wrong?" I croak. My voice is still hoarse, but the tonic from the healers has finally started working, and the pain has all but disappeared.

"What do you mean?" he grumbles.

"I've slept next to you for months," I murmur, "and now that we're back in the castle, it's just over?"

"That's why you're upset?" Guilt laces his voice, and his fingers press more firmly into my face.

"Of course, Weston! Today was the worst day of my life. I've lost my parents, my friends, my guard. I've been thrust into a position that, for my whole life, I've been made to feel like I would never do well in, and now in the blink of an eye, the entire kingdom is my responsibility. You're all I have left, and I've spent almost every moment with you since you took me off that beach, and now you don't want to be near me?"

My chest rises and falls with rapid breaths as I try and fail to squash down my feelings.

"No, Lennox, that is not at all how I feel. It's killing me that I can't touch you, not just because you're the queen and I'm your guard, but because I don't want to hurt you, not after everything you endured today. Don't ever think that I want to be anywhere but at your side."

The mattress dips as he leans closer, and his voice dips lower. "In my attempt not to hurt you, I ended up hurting you in a different way. I'm sorry. You have to know I never want to. But sweetheart, this isn't my ship. It's not my bed. Like you just said, today was one I never want to relive ever again. Not only was it the worst day of your life, but it was the worst of mine. I watched you die once before, and this time, I didn't think you were coming back to me.

"I am not strong enough to do it again, and all I want to do is hold on to you and never let you go. But I can't, not around anyone else. I already jeopardized enough back in that throne room today, but I didn't give a fuck who saw. I wasn't going to let you die alone or in anyone else's arms. You're mine, and if those were our final moments, I wasn't going to let duty and titles take them away from us.

"But they weren't, thank the gods, and now, learning to navigate this together is going to be a challenge. Things are going to be different from what they were. They have to be. And after the day you had, I didn't want to assume you wanted things to be just as they were when it was just you and me. I didn't want to overwhelm you or pressure you and especially didn't want to do anything that could hurt you. I should have asked. I'm sorry I didn't. But Lennox, never assume that anything has changed for me. It never will. I swore it to you. I keep my word."

I sniffle again, wishing I could really see his face, and unable to form any coherent thoughts after everything his words made me feel. He told me recently that he loved me like the men in my books, unconditionally and ardently, and I believe him. It will never change. The trauma from the day overshadowed what I should never have questioned.

"Will you just lie with me?" I ask, my voice small. "Please?"

He leans over me again, barely a breath away, and the warmth of his words melts away the worry coiling inside of me. "Of course, my queen. There's nowhere in this world or any other I would rather be." Weston kisses me gently before standing and rounding the other side of the bed.

"No outdoor clothes," I say into the darkness, and his low chuckle meets my ears.

"You must be feeling better. You're getting more of that tonic in the morning."

The sound of his belt being unbuckled rings through the quiet as he leans his sword against the bedside table. There's a rustle of fabric as he steps out of his boots and tosses his clothes to the floor before lifting the sheet and sliding in beside me.

Warmth emanates from his bare skin as I scoot my body closer and feel the pillows shift as he tugs them toward the center so I can still rest the muscles in my neck. The moment my body presses into his side, I let out a heavy breath, filled with all the worries and anxieties I have been holding in while he has been doing his duty as the First Guard.

He's back, and I feel like I'm home, like we're still on the ship, soaking in as much of each other as we can. Turning to the side, I lay my head on his chest, ignoring any pain from the movement, and listen to the slow and steady beating of his heart. Neither of us moves for a while, until Weston's fingers find my hair and he slowly strokes it, further lulling me into a deeper calm.

"This wasn't the new start at home I expected," I whisper.

"It wasn't for me either," he answers, "but I still have you. You're what I need."

"Me too, Weston," I say, and close my eyes, focusing on his rhythmic breathing, and the fact that I still can. "All I need is you."

CHAPTER THIRTY-THREE

For a few moments before I open my eyes, as I lay with my cheek pressed into Weston's chest, I forget everything that has happened. It feels like we're back in Dawnlin, waking up in the morning, unaware of what the day has in store for us. But then I feel the chill in the air against my skin, and a sharp pain in my neck, and everything comes rushing back.

I am the queen.

My father is dead.

I have a kingdom to run, but the healers, who I'm sure will bring me another dose of the pain tonic as soon as I send for it, require me to rest. I let out a deep sigh and open my eyes. The dim, grey light from the windows is still too bright for how exhausted I am.

I startle as my gaze falls on the warm body lying next to me, and stifle a gasp.

"Weston!" I hiss as my fingertips itch to touch his skin. Black and blue patches cover his entire torso, with red and swollen lumps in places they weren't before. Blood soaked bandages cover numerous gashes that clearly bled through the night. Stitches bring together the deeper wounds on his face, his arms. The skin across his knuckles is torn, and the beginnings of angry scabs match those of the rings around his wrists where he fought against the manacles.

My mouth falls open as I pull away, my hands hovering over him, afraid to touch him anywhere.

He lets out a gruff sound, and the arm snaked around my hips tightens, pulling me against him again.

"Don't run away. I'm fine." His voice is thick with sleep, and his eyes remain closed. I can't help but gawk at the evidence of what he told me last night.

I knew he fought to get to me. I could hear it. I could hear the guards beating him at Brynne and Guthrie's command, and his roars as he took on every single one of them. I believed what he said because I knew he would never just let anyone harm me, not after he was willing to give up his life, to become the Guardian by sliding his sword through Dane's throat, just to save me. Now though, no one would question his devotion to his oath, his duty, or his love for me.

I press a firm kiss against his ribs, and gently rest my hand on his abdomen.

This man will sacrifice everything for me. Being back here, in my rooms, in my bed, the place that I've spent the most time and felt aching waves of loneliness over the years, makes me realize how much I truly need him. How much I love him.

I am the queen now, and there is no question in my mind that I need to protect him the same way he would protect me. I close my eyes and drift back to sleep, silently making my own oath to him to do just that.

Weston takes the orders from the healers seriously and confines me to my rooms. Unless they are examining me for healing progress, bringing a pain tonic, or delivering meals, no one is allowed inside. Days pass, and we stay locked away together, allowing each of our bodies the rest it needs. Weston barely looks phased by his injuries, but doesn't let me do much besides lay with him and sit up to eat until I can move more freely and speak without wincing.

Every morning, he dresses in his uniform and leaves for hours as the staff questioning continues. He won't be satisfied until he feels no traitor has slipped through unnoticed, and has been busy restructuring the guards to ensure the castle is fortified with men who care for the kingdom, but even more so, are loyal to me.

One morning after the sheets were already cold where he slept, I woke to a stack of books and a note that read "This time, tell me what you're reading." I spent the afternoon getting lost in the stories. He must have snuck down to Tila's workroom because *The Maiden's Moonlit Venture* was sitting on the top of the pile. My cheeks heated and I couldn't help but smile as I recalled the last time I read that book, the night he returned from his first shift and the first night I knew there was something more forming between us.

A few days after, Weston and I sit together, on the settee after he returned from his morning with the guards. His arm rests casually along the back as he reads security reports from across Blackwood. I'm tucked into his side, reading a new book he brought back from the library in the city and drinking some tea filled with honey that Roxyana says will soothe my palate.

There's a soft knock at the door, and I turn my neck slowly to watch Weston rise and stride across the room. He unlatches the bolt and opens the door just enough to see, but uses his body to shield anyone from looking inside or getting past him.

"Is the queen open to a visitor?"

The familiar voice makes my chest warm with comfort, and I can't help the smile that turns up my lips. Weston looks over his shoulder at me for permission, and I chuckle at the thought that he would kick his own father out if I gave the word.

"Of course, Edmond. Come in."

I pull closed the sides of the warm robe I have over my nightgown. With no desire to leave, I haven't dressed as the queen should, and only did enough to keep the chill away. Weston holds the door open wider and steps to the side, allowing his father to enter before closing it and sliding the lock into place once more.

I set aside the book and smile up at Edmond as he takes a seat across the room in the chair next to the hearth. It has been difficult to feel happiness in the aftermath of everything. I've been thankful to feel safe and whole spending every day alongside Weston, but seeing Edmond brings me a little joy I know I've been missing.

Instead of returning to his seat beside me, Weston stands just behind the settee, his arms locked behind his back and the stoic look of the First Guard on his face. I pull my eyes away from him and look back to Edmond, who's gaze jumps between us with a soft smile on his face.

"After the events of the past days," Edmond starts, "I'm glad to see you both looking well. At least better than before."

With as observational as Edmond is and has taught me to be, it's unlikely he missed the ring of dark bruises around my neck and the bloodshot color to my eyes from losing so much air. The healers have assured me both will improve with time, but I can imagine for someone who saw me healthy every day, it might look shocking.

"Much better," I say. "The healers have been very attentive."

"As they should, Your Majesty," Edmond says with a nod. "And you, son?" He looks to Weston behind me. His eyes are hopeful, yet misted over, the same way he looked when he first told me about his son in the library all that time ago.

"I'm fine," Weston says, then clears his throat. "It's good to see you, Pop."

Edmond's smile grows wider, before he leans back into the cushions of the chair and props his head on his hand in the thoughtful way he always does.

"I'm glad to hear it. Though it has been quite a while now, I do still believe I know you better than you sometimes know yourself." He looks back to me. "*Both* of you. Neither of you are fooling me. Do not be formal on my account."

My mouth parts in surprise, and I don't move, not until I hear heavy footsteps round the settee. Weston falls back into his seat beside me and crosses his ankle over his knee as his hand comes to rest on the inside of my thigh.

"I assumed as much." Edmond chuckles lightly, but his gaze stays assessing, bouncing from the lack of space separating our bodies, and the comfortable, albeit too intimate way Weston's hands are on me. My cheeks heat at the thought of what is going through Edmond's mind.

"Did you come for a visit, or just to prove yourself right?" I can hear the smile in Weston's voice, and my stomach tumbles at the ease and familiarity growing in this room.

"You should know, my boy, I do not need to see anything to know I am right. Although, seeing with my own eyes brings me joy, for many reasons. Can't a father want to behold the son he hasn't seen for close to twenty-three years? Or visit with his dear queen who has been gone for far too long?"

My chest clenches and I fight back a smile. Even though I welcomed the joy when Edmond walked in the room, it still feels wrong amidst all this sadness and loss. "I think we both know you better than that. What's on your mind, Edmond?"

"Ah, yes. Well, as you may know, Your Majesty—"

"Lennox, Edmond. You've always called me Lennox."

"I have, however, this occasion will call for the formality, as you will see in a moment."

The quiet feeling of being disobedient as a child prickles at my skin, but I squash it down. "I'm sorry I interrupted, that was rude of me. You taught me better than that. Please continue."

"Of course, Your Majesty. With the…recent events, and the passing of your father, Blackwood now falls to you, something of which I am sure you are aware as we have been preparing you for it since childhood."

"I am aware," I nod. "Although I was not expecting it so soon."

"None ever are. But that leads me to the topic of discussion for today. Steps need to be taken, procedures initiated to have a successful transition into your reign. First, the entire kingdom will need to be notified that the king has passed. It is required in order to begin the mourning period before planning the funeral and your coronation."

My head spins as the reality I've hidden from between the pages of my books comes crushing down on me. I blink at him rapidly as I try to process all the things I have been avoiding thinking about, and now, I can't any longer.

"You will need to select your advisors and make any changes to the staff for how you would like the castle run. The other kingdoms will also need to be notified about the conveyance of power, and no doubt there will be many who want to speak to the new queen."

Reeling, I shake my head, and my brows furrow. "Of course. I knew all of this would come, I just didn't want to think about it yet. Would you mind if we started tomorrow? Of course, you are the one I trust above everyone else, and there is no question that I choose you, Edmond."

"Yes, well," he says with a small nod. "I would be remiss if I said I did not know you would choose me, but I am afraid, Your Majesty, I have to decline and offer my formal resignation from duties for the kingdom."

My jaw falls open, and I gape silently at him.

Resign? How could Edmond resign? In the time I need him the most, the time I need my tutor, my advisor, the man who shaped me into the future ruler, he's leaving? Weston's hand tenses on my thigh, but he says nothing.

"I don't understand," I say, shaking my head slightly. "Did I do something? Did something happen before we came back?"

"Nothing you did could have affected my decision, Your Majesty. However, something *did* in fact happen."

Edmond reaches beneath his coat, the same way he did when he pulled out my mother's diary, but instead, my breath catches in my throat when I see what he's holding.

Weston jumps to his feet and we both stare at the lump of familiar fabric, this time not dangling and empty, but round and full, with a golden glow emanating from above the golden tassel that ties it closed.

"What are you doing with that?" Weston growls. "I've been searching for it, and you've had it this entire time?"

"I see your time away did not change your ferocity," Edmond says. I would laugh if I wasn't in complete disbelief of what Edmond is holding, and can do nothing other than stare and wait for an explanation. "You may compose yourself. I simply did not want it falling into the hands of someone who did not know what it meant, or—" Edmond's voice trails off and his face softens as he looks at his son. "Someone who did, but did not deserve to have that decision made for them without the proper knowledge."

"Edmond, what are you saying?" I whisper, and fix my eyes on the pouch that brought us here mere days ago, the one that holds the power to give hope or take it away. The one the Castaways had been searching to fill for years.

Edmond smiles at me softly, as if he knows I've figured it out.

I need to hear the words, the truth. Weston needs to hear it.

"I cannot continue with my duties in Blackwood, because I have new responsibilities and duties, for Dawnlin. As the Guardian."

My hand flies to my mouth as I can't hold back the gasp this time. Weston's arms lift, his hands settling on the back of his head as his fingers grip his hair. The look of shock and disbelief quickly overtakes his expression.

"What do you mean, as the Guardian?" Weston barks.

"Let me explain—"

"How do you know what that is?" he says. "How did you even know he had it to take it?" Weston gestures to the pouch still in Edmond's hands.

"My boy," he says gently, "I know far more than I have ever been able to tell you."

Been able to tell you.

That can only mean one thing.

"Edmond...you've been to Dawnlin?" I ask breathlessly.

"*What?*" Weston snaps, his head whipping back and forth between us. "When? I would have known. How did you keep it from me?"

"Please, son, sit. I will tell you everything you wish to know, now that I can."

Weston lets out a sigh as he drops heavily down beside me. He leans forward, resting his elbows on his bent knees and holding his head in his hands. Reaching out, I graze my fingernails across his low back, reminding him with the touch that he craves that he's not alone in all of this. With as shocking as it is for me to learn that Edmond only told me about Dawnlin because he had been there, I can imagine it is worse for him.

Once Edmond determines we have settled, he starts.

"I am now the Guardian of Dawnlin. The magic of the island that lies within this dust will bring me back to it, and I will be ready and waiting for the next call."

"But how?" I ask, unable to hide the disbelief in my voice. "You didn't kill Dane. My father did, and ultimately Dane was responsible for his death. How then are you the Guardian?"

"It is interesting that on an island that helps bring about life, you believe that death creates its protector." Edmond looks blankly at me, the same way he did growing up when he was trying to get me to think about something. I blink at him, keeping my mouth sealed shut, hoping he will continue explaining, and am relieved when he does.

"The magic of Dawnlin does not lie with the person who is granted the title of Guardian. It lies with the magic inside this pouch. Once there was no longer a Guardian of Dawnlin, the moment I obtained the vessel that holds the magic, I became the new Guardian."

My jaw slackens as his words hit me. All this time, the Castaways thought the Guardian was created by the death of the previous one. How could they not? Sig and Weston had no other knowledge of this place, only what they saw happen before their eyes. But they were wrong.

"It was with the dust all along?" I ask. "It wasn't because Dane killed the previous Guardian?"

Edmond shakes his head. "No, Your Majesty. It was because he was the first to procure the dust."

Weston's face falls into his hands, and his frustrated growl echoes through the room. "This entire time, I could have fucking killed him, and it wouldn't have meant anything. We could have rid the island of him, and it would have been done."

"But you know you would have grabbed the pouch first," I say as my hand flattens on his back. "You wouldn't have let anyone else take it."

He turns his head slightly and shoots me a look, which I return.

"You know I'm right."

Shoulders rising and falling with a heavy sigh, he looks forward again, his hands still wringing through his hair.

"Which," Edmond interjects, "is why I could not allow that to happen."

Both our heads snap toward him, only to find a satisfied smile.

Weston drops his hands as his back straightens. "You did it so I wouldn't become the Guardian?"

"I did it because I thought neither of you should become the Guardian. But, I could not let my son, who has already sacrificed so much, lose his chance at a normal life and happiness. I did not want that decision taken away from you without your knowledge, especially after the last twenty or so years."

My throat tightens, and I swallow down the lump. Edmond wasn't there. He didn't see the way Weston gave himself to his crew, and sacrificed everything he wanted to keep them all safe, but he knows that the man who left his kingdom to help his best friend have happiness once again deserves his turn to have the same.

"*How* do you know this, Pop?" Weston implores. "How did I never know you went to Dawnlin?"

"You were very young when I left, and I was not gone for long." Edmond's face falls slightly, but he tries to hide it with a soft smile. "I returned just after your mother died."

Weston's mouth falls open and his eyes widen in realization. The nightmares, the ones he told me about where he relives the night his mother died.

Please don't leave.

He was begging his father to stay, begging Edmond to stay, because he was leaving to call the Guardian. He was trying to find the healing waters to save her life, but he was too late.

And he could never speak of it.

"You got them," I say, my voice barely a whisper. "You were worthy."

Edmond nods solemnly. "I was, but by the time I returned, my love was already gone. I never got to say goodbye, nor could I ever utter a word as to where I was or why."

Weston's jaw ticks at his father's recollection of that night, which is so different from the one the once young boy remembers. "You still haven't explained how you know all of this. There's nothing written anywhere on that island. We checked everywhere, and everything written in this kingdom is too vague."

"Neither of you will be surprised to hear that I simply talked to the man. Though I was pressed for time, I still needed to know as much as I could about the magic I was about to trust, and Horace agreed."

"Horace?" I ask. "Who is Horace?"

"The Guardian before, I am assuming the same one who brought you." He nods to Weston. "He did not hold back, of course, knowing I could not speak of the magic once I returned to our world. He seemed very obliged to talk about it with someone. It makes sense that most who seek out Dawnlin are singularly focused. He was very kind and educational."

"So you knew that the dust decides the next Guardian," Weston says. "But you also knew how to replenish it."

"I did."

"Light always finds a way," I say, and Edmond's smile widens.

"I am delighted to see my lesson stuck. It was a rather useful metaphor, for more than just providing you with the knowledge of how to get home."

"But how did you know we would need to know that?" Weston asks. "How did you know the dust would run out?"

"One can never be unprepared for all possibilities. Without being able to speak of Dawnlin more than telling the well-known myth, I had to ensure that in the event you could not return, time would give you the way home. I had to come to terms with the fact that I might not be able to see you if the worst did happen. And so it did. But as I said, it was a useful lesson in more than one way."

"But we can talk about it now. Why? Why couldn't I say its name when I tried days ago, but now, there's nothing stopping us?" Weston asks.

"I assume it is because I am the Guardian, and you two already know about the island, have been there, and are not blind to the secrets. I would assume if someone who knows nothing of the island were to walk in, you would be bound to secrecy once more."

"I have a question," I ask, falling back so easily into my learned patterns with my tutor.

"Your Majesty, please." Edmond bows his head slightly, urging me to continue.

I search his face, trying to read the man who knows so well how to hide his true intentions, but I don't want him to hide behind anything right now. I want to know the truth. "You sent me to bring him home."

Weston's gaze pins his father to the chair, and I know he wants to hear the answer as well.

"I sent you to help your mother," Edmond says. "I would be insincere if I said that I didn't have hope that with you there, he might also find a way home. If a way home was not possible after he had been gone for so long, then at least he would no longer be alone."

"But why me?"

Edmond clasps his hands in his lap, the same way he does whenever he gives me a lengthy explanation.

"You two share quite a few similarities that, based on your familiarity with each other, you have already noticed. Fiercely loyal. Stubborn. Intelligent. But I held onto hope that your tender heart would give him a reason to show the one he keeps hidden away under his rough exterior."

Weston grunts in response, and Edmond shoots me a look as if to say, 'See?'

My nose burns and my eyes well with tears, but Weston shakes his head and huffs a laugh.

"You've always been a meddling son of a bitch, Pop."

"Weston!" I shove his shoulder, and he finally sits back, relaxing into the cushions and pressing his side against mine once more.

"Don't punish him for his honesty, Your Majesty. He knows me well. I did indeed hope you two would at least develop a friendship with your shared goals and similar history."

"You knew I wouldn't age," Weston says, a statement, not a question.

"I did. That is one of the things Horace explained. The land is timeless."

Silence falls between us as the heaviness of the conversation settles in the room. Now that we know Edmond is the Guardian, that he's been bound to secrecy of his knowledge and has influenced our actions up until this point, there's only one more thing to discuss.

And no one wants to be the one to bring it up.

Weston finally breaks the silence, and I feel a pang in my chest at his words.

"So I finally come home, and I'm just supposed to say goodbye to you too? Again?" His voice is thick and laced with pain I know he's trying to hide. He's lost his oldest friend, his crew, and now his father, all within a few days. Some goodbyes we expected, but others have been unexpected and difficult to accept.

"Unfortunately, yes." Edmond's jaw tenses, and it hits me like a bolt of lightning. I see so much of Weston in him, things I didn't realize before, but there is no doubt at all, despite their differences in appearance, that Weston is Edmond's son.

"Although," Edmond continues, "I do expect things will be quite different now. While I may not reside at the castle, I believe we will see each other again, however frequently both your and my responsibilities allow."

Sadness wraps around me, and I let my shoulders sag under the weight. It isn't just Weston losing him; it's me too. Edmond was the only remaining family either of us had, and now we only have each other. I lean back, trying to keep him from seeing my reaction to Edmond's news. Weston always takes on the emotional burden of those he cares about, and I don't want to cause him more pain, even though we both are losing everything. Together.

"Besides." Edmond presses his hands into his knees and pushes to stand. "It is high time you started your own lives. It will bring me great happiness to continue to watch you both do so, however you choose."

Tears blur my vision once again, and I know if I blink they will fall.

"Thank you, Edmond. For everything. All of it."

Looking toward Weston, I find him already watching me, and I turn away with the fear that I'll start crying too hard if I keep looking. "I'll miss you."

"And I you, Your Majesty. May I join you for a meal tonight, before I ready my things, and set my affairs in order? I would like to be present for the king's funeral, but I do so want to hear about your time on Dawnlin."

"No, you don't," Weston says with a wince, and a burst of giggles erupts from my chest.

"Oh, you mean you don't want to tell him about how you stole my dagger and then used it to take me captive?"

He scrubs his palm down his face. "You were trying to stab me! What did you want me to do?"

"Not take me captive, that's first of all."

"It was for your own good," he mumbles, and I laugh, before looking back to Edmond, to find his eyes shining as he watches us bicker.

"Well," he breathes and clasps his hands together. "It seems we will have quite a bit to talk about over dinner."

"At least she'll be eating this time." Weston shoots Edmond a glare and is only met with a beaming smile.

"I'm looking forward to hearing all the details."

"Maybe not all of them," Weston murmurs so only I can hear, and I try to stifle a smile.

Edmond crosses the room and unbolts the door before turning back to me and dropping into a deep bow. "Your Majesty."

"See you soon, Edmond."

The door closes behind him, and I sag into Weston's side, pressing my cheek against his chest.

"The Guardian," I murmur, and he lets out a sigh.

"Yeah."

The silence is heavy, marred only by the crackle of the dwindling fire. After all the worry about becoming the Guardian, or doing everything to prevent it from happening, the magic still took one of the people closest to me.

But it didn't take Weston.

"I'm sad to see him go, but I understand why he did it. I would have lost you," I whisper as I play with a button on his shirt.

His hand cups my cheek, and his fingers wind through the hair at the back of my head.

"You'll never lose me." He tilts my neck gently then leans forward, giving me a soft kiss before pulling away slightly.

"I had to deal with the loss of my father a long time ago. I was so happy to finally see him again, and make up for the time we lost together. Though now we can't, this feels less final than when I accepted his loss before. I'm still sad."

I search his eyes and see the sadness there, no longer hidden from me, and it makes my own break through.

"Why are we losing everyone around us?"

"Some people are only meant to be in our lives for a short period of time. They show up when we need them, or when they need us, and then life goes on. Not every person is meant to be forever. Maybe Pop has taught us everything we need to know, and now he can move on to help the next person."

Weston shifts his body and lifts his legs so he's lying along the length of the settee, arms flexing as he lifts me and pulls me over him. I sink into the back cushions and wrap myself around his body, soaking up his warmth and listening to the beat of his heart under my ear.

"I do still need to talk to him though," he says, his low voice grumbling in his chest. He lazily strokes the skin down the length of my arm, sending tingles cascading across my skin. I close my eyes and try not to let the sadness about letting people go take over, especially when I have the one I need right beside me. "He might be a meddler, but I have a lot to thank him for."

CHAPTER THIRTY-FOUR

A thick gold frame surrounds my clear reflection as I nervously smooth out the wrinkles in the first dress I've worn in years. Tila will scold me if I look like a mess the first time I emerge from this room as queen. The dress is simple, but detailed enough so that everyone who was not in the throne room, everyone who is seeing me for the first time will have no doubts that things have changed.

The woman staring back at me isn't the girl who stood here years ago, getting ready to leave her kingdom for a chance at a better life. Though she looks almost the same, I can see the subtle differences. The sun-kissed skin that will surely fade the longer she is away from true sunlight. The set of her shoulders pulled back and ready to speak her mind. The glitter in her eye that has known hope but has also seen despair.

She's endured so much in such a short time. She's learned to trust, been betrayed, and learned to trust again. She's learned to love and be loved, not only by a man, but by friends who made her feel whole. She's lived and hoped and grown, all because she found the strength inside herself to leave the place that held her back, and find something more.

And now she's the queen.

I wasn't prepared for my life to change so drastically before I even had time to catch my breath or readjust to the cold, but I have no choice now.

A tall, broad frame appears in the reflection behind me, and I feel Weston's warm hands settle on the curve of my hips. He leans down and presses a kiss into the side of my neck, right over the skin that is still purple and blue.

"You look beautiful, my queen," he murmurs against my skin, and goosebumps cover all the exposed flesh that peeks out of the tight bodice. He presses another kiss just above the last, as his arms circle my middle and pull me against his body. Resting his cheek on my hair, he meets my gaze in the mirror.

"I can hear you thinking."

I grasp his forearms tightly and let out a heavy sigh. "I'm not ready to do this."

"You don't have to," he murmurs. "I will take care of everything as long as you give me permission."

"But I need to. I will regret it if I don't."

His eyes soften as he holds my gaze in the mirror, and I try not to notice the nerves etched into my face.

"It's normal to doubt yourself and feel you can't do something, while still staying strong and confident on the outside. If you only knew how many times I look like I know what I'm doing, but inside is a raging storm. You've already seen some."

I think back to what times he might be referencing, because I've never thought Weston didn't have every confidence in his decisions or his abilities. Even when he had the tip of his sword pressed into Dane's neck, he looked as sure as ever. But back at the ship, back in the infirmary, he looked ready to explode, and couldn't even speak to me. My chest tightens at the thought that he was suffering inside more than he was showing.

His thumb slides across the dress at my waist, his slow caress a comfort. "It's alright to feel like you're falling. No one needs to know except for the person standing behind, ready to catch you."

My voice is small when I answer. "I might need you to catch me."

"Always, my queen."

I straighten, and Weston follows suit, but one hand stays pressed into the small of my back. "Alright. Let's go."

He leads me through the room and opens the door widely, stepping to the side and waiting for me to pass. The moment we are out in the open, his hand drops away, and he lets me take the lead, falling into step closely behind. Our footsteps echo in sync on the stone, and I try to pretend that this is just another walk on the island, back before we knew each other intimately, when he always stood at my back to make sure I didn't actually fall.

I've been dreading this moment for days and doing my best not to think about it as it loomed over us, but I need to move forward. Move on. I'd gone my entire life without being in this part of the castle, and now, after everything and the memories it holds, I want to stay away from it for another twenty-three years. Unfortunately, there is no other option.

The corridors leading toward the dungeon get colder as we descend, and I'm grateful for the thick fabric and long sleeves that help ward off the chill. That we survived down here in the cold after leaving the humid heat of the island still amazes me, and I make a mental note to tell Weston to ensure the prisoners are kept warm.

They may be traitors, but I'm not a monster. That isn't the queen I want to be.

A new set of guards was assigned to the dungeon antechamber after Weston questioned the involvement of the previous set, and he must have made sure they were aware we were coming. When I step into the doorway, they are already standing at attention, waiting for us to pass through.

"My queen," Weston mumbles, and I step to the side, giving him just enough room to pass by. He strides across the room and pulls open the dungeon door before stepping to the side and ushering me through.

"Your Majesty," the guards say in unison as they each fall into a deep bow when I pass by. The keys on a large ring jingle as the guard closest to him reaches out and hands them to Weston, before he wordlessly leads me through the corridor. I follow a few paces behind, trying to slow my breathing and push away the memories of Weston being overpowered and beaten the last time I walked through these halls.

"Back away from the bars!" Weston shouts, the threat of enforcement clear in his voice. He turns back toward me, and his voice lowers to a murmur. "Stand near the wall as far from the cell as you can."

I nod, and my agreement must be enough for him because he turns back and continues to lead us through the dark and frigid hallway.

"On your feet for your queen!" he barks again. The command is followed by the scuffle of movement from some cells, but it is obvious it did not come from all of them.

I pull my shoulders back as we walk, keeping my chin held high. I refuse to let any of them see any of the vulnerability I feel coursing through my body. It will also ensure that they see firsthand what I endured and survived in their failed attack.

As I pass by, I look into each cell but don't recognize most of the guards locked away. Some cells have multiple men inside, despite Weston's command to keep them separate, and it makes me sick to my stomach to think that we didn't have enough cells for the number of guards involved in the plot.

When I see Storm lying across the floor, staring at the ceiling with his head resting on his hands, I scowl. Of course he isn't on his feet. I'm not his queen. Storm isn't from Blackwood. I knew the moment I shook his hand back at camp that it was customary to another kingdom. So why was he involved? Why, after all that time on Dawnlin, did he follow Dane like this?

We pass Guthrie, who also refused to stand, but unlike Storm, he sits with his back pressed to the stone wall, sneering. His beady eyes track me as we walk by, and I don't break the contact. He deserves to know that he didn't break me; that his words were only that, words. He may have been a snake, waiting for the right time to strike, but in the end, he did not win.

Weston slows as we approach the last cell, and I already know who I am about to come face to face with: one of the three people I thought cared about me for most of my life.

Surprisingly, Brynne is actually standing with her gaze trained forward and her hands held behind her back. When we stop in front of the thick iron bars, I step back as Weston instructed, giving him the foreground, but staying directly in front of her.

I want to look into her eyes as she tells me everything.

Or lies to my face.

"It is only because of the mercy shown by your queen that you are able to plead your case," Weston says as he steps closer to her cell. His eyes narrow, and she refuses to look at him. "Your time starts now."

"I have nothing to say." Her tone is sharp, her mouth forming a line, but her face gives away nothing.

"I find that hard to believe. You manipulated the queen for years, lied to the crown, plotted to overthrow the king, and then murder the heir. Start talking."

"I don't deny it, and I know nothing I say will change whatever decision I'm sure you have already made for me. I know how this works." Her stony gaze stays locked on the wall above me, and she looks completely unfazed that her life is about to change.

When I told Weston I wanted to be here for the questioning instead of having him report the details to me, I swore I was only going to listen. I didn't want to get involved. The weight of having some of my greatest fears realized, that she had been plotting against me for years and that our relationship, our friendship, was never real and was only part of her duty, her fake duty at that, was too much for me to handle.

But now that I stare her down, and recall the last conversation we had about her being proud of me, of wanting me to find Dawnlin, of worrying for my safety, all I feel is hatred.

"What kingdom are you from?" I snap. Her eyes fall to mine, but she stays silent.

"After what you did to me," I snap, taking two quick steps toward the bars, "the bare minimum you owe me is answers." From the corner of my eye, I watch Weston shift closer to my side, but my eyes stay trained on her.

"Nafria."

"How long were you…there?" I feel the tug of something in my throat when I try to utter Dawnlin's name, and I know instantly it is the magic, preventing me from spilling secrets to those who can hear from the other cells.

"I don't know exactly. Eight? Ten years? It wasn't easy to keep track."

"Why did you do it?" I grind out. It's the only question I really want answered. Why? Why did she choose me to be the victim of her lies and deceit, especially when I was so young? I'd done nothing but look up to her.

She glares at me, her jaw clenching and unclenching as the seconds drag on.

Weston loses his patience, and his growl echoes off the stone. "Your queen asked you why you manipulated and betrayed her. Give her a fucking answer."

"Well, that's just it, isn't it?" Brynne snaps, finally turning to address him. "She wouldn't have any clue about the real motivations behind what I did, because she was always going to be the queen. She sits here with her fancy clothes, in her big castle, with every need met.

She never even had to leave to work for what she wanted. She doesn't know what it is like to have nothing, to fight just to live. When someone offered me the opportunity for us to switch places, I fucking took it. Who cares if one little spoiled princess had to die to get what I wanted? It was worth it."

Weston's eyes darken at the mention of my death, and I can almost feel the tension roiling off his body.

"He offered you my kingdom," I say directly.

"He loved me!" she cries, her stony mask finally cracking, as she turns her attention back to me. Her eyes glaze over, and there's a slight quiver to her chin, but she doesn't stop. "We were going to sit on the throne together. That is what all of this was for—to finally have my place, a place that I *earned*, alongside him!"

"He didn't love you," I grind out. "He used you."

She scoffs. "How would you know? You weren't there. You know nothing!"

A bitter laugh erupts from my throat, and I try hard not to look at Weston. He knows what Dane was to me before him. He watched it all. I'm not hiding anything from him, but I still don't like speaking about it in front of him.

Right now, I have no choice.

"I know more than you think. I know he was great at making you feel loved and seen, and giving you so many promises for what your future could be. He made you feel needed and wanted, but every single touch, every single word, was all a plot to get to his end. His goal. Which was never you or me. It was my mother."

"It wasn't." Her voice trembles through her gritted teeth. "He only saw her as his path to the throne. He told me the exact plan!"

I laugh again, this time with the bitterness gone and replaced by utter disbelief. "And I thought he had *me* fooled." I shake my head, my jaw slackened as everything I want to say to her races through my mind, but I settle on one last question.

"Was any of it real?"

Her gaze hardens, and she shakes her head.

"No."

Nodding slowly, I choose my next words carefully, and I barely recognize my icy voice as it falls on my ears.

"I thought you were my friend, Brynne. The one person who stood behind me for more than just her duty. I trusted you. I cared about you. But once again, I was deceived because I was weak and naïve. Despite all that, you helped teach me a valuable lesson. I won't ever let anyone walk into this castle or my life ever again without being picked apart."

I square my shoulders toward her and relax my face as I try to hide the flame of anger that is threatening to burn into an inferno. This next command isn't coming from Lennox. It is coming from the queen, and I refuse to let my emotions bleed through.

"Briony Couling, you are henceforth sentenced to exile. You are stripped of your rights and protections of the kingdom of Blackwood. You are dishonorably discharged from the position you falsely obtained as the Second Guard, and by admission of guilt, you are convicted of conspiring against the crown, and assisting in regicide."

The moment the formality has left my lips, my voice drops low, my tone so deadly I barely recognize it. All the fury I suppressed as the queen surges to the surface, as Lennox stands tall in her place.

"You are a fucked up, miserable, lonely person, who cared more about herself than being a decent human being. And now, you're going to spend the rest of your life in exile. I pray to the gods that you never have a day of peace knowing that I won, and you didn't."

Weston clears his throat beside me. "My queen, I hear Berrendahr has a very secure island prison for exiled civilians."

A laugh bubbles out of my chest.

What sweet justice, sending Brynne to an island prison where she will live the rest of her life, just as she and Dane left us to.

"Send her immediately. Tell Signee to have fun with her." I step toward the bars again and see tears welling in Brynne's eyes. "He may have manipulated and used you too, but I don't feel even the smallest bit of sympathy. Not when you were responsible for killing my father, almost killing me, sentencing my mother to death, and ruining the lives of everyone I love. You deserve this future. You chose this, and I won't miss you, Brynne."

I turn on my heel and stalk back down the hallway, but stop short when I come to Guthrie. Weston doesn't miss a beat, matching my pace and keeping his distance with my abrupt stop.

"What are your commands for the rest of them, my queen?"

"I'll hear their cases individually, then make my decision starting tomorrow."

"And with him?"

I turn and glare at a man I barely know, but who doesn't deserve to disgrace the uniform he still wears.

"Exile. Get him out of my kingdom." I start forward again, but before I make it more than a few paces, I stop, turning quickly to approach the bars. Looking down my nose at the man who has been glaring at me with hatred, one corner of my lips turns up in a smug smirk. "I guess I'm not a piss-poor excuse for a queen after all."

His eyes narrow, but I don't stay long enough to let him respond. I turn on my heel and continue onward. We haven't even been here an hour, but I feel emotionally drained. I have one more cell to stop at before I cannot handle any more duties for the day.

He's still lying on the ground when I approach, and even though I know he sees me, he doesn't move a muscle.

"Why?" It's all I ask, all I need to know. I barely knew Storm, but I watched as he walked around the island, hunting the Castaways. Hunting me. Why did he care so much that he was willing to go along with Dane's plan? What was in it for him?

"He promised me money. Land. A title."

While I was furious with Brynne, I feel nothing at Storm's response. He did this for wealth, and knowing the island kept the healing waters from him, making it clear that it didn't trust him to find them, I can't say I'm surprised.

"That's all?"

"It was enough for me."

I make a sound of disgust, and step away, refusing to give him another moment of my energy. Someone who will play along with a plot to murder innocent people solely for material things doesn't deserve it.

I hold my head high, and barrel out of the dungeons, the blur of the cells and the slam of the doors behind me the only thing I hear until I am back in the regular halls of my castle. I can feel Weston behind me. His presence is only slightly calming to the raging chaos inside me.

It hits me how different I feel as my footsteps pound on the stone floor. I've only ever shown rage like that to a few people, and one of them is still standing behind me. If I had before, no one would have listened, but now? Now they do. Because it isn't the princess speaking, or just Lennox. It's the queen, and it feels different. Like Weston said, I have always been the queen, but now, everyone around me sees it.

Weston's low grumble pulls me from my thoughts, and my already pounding heart quickens even more. This time, it's not with fury, but with fear as what he says and the implications of it register.

"Get back to your room. *Now.*"

CHAPTER THIRTY-FIVE

The urgency in Weston's voice is unmistakable. His tone isn't foreign to me, and it makes my spine stiffen. I don't question his command and instead keep my expression blank and do what he said. Something tipped him off, making him concerned for my safety. I don't know what it was. Nothing I heard or saw gave me any pause, but he's different. This is his duty, his training, his responsibility, and I know he is being even more vigilant than normal after what happened days ago.

Weaving through the hallways, I never slow, and instead speed up just slightly. Weston matches my pace, and I feel a flash of relief when my door comes into sight. My composed facade falls the moment I step through the doorway, and I spin around, the fabric of the large skirt rustling just as the lock slams back into place.

"What's wro—"

Weston's lips crash into mine, cutting my words off and stealing my breath away. His hands wrap around my face, and his thumb presses into my chin, gently coaxing my mouth open. I sigh into his kiss, and it's obvious how wrong I was.

His voice wasn't filled with urgency out of protection.

It was out of desire.

His tongue dives into my mouth, insistently stroking against mine and a flicker of longing lights inside of me. The last time he kissed me like this was when we stood on the deck of his ship, right before we came home. Too much has happened since then, and I could tell he was being gentle with me after all the abuse my body endured.

Something changed his mind.

That flicker of desire blazes when he turns me around, never breaking the kiss even as he walks me backward until my back hits the wall next to the door. His lips and tongue are demanding, his grip possessive as he presses his body into mine. I fist the uniform at his sides, and tug him closer, encouraging him even more. When he tears his mouth away from mine, I have to gasp for a breath. My chest heaves, pushing against his torso as he presses fierce kisses into my jaw before trailing them down my neck.

"I don't think I have ever wanted to fuck you more, my queen," he growls into my skin.

"I doubt that," I get out between pants. His tongue swirls over a sensitive spot on my neck before he sucks it between his teeth, and I let out a low moan.

The responding chuckle is low and sultry, and I don't know what to focus on. Between his demanding tongue and lips, the desire in his voice, and the pressure of his hands on my body, pushing me into the wall as firmly as he is gripping me, I'm completely overwhelmed.

"What did I do?" My voice is breathy as my chest rises and falls rapidly, trying to catch up to what he stole with his mouth moments ago.

"Exist." He lets out a hot sigh against my skin before trailing his lips across my exposed collarbone. "And then showed me that fire the I fell in love with." I huff out a laugh and my head falls back, exposing more of my neck to him as he continues licking and sucking the skin down my chest. My back arches slightly, the movement involuntary the closer he gets to my breast, and I feel my hardened nipples rubbing against the tight bodice.

A low rumble from deep in his chest meets my ears as soon as he notices the shift of my body. "I can't decide if I like it better directed at someone else, or at me. Might have to test it a few more times so I can decide."

Unrelenting hands slide across the bodice of my dress to the back, and I feel myself tugged away from the wall, just enough to give his hands space. The bodice loosens barely a moment later, the top falling forward and exposing my peaked nipples over the edge. My back presses into the wall once again, as one hand splays across the front of my hip, holding me in place as he nips at the skin on the top of my breast.

"Did you take your pain tonic this morning?" he asks as he straightens to his full height, his eyes scanning mine waiting for an answer.

"Yes." I don't look away. I'm being honest, I took it, the same as I have every morning and evening since the incident in the throne room, but I know it's the exact answer he's looking for. I know he's tired of treating me like I'm going to break, but he still doesn't want me to be in any pain.

His eyes darken as he slowly closes the space between us.

"Good girl."

The free hand fists in the hair at the nape of my neck, tugging gently to angle my head to his before his lips find mine again. Our tongues dance together as he continues to devour me, as if he never stopped, as if he will cease to exist if he doesn't consume me.

My skin buzzes with anticipation as the hand on my hip slides up my stomach before wrapping around the top of my dress, and yanking it down further loosening it. Deft fingers find my hardened nipple, and I hum against his tongue, just before he rolls it firmly between his finger and thumb causing heat to pool between my thighs. I moan into his mouth and he breaks away with a low chuckle.

"Shh," he says against my lips. "Someone will hear you."

My head feels hazy, and I can barely focus on his words instead of the touch of his hand. His fingers release my nipple, leaving my heavy breasts falling out of the top of my dress, as his hand slides down the front of my dress, his fingers fisting the fabric as he bunches up the skirt.

He seals his lips over mine again, but when his soft command finally registers in my mind, I shake my head and push him away.

"Doesn't that feel wrong?"

My whole body shudders as his fingers find my skin beneath the hem of my bunched dress. The barest brush of his fingertips up my inner thigh turns my insides molten, making it almost impossible to focus on what I was saying.

"Nothing with you ever feels wrong, Lennox." His teal eyes bore into mine, and I latch onto them and stare back.

"That's not what I mean."

There's a flash of hurt in his eyes. "Then what do you mean?"

The hurt is replaced by darkened desire once again as his fingers slide beneath the lace edge of my undergarments above my thigh, and a shuddering breath escapes my chest.

"I don't like hiding."

The muscle in his cheek flickers as he clenches his jaw. "You know that if anyone finds out that an unmarried queen is fucking her guard, it will diminish any future marriage prospects. I will not do anything that will jeopardize your opportunities as queen, especially if it is for the good of the kingdom. I'm not worth that."

My eyes widen in shock but also anger. "You're not—" I sputter, but he presses a finger to my lips.

"In whatever way you'll have me. That was my promise. I intend to keep it."

Pushing his arm away from my face, glare at him. "I'm the queen. I can do what I want and change any tradition or rule that I want. My father didn't marry for an alliance, so why would the queen be required to?"

He lets out a breath through his nose. "No, he didn't. But you're not your father. Do what *you* think is best for the kingdom."

I fist the shirt at his chest again, holding him firmly and looking him square in the eye, pleading with him to understand all the emotion and love behind my words. "But you're what's best for me."

He shakes his head, his eyes squeezing shut like it pains him to even think about the consequences of any decision. When his eyes fly open a moment later, every feeling his gaze held is gone, and the desire I get lost in is back in place.

"That's enough talking," he grumbles, and his mouth presses into mine, his tongue filling me so even if I tried, I couldn't speak anymore.

Pleasure and anticipation throbs through my core as his hand finally slips beneath the lace and finds the wet heat at the apex of my thighs.

"You're already soaked for me," he grumbles as his fingers stroke me tenderly. My body screams for him to fill me, to press inside and touch me where I want him most. Pleading for any bit of pressure, my back arches and my hips press into his hand, but he pulls back as far as the fabric will allow, refusing to give me what I want. His tongue dives deep, silencing a whimper as a single finger circles just inside my entrance, making my whole body jolt. My knees weaken, threatening to buckle beneath me. Grabbing hold of the corded muscle in both of his arms, I squeeze tightly, holding myself upright as my mind spins, lost in all the sensation.

The moment two fingers press inside me, he breaks the kiss, his jaw clenching as he watches my head fall back in pleasure. When they curl inside me, stroking something that sends lightning shooting through my spine, I can't stop the cry that rips from my throat.

"That wasn't quiet, my queen."

"I don't care," I gasp and squeeze his arms tighter. "Fuck." The heel of his palm presses into me and rubs rhythmically with the slow slide of his fingers that continue to curl against me, pressing firmly before sliding out again.

Without stopping the delicious pleasure from his fingers, his other arm snakes down, looping under my knee and hiking my leg over his waist. Tilting my hips, he presses into me again, his fingers sinking impossibly deeper and his palm giving my throbbing clit even more pressure.

"Oh gods," I moan, and force my eyelids to open, even just a little, so I can see if this is doing to him everything it's doing to me.

And I do. I know he wants me. It's clear in the darkness of his eyes, his widened pupils, and the firm set of his brow, but I also know he's trying to distract me from whatever possibilities of the future that keep playing through his mind. They plagued him back on Dawnlin, and it took me too long to get him to forget them all and accept me as just Lennox. Not the queen of his kingdom, not the daughter of his friend.

He finally saw me for me. He saw that despite the lies he told himself about his duty and expectations, he could have me, and more than that, I wanted him to.

Maybe it's being back in Blackwood. Maybe it's watching me act like a queen. Maybe it's knowing my father died with the understanding that our relationship was more than that of a princess and her guard, just like Weston said he would. Maybe it's feeling that the choices were not our own, that Edmond meddled and forced us together. Maybe he's worried that no one else would accept our being together.

Whatever the worry, I can't let him pull away from me, not after everything we've built with each other. The love, the trust, the devotion. It's too much and too perfect to let it be ripped away.

Unwrapping my fingers from their tight grip on his arms, I grab the collar of his shirt and with all the force I can muster pull him forward. His hand slams into the wall beside my head, catching himself and righting his balance so he doesn't crush me, but my tactic works. I got his attention.

"Listen to me. You're wrong." I steel my voice, trying to make it as strong as I can while he's still making my toes curl in my boots.

"I'm always right, remember?"

"You're not now." The words come out harsh as I glare at him, but it only lasts for a second before my eyes fall closed, and my head tilts back as a wave of pleasure crashes through me from the stroke of his fingers against my walls. Clearing my throat, I force my eyes back open, and try to keep my voice from being overtaken by the pleasure he's coaxing from me. "You know this is more than just a queen fucking her guard. I love you, and you love me. Whatever self-sacrificial grumpy Captain bullshit you're trying to pull will not work on me. So drop it, and fuck your queen."

The teal in his eyes all but disappears, as carnal desire takes over. Jaw tightening, and eyes darting between mine, his hand shifts between my legs, and his thumb finds the right spot. My mouth falls open in a silent whimper as he rolls it in a tight circle, again and again, daring me to be the one to break, but I refuse to look away.

"I decided." His chest heaves and it almost sounds like a snarl. "Directed at me. I only want it directed at me." His body cages mine, pinning his hand between us and making every motion reverberate between our bodies. "Now fuck my hand, my queen, so I can watch that fire consume you before I get to."

My core clenches around his fingers, and his chest grumbles as he presses his forehead into mine, our gazes staying locked on each other. Following his command, my hips move as if on their own, rocking and riding his thick fingers as hard as I can until the pressure building at the base of my spine intensifies. My teeth sink into my lower lip as my hips continue to work. He leans forward, taking my lip between his own teeth and tugging it free of mine. Hunger flares in his eyes, and I can't stop it. My hips buck against his hand as the last hold I had on the waves of pleasure consuming me breaks.

Head falling back, eyes squeezing shut, I can't stop the feral cry that escapes me. Weston's warm palm presses over my mouth, dulling the guttural moans ripping from my throat, which only serves as fuel to the already blazing fire.

My chest heaves as the last waves of my release calm, and my limbs quiver beneath me. When Weston drops to his knees, the pressure of his body no longer holding me upright, I feel like I'm going to fall, but he doesn't let me. Splaying his hand across my low abdomen, he holds the hem of my dress out of his way, giving him a clear view of his fingers still sunken inside me.

They slide out slowly, hooking in the soaked fabric to pull it to the side. His head disappears beneath the bunch of the dress, and all I feel is the long, luxurious caress of his flattened tongue on my swollen and sensitive core.

I whimper softly, just before he leans back, lifting his gaze upward as a devious grin breaks across his face.

"Don't make a sound."

Clamping my lips shut, I breathe through my nose, trying to stay quiet and also slow my rapid breaths, but it doesn't work. The moment his lips clamp around my clit, sucking at the same time that his tongue flicks out repeatedly, my knees buckle. My hands fly out, reaching to steady myself on him as he presses his face deeper into my core. His splayed hand presses more firmly into my abdomen, sending a fresh wave of pleasure through me so intense that I have to fist my fingers in his hair to keep myself upright.

"Weston," I pant in a whisper, and he flicks again, before moving down to lavishly lap up the mess he made of me a moment ago. Despite his command, I can't stop the cry as it rips through my throat. It's met with a growl that only worsens my need to scream as the vibrations send my inner walls fluttering, begging for his thick cock.

"Inside me. Now—"

Knock, knock, knock.

This time it's my hand that slaps over my mouth, as both our heads snap to the door mere inches away from where I'm pressed against the wall.

"Fuck," I mouth as he stands and drops my dress to the ground.

"Turn around." His words are barely a whisper, but I hear them. Spinning until my back is to him, he tugs the bodice back into place, his fingers finding the ties and deftly tightening them.

The knocks sound again just as he finishes the knot. He points across the room to the empty chair by the hearth and nudges the curve of my ass. Crossing the room quickly, I sink into the chair by the hearth, taking a deep breath. My cheeks are hot, but I school my features to hide the fact that I just had the face of the First Guard between my thighs, even though I feel like it is written all over mine.

Resting my chin on my shoulder, my eyes fall on Weston, standing behind the door with one hand resting on the handle. His lips twist into a smug smirk and I bite my lip to stifle a smile as he reaches down to adjust himself. Heat flashes in my face again as his gaze holds mine and his tongue flicks out, leisurely licking his lips, before sliding the bolt and yanking open the door.

"Good morning, Tila," Weston mutters, and opens the door wider. "What a pleasant surprise."

I roll my lips together, trying to suppress the giggle that only worsen's with her reply.

"I'm sure it was." Stepping further into the room, she drops into a low curtsey.

"I didn't realize we had to meet this morning," I say. "I would have met you in your workroom like I normally do."

She rises and clasps her hands together in front of her. "You don't have a formalized schedule yet, Your Majesty, however, our work today is time sensitive so we must not delay." Turning to Weston beside her, she smiles up at him sweetly. "You may go, mister Rowe."

Weston's jaw slackens as he looks down at her before turning his stunned expression to me. As the captain and First Guard, I can't imagine there were many times someone dismissed him from a room, especially someone like Tila.

I shove my tongue into my cheek before nodding. "I'll be fine, *mister Rowe*. You can return to your chambers and return in a while. About how long, Tila?"

"Should be no more than an hour."

I smirk at him, and he crosses his arms, trying not to smile. "Should be enough time to take care of what you need."

"We will finish that discussion later, my queen." The intensity of his gaze shows all the promise of finishing what was interrupted, as he hinges at his hips and drops into a low bow. My heart stutters as I watch him rise to his full height once more, his eyes never leaving mine.

It's the first time he's ever done that, and I don't like it. He's knelt before me, when he swore his oath, and back in the throne room, but that felt different. That felt personal and intimate. This bow, this outward sign of the hierarchy between our positions makes a pit form deep in my stomach. It's too formal, too stifling. Too fake.

And the second he does it, after just having told me we need to keep everything between us a secret, constructs a prison around every real feeling I have for him and he has for me, and locks them away until either of us decide its time to break free of it. I never want to see him do it again.

But I know he will. He has to.

For now.

Tila walks toward my closet and pulls out a small stool that she sets in front of my mirror.

"No ladies today?" Crossing the room, I note that her assistants who have been helping her dress me for years are absent. It's just the two of us, and probably better after what she could have stumbled in on.

"Not today, Your Majesty. I assumed you were still recovering and would want no one to hover." She glances over at me as I approach the stool, ready to step on. "Fix your skirts, dear."

My face bursts into flames and my head snaps down to find exactly what Tila is talking about. In the haste to look like nothing was going on behind my closed doors, my underskirts tangled up in themselves, making it painstakingly obvious what we had been doing. Not to mention, the entire top layer of fabric is wrinkled from where Weston had it bunched in his fist.

Fuck.

I scramble to straighten myself, smoothing out what rumples I can, and completely avoid eye contact with her once I'm done. This is exactly what Weston was talking about, exactly what he didn't want to happen. I told him I didn't care, but he clearly does, and that's a conversation we will have, just not today. As long as this didn't just ruin it.

I trust Tila, I don't think she will gossip, but what if her assistants *had* come today? This secret relationship between us wouldn't be so secret anymore.

I clear my throat and step onto the stool as she disappears into my closet, only to reemerge a few moments later, her arms laden with dresses.

"Tila," I start "Whatever you——"

She holds a hand up and looks away, stopping me before I can even start. "There is no need for worry, Your Majesty. Who the queen allows into her bed is no concern of mine." My slow exhale is filled with relief as she strides past me and drapes the dresses over the back of the settee. "I'm just glad you learned what you needed to from those books. Gods know Edmond would not have been up for explaining, and now given the...situation... I'm sure that was for the best."

Now that the person I'm allowing into my bed is Edmond's son.

Lessons I endured about the importance of continuing the Holt family line, and the importance of producing an heir were uncomfortable enough with my tutor who was like a grandfather to me. I don't know if I could have faced him alongside Weston if he had been the one to try to explain the logistics. But the thought flitters away as quickly as it came, as the more important one pulls all my focus.

A laugh bubbles out of my throat as I gape at Tila. "I knew it! You knew I was taking them!"

She scoffs. "Of course I did, dear. I made sure to weed out the ones that were less than entertaining." Her conspiratorial wink sends me into another fit of giggles, but she claps her hands, bringing us back to the task at hand. "Now, we must not waste time. We are not creating anything new, as time will not allow it. We will have to work with something you already have and make alterations if necessary."

My brows furrow as I catch her eye in the mirror. "What are we preparing for? I haven't approved anything or heard any news."

Tila's gaze softens, sympathy coating her features, and her voice is gentle, as if speaking to a scared child.

"Your Majesty, this one requires no approval. We need to make sure you are appropriately dressed for your father's funeral."

CHAPTER THIRTY-SIX

Raindrops patter against the windowpane as thunder rattles the glass before me. The weather is fitting for a funeral, especially my father's. Weston wasn't here as I dressed this morning, no doubt making sure all the preparations were complete before I even stepped foot out of this room. It's the first day since we landed back in Blackwood that anyone is actually leaving the castle grounds, and if I thought he was protective before, after my life was threatened at the literal hands of someone I knew, he might be insufferable now.

I stare through the water-speckled window out over the grounds, but can see nothing more than fog-filled trees and the castle wall. Cold seeps in through the seams, and I wrap my arms around myself to suppress a shiver.

I miss Dawnlin.

For more than just the beauty and weather.

Gently closing my eyes, I try to remember the feel of the warmth from the suns on my skin, the fragrant smell of the plants, and the crash of the waves. Anything. I'd welcome anything that could wash away the cold and dreariness in front of me now, even if only for a few moments.

We knew life would be different when we returned to Blackwood, but neither of us expected this. Becoming queen was a distant future, one I knew was coming, but thought with as young as my father was when he became king, that I would live an entire life as a princess before I took the throne. I would have time to adjust, time to speak to my father about making significant changes, and I would do so with Weston by my side.

I wasn't expecting to be standing in a funeral gown, and finally being presented to the kingdom on the same day I have to bury my father. This wasn't at all the way I thought the kingdom would finally see the princess, but today they will finally see me.

The door opens behind me, and I know the person walking through is Weston without looking. My body knows it's him. My skin tingles, now not just from the cold, but with an awareness of his proximity. I keep my eyes fixed on the view and the rain, trying to steel myself against all the overwhelming emotions that are sure to surface today.

Weston's steady footsteps echo through the room, and my body thrums with energy when he stops next to me, sliding his hand onto my lower back.

"Are you ready?" he murmurs.

My gaze stays transfixed on the view, and my stomach churns at the thought of leaving this room. "No. Are you?"

"No."

I lean into his touch, and his hand slides across my back, wrapping around the opposite side of my waist and tucking me into his side.

"I never thought I would have to bury him," he says, his voice barely a whisper. "Not after an attack like that. I always thought I would die protecting him. It's what I swore to do. Every second of today is going to be a constant reminder of many things. With every step, I'm going to be reminded that I failed him."

I shake my head. "You didn't fail, Weston. You fought. You fought for me, and he saw that. You're one man, one who was in chains. None of what happened falls on your shoulders. It falls on Dane's." When he says nothing, I continue. "He didn't blame you. Instead, he shocked us both and encouraged you."

He lets out a sigh. "Doesn't make it any easier."

I turn toward him, tipping my chin up to look into his stoic face. "Well, then, let's get it over with."

The glint of shining metal catches my eye, and I look down, finding his First Guard uniform completely transformed. Armor similar to what Brynne wore so often covers his body, with the seal of Blackwood plainly in the center of his chest to match the polished golden band on his finger.

From the moment I met him, I knew he was strong and commanding, but this? It takes my breath away. Even after knowing who he is and what position he holds for all this time, it isn't until I see him, fully dressed, his gleaming sword at his side, ready to go into battle for me, that it finally sinks in.

Weston is just as integral to this kingdom as I am. Sworn to protect me, but promised to love me.

He's mine, in duty and in heart, and all the ways that matter, even if it only ever stays between us.

"I have something for you." His words jar me from my thoughts, and I pry my gaze away from his armor. He reaches behind him, pulling something from his belt before extending his hand to me.

My dagger.

Its whereabouts hadn't crossed my mind once in the aftermath of everything. After years of feeling secure and safe with it tucked into my waistband, then trying to get it back when I didn't have it, in the last week, I hadn't even missed it. Not once. The man standing in front of me makes me feel safer than any blade ever could, but I'm still glad to have it back. After everything it has helped me through, I can't part with it, nor am I allowed to officially and traditionally now as the queen.

"Thank you."

He flips the blade, so the hilt is extended toward me, and I take it, sliding it into the secret pocket of the dress that Tila ensured was there. It will take getting used to not having it in my waistband whenever I am in a dress, which I suspect might have to be more often now. Tila can get over it, because I know I'll be in my training pants as much as I can.

"I figured you wanted it back. I didn't want you thinking I took it away again."

I chuckle softly. "Well, I don't want to stab you with it this time."

The corner of his lips tips up into a smirk. "Maybe I should have hidden it under my pillow and made you try to take it." I shove him playfully, and his smile widens. "You're required to have it anyway before we step foot outside."

"Says who? I make the rules here."

He leans forward, and there's a low grumble in his throat. "Says me." He presses a chaste kiss to my lips, and I roll my eyes.

"You're going to be right there."

His gaze falls, and the muscle in his cheek flickers. "I was right there last time too. I still couldn't protect you."

"So, this guilt you're feeling isn't just about my father, then?"

His throat bobs, but he ignores the question. "Do we need to go over the routes again?"

"No, we don't." I reach up and cup his cheek, forcing him to meet my eyes. "Weston. Everything will be fine. It's a funeral, not a rowdy celebration."

"Right, and anyone who is unhappy about the royal family could try to hurt you."

"You know I can protect myself."

"I know," he grumbles, then pauses. "I just can't let it happen again."

My thumb brushes against his stubble, and he leans into my touch just ever so slightly. "You won't."

A few heartbeats pass in silence before he speaks again. "There's something else."

His hand dips into the pocket of his pants, and his clenched fist comes out slowly. When he turns it over, opening his fingers to show me what is inside, I choke on my breath.

"Weston," I say warily. An entirely new set of emotions rises in my chest, all of them mingling together, making them difficult to identify. Panic? Fear? Excitement? Longing? My chest rises and falls rapidly as I snap my eyes to his, only to find him shaking his head.

"It's not what you think."

"What I think is that's a ring, and you're giving it to me. I don't know what that means. I need you to explain."

"Sweetheart, if I am ever fortunate enough to give you one of these, you'll know exactly what it means."

His hand falls from my waist and slides down the length of my arm until his fingers wrap around my wrist. Lifting my hand and turning my palm upward, he presses the ring into my skin, and I feel a twinge of disappointment.

"It's your mother's. The one Dane stole." He closes my fingers around it, and the warm metal feels foreign pressed into my palm. "I thought you might want it."

Swallowing down the lump forming in my throat, I stare at my closed hand as he wraps both of his hands firmly around it and presses a kiss to my fingers.

"I think she should have it," I whisper. "Father would have wanted her to have it back."

He nods slightly, and I ignore the squeeze in my chest as I let my tightly clasped fist fall. Of the myriad of emotions I expected to feel today, what's coursing through me right now wasn't even close. I push away the thoughts of what it would look like if this weren't my mother's. So long ago I'd been so concerned about marriage alliances and meeting potential suitors from other kingdoms. I'd accepted it was likely I would not marry for love, but right now, all I can think, all I can feel, is how much I want a ring from the man that stands before me.

Clearing my throat breaks me out of the trance, and I'm no longer lost in my thoughts of what could be. I start across the room and pause, just for a moment, to glance in the mirror and make sure I still look how I did when Tila left me. The dress is an old one from my closet, but still fits. The thick black fabric is fitting for the occasion and the weather. Long, tight sleeves will keep the chill off my skin, even though the neckline plunges to be a little more revealing than when I wore it years ago. Tila thought it might not be the best first impression to the kingdom, but I disagreed.

I wanted it to be revealing. I didn't want to hide myself under layers of fabric and veils. I wanted my people to see their queen, complete with the ring of brownish yellow bruises that are slowly healing around my neck.

I want them to see what I endured; what I am willing to endure for them.

Burying my father. Fighting off an attacker. Surviving.

They don't know me, so they have nothing to judge me by beyond what they see from this point forward. I want them to see someone who is strong, even if I feel anything but strong today.

I turn my head, eyeing the low, tight bun Addy helped me with, and making sure no stray strands are out of place. I didn't want to deal with my unruly waves in the rain. I don't need a distraction. I want to focus, get through this, and move on.

With one last look, I find Weston's gaze in the mirror.

"Let's go."

When we emerge into the hallway, the air feels different. I don't hesitate, not like before, or like all the times in the past that I walked by her closed door. I don't rush past. I don't avoid looking. I walk straight to her door, gripping the handle tightly, and push it open.

The scene before me is the same as it has been every time I've been brave enough to enter this room, hell, to even look into this room. But this time, I am not the same.

I round the bed, coming alongside her and take her hand. The warmth of her fingers catches me off guard, especially after the chill from my room, but it feels right. It feels like the last piece of me that I had been missing.

"You lost this, Mother. I wanted you to have it back."

I slide the ring on her finger, straightening it so the stone faces the ceiling, but I don't drop her hand. Instead, I squeeze it tighter.

"I have to bury Father today," I mutter, and huff a sad laugh. "I honestly thought you would be first. I never would have guessed it would end up this way."

Emotion swells in my chest, and my gaze snaps up, searching for Weston. I find him leaning against the door frame, his arms crossed over his chest and armor glinting in the flickering flames as he watches me. He gives me a reassuring nod, and I inhale a shuddering breath before looking back at her serene face again.

"I tried to save you. We both did, but things didn't go the way we hoped. We held onto it for as long as we could, but in the end it wasn't up to us. At least the hope brought us home, but it was empty-handed. And now Father is gone. He held onto hope for you too, but I think…"

My voice trails off, and my eyes fill with tears.

"I think it's time to let you go. You've held on for so long. I know you wanted to have a life together, and wanted one with him, but he's gone now. It isn't fair to keep you here when you could be with him on the other side."

I squeeze her hand tightly as a tear falls silently onto the bedding, followed by another. I inhale another harsh breath and let everything I want to say to her come out, because this is probably my last chance.

"I hope that one day I can be the mother you always wanted to be. I'm sorry you never got to experience that. I know how much it meant to you. I promise your memory will live on. In me, in this kingdom, in the future generations of Blackwood. Even though I never got to meet you, I feel like the pieces I have gotten were better than the hopeless grief I had before."

I smooth her hand on her abdomen, and the light from the candles glints off the stone.

"Until we meet again." I stand quickly and walk straight for the door, but Weston doesn't move. Instead, he steps forward, wrapping his arms around me, and holds me tight. I press my forehead against the cold metal covering his chest. The armor that protects him is blocking me from having the comfort of his warm body that I am craving.

After Dawnlin deemed me unworthy, I knew I would eventually have to say goodbye to my mother, and this time, for good. Despite being prepared, I knew it would still hurt, but I never thought I would have to do it on the same day I buried my other parent.

"I'll tell the healers tonight that it's time."

I feel him nod against my head, but it takes me off guard when he speaks because it isn't directed at me.

"You would have made a great mother, Lyla. But you can leave knowing I will take care of her. Even though you never got to meet her, she is still very much your daughter. I swear it."

My fingertips dig into his hips as I squeeze my eyes shut, completely uncaring that the wetness coating my eyelashes is, once again, going to destroy Tila's work. I allow myself only a few seconds of despair and pain before I sniffle and push myself away from Weston.

"Alright," I say, setting my jaw and looking at him directly. "Time to bury my father."

CHAPTER THIRTY-SEVEN

Father's open coffin sits atop a carriage in the entrance hall, on display so everyone in the castle could say their final goodbyes. I'm the last one left. Guards stand surrounding the black wooden box, their faces solemn, but their bodies still held at attention out of respect for their king.

Edmond waits beside it, along with mister Mason, the man my father chose to manage the daily business of the castle. Both dip into low bows as I approach, and the sadness in their faces is unmistakable as they rise and meet my gaze.

"If your majesty would like any more time before it is sealed, we will all take leave," Edmond says calmly.

"There's no need for everyone to leave. I will not take long." Stopping just an arm's length away from the foot of the wooden box, look over my shoulder at Weston. Jaw clenched tight, with sorrow etched into his features, he looks upon his lifelong friend. "Mister Rowe, if you'd like some time."

"Thank you, my queen," he murmurs with a bow of his head. His hands stay clasped behind his back as he steps past me and approaches the side of the carriage. No one but me can see the whites of his knuckles from his clenched fists, or the tension in his shoulders as he takes in my father's body.

It takes every strength I have not to reach out and take his hand, to hold him, and touch him like I know he needs to feel comforted, but I can't. Not here, not with all the watchful eyes of the guards and staff anywhere you look. But he knows I can't because he doesn't want me to.

My throat tightens. The emotions of this moment are too much for me to keep down, and it isn't from what most onlookers would think. It's from having to watch Weston in pain, going through this alone, and knowing there is nothing I can do to help him.

After Tila interrupted us the other morning, the conversation hadn't come up again. We don't agree at all about how to move forward, but once all the formalities are over, and the calm has somewhat returned, we will discuss it again. I know his duty is important to him, but I also know he cares for me more than it. He proved that when he tried to get to me instead of my father. He deserves to be loved loudly, publicly, and not hidden away as an illegitimate secret.

I don't want to live a life filled with hiding and secrets, and I don't care about alliances or marriage pacts. I want to prove myself to other kingdoms by being me, by being a strong queen, not fucking a low-born prince just to keep peace.

My father and mother did it. They always chose love, even when it felt hopeless.

They aren't the only ones.

I can do it too.

Maybe that love is what made my mother hold on, or maybe it was her deep, hopeful love for me and the life we would share.

Weston and I have endured hopelessness, betrayal, death, and despair, and our love never wavered. If all of that brought us together, helping me find him and finally have the love I've always wanted, why would I hide it away and pretend it didn't exist?

His selflessness is almost a fault. Everyone else's needs are more important than his own. Blackwood, the Castaways, and me. He's constantly choosing everyone around him, but he's never had someone choose him.

He is my choice, and more than the fact that I can't do any of this without him, I don't want to.

"My king," Weston grumbles, and bends into a deep bow. When he rises, he wastes no time stepping back into place behind me, and I can't miss the hard set of his jaw and the pain in his eyes.

Now it's my turn.

I can't avoid it any longer, despite how much I want to just escape and let the entire day happen without me. My days of escaping are over, as are my days of having a living parent, because this is it. This is the last moment I will ever see my father.

Stepping up to the side of the carriage, I drag my eyes up his lifeless body to his face. The healers did well at making him look at peace, of erasing the final terrorizing moments of his life. You'd never know by looking at him now that he died at the hands of someone who was trying to take everything from him.

My gaze trails away from his face and down to the hands resting on his chest. They are clasped around his dagger, the gold dull without the touch of light from the darkened rain clouds covering the sky. Edmond asked if there was anything I wanted to keep that would not be buried with him, but I declined.

The only thing he valued besides his dagger was his own ring, but I couldn't take it from him. It wasn't a piece of history, or a symbol from Blackwood. That ring symbolizes the love he had for my mother, and the hope he held on to for so long. It shouldn't ever leave him, just like she never did. I returned hers this morning, and now, they both are whole once again.

The length of his polished blade shines against his pristine burial clothing, and its presence is the last tradition he will take part in as king. Presented to him at his own ceremony, his dagger was the same symbol of protection; for himself, for the kingdom, and now is there to protect him even in the afterlife.

It had done its job.

Not a single trace of Dane's blood soils the blade or the hilt, but I know it was there. I saw it with my own eyes as he fell to the floor after plunging it through Dane's back, the same way Weston threatened back in Dawnlin. Dane had been so focused on me, on exacting his revenge, that he didn't consider the king having the same protections I would. Ultimately, that mistake wrote his demise.

"Goodbye, Father."

The two words are all I can mutter. How can you put into words the years of inner turmoil, the feelings of inadequacy, and abandonment? It's all I feel as I look upon his face for the final time, despite his explanation, despite his apology. Those feelings don't just go away because he's no longer in this world.

Stepping back from the carriage, I clear my throat before looking back toward Edmond and Mason. "Seal it."

"Yes, Your Majesty," the guards murmur, and spring into action around us. My body jolts slightly as the wooden lid slams into place as they lock it firmly, and I feel Weston take half a step closer to me, his presence comforting with the storm that is brewing in my mind.

Now, the only time he will ever look down on me is when I pass his portrait in the castle.

The scent of musky, damp earth fills the entrance hall when the guards open the wide, black wooden doors. Dark grey clouds hover low as a misty rain slants through the air, soaking the stone walkway just outside. An involuntary shiver courses through me, not only from the cold that now seeps into the room, but from the anticipation of what is about to happen. When I step foot out of those doors, the kingdom will know who I am. They will finally see me, Lennox. Once it's done, there's no going back.

Edmond, Weston and I repeatedly reviewed what was to come next, knowing full well I might forget everything the moment I stepped outside under the scrutiny of the kingdom. Weston will be right behind me, but I don't want my first impression to be that of a naïve, stumbling little girl dropped into a position she wasn't prepared for.

I know the procession, the ceremony, the expectations, and now I just need to go through the motions.

The guards wheel my father's carriage out of the entryway, and within a few moments, it is hooked to the horses that will pull it in the procession through the city.

"Are you ready?" Weston mutters, and I nod, keeping my stare locked on the carriage. Hands linked behind me, I set my shoulders and take a deep breath, waiting for the procession to begin.

"Forward!" Weston calls, and the guards file out of the doorway and line the courtyard on either side of the carriage.

I startle when I feel his fingers lace with mine, squeezing tightly before falling away. The gesture makes my heart ache, not only because I know he's reminding me he's going through this with me, but also at how much of a risk he just took, showing any sort of affection to me out in public.

The carriage driver calls out, spurring the horses into movement, and the wheels begin to slowly roll forward. Rain patters on the wooden surface, the coffin laid in the open air for every gathered citizen to watch pass by.

Inhaling one final shuddering breath, I take my first steps to follow.

The hinges on the rarely used castle gates squeal as the large entrance gates open before us, and the guards file out onto the road. Their formation is pristine, as if they had been practicing for such an event. There was no way for them to be this prepared, and I can only assume such perfection is a testament to Weston's leadership and direction of his men. The driver shakes the reins, and the horses begin to walk, following behind the first set of guards.

This is my cue.

This procession is the last ceremony my father's body will partake in; the last time his people will see him as king. Once he is buried, as the heir, I will take his place in the carriage, symbolizing a seamless transition of the royal line before the people. It's simple enough, but nerves still course through my body as I step past the entryway, out into the open.

The cobblestones beneath my feet feel familiar, despite only traversing them for the first time almost two years ago, and rarely since then. As I step through the gates into the city that I can't wait to get to know, my steps almost falter, and I have to fight to keep my head trained forward.

People.

Enormous crowds line the street, every person clad in dark clothes, squeezing together, taking up all available space, and braving the weather to pay respects to their king, and no doubt, to lay eyes on the new queen.

I swallow the lump in my throat as whispers carry on the wind, and from the corner of my eye, I see glances exchanged and fingers pointed in my direction.

I focus back on the carriage, trying not to let my insecurities overtake me. There's no way to know if it is the sight of me for the first time, or the ring of healing bruises around my neck that has them talking. I may never know, and I don't need to. I'm their queen, and I want them to get to know me, just as they did my father.

That's the queen I want to be, no longer hidden away behind the walls.

The rest of the walk to the royal cemetery passes by in a blur of raindrops, whispers, and crowds of people. Besides the sound of Weston's sure gait behind me, the only thing that keeps me from wanting to shrink away is knowing that every step I take is one closer to being through with this.

The rain doesn't slow, and by the time the carriage enters the royal cemetery, my dress is completely soaked through. Curled tendrils escaped my bun and fall around my face, and my drenched hair is plastered to my head. When I lay eyes on the polished stone building for the first time, it hits me how many of my relatives are buried here, people I will never know, and soon, it will hold two more.

I hardly see the guards lifting the coffin from the carriage and walking it inside the waiting open doorway. I don't even remember I'm supposed to move until Weston nudges me from behind, urging me to follow.

How long before I do this again with my mother after the healers stopped providing her with care? Would it be in days? Weeks? Months? How long will her body continue to hold on?

How did I end up alone?

The thought crashes through me and opens a pit in my stomach. As I walk toward the mausoleum, the faces of everyone I've lost in such a short time flash through my mind.

But I'm not alone. I have Weston, and maybe someday we will see some Castaways again. Edmond may be leaving, and Brynne exiled, but Tila is still here. We will make a new life, one that we want, one that looks like the dreams I've always had. As long as I can convince him, like I did before, to stop letting our duty get in the way of what we have, we can have it all.

I did it once, so I can do it again.

Not a single word is uttered, not a prayer or a chant, until the stone door closes. The loud boom rings in my ears and casts the room in silence. It is only then that the first tear falls, and I swipe it away angrily.

I do not want to cry today. How could I? He was a father in name only, and today I'm saying goodbye to the life he created for me. With the closure of that stone door, my new life can begin, one that I choose, that he never trusted me to have.

He may have had his reasons, and used his dying breath to at least explain, though not to ask for forgiveness. Deep down somewhere I may even forgive him for it, but it doesn't change every minute that I felt the effects of his neglect, his ignorance, his pressure. It doesn't give back everything else that was taken from me over the course of my life. It doesn't change that he wouldn't look at me, or speak to me, that he hid me away. It doesn't change the depths of my loneliness and the constant worry with every person I meet if our relationship is real, or only built on my title.

It doesn't change the feelings of inadequacy, the fear of doing anything wrong, of being a terrible representation of Blackwood, and because of all that, trying to prove myself with everything I did, only to be shut down.

He may have had his reasons for what he did, and he may have been sorry for them, but that doesn't invalidate any of what I endured. What I *survived*. And what gave me the strength to do everything I did from the moment I stepped out of that castle.

A heavy sigh escapes my chest, and another tear falls. I swipe it away just as harshly as the first, and stare at the shiny polished stone as the words spoken for my father sound like a low hum in my ears.

I'm jarred from my trance when Weston's arms wrap tightly around my shoulders. Glancing around the dim room, I realize we are alone, the door just barely cracked behind us. My back sinks into his chest, and he holds me tighter, supporting the weight of this heavy burden on my body, and nuzzling his cheek into my damp hair.

"He never wanted you to go through this, to be a young queen like he was. He never wanted you to carry that burden and have your life devoted to something else." His voice is low, and the rumble in his chest against my back is comforting.

"Sometimes no matter how bad we want something, it isn't meant to be," I whisper.

"In this case, I guess not. But that doesn't mean it isn't the way it was supposed to happen." He presses a kiss to my hair, and we stand clutching each other, staring at the letters of my father's name, carved into the surface of the stone. There's a space below it for my mother, ready for her to be buried alongside him, and I feel a pang in my chest.

I don't wipe the last tear. I let it linger on my cheek as I straighten my shoulders and step out of Weston's arms. No one will notice it in the rain, and if they do, at least they will know their queen isn't cold and heartless. They'll know I am a person, with feelings and loves and cares, the same as them, and hopefully they will know that because I care about mine, I will also care about theirs.

Holding my head high, I descend the stone steps and walk through the aisle of guards lining the path back to the gate. What comes next is extremely important to the kingdom, to the people who came out to pay their respects to their late king.

Now, there's no one in front of me, no one ahead in line. There's only me riding in the royal carriage. I round the back of it, feeling Weston come alongside me. He extends his hand, and I take it, feeling the tingle where our skin touches and relishing one of the few times where I can touch him in public without rousing suspicion. Just as I'm about to step into the carriage, he drops my hand and thrusts his body in front of me, blocking me from the view of the crowd.

"Your Majesty!"

The cry reaches my ears, and I know it is coming from somewhere behind, but closer than it should be if it were from the crowd. I turn toward Weston, trying to see past his shoulders as a hooded woman hurriedly approaches the carriage. My heart pounds in my ears, the pace quickening as I try to see who is coming, and why. What would anyone have to say to me, right now of all times? Is this one of the security instances that Weston and Edmond prepared me for? Tension pulls at my shoulders as Weston issues a command.

"Stop right there." His hand rests on the hilt of his sword, and his shoulders pull back beneath his armor.

"Your Majesty, I'm so sorry."

That voice. I know that voice.

Then it clicks.

"Mister Rowe, wait." I rest my hand on his shoulder, hoping it will relax him, and he halts. His body still guards me from the woman now standing in front of him, but he doesn't look as if he's going to draw his sword on her. I peer past his shoulder and as she lowers her hood, I find the shocked face of a woman I've come to know.

"Estelle," I breathe, then look to Weston. "She's alright," I murmur, "you met her already." But he doesn't relax, and instead stays still as a statue between us.

Dropping her gaze, she sinks into a deep curtsey before us. When she rises again, her eyes are still full of shock, her brows drawn in as she stumbles through her words.

"Your Majesty, I am so sorry. I—I didn't know. I didn't know it was you."

I smile softly and her brow relaxes slightly. "It's alright, Estelle. No one knew. That's the way I wanted it to be."

"So," she says, her head shaking slightly as she pieces it together. "So you're not Addy. You're the queen."

I nudge Weston to the side, and he reluctantly moves, giving me enough room to step to the ground and extend my hand toward her.

"Hi Estelle, I'm Lennox. It's nice to officially meet you."

She hesitates before slowly extending her hand and gently taking mine. "I'm honored to know you, Your Majesty. I didn't before, but now, seeing who you are, I have no fears at all that the kingdom is in your hands."

Gratitude and pride well in my chest, and the words stick in my throat as I try to respond.

"Thank you, Estelle. That means a great deal to me."

She releases my hand before dropping into another deep curtsey. "If you need anything at all, just send word."

"If I need anything, I'll come see you myself." She returns my smile warmly before stepping away and joining a group at the edge of the road. They all look at her, some flabbergasted, some nervous, but when I raise my hand in a wave at the little girl clutching her father's neck, their expressions change, and the beaming smiles that return makes me feel warm despite my cold, wet clothes.

I can do this. I can be the kind of queen whose people know she cares for them, and hopefully earns the same back. I just need to be myself, not who anyone else wants me to be, or who I thought they wanted me to be. Just Lennox. My time on Dawnlin showed me I can let people in, and let them see who I am, and that who I am is enough to be loved.

My people will see it too.

"My queen," Weston grumbles, and extends his hand to me again. This time, I don't stop. I take it, stepping into the carriage and sitting down on the soaked fabric as the now heavy mist falls around us.

Weston slams the door of the carriage behind me and takes his place at the door. His eyes never leave the crowd as he scans for threats in this last section of the ceremony.

The horses walk, and the carriage jolts slowly forward. My transition in front of the kingdom is complete, and now we will proceed through the streets until we're back home.

The farther from the cemetery we are, the more the mood of the crowd changes. While we are in the midst of the month long mourning period after the death of a king or queen, it doesn't stop my people from expressing their thoughts about having a new queen.

My jaw slackens as I stare into the crowd, stunned. People of all ages wave as I pass, and the pointing I thought was surely out of disappointment, doesn't feel that way now. It feels like acceptance, and the weight of worry lifts from my shoulders as I smile softly back, acknowledging the waving children with a flutter of my fingers or a nod of my head.

We round a corner, heading down the final long stretch of road that leads back to the castle gate, and the closer we get, the more the crowds grow. With every cheer and wave, I want to cry for a different reason, as I see the people spilling over the edges of the streets, even down the alleyways attempting to see me.

My skin prickles as I recognize where we are, and know what is approaching. I see the entrance to the alley that changed the trajectory of my life, and I can't help but want a glimpse at the fountain that now holds a special place in my heart and will always bring up fond memories.

As we pass the alley, and my eyes fall on it, a sharp gasp rips from my throat. I turn in my seat, craning my neck to try to get a better view, all while trying not to draw the attention of the faces packed around it.

My gasp must have caught Weston's attention, because when I glance down, he's looking up at me, his brows drawn as he takes in the surprise I am sure is written all over me. I tear my gaze away from him and look back to the alley, and from the corner of my eye, see him do the same before his head snaps back toward me.

My jaw slackens as I take it in, the symbol of the place I love, that brought me hope, and a family. Brought me Weston. The symbol that I thought lost its magic because of its aged and decrepit appearance. There's no mistaking that this isn't the same fountain that brought me to Dawnlin.

Because *this* fountain is flowing.

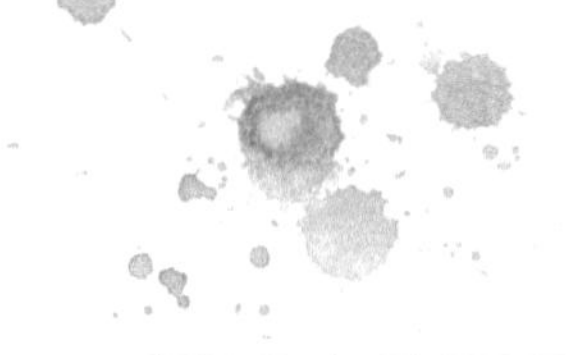

CHAPTER
THIRTY-EIGHT

I don't wait for the carriage to come to a complete stop before I throw open the door and run down the steps. I don't even let Weston help me out, like I'm sure he was prepared to do. Instead, I traipse through the entrance hall with one solitary focus: getting somewhere we can freely talk, where we won't be hindered by the magic binding our speech.

What could this mean?

Why is the fountain so different, and so suddenly?

Is the change because of the magic? Or am I holding onto hope when the change can be explained by something as simple as the city preparing for the king's funeral?

I can feel Weston right behind me, his loud steps pounding to keep pace with mine as I wordlessly speed through the castle. I don't head to my room. It's too far away, and I need to talk to him now, so I turn off and head to a room I haven't been in for years.

The familiar smell of leather-bound pages calms my rapid breathing ever so slightly as I push open the door to the library. Weston catches it just before it closes, and I whirl on him as he slides the lock into place.

"Did you see it? Did you see the fountain?"

He nods and presses a finger to his lips. Stepping past me, he makes his way around the library, checking down every aisle of shelves and behind every armchair to ensure we're alone before walking back to me.

"I saw."

"It's nothing like it was before. The water, the stone, it—"

"It is," he says, pointing toward the city, where it lies outside of the walls, surrounded by my people walking past it on their way home with no idea of the magic they are so close to. "That is what I remember. It's what the fountain looked like when I called the Guardian. It wasn't the decaying thing that brought us home." His voice is different. Urgent. Hopeful. And I can't deny I feel the same thing.

Something happened.

Something is different.

Taking a step closer, my eyes search his. "What do you think it means?"

He rubs his palm over his slackened jaw. "I don't know. But it has to mean something. The magic was always intentional. I have to believe that includes the fountain."

"What if…" My voice trails off as I try to remember every thought I had about the fountain and the magic. What we just learned from Edmond turned everything we thought we knew upside down, and I'm realizing that might happen once again.

But what if it is exactly how I thought all that time ago?

I squeeze my eyes shut and take a quick breath before starting again. "When I first found the fountain, the way the fountain looked surprised me. It wasn't the same as the story that led me there. It was broken…not flowing. I thought it was a sign that the magic had dried up, and even if I figured out how to call the Guardian, it wouldn't work. But it did, and when I went to Berrendahr, the fountain looked the same as the one here. Before, when you saw it, nothing had changed. It was the way the story had depicted. What if it deteriorated because of Dane?"

His eyes snap to mine, and I can see him working through the possibility. My stomach rolls and my skin tingles as my thoughts come tumbling out of my mouth.

"Dane cheated the magic when he became the Guardian. The person who tried to take from the island was the one in control of it all. What if that changed the magic? Dawnlin didn't trust him. What if it was because of him all along?"

"And now he's gone," Weston murmurs.

"Now he's gone," I agree, and I can feel the excitement raging inside me, begging to come out. "He's not the Guardian anymore. Edmond is. Someone who truly cares about Dawnlin and the myth staying alive is back in control. He made sure we knew about the healing waters. He truly wants to give people hope. He's not someone who was trying to take for himself."

His hands rest on his hips as he nods slowly. "The island knows. It knows the threat is gone, and it doesn't have to protect itself from him anymore."

"Exactly. It trusts Edmond now. Not only is he the new Guardian, but he has been there before. He was worthy, Weston. It's no longer being cheated."

"Maybe the next person who finds it will actually have hope," he grumbles. There's a glimmer of sadness in his eyes. We all had hope, but couldn't save who we came there to save, all because of what Dane planned, and what Storm and Brynne did to ensure it happened. They all plotted to steal from the island and use the magic for their own gain. Everyone else came there with genuine intentions, but because of them, the island hid everything to protect it. Dawnlin didn't have to protect itself any longer, not unless someone new and untrustworthy came along. It had Edmond now, the most honorable and observant man that could be in charge of guarding the magic.

But what if *everything* is different now? What if now that the magic is safe and restored, all of us who Dawnlin denied could have a second chance?

"Weston," I murmur, biting my lower lip nervously before looking up to catch his eye. "Do you think we should go back?"

His hands find my face, his thumbs brushing my cheeks as he tilts my chin up to see me more clearly.

"Lennox, you're the queen now. We can't go back."

"Not to stay," I say quickly. "We'll never be trapped there again. Edmond wouldn't allow it."

"Then what are you saying." It's not a question, more of a statement, a plea for an explanation.

I inhale shakily as tears well in my eyes, and his face softens at the sight. "I buried my father today. The entire time I wondered how soon it would be until I had to do this all over again with her. I know I said I would talk to the healers tonight about letting her go, but then I saw the fountain and I..." I trail off, my eyes searching his face, trying to find any sort of reaction to what I'm saying, but he gives nothing away. "Weston, I can't give up yet. I have to try one more time. I have to know if I'm truly not worthy of helping her." A sob bursts from my chest, and he leans forward, his gaze intense as his eyes bounce between mine.

"I don't care what Dawnlin says, you are worthy, Lennox. We all were."

I sniffle, letting the tears fall freely down my cheeks, and he swipes them away with his thumbs. "If we all were...are, then we have to go back. If we are right, and it was all because of Dane, now that he's gone, maybe we can save her."

His jaw works tightly, and a fire lights in his eyes. "You want to leave and come right back?"

I nod as much as I can with his hands still clutching my face. "How long was Edmond gone? When he left for your mother?"

Weston's eyes trail away as he thinks back to his childhood. It was so long ago, back during a time that clearly was emotionally tumultuous for him, so he might not remember. He may have blocked out all the details surrounding his mother's death, except for the ones that come back to him when he sleeps.

"It was only a day, maybe two, although he spoke as if barely any time had passed at all. We know time doesn't match up. It's possible he left and came right back after the mountain."

"If we do the same, then we would only be gone for a day. We can easily disguise our absence as grieving in my chambers." The words fly out of my mouth as my excitement heightens. "I haven't chosen my advisors yet. I need to leave someone in charge."

"Tell me who and I will notify them while you change."

I look down at my still-sopping dress, having completely forgotten from the new development that the fabric is still heavy with rain and sticks to my skin. Weston is always two steps ahead, because changing to go back to Dawnlin had been the farthest thing from my mind.

"Tila," I say, looking up from the folds of my skirt. "I trust her to keep things in order."

Nodding firmly, he shifts toward me, and one hand sinks into the damp hair at the nape of my neck. A shiver courses through my body as I look up into his face.

Jaw tight, and his eyes searching mine, his voice drops to a low grumble. "Are you sure you want to do this?"

"I don't want to. I *need* to."

Something flickers in his eyes, but his expression remains unchanged. My mouth falls open, about to ask him what is wrong, but before I can utter a sound, his mouth is on mine. Fingers fist in my hair as his lips coax mine open and his tongue sweeps inside, deepening the kiss. Matching every movement, every stroke, I sink into him, trailing my hands up his body and clutching his armor to pull him closer. Lifting onto my toes, I press my body into his. After the morning filled with despair, the desire he's sparking to life inside me is warm and welcome, but he breaks the kiss, pulling away slightly and trailing his nose down mine until our foreheads press together.

"I love you," he murmurs, and my stomach tumbles in response. I'm still not used to hearing him say those words, and after years of wanting and hoping to be loved and believing it would never happen, a tiny sliver deep inside me still has a hard time believing them. "No matter what happens, I will always love you."

"I know," I reassure him and myself. My voice is breathless from the intensity of the kiss, and I try to lean back to meet his eye, but his arm flexes around me, clutching me so tightly that I can barely move. The hand sunken in my hair slides down my neck, the warmth from his palm and fingertips burning a trail down my icy skin until it settles on my chest, flattening right over my heart.

"You hear me say the words, but I want you to feel it. In here, understand?" He presses more firmly into my chest, and from every place our bodies touch, I can feel the tension roiling through him.

"Weston, what's going on?" Fighting against his strength, I lean back enough that I can look into his eyes, and see the dark depths of teal staring back at me with words unsaid. I search his face for an answer, but he ignores my question.

"Until my dying breath, remember?"

"I remember," I breathe, and his lips crush mine again. His movements are more insistent, more urgent as his body towers over mine, walking me backward until the back of my legs bumps the side of the desk where Edmond and I spent so many years, preparing me for this day.

His tongue delves deeply as he crouches before me, just enough for his hands to fall to my thighs, sliding around until they grip my ass and lift me onto the edge of the desk. Parting my legs, he steps between my knees and grips my hips, sliding my body to the edge of the desk until

I'm flush against him. Heat pools in my core as he presses into me, and despite the mounds of fabric and armor between us, every movement sends a shock of pleasure through me.

I moan into his mouth when he slides a hand down my thigh, hiking my knee up onto his torso and giving him more room to get as close to me as his uniform will allow. Finally breaking away from the kiss, the stubble of his beard scrapes my skin as his lips brush over my chin and down my neck, leaving a burning trail of kisses in their wake.

"I love you." His voice rumbles against the bare skin at the crook of my neck, and the throbbing between my thighs only worsens as I wrap my arm around his neck and clutch him closer.

"Weston," I moan, as he slides the hem of the dress up, letting it pool at my waist.

"Yes, my queen?" His teeth nip at the skin on my neck at the same time as his thumb brushes my inner thigh, and I almost combust as I squeeze my eyes shut and force out the next words.

"Weston, we can't do this right now." Pain lances through my chest the second they come out of my mouth, because all I want is to be wrapped in his arms, to be full of him, and safe. To have forgotten all the thoughts and worries and emotions that came from this day, but this day isn't over. Not after what we discovered.

His body stills, and a deep sigh heaves from his chest into my neck. My dress drops back down as his arms slide back around my waist, his muscles tightening as he crushes me to him. He inhales deeply but doesn't let go. Skating my fingers along his head and weaving them through his hair, I stroke gently, hoping it will help whatever turmoil he has going on inside his head.

"I'm sorry," he murmurs, the sound muffled from where his lips are still pressed into my skin.

"Don't be," I whisper, but the moment he lets go and straightens before me, a pit hollows out my stomach. This tender moment is gone, at my request, and the intensity I've grown to love takes over.

The captain is back.

"We need to wait until the crowds have dispersed. The rain should help clear them quickly, but we can't risk having too many people around. Now that everyone has seen you, they will no doubt watch wherever you go. We can't disappear in an alleyway and risk someone noticing, so we are going to have to be discreet."

"Right," I say with a nod.

"And we're doing this the right way. We're not cheating the magic. We're not telling Pop we're going back. We're going to call the Guardian like we should."

"I agree. I want to do this right."

He leans in and presses a hard kiss to my lips again before pulling away quickly. I take his outstretched hands as he helps me lower myself off the edge of the desk, and set my skirts right before brushing a loosened strand of hair off of my face.

"Go get dressed, sweetheart. Let's go back to Dawnlin."

CHAPTER
THIRTY-NINE

*S*neaking out of the castle was difficult and nerve-wracking before, back when I had someone to answer to if I was caught. Now, there is no one. I am the queen, so planning to sneak out knowing there will be no repercussions makes my stomach turn with a different uneasiness. No one can know we are gone. If we are caught, rumors are sure to spread about where we were going, and why the queen was sneaking away.

Weston used the excuse we devised about observing the mourning period and played up my overwhelming emotions from the funeral when he instructed the guards to leave me alone. Hopefully, if we've calculated the approximate timing correctly, we won't be gone long enough for anyone to come looking.

The soft click of the door sounds behind me as I shove my hair deep into the hood of my cloak and pull it low over my eyes. I don't have to guess who entered the room without knocking. There's only one person who is comfortable enough with me to do that.

"Did anyone question you?" I ask as Weston crosses the room, his figure coming to a halt beside me in the mirror.

He scoffs. "Of course not. Now that the traitors have been rooted out, the guards we have left are good and loyal men. They respect the crown, and care about the kingdom and their role here. They understand the command structure."

My eyes graze over his reflection, taking in the thick tunic and pants that have replaced his guard's uniform and armor. The fabric pulls across his chest and leaves nothing to the imagination regarding his strength as it curves over the muscles in his shoulders and arms. His cloak hangs from his clenched fist, ready to conceal him better as soon as he deems my disguise enough.

"Has anyone pushed back against your authority? Or questioned why you, you know, haven't changed?"

It has been one of my biggest worries since being back in Blackwood, now without my father and his to protect us from any questioning. The guards he knew from before saved our lives, but the concern that they want answers as to why he hasn't aged has been heavy on my mind.

"The ones who know me haven't. I can tell they're confused, but no one has said a word. Maybe one day they'll ask, but we both know I can't tell them the truth."

"Maybe we need to come up with a story then." I straighten the uniform skirt and turn toward him.

"I will come up with something. You don't have to worry about it. Are you ready for the next part?"

I nod and check myself in the mirror one more time. I didn't bother disguising myself as much as before, foregoing coloring my hair and instead making sure none of it was visible under the cloak. The staff uniform shouldn't draw any unwanted attention, because it isn't abnormal for those who work here to leave the castle and come back the next day. Our plan is to make it look like Weston is taking his evening off with a woman who works in the castle, and I feel an odd twinge of jealousy at the thought, despite the woman being me.

Weston pulls the cloak tighter around my shoulders and fastens the next clasp, hiding a little more of my frame. He scans his work and mine until he seems satisfied I'm adequately disguised, but his hands stay clasped around the edges of the cloak.

"You have your dagger?" he grumbles.

"Yes."

"I don't expect there to be any problems, but you know what to do if there are."

I roll my eyes. "Weston. Dane is gone. Brynne and Storm are exiled. You've questioned every other person in this castle personally. My people may know what I look like now, but there's no other reason to think there will be a threat. The only reason we are hiding is that we don't want anyone following us and finding out about Dawnlin. You know I don't want to spend my life locked away behind the castle walls anymore. I won't be afraid to be around my people. You don't need to worry."

Releasing the cloak, his hand slides around my waist. "When it comes to you and your safety, I will always worry."

Even though it can be so frustrating, I know his protectiveness is part of how he shows he cares. Nothing I can say will ever stop it. I've already tried. But maybe tonight I don't have to stop it, and instead distract it.

"I know we have to make sure everything looks real to the guards, but maybe we could pretend like it actually is. For one night, we can just be two people without titles and duty and expectations, and just enjoy our life. Even if it is a ruse."

My mind drifts back to the night Dane took me to the tavern for the first time, and I watched the patrons living happily without inhibitions. The longing I felt that night hits me square in the chest. How I wanted so badly to be as carefree as the other patrons, not having anyone take a second glance if I wanted to have more than one drink or sit in a man's lap. Stupidly, I thought I wanted all of that with Dane, but now, I can't see any of it with anyone but Weston.

He thinks we need to hide the love between us for the sake of the kingdom's future, and I wish with every part of my being that I can convince him otherwise. But for now, I have tonight, and this plan we've concocted to go unnoticed, and I can hold on to the thrill from the show we are about to put on.

The corner of his mouth turns up slightly. "Just because we're tricking the guards doesn't mean it isn't real, Lennox." He tugs me closer and slides both his hands around my waist to settle low on my back. Desire burns in his eyes as his voice drops impossibly low. "It is very real how much I want everyone to see that you're mine, how I want all the other men to see my hands on your body, and know they can never touch what I have. It is very real how much I struggle to push away the thoughts that run though my mind every moment you're around me, distracting me from what I should be doing because all I can think about are ways to make you moan my name like I am so fond of you doing."

My breath hitches as his hands slide down the curve of my ass, gripping me firmly and pulling me flush against him. His smirk deepens as he takes in my heaving chest before his eyes meet mine. "None of what we're about to do is fake for me, sweetheart."

Rising onto my toes, I fist the tunic at his chest for balance and lift my chin. The hood falls back, and he tracks the movement before his gaze trails over every inch of my face. He knows exactly what I want, and thank the gods, doesn't make me wait for it. He presses a slow, luxurious kiss to my lips before straightening again, and tugging my hood back in place.

I fold my fingers through his and follow as he leads me to the door. Peeking his head out of a small opening, he looks back and forth, checking the corridor to make sure there are no lingering guards or late-night staff. I sent Addy home hours ago, using the same excuse that I needed time alone for a few days and could take care of myself.

When Weston decides we're safe to start the first step of the plan, he pulls me through the door, latching it closed behind us, and briskly walks straight for the staff staircase. The route we planned is the same as the one I used to leave, the one with the shortest and most direct path to the city, as well as the most shadow-filled corners once we're outside.

Wrapping his arm firmly around my shoulder, he tugs me into his side, angling my body so I can easily hide my face in his clothes. He walks casually, trying to look as inconspicuous as the newly returned First Guard can, but the tension in his body is unmistakable. Head turning constantly, he scans the area, taking in everything to ensure we aren't discovered.

"Ready?" he murmurs as we approach the door that leads to the courtyard and gate.

"For you to ravish me in front of the guards?" I joke, keeping my voice barely above a whisper. "Stass would wholeheartedly approve of this plan."

My chest warms at his low chuckle, just before a burst of cold air chills me again when he opens the door in front of us. I barely have time to react to the cold as he tugs me outside, flinging the door shut behind us, and spinning my body into the dark alcove.

A flicker of excitement stirs in my belly as my back slams into the stone wall, and my eyes lift to Weston's smirking face. Shadows caress his features as his body surrounds mine, both working to block the view of the guards stationed on the other side of his broad frame. The pads of his fingers gently tilt my chin until my lips touch his waiting mouth. He parts my lips, and my whole body quivers when his tongue barely brushes against mine. When he steps even closer and his body crushes me against the stone, I let out a sigh and tilt my head even farther back to meet every motion.

Weston kisses me like it's the first time, with all the desire and love that he poured into it before, but this time, he's not pulling away.

And he's right. None of it is fake. It's just a secret.

His mouth is unwavering as his hands roam over my body, gripping my hips firmly. Heat flames under my skin, and I let out a soft moan into his mouth as his thumbs find the soft flesh just beneath the bone, kneading soft circles and making me want his hands in other places.

A low chuckle rumbles in his throat as he breaks the kiss, and I can feel his smile against my lips. He barely stops for a moment before his lips are on me again, trailing kisses along my jaw. I keep my face turned into the warmth of his neck, inhaling him deeply until I feel the tickle of his breath against my ear.

"Laugh."

The giggle that erupts from my throat is from more than just following his command. It's as if time stood still in the last few moments, and I've been so lost in Weston's attention that I almost forgot there was more we have to accomplish, more to the ruse we are acting out.

Focus, Lennox.

His smile widens against my skin, and when his tongue flicks out, licking and sucking the sensitive spot beneath my earlobe, another uncontrollable wave of giggles overcomes me. He hums appreciatively against my skin before his lips drag back up to my ear.

"Every sound that comes out of that pretty mouth makes my cock stiffen. Any more and my guards will have no choice but to see how hard I am for you."

I suck in a quick breath, and he grumbles at the sound. My hands fist in his clothes as I pull him closer to me and angle my face so now I can whisper in his ear.

"If we didn't have somewhere to be, I'd be bringing you to bed right now."

Leaning back just enough so he can see my face again, he lets out a sigh, and worry races through me. It almost seems…sad. But it's gone in a second when he captures my chin in the crook of his hand, his thumb and his fingers pressing into my jaw, and pulling me in for another fierce kiss.

"I love you," he murmurs. "Time for the next step."

He pulls away abruptly, straightening until he towers over me again, and shifts to make sure I'm still shielded from any wandering eyes. He tugs my hood down a little farther over my face, then grabs my wrist, pulling me into his side and wrapping his arm around my shoulder. I curl into him, dipping my chin toward his chest and following the guidance of his body as we saunter toward the gate. His chest vibrates under my cheek as he grumbles a quick greeting.

"Gentlemen."

"Sir." A few other voices murmur a greeting, and I mentally tally the number of guards we have to worry about when the first one speaks again.

"Night off?"

"First one in over a week," Weston says, all his normal confidence coating his voice. "The queen is in her rooms. All entrances should be closed down for the night. If anything happens, ONeal is in command."

"Yes, sir," the man says again, followed by the clank of the lock and high-pitched squeal of the hinges. "Enjoy your evening, Rowe. Miss."

"We will," Weston mutters, and his arm tightens around me. I let out another playful giggle, a planned one this time, and sink into him more, hoping that whatever look is on Weston's face helps play into the scheme.

Weston's body guides me through the gate so I don't have to see where I'm walking. Hopefully to all the guards, it looks more like I don't want anyone to know who is sneaking off with the First Guard on his first night off, and less like the queen is hiding beneath a staff uniform.

My boots pound on the cobblestones once we step outside the grounds, and Weston's hand lifts from my shoulders. I assume he is signaling to the guards behind us it is safe to close the gate, and let out a deep breath when I hear the clang of the lock reverberate behind us.

We made it.

The mist and rain from earlier in the day have stopped, but the bitter wet chill in the air cuts through my clothes once we are out from behind the protection of the looming castle. I shiver, tugging my cloak more firmly around my shoulders and Weston leans closer.

"Almost there."

I wait until we're a few blocks away before straightening myself so I can walk normally. My hood still hangs low over my face, but at least I can see. I know the way, but the walk feels different this time. Very few people are out tonight, probably because of the worsened cold and late hour, but I still keep my gaze down. Now that the kingdom has seen me, I can't take any chances.

Not tonight.

The darkened entry of the alley comes into view ahead, and the closer we get, the easier it is to hear. The unfamiliar rush of the flowing fountain and the water rippling in the pool stands out over the otherwise still night.

Neither of us utters a word, but our pace quickens together. Weston's arm drops away from my shoulders only to clutch my hand and lead me around the corner and into the dark space. The bright white stone almost glows in the dim hue of the moon through the clouds, illuminating the air around it.

My heart pounds in my chest as we stop before it.

The fountain, the same one that brought each of us to Dawnlin and back again, looks nothing like it did mere days ago.

Gone are the packed dirt and sludge-covered surfaces, the cracks and nicks in the stone. Pristine white carvings with smooth surfaces depicting every manner of life and magic are clear as if it were in daylight. The water cascading through the openings in the mountain and into the pool below is clean and clear.

It looks exactly as I expected it to when I first realized the fountain was the key.

It looks *alive.*

As if something breathed life back into it, the same way the healing waters would. The magic is back.

We might actually have a chance.

Weston releases my hand and roams around the alley, peering behind anything that could hide someone, and looking in every shadowed corner to make sure we are alone, the same way Dane did the first time he whisked me away.

While Dane was the one who caused the heightened level of caution, Weston learned his lesson. This time, he isn't willing to take a chance that someone would harm the magic, not after we are so close.

"We're alone," he murmurs and is back at my side in an instant.

"We need to call Edmond." The breathiness in my voice betrays my excitement, and I look up at him. "Do you remember how?"

He nods, his brow furrowing. "Tears."

His chin dips, and his teal eyes meet mine, and in the moment as I look up at the man I love, tears feel completely impossible. Dawnlin already gave me almost everything I hoped for. It gave me a new family, one that I chose. It gave me freedom and the power to make my own decisions. It gave me love and a future I never thought I would have. Though I left wanting to cure my mother, and have a life with a parent I never knew, I was grateful for what I walked away with, even if letting go of the others and of the hope for saving her hurt more than any pain I ever knew.

The last time I knelt at this fountain, I was filled with hopelessness.

But when I look into Weston's face, when I feel the brush of his fingers against mine, I don't feel sad or hopeless at all.

Which makes panic rise in my chest.

If I can't cry, we can't call the Guardian. I've never seen Weston shed a tear, only felt the ones that fell on my cheeks when he thought I died in his arms. How can we go to Dawnlin if we're no longer hopeless?

"What are you thinking?" he asks, and I let out the breath I was holding.

"I don't know if I can do it. I..." My words trail off as I try to piece together all the emotions surging through me. "I think this is the first time I've ever been in my kingdom and didn't feel completely hopeless. Not anymore. Not with you here. Even if I could get a single tear to fall, deep down, the same feeling isn't there. Just a tear might not be enough for the magic."

I watch the column of his throat bob with a hard swallow, and he reaches up, his palm cupping my cheek. "I feel the same."

Leaning into his touch, I sigh deeply, my shoulders falling as if they no longer have to hold up the invisible weight I have been carrying. A quiet calm settles between us, punctuated only by the trickling of water in the fountain.

This was it. This was our chance to save her. Both of us sacrificed pieces of ourselves to do so, and now, all because we found each other, found happiness, we lost our chance to help her. I know it isn't a waste, and deep down, I want to think she would agree, especially knowing how my father left this world wishing only that we lived. But the piece of me that hoped for her to be part of my life aches.

"I don't want to give up on her," I murmur, "but maybe now that my father is gone, they can be together again. She would be happier, and so would he, after holding onto hope for so long. Even if we could get back, would it be selfish to keep her here and away from who she loves?"

He turns toward me, taking my other hand in his, and the thumb still on my cheek strokes my skin softly. "She loved you too, Lennox. Don't forget that. But holding onto hope isn't selfish. It's part of being human. Letting go isn't selfish either. There's no right or wrong answer in death. Life as well as the end of it, will be how it is meant to be."

How it is meant to be.

Everything that has happened in my life, all these ripple effects that have made me who I am and gotten me to where I stand, were all meant to be. I thought I could change things, control them, make what I wanted to happen when I wanted to, but time and time again, I was humbled. The island proved me wrong every time I thought I knew what was coming, and my world was turned upside down. My life here proved me wrong, when everything I expected to have or return to didn't end up at all how I pictured.

Because it all happened how it was meant to be.

Dawnlin gave me hope. Edmond led me to it. But even after everything, I still couldn't bring the waters back to her.

It's time for it to end.

"If there's no way we can help her, and no healing waters, then I think it is time I let her go." His lips tip up into a sad smile, no doubt understanding what I'm feeling after he too has had to let both of his parents go.

"I'm sorry, sweetheart."

Turning away, my eyes fall on the fountain again. This piece of stone has brought me so much misery yet so much happiness, and now my journey with it has come to an end. Edmond will be there, for whoever finds it that needs it in the future, and I know without a doubt that their experience will be more fruitful than ours.

"I tried," I whisper. Whether it is to the island, or to my mother, I'm unsure. I stare fixated on the water cascading down before me, so much like the waterfall that hid the island's secrets. Reaching out, I run my fingers through it, wanting to commit those moments to memory one final time.

Mouth falling open, my eyes widen, and a gasp rips from my throat as I take in the sight before me.

It's glowing. My hand cuts a break in the water's flow, and everywhere it touches my skin glows gold, the same as it had when my tears fell into it almost two years ago.

I yank my hand from the stream and reach out to grab Weston, yanking him closer to the fountain.

"Weston, look!"

Extending my hand, my fingertips disappear under the stream of water, and it happens again. The glowing water cascades off my skin, down into the pool below before fading once more.

"Does yours too?" I ask and tug his hand toward the stream, immersing it in the water beside mine. My eyes widen and my stomach tumbles as I watch the water around his hand glow, the same as mine.

"Why is it doing that?" I ask, looking around to see if there are any other changes, anything that could tell us what this means and why it is so different from before.

"I should have known that you two would be the first to call me."

We both whip around to find Edmond, cloaked in a robe similar to the one Dane wore when he was called. He stands behind us, hands clasped in front of him, with a soft smile on his face as he waits for our response.

"Pop," Weston breathes, and Edmond smiles wider. "That worked? The magic called you?"

"It did. I felt the pull, and here I am."

"But we didn't shed tears," I say. "How did we call you without them?"

Edmond barely shrugs. "Maybe the magic recognizes it already allowed you to the island once before, and you left empty-handed."

"It's giving us a second chance?" Hope bursts through my chest, and I look up at Weston as a grin tugs at my lips. I squeeze his arm, and he looks down at me with a smile, but my excitement falters. There's something more behind his eyes, and I can't figure it out, something I feel like he isn't telling me. I hold his gaze, searching his eyes, but he looks down at where my hand is wrapped around his arm, and instead reaches over and clasps our hands together.

"It would seem so," Edmond says, his eyes bouncing between us. "Are you ready to return?"

"Yes," Weston says, taking long strides toward his father and pulling me alongside him. He wraps his arms around my shoulders and gives Edmond a firm nod.

Edmond places his hand gently on my back, and I watch as his other hand reaches into the loosely open pouch that dangles from his belt. The glowing, fragrant dust that caused us so much trouble pools in his palm, and I squeeze my eyes shut, turning to sink my face into Weston's chest as I feel the magic of Dawnlin wash over us.

CHAPTER FORTY

Heat and moisture in the air surround me, and I know instantly that we are back in Dawnlin. Before I can even open my eyes, I feel Weston's hands at the clasp of my cloak, his deft fingers undoing it and pulling it from my shoulders in anticipation of the change in weather. He tosses it to the ground on the side of the plateau before pulling his off and tossing it away as well. We didn't dress for Dawnlin. The cold in Blackwood wouldn't have allowed it, and it would have made it too suspicious as we tried to sneak past the guards, but the moment his garment hits the floor, excitement courses through me again.

"Are you both alright?" Edmond asks as he takes a step back, pulling off his cloak and draping it over his arm.

"I'm alright." I finally take a moment to catch my breath, though my body hasn't yet forgotten how long I spent here, and it isn't difficult like it was the first time. I glance around at the same view that enraptured me before and note the oddly uneasy feeling in my stomach. It was mere days ago that we were trying so hard to leave, and I'm already back in a place I thought would be my home forever.

Not for long.

Weston stays quiet beside me, and I look up, squinting into the bright rays of the suns, trying to see if there's something stopping him from answering his father.

"Are you all right?" I ask quietly. My eyes catch on the tick of a muscle in his jaw before he nods, looking down at the ground between us.

"Yes."

I barely can get a sound out to ask something more, to figure out why he's behaving so oddly…or more like he used to, but Edmond interjects.

"Then let us head to the mountain. I am sure you both know the way." Edmond gestures down the pathway with a smile, and Weston's hand settles firmly in the small of my back. He leads me down the path, and I struggle to keep up with his brisk pace. I sneak glances at him as we walk, trying to catch any sort of clue or expression that could give me insight as to what is going on in his mind.

Something doesn't feel right. He's quiet and tense, but it's not just him that feels different. The island does too, and I can't figure out why. Maybe it is because of the new Guardian, this being the first time he has stepped foot on the island since the magic claimed him. Or maybe this is how it was supposed to feel, before the magic was cheated.

Pushing all the thoughts aside, I focus on the reason we're here, not Weston's mood, not Dane changing the magic. We got a second chance, and all I need to think about is whether I will be worthy or not. As we weave down the familiar trodden path, I feel a pang of sadness. We don't have to hurry, don't have to look around or watch our movements. There's no one we are going to run into, no Voyager hunting us down, no Dane to contend with. There's only Dawnlin, and whatever obstacles we may run into the closer we get to the mountain.

It makes me miss everyone even more and feel guilty that, with all the developments in my kingdom, I've barely thought about anyone.

I won't do that again, starting the moment we get home.

No one speaks as we traipse through the calm path, and I scan the surroundings in anticipation of the island changing beneath our feet. Despite having found the waters before, we still can't be too comfortable, and it's hard to let go of the heightened awareness that I've become so accustomed to here. We curve around the marsh, approaching the spot Weston and I met Mara and Roley barely over two weeks ago, and the sound of the rushing river below roars in the distance, just as the bridge comes into view.

Weston almost stumbles over me as my body jolts to a halt. My eyes widen and my jaw falls open as I take in every detail.

What the fuck?

"Lennox, what's wrong?" Weston grumbles beside me, and I slowly raise my hand to point to what my mind can't wrap around.

"The bridge. It's perfect." The words leave my lips in a rush, and Weston's head snaps toward it in response. The moment he sees it, he takes a hesitant step forward, like he too can't believe what is right before his eyes, how different it is from what he's known to be here for twenty years.

Brushing past him, I run to the edge of the bridge, forcing myself to stop at the entrance and peer across. My hands wrap hesitantly around the thick rope, as if it is going to disappear if I touch it. The fibers are firm and solid beneath my fingertips, with no frays or wear from years of being exposed to the elements. The wooden boards—the ones I almost fell through to a premature death—aren't the same at all. It's as if no one has ever walked across them before. Thick and solid, evenly spaced and polished, even the gaping hole where my body dangled above the monsters is nowhere in sight.

The monsters.

I bolt to the side and clamber up the boulder next to the bridge, leaning over the edge of the rock as far as I can to peer into the river below. Weston's hands grip my hips to keep me stable and stop me from leaning too far, but I don't need to get any farther. The breath is sucked from my lungs, and my eyes take in the gently flowing water, clear and sparkling underneath the evening sunlight.

Whipping my head over my shoulder, my voice rises, matching the mixture of confusion and excitement at war inside of me. "They're gone. The monsters are gone!"

"Where the hell would they go?" He leans over me to look into the canyon himself before muttering under his breath. "Shit."

"I was right." I spin around and slide down the side of the rock, dusting the dirt and stray gravel off my backside quickly. "The island was protecting the waters. All the dangers, all the changes, it was all because of Dane. Now that he's not here to protect against, it's like the island is restored."

"So it all disappeared," he murmurs, catching my gaze before we both look back toward Edmond.

"Is there something you're looking for?" he asks, a look of confusion on his face.

"I'll explain after, Pop." Weston takes my hand again, lacing his fingers through mine and tugging me back toward the path. "We need to get to the mountain."

We walk faster than before, and my legs burn with exertion as I try to keep up with Weston's long strides. The twists and turns wind us alongside the forest and bring us to the same spot I stood when I figured out the clues, when I saw the symbol of Dawnlin from the opposite side of the lagoon.

But just as the island had shockingly changed back at the bridge, the sight before us holds no symbol, no sign that anything is hidden, because on the other side of the lagoon, the mountain isn't the same one we left behind.

My jaw falls open, and I tug on Weston's arm, pulling him to a stop. "Look!"

The waterfall no longer conceals the entrance. The powerful wall of water that hid the doors now splits in two, the cascading veils following the curve of the stone door that sits between them. The stone bridge is exactly the same, arching over the river and second set of falls and caves that the waterfall creates, but this time, it's not just a bridge. Another stone walkway connects to the side, extending right to the base of the platform, as if the island never wanted to hide the entrance from anyone.

Because it never had to.

A disbelieving laugh bubbles from my chest, and tears well in my eyes.

"You both know what to do," Edmond says from beside us. "I will see you when you return."

I can't wait another second. Hope swells in my chest, and a grin splits my face as the feeling of triumph overwhelms me. This feels real and so much different from the last time I gazed out over the lagoon after my map led me to it. Squeezing Weston's hand, I take off running. My knees kick up the length of my skirts, and I wish, if not for this moment alone, that I had worn pants. Weston matches my pace, reaching out to catch me when I stumble on some stray rocks as we get closer, then urging me on once more.

Not once did the island trap us.

Not once did our course change.

There was no flicker of a fin in the lagoon, no snap of a monster from the canyon.

The island brought us back to get the healing waters, and isn't protecting them any longer.

Maybe we will be worthy after all.

Water glistens on the slick stone bridge, and Weston slows us to a walk so we can cross it without risking a fall. I take in the sight of the new twin waterfalls cascading on either side of us as we slowly cross the new pathway to the platform. Our boots barely meet the ground before a loud crack echoes around us, and a gap appears between the two stone doors as they swing inside, signaling torches to light down the tunnel.

"I can't believe it. It was supposed to be easy," I breathe. My chest still heaves from the run, and now from the anticipation of the chambers that await. I flex my fingers as the tips begin to tingle, curling them into fists to fight the eruption of emotions. Weston reaches over, taking my hands in his and turns me to face him.

"Lennox."

I drag my focus away from the entrance and bring it back to him. He brushes a strand of hair off my face, and his fingers wrap around my head, but he says nothing, only looks at me with longing and hesitancy. It's a look I am familiar with. It's the same way he looked at me before the night he saved me and got down on a knee to swear his oath.

"What's wrong, Weston? You're acting strange." My eyes search his, but his only grow more intense. His other hand finds my face and tilts my neck gently as he takes a step to close the gap between us.

"Nothing is wrong," he grumbles, but something deep in my stomach tells me I can't believe him. "Just remember, nothing could ever happen that will change how much I love you. Not here, not in Blackwood. Without you, I had no purpose, and you will be what I live and breathe for. My life isn't worth anything without you in it."

"Weston, you're scaring me," I mutter just before he crushes me in a kiss, leaving me breathless before pulling away and grabbing my hand. My mind spins with his words and the look on his face, but he doesn't give me a chance to do anything about it. Before I have time to think, or even try to decipher what he could be talking about in this moment we've both spent years waiting for, he takes the first step into the mountain, and the stone doors slam shut behind us.

CHAPTER FORTY-ONE

Every thought I had a moment ago disappears as we are plunged into darkness and my focus shifts to the torches before us. The magic humming in the mountain feels different from the last time I walked through that stone door, and this time, I'm not alone. I know what lies ahead, what will be asked of me and what the magic will decide. The chamber, the carving, being judged on my worth, but even though I know what lies ahead, it doesn't quell my nerves.

A prickle of uncertainty tickles the back of my neck as we stand side by side and look down the never-ending tunnel. I don't want to go through this just to be told I am unworthy again. The blow would be devastating, especially now that I am the queen and am already starting off my reign enveloped by darkness instead of light.

But would the island have let us back if there was a chance that we weren't worthy?

There's only one way to know.

My fingers ache as I grip Weston's hand as tightly as I can when he takes the first step forward. I follow his cue, and we walk, hand in hand, into the darkness with the flare of torches lighting before us down the endlessly winding path. I haven't even considered how long this portion of our return would take. Every time before, it had taken the entire day to get through the mountain. Now that there is nothing to protect against, no Castaways to get into position on the collection beach, would it be the same?

Neither of us speaks. The only sound beside the flickering of flame is the rhythmic thud of our boots against the ground. Tension emanates from Weston's body the farther we go. I can feel it in his stilted gait, and the way he clutches my hand.

He shouldn't be this worried, this uncomfortable, this…nervous. We finally made it. Years of sacrifice on his part and loneliness on mine brought us to this second chance, to get the healing waters and save my mother.

The final torches light ahead, and the darkness beyond tells me we've reached the chamber, the step through the portal one of the ultimate tests to show we trust Dawnlin and accept whatever it has in store for us.

But this time, it isn't Weston leading me forward. It's me pulling him.

I step into the darkness, tugging him behind me, and the circular room illuminates around us. The names carved into the walls look the same as before, even though I know there are new names scattered around, from Taril and every Voyager who couldn't leave without trying.

As I look around the room, the sinking feeling I left with comes back to me in full force, and the fear of being unworthy again is stifling. Underneath it all, there's something I didn't think I could have again if I ever came back here. A glimmer of hope.

We step into the middle of the room, silently standing side by side. Dawnlin knows we are here, but it is different from last time. The fountain didn't need our tears to bring us back, so the mountain might not be the same either. I don't know if I should speak or go straight to the basin, so I opt to do nothing, waiting for the island to see that I'm laying all my trust and guidance on it.

The boom of the voice makes my body jolt, even though I knew it would come, *hoped* it would come. I hold my breath, straining to keep myself under control as I listen to the words, and lay my fate in Dawnlin's hands.

To the heart of Dawnlin you return
The healing waters you hope to earn.
Deemed unworthy once before,
Unable to heal whom you adore.

Carved already the name in stone,
The magic tied to them alone.
To the basin you may advance,
Full of hope for another chance.

But blood and waters were not exchanged,
The question now, has fate rearranged?
To the same terms you must agree
For the isle of Dawnlin to hear your plea.

A fresh drop of blood must be obtained
To weigh whether intentions have been feigned.
If deemed worthy, the waters will flow,
And Dawnlin's final answer, you will know.

Weston's hand falls between us as I reach to my waistband and yank my dagger free. My feet have a mind of their own as I almost run across the chamber, climbing the steps and reaching the basin in barely a breath. I grip the curved lip of smooth stone and I peer inside, before pulling my eyes up to the dry spout above.

I have to know.

I have to know if all the suffering after the island denied me before was only because of Dane's betrayal. Countless hours of self-doubt, questioning myself, my value, my morals, my motivations. Was I, Lennox Holt, worthy of saving her all along, but the magic used this one final stipulation as a last defense against the waters falling into the wrong hands? Was everything Weston and Sig did born of good intention, but unnecessary because no one would be granted it as long as Dane was trying to steal it?

If those waters flowed, every single Voyager and Castaway needed to be tracked down and given the chance to come back, because if it was all Dawnlin protecting itself, each of them could have their hope restored.

But if it wasn't, if I truly am not worthy of saving my mother, then it all ends here, with this final drop of blood.

I raise my dagger, pressing the sharp edge into my now outstretched palm, but just as I am about break the skin, the boom of the voice startles me and I freeze once again.

The agreement unfair lest you're reminded of terms
Your drop of blood wholeheartedly affirms.
Should you choose another course,
One term the magic must still enforce.

Unable to speak if your return is too late,
And your loved one has already met their fate.
If the waters are used and all terms are met,
All memory of Dawnlin you will forget.

The sharp clatter of my blade falling into the basin echoes through the chamber, but I can barely hear it over the ringing in my ears. My fingertips tingle, the numbness spreading into my hands as they fall to the edge of the basin, gripping it so tightly that my fingernails break under the pressure. My head spins as my chest heaves, my breaths so harsh that the only thing keeping me upright is my grip on the stone.

Everything. I'd forget everything.

Flashes from the last time I stood at this basin come flooding back to me. The voice, the terms, the decision, the slicing of my palm. Nothing has changed. The bargain is the same as before, only this time, I have more to lose.

All memory of Dawnlin will cease to exist.

A sob rips through my chest, and I slap a hand over my mouth to stifle it. How stupid I was to think that forgetting Dane and the Voyagers would be difficult. Back then, I thought it was the most life-altering decision, but still was able to slice through my skin and live with the fact that I might not remember him.

This…this is excruciating. Impossible.

Hopeless.

My shoulders slump in defeat as my head hangs between them. Tears blur my vision, pooling swiftly until there's nothing I can do to stop it. They fall, and the moment they strike the empty stone basin, it's like my chest cleaves in two.

How can I choose my mother over Weston? How can I let go of the only family I have left, and snuff the hopes and dreams she had for a life with me, her only daughter? After all this time, all the trials, all the sacrifice, the death, I can't just give up on her.

But how can I lose the love of my life? How can I leave him completely alone, with no father, no friends, no one to spend the life he also sacrificed? How can I trade one love for another?

My knees tremble at the thought of leaving him alone and losing him. But just as terrifying is the thought of choosing to end the life my mother kept clutched in her perpetual sleep, and turning away from the second chance the island is giving me.

The strong and determined Lennox that walked into this mountain the first time is nowhere in sight. I was prepared to forget it all before, prepared to do anything to have a loving parent, to know what true and unconditional love feels like, because somewhere deep inside, I think I knew that the love I thought I had from Dane wasn't true.

But Weston? Weston's love is. It is true, and deep, and unrelenting. It is selfless and undeniable, and pure. As is mine for him.

The sob is louder this time, almost equaling the sound of my pounding heart. I reach up to press my palm over it, trying to force the stabbing pain away as my breaths become short and stilted, and tears continue to stream down my face.

Then it clicks.

My gaze flies to my hand, pressed into my chest, over my heart.

He knew.

Whirling back toward the center of the room, my eyes find his, my jaw slack with disbelief as I take in the look of complete and utter devastation on his face.

"You remembered." My voice is watery and barely audible. "That's why you…you said…all those things. You remembered that if I went through with this, I would forget you."

His throat bobs, and his jaw tightens, but he doesn't say a word. He nods his head only once, and it feels like the ground shakes beneath me. I thought I would be angry, thought the moment he told me he knew, I would rage at him, like I'd done so many times before, but the anger doesn't come. Instead, it is replaced with soul-crushing anguish, the heartbreak instead taking over me with full force.

"How could you, Weston?" I scream. My voice cracks as I fall apart in front of him, but his gaze holds firm, and he doesn't shy away. "How could you let me come back here if you knew I would forget it all? Why didn't you tell me? Why didn't you stop me?"

I don't know when I moved. My mind didn't register my feet moving at all, taking me down the steps and across the chamber, but now, I stand before him, his clothes fisted in my hands as I shake him with all my strength and wail every question.

He doesn't fight me, doesn't yell back like he's done before time and time again as our stubbornness butted heads against each other. I want him to yell, to scream, to fight with me. I want him to stoke the anger that is so easy to hide behind, because it hurts less than the misery I'm feeling knowing he let me come here to sacrifice him. The sorry in his eyes only deepens as he dips his chin, his gaze still locked on mine.

"How could I stop you?"

His voice is a soft caress, the direct opposite of my frantic screaming, and it shatters me into pieces.

"You just stop me! You say, 'Lennox, are you sure you want to forget everything?' Do I have to make you repeat after me?"

His hand cups my face, and his thumb rubs soft strokes over my cheekbone. "How could I be selfish and tell you to give up the chance to save your mother, the same person I came here to save? How could I take her away?"

"Because it would take away you!" My shriek echoes off the walls of the chamber and is followed by my sobbing through gritted teeth and a clenched jaw.

His other hand settles on my face, and he leans in close, clutching me to him. His brows crinkle in the middle as he begs me silently to listen.

"Then let me do this for you."

Mouth falling open, I gape at him, sheer horror etched onto my face.

Let Weston forget? After all he's done, all he's sacrificed, the life he left behind, how could I decide to let him forget? It wouldn't only be me he lost. He spent twenty years with a family he could find back in our world, start a new life with. He would lose every single one of them if he took my place, my responsibility.

My duty.

Why is he offering to give up even more of his life for me?

Because he swore he would.

The last thread of control I have snaps, and I feel it reverberate through me like the explosion in the mountain. I claw at his wrists, trying to hang on to him, to ground myself, as my knees give out beneath me.

I can't breathe.

I can't think.

All I can do is stare back into those teal eyes, the ones that brought me back to life in so many ways, and beg them to save me once more.

"Lennox, sweetheart, you need to breathe."

A sound like I've never made before rips from my chest as I try to suck in air. This feels worse than drowning, worse than giving up hope on my mother. I can't feel my hands, my legs, my feet. My chest feels like it is caving in on itself, my breaths so shallow and sobs so deep that I can't move.

I'm dying.

I always wondered what would pull me into the next life, and after facing death so many times on this very island and at the hands of others back home, I never thought it would be from a broken heart and an impossible choice.

Weston lowers us to the floor and kneels before scooping me into his arms and crushing me against his chest. The moment he takes over, holding me when I cannot hold myself, I completely break.

Pain erupts in my fingers as I clutch onto him, squeezing and grabbing anything I can reach to stop feeling like I'm falling. His clothes, his neck, his shoulders, his arms. My limbs move erratically, grasping at anything and unable to be controlled by my spiraling mind.

"Shhh," he croons into my ear. His hand strokes my hair as he rocks me slowly. "Breathe, Lennox, breathe."

I try to follow his command, but I can't. All I can think about is that these could be the last moments that either of us remembers each other. These could be our last touches, our last caresses, our last words spoken, before they disappear forever. Our entire love story vanished, leaving the other miserable and alone to watch as they are forgotten and unable to ever speak of it.

"I—I—I…can't," I stutter, and press my forehead into his chest.

"You can. You are the strongest person I know. You have survived worse than this. You can breathe, baby. Please breathe."

"I can't let you go, too," I cry, each word punctuated by a sob.

Is this how my life is truly meant to be? Am I destined to be alone? Every person I have needed or ever grown close to has been ripped away from me. Just when I think I have finally found a place where I belong, both in the arms of someone else and within myself, once again it's slipping through my fingers.

Weston or me. This choice is impossible. I can't make it.

But I can't let him make it for me.

"You aren't letting me go," he grumbles, and his hand settles on the side of my neck, pushing me back slightly so he can look into my eyes. "You aren't letting me go. I will still be there, by your side, whether or not you remember me. Until the breath stills in my lungs."

"It's not fair," I choke out, and a sad smile tips the corner of his lips.

"Nothing in life is fair, sweetheart. The one I've lived is proof of that." He dips his face toward mine, the sincerity in his gaze piercing. "But every unfair second of it I struggled through was worth it because it brought me to you. Now breathe. In."

I finally suck in a short, stuttered breath, keeping my eyes locked on his while I do.

"Again," he commands as his hand strokes circles on my back. I follow his orders, the second breath barely easier than the last, but I will myself to try.

"Keep breathing," he says, and I do, refusing to look away from him, and trying to soak in the feeling of his touch, because either way, I lose it forever.

"We don't have to decide right now," he murmurs, and my measured breaths stop.

"Yes, we do, Weston. We're in the mountain!" I gesture around us incredulously, flinging my hand toward the wall nearest us, and he catches my wrist, bringing my hand back to rest on his chest.

"What I mean is, we can both try, and when we go back, we can decide then. All of this worry might be for nothing. We could still be unworthy."

A harsh laugh escapes me. "That would make all of this easier."

"Maybe in the moment, but not really. You would still have to say goodbye to Lyla."

A fresh wave of tears fills my eyes, and he leans forward, pressing a firm kiss to my forehead.

"Whatever happens, you aren't losing me, Lennox. I will be right behind you, like I swore I would."

We sit on the floor of the chamber, clutching each other in silence until my breaths become steady once again, though still broken by the occasional stuttered inhale. The panic has quieted, and despite the steady hum of anguish and worry just beneath the surface, in this moment, with this breath, I no longer feel like I'm imploding.

I'm just numb. Numb and angry with myself that I didn't remember such a crucial detail to the bargain I so willingly made with Danwlin once before. Maybe if I had, we never would have gone back to the fountain, or never would have let Edmond sweep us away after admitting that we were happy without having the second chance we thought we wanted.

But that was not how this night was to be, and nothing will change where we are and the choice that now sits before us. Though everything feels out of my control, I hold on tightly to the one thing I can.

"I want to do this together," I whisper.

"Anything you want, my queen." He presses a soft kiss to my lips, and I feel a crippling pang in my chest. The sobs rear up again, but I squash them down, doing what Weston commanded me, and focusing on my breath. His arms loosen and he takes my hands, helping me to my feet as he stands beside me, waiting to make sure I no longer feel ready to collapse under the weight of this night.

We walk slowly together, hand in hand, across the chamber and climb the steps up onto the dais. Light still illuminates the empty basin, and I reach inside, grabbing the hilt of my dagger before turning toward Weston. He lifts his hand, holding his open palm out to me, and I take a deep breath before wrapping my fingers around his. The tip of my blade trails along his skin, and blood blooms in its wake; the blood that will seal the promise to the island and upend our lives, all to save my mother's.

When it is my turn, I don't hesitate, dragging the same tip of the blade across my palm and watching a similar deep crimson puddle form.

"Ready?" I whisper and look up at him.

He nods, refusing to look away as he extends his hand over the basin. I mimic the motion and in the same breath, our hands turn over, and the blood falls to the stone.

From the corner of my eye, I see the droplets disappear, but I can't look away from Weston. Warmth coats my palm, and when he takes my hand in his, I finally pull my eyes away to see both our wounds knitting together with a flash of a golden glow, sealing the deal the same way it is sealing our fate.

The voice booms around us, and he sidles closer, his side pressed into mine as we wait for the next direction.

To those deemed worthy, healing waters will flow,
For what's held in all hearts, the isle does know.
Don't lose hope, as has been discussed.
In the magic of Dawnlin, you must trust.

A small glass vial appears before each of us, and my hand shakes as I reach down to pick it up. The glass is cool against my fingertips, and I watch as Weston does the same, but nods toward me.

"You first."

The breath stills in my chest as I drag my eyes to the spout. I begged for it to flow before, pleaded with Dawnlin to find me worthy, but this time, I don't know what I want. If it doesn't, I lose my mother, but if it does, I lose the one true love in my life, the man who chose me, and sacrificed for me. Who saved my life and protected me. The man who would lay down his own, in death and in the midst of this twisted magic, for me, so that I don't have to suffer.

The glass jostles in my trembling hands as I lift the vial to the spout. This is it. This is the moment that decides my fate. Blood rushes in my ears, the roaring blocking out everything except the feel of Weston pressed into me, and the hole in the stone wall. My chest burns from holding my breath as I wait for something or nothing to happen. Just when I think that, once again, I am unworthy, that all the worries that just broke me and the tears shed were unnecessary, my body feels like it has been crushed once again.

Because I'm worthy, and the waters flow.

CHAPTER FORTY-TWO

The press of Weston's hand into the small of my back is the only way I know that all of this is real. It isn't a nightmare that I can't pull myself out of, like the ones that plagued me until I spent every night sleeping beside him. He guides me through the stone archway, but I can barely focus on the fact that we are leaving the mountain. Everything surrounding us as we traipse through the tunnel is a blur, because I can only see the two matching vials I hold, one in each hand.

His and mine.

It was no longer a question or a worry. After all this time, both of us were deemed worthy by Dawnlin to save my mother.

But how can we possibly choose who will be the one to do it?

I can't pull my eyes away from the sparkling liquid in the corked glass that swirls and jostles with every dragging step I take. My boot catches on a rock jutting from the ground, and I barely flinch as I stumble forward, because Weston is right there to catch me. He always is, in more ways than just catching me before I literally hit the ground.

His arm wraps around my back, his hand settling on my hip as he supports me, holding me upright as my body literally bears the crushing weight of this decision. The magic of the portal surrounds me, pressing into my skin as we step through, and it is only then that I look up, blinking into the bright light of the pink and orange sunset that fills the sky.

But we aren't on the beach. My boots don't sink into the sand as I step forward toward the crash of the waves. Instead, they are planted on the stone surface of the platform, the same place we had entered, as the twin waterfalls cascade on either side of us. Edmond stands a few paces away, his hands clasped in front of him, clearly waiting for our return.

Everything feels hollow as I lean into Weston for support when he urges me forward toward his father. My feet move on their own, pulling me away from the mountain, back toward my kingdom where the reality of this decision will be too much to bear. My steps falter, the soles of my boots slipping on the slick surface beneath them, and I almost fall to my knees.

Part of me doesn't care. Part of me wants to feel the pain of my knees hitting the ground. It would let me feel something, anything other than this hollow ache and churning stomach that have been with me since the moment I could breathe again in Weston's arms. But as he always does, he doesn't let me fall. Weston catches me, then bends to hook his arm under the crook of my knees before hoisting me into his arms.

Shoulders caving in on themselves, I immediately shrug against him, pressing my cheek into his chest before my muscles surrender and I fall like a dead weight. A single tear trails down my cheek, and I coil my arms into my abdomen, clutching the vials as tight as the exhaustion will let me.

"I can't go back yet," I murmur, knowing that he likely didn't hear me from the roar of the crashing water around us.

He leans forward, angling his ear toward my lips and grumbles, "Tell me again."

It takes every ounce of strength I can muster right now to find my voice, and try to keep it from cracking under the pain, but try as I might, it disobeys me and does, anyway. "I can't leave yet. Take me home."

He nods before turning to press a kiss to my forehead and straightening once more as he strides across the platform, gesturing to Edmond to follow him to the opposite side of the bridge.

"May I ask if you were successful?" Edmond says once we are back on solid ground, and I feel Weston nod.

"We were this time."

My lip trembles, and my hands tighten around the glass.

"Ah, I see. Are you ready to return then?" Edmond asks.

"No, Pop. We're staying the night. There's a ship in the cove, well, there was. Hopefully, it is still there. That's where I lived. That's where we'll be."

"I will be here when you are ready."

"There's space on my ship. Where are you going to stay?"

"In the Guardian's home, of course."

If I had the energy to respond, I would ask Edmond about the Guardian's home, but I can't. It doesn't surprise me, though, that while I spent so much time trying to figure out if there was any specific place for the Guardian while I searched for answers on the island, Edmond already knew them, just from spending a few hours with Horace. While it feels like a dagger to the stomach knowing I am losing yet another important person in my life, it brings me joy Edmond is now the Guardian of Dawnlin. It feels like the magic is right again, and all the lost knowledge has been found.

"Goodnight, Pop."

Weston cradles me closer as he walks along the path through the trees. I don't move or make a sound. Instead, my eyes flutter closed, and I just listen to the rustle of the leaves and the pounding of his heart. After a few minutes, the comforting sound of waves crashing hits my ears, and when his pace doesn't slow, I know the ship must still be there, waiting for us. Maybe it never left, or maybe the island brought it back the moment it knew I wasn't ready to leave.

The pounding of Weston's boots on the gangway is loud, and I let out a deep sigh.

Home. This ship is the only place that has truly ever felt like home.

And I might forget it forever.

I finally peek out from where I've stayed tucked away, and see that it's almost dark now, the suns having fallen enough to barely peek over the horizon. Torches whoosh around us as they catch fire, lighting the deck as Weston steps onto it, and I let out a breath heavy with exhaustion.

Today has been too much. All I want is to curl into Weston's body, close my eyes and fall asleep, making all my problems disappear. But at the same time, I want to stay awake, soaking up every second, every movement, every touch, every sound, out of fear of never having them again.

We descend the steps, turn down the hallway, and head straight to our room. The ship is silent, and just like the last time we were alone and it was this quiet, I don't like it. But I need to be alone with him. I need time to figure this out, without the pressure of running a kingdom and rebuilding everything after my father's death.

I need him, and only him, with no distractions.

The lanterns flicker to life the moment we step inside our room, and as I take it all in, a fresh wave of grief washes over me.

"Let me run you a bath," Weston says, his voice cutting through my spiraling thoughts. "And I'll get us something to eat."

I barely nod, and I don't know if he even sees it. I'm too upset, too completely paralyzed by what happened tonight to coax my voice to life. He sets me down softly in his chair, and his hands are gentle as he takes the vials out of mine, placing them on the desk behind me with a soft thud. My shoulders sink, and I curl in on myself as I wrap my arms around my torso, trying to fight the sinking feeling deep in my stomach.

Memories flash repeatedly in my mind at the sound of rushing water and the filling tub, and my chin quivers. Squeezing my eyes shut, I replay them all: struggling to sleep after his first shift as I listened to him bathe, trying to convince him we were friends before he promised to take me to the island and tell me more of the truth, lazily soaking in the hot water with him after letting him consume my body and take everything I had left to give.

They'll all be gone. Every single one of those memories. I had to fight so hard to make all of them happen, all for different reasons, and now, it feels like it was pointless, because either he or I won't remember a thing.

Blurred boots appear in my tear-filled line of sight as he steps back in front of me and gently takes my hands, pulling me to stand. Every movement is quick but caring, purposeful but compassionate. He pulls the dagger from my waistband, setting it next to the vials before loosening the laces on my bodice, tugging and sliding the material over my skin until I'm freed from the staff uniform.

Where just hours ago this would have made me want to drag him straight to bed, it's different now. His actions aren't full of lust and desire. They're filled with comfort and understanding and love. He knows the decision that lies before me. He made it mine, but that doesn't mean he will not help me through it.

My skirt falls to the floor next, and I grip his forearms as I step out of it, and he makes quick work of my undergarments before sweeping me up into his arms again and walking me over to the tub. My skin screams as he slowly lowers me into the water, but I welcome the heat. I want to feel a different pain and am grateful for the distraction as I pull my knees to my chest and rest my chin on them.

"I'll be back in a few minutes," he murmurs, pressing a kiss into my hair. I don't watch as he walks away. I can't bear the sight of it, but when the door clicks behind him, the room falls into a deafening silence.

The last time I was alone like this, in this room, was when Weston left to bring Fin back home.

Fin.

My heart breaks again, as flashes of his smiling face and tight hugs surface in my memory. It feels like a curse that I'm bringing upon myself, as my mind reminds me of every person I will no longer have. Anger bubbles in my chest, but not at Dawnlin.

It's at myself.

How could I have forgotten such a crucial detail in the bargain I struck? How could I have been so focused on myself, on finding love and family, that I didn't remember something that would change the course of our entire lives?

If I had, maybe I never would have decided to come back. Maybe I would have followed through with my plan and spoken to the healers instead of the Guardian tonight. I wouldn't have talked Weston into sneaking me out of the castle and bringing me to the fountain, now that it is so obvious to me he didn't want to.

I haven't made a decision. I still could leave here and follow through. I could let her go. But would I? Would Weston even let me?

I know he said it was my decision, but would he accept it? He was worthy the same as I was. One of those vials belongs to him. Even if I say I want to let her go, to let her be with my father, he could still decide to fulfill his promise to his king and use his healing waters to save her.

He would do it so that I didn't have to suffer without her, but he isn't considering how much I would suffer if I had to watch him forget. If I had to live every day, watching him serve the crown, serve me, and only remember his life as the First Guard.

Tears well in my eyes and I hug my knees tighter trying to ease the pressure of the gaping hole in my chest.

I couldn't do it. I couldn't live every day watching him forget me and everyone else he cares for. He wouldn't remember Sig, or Jorn, or how he was the beloved Captain to everyone on this ship.

Without a second thought, he would give up his life for me, again.

But I can't let him do it, selfishly, but also not.

I never thought I would have to choose between the man I love and the mother I always wanted.

When we found the dust, and decided to go back to my kingdom, I wasn't expecting to have everyone that was supposed to stand beside me and help me as queen completely disappear. My father, Edmond, Brynne. Almost everyone I trusted, or thought I trusted, is gone.

Weston would never leave his position as First Guard. I know firsthand how much he values his duty and his oath, and he would trust no one else with my protection. He was the one who said that his title is the only thing ensuring that we can be together, in whatever capacity that would allow.

If I say goodbye to my mother, then I say goodbye to the last person who could help me fulfill my potential and ensure I don't succumb to the pressures and expectations of a new ruler. If I don't heal her, I have no one left to appoint as an advisor, to give me guidance or direction from their own experience. My kingdom could fall, and it would be entirely my fault.

The only person who has been queen, who knows what it is like and what it requires, is her.

If I let her go, I would be dooming all of my people to the reign of a naïve queen, who only just ever found enough strength to step foot outside the castle walls. There would be no one there to inspire confidence in my people, no one to support and vouch for me, no one to calm the nerves or stop the mistreatment of other kings and queens. We've already had one, and that was while my father still sat on the throne. How easily could a mutiny start amongst *my* guards if it were just me?

The thoughts swirl in my mind, and bile bites at the back of my throat as I consider it all. How am I supposed to choose between what is best for my kingdom, and what is best for me?

Are they the same?

The sound of clothing hitting the ground beside me pulls me out of my thought spiral. I'd been so lost in my mind that I hadn't even heard him come back into the room. Weston steps into the tub behind me, slowly sinking into the water and extending his legs on either side of me. The surface of the water ripples and sloshes around us as he sidles up to me, and I let out a sigh as his lips press firmly into my shoulder. His hands slide up my back, working and kneading the muscles along my spine, before they slow at the base of my neck.

With our disappearance from the castle tonight, I missed my evening dose of the pain medication, but the stiff muscles and soreness has been the last thing on my mind. Tears bite at my eyes when I feel the tips of Weston's fingers press into the muscles at the back of my neck, slowly circling around to the front, followed by the familiar tingling warmth of the salve.

He hates using the magic that Dawnlin offered us during our time here, but he never hesitated using it for me. I can't imagine how much it has been gnawing at him, wishing he could do something to help rid me of the injury. He saw his opportunity, and took it, and while it stopped bothering me mentally, at least now I know he is satisfied.

"Thank you," I whisper, and feel him let out a hot sigh against my skin just as the last tingling of the salve dissipates. He settles his chin into my shoulder, and I tilt my head, resting it against his.

"I'm sorry I didn't tell you," he mumbles, and I feel a pang in my chest. "I didn't want to influence your decision. It's not my place to try to persuade you either way, and I didn't want you to feel like I was."

I shake my head. "You're wrong. It *is* your place, because you're mine and I'm yours. That means you talk to me, Weston. Not hide things from me."

"I wasn't trying to hide it." The water sloshes as his arms wrap around my middle and clench tightly. "I truly didn't know if you remembered, and still wanted to try. I couldn't leave Blackwood and get to the mountain without you knowing my feelings for you. You have to know that whatever you decide, they won't change."

"We decide. Not just me."

His lips press into my shoulder again, and he mutters against my skin. "It's not my decision, my queen. But I will shoulder the burden for you time and time again, for as many stars as there are in the sky so you never have to feel the way you felt today."

I suck in a sharp breath and swallow down the lump in my throat. "I don't think there's a path I can choose where I wouldn't feel that way."

The muscles in his arms ripple as leans back, pulling me along with him until I'm settled against his chest with my head in the crook of his neck.

"We have time," he says. "We don't need to decide tonight. Lyla has held on this long, we can look at all the possibilities."

I don't respond, because he must know that I've been analyzing the possibilities since the moment he left me alone, and I'm just as lost as I was when I heard the reminder from the island.

The deafening silence settles into a comfortable one, and I close my eyes, just breathing and feeling. The heat from the water, the firmness of his body, the safety and protection in his arms.

I try not to think, but with the gravity of this choice and all the new ones that have come up, I can't get this thought out of my mind.

"We have to find all the others. We have to bring them back so they can try too."

"I agree," he grumbles.

I swallow hard. "Only you can do that." My voice is barely a whisper, and, despite my effort, cracks on the last word.

He releases a deep sigh.

"I know."

Weston's hold on me doesn't loosen as we sit in the cooling water and listen to the comforting sounds of the ship. My muscles still feel taut despite the work of his powerful hands, and my chest is as full of turmoil as it was before.

I don't want to cry anymore. I want to be strong, even though I feel anything but. More than anything, I just want to escape the prison of my mind and fate, even if it is just for a little while. I want to feel whole, and safe, and loved.

Because it might be the last time I ever do.

Squeezing my eyes shut, a single tear escapes one corner.

"I need you to love me," I whisper softly.

He shifts behind me, sitting us upright and sending the water cascading over the sides of the tub as he turns my body until I'm facing him. Taking my face in his hands, I can barely meet his eyes because the earnestness I find there feels like a dagger to my chest.

"Lennox, I do love you. I love you with every part of me, to the depths of my soul. I love you more than I have ever loved anyone in my short and long life. More than my mother, my father, my best friend, my family here. You gave me purpose, and hope for a life that I thought was well over. I will never stop loving you, never stop showing you that you are mine, and that I would do anything for you, in any time, any place. You don't need me to love you, because I already do, and no matter how many more challenges we face, that will never change."

My face crumbles at his words, and I drop my chin to my chest to try to hide it. I can't contain the sob that built up inside me the longer he spoke, and the mangled sound punctuates the quiet room.

His reassurance is exactly the problem. Deep in my soul, I know he means every word. I know he loves me, the same as he knows I love him. And it's exactly why this choice is tearing me apart piece by piece.

"I know you do," I say, my words mangled by the effort it is taking not to break into another fit of tears. "That's not what I mean."

I lift my chin to meet his gaze, only to find him watching me, his face pleading for me to believe his words. His eyes take in my tears, my swollen eyes, my quivering lips.

"Then tell me what you mean, sweetheart."

My limbs tremble as I reach out and settle my hands at the curve of his neck, stroking his skin with one thumb. My eyes dart down to his mouth, before meeting those beautiful teal depths again. "I need you to love me."

He doesn't hesitate, only leans in and presses the softest brush of a kiss to my lips.

"I will do anything for you, my queen."

CHAPTER FORTY-THREE

Heat smolders in his eyes, but the way Weston looks at me is with more than just desire. Rivulets of water cascade down his naked flesh, splashing into the tub as he grips both sides and stands. His movements aren't hasty, they're purposeful as he steps over the side, toweling off before reaching his hands out to help me to my feet.

Weston never wants to see me in pain, and he knows that what I've asked for is the only balm that will soothe the wounds that are actively bruising and bleeding my heart. He never makes me wait, or makes me question whether or not he wants to touch me or be with me, but this time feels different. Each touch and caress is reverent and unhurried, but enough that I'm not left feeling empty.

His hands are gentle as he towels off my hair, then slides the plush fabric down the length of my skin. I close my eyes, reveling in the feel of him caring for me, and try to focus only on that. Not tomorrow, not the future. Only Weston.

He lifts my chin gently, and my eyelids barely flutter open before they are closing again as he dips his face to mine, sweeping me into a soft, sensual kiss. With his arms wrapped around my middle, he lifts me until our chests press together, our bodies molding and fitting with one another as if we were always meant to be.

My arms fall gently around his neck, and a soft sigh escapes my lips when his tongue brushes against mine, asking, seeking, yearning, and I let him. My thoughts dim under the heat of his skin, and the deepening of his kiss, and I don't realize he's carried me across the room until my back settles on the cool sheets of his bed.

Our bed.

For the last time.

He never breaks contact as he lowers himself over me, his bare skin caressing every inch of mine. Strong arms encircle me, muscles tightening as he clutches me to him, his kiss still slow and constant, as if we have all the time in the world.

Turning away slightly, I break the seal of our kiss, and our chests heave against each other, my body relishing and also fighting against the crushing weight of him. When he presses his forehead against mine, I break the silence.

"I love you," I whisper, and almost wince as I can hear the tears I'm holding back in my broken voice. His hand moves to my face, his thumb brushing the swollen pout of my bottom lip, but his eyes dart between mine as his brow furrows.

"Don't say that like you're telling me goodbye." The low rumble in his chest and the earnest look on his face almost breaks the dam holding my tears back, and it takes everything in me to keep them at bay, to just focus on him. His heat, his weight, his smell. Trying to memorize everything in case it all disappears.

"Lennox," he says, snapping me out of my thoughts, and I focus back on his face. "We aren't saying goodbye."

"Weston—"

"No. I said it's your decision whichever way we do this, but this is not goodbye. Tonight is not goodbye. Do you understand me?"

My throat tightens as a traitorous tear escapes the corner of my eye, but I don't answer. I can't. Not when everything about this night and the way he is holding me feels exactly like a goodbye.

His face hardens, the commanding look of the stoic captain I fell in love with firmly in place. "I need to hear you say it. Tell me you understand."

I swallow hard, my voice watery when I can finally speak. "I understand."

As if to seal the agreement between us, his lips mold over mine, the fire behind his words burning into me, and I kiss him back with all the same heat and intensity. He pulls away, his face softening again as he presses slow kisses to my face, my jaw, my neck, slowly winding his way down my body. His hands never leave me. They explore my skin, holding and caressing as if I'm the most precious thing in the world to him. The brush of his fingertips lights a fire in their wake, and my core throbs and flutters the closer he gets, but he doesn't hurry.

Instead, he savors me. With every brush of his lips, his tongue, his fingers, he breaks me and builds me back up again, until all of my worry and anguish is replaced by his all-consuming love.

"So fucking beautiful," he grumbles against my inner thigh, and my chest swells when he moves to the other side. "So fucking perfect." My body writhes and shakes as he finds my wet heat, worshiping me with his mouth and tongue, as his soft words of endearment and encouragement mix with my whimpers of uncontrollable pleasure.

When I feel as if I'm going to split in two, both from his body and the swell of emotions he's pulling from me, I reach for his hand, pulling it away from where it is planted firmly on my hip, and tug him toward me.

"I need you," I pant, the words almost a plea. His eyes meet mine from where his chin rests on my stomach, and the passion in his gaze makes my heart pound in my chest. "I need you inside me."

"There is no place in this world, or our world I would rather be, my queen."

Sitting back on his heels, he grips my hips and slides me toward him before wrapping my legs around his back and angling my body the way he wants me. Unable to tear my eyes away, I watch every movement as he reaches down, fingers wrapping around his thick cock, hard and ready after all the time he already spent pleasuring my body. He lines himself up, his tip teasing my entrance, and my breaths grow rapid with expectation of him filling me.

The thick muscles in his thighs ripple as his hips flex forward, so slowly and torturously stretching and filling me, that I can't stop the low moan that rumbles in my throat. I bite my lip to stifle a cry when his hands find the curve of my ass and lift, pulling me closer and holding my hips off the bed as he sinks impossibly deeper. My hands fist in the sheets as he finds a rhythm; a slow thrust and retreat, the fullness everything that I was begging him for.

He's not frantic or hurried, but like Weston always does, he pours all his emotions into his touch. Every deep stroke feels like something new. It feels like uncertainty and fear and worry, but most of all it feels like love.

And even though he said it isn't, it feels like goodbye.

He catches me watching, unable to look away from where the deep cut of his muscles guides my gaze to his cock, especially as it slowly sinks inside of me.

"You can watch me take you all you want, sweetheart," he says, followed by a low grunt as he hits me impossibly deeper. The muscles in his abdomen ripple, and sweat glistens on his skin, sparkling over every surface and making even the mangled flesh of his scar beautiful in the moonlight.

"Watch me remind you that this is mine. Your cries are mine, your pleasure is mine, your body is mine." He leans forward, setting both hands on either side of my head, but his hips do not stop their decadent torture. He lowers his face until his lips are barely a breath away. "Your heart is mine."

"And yours is mine," I whisper as I stare into his eyes.

"For eternity."

His mouth drops to mine, and he kisses me fiercely, crushing himself to me, and devouring me in every way he can. Fire licks up my spine as he rocks into me, the pressure of his hips hitting me just right as his thick cock still slowly slides in and out. But when the building pressure makes my back arch into him, feeling like I'm going to implode, he pulls back, leaving me wanting until our bodies are tangled in a new way and he slides into me once more.

Over and over again, he brings me to the pinnacle of pleasure, loving me like I said I needed. Silent tears trail from the corners of my eyes, and my chest squeezes as he whispers soft words in my ear, promises that I know neither of us should make tonight. He loves me, despite everything inside me that wants to break and mourn the version of me that won't remember any of this, or the one that will never have it again.

When my limbs are shaking, and my chest heaving, unable to take the onslaught of physical and emotional bliss any longer, my hand wraps around his wrist, squeezing tight until his movements still.

"Weston, please." My words are almost a whine, and I see a flicker of anguish in his eyes as he slides out of me, before turning me onto my back so our chests press together once more.

I almost feel like I will tip over the edge as his cock thrusts inside me once more, and I gasp at the shock that the contact with my swollen core sends through me. His hands skate up my sides and push my arms above my head, his fingers tickling my skin until they lace between mine. He squeezes my hands tightly, pressing them into the soft mattress above, and his nose strokes down the length of mine.

"Hold on to me." His chest rumbles with the command, and I nod fiercely, squeezing his hands in mine and pinning my knees to his sides, drawing him even deeper. "Don't ever let go."

Our bodies move together, each movement in perfect harmony until we are consumed by moans and cries and whispers. We're all hands and tongues and hips, as the slow and tender rocking turns into frenzied, burning desire. Pressure and heat build until I don't think I can hold on any longer, and the voice that is my calm in all the chaos of my world and my mind breaks through the periphery.

"Let it go, Lennox. Come with me, my queen."

My toes curl and my back arches, pushing my hips harder onto him as I come undone, fueled even harder by the fierce rock of Weston's cock into me, and the feral roar into the crook of my neck as his hot release spills inside me. Heat blooms in my belly and between my thighs as my limbs collapse, my fingers unable to move from squeezing his hands so tightly. He releases my hands and cups my face, kissing me deeply, clutching me as if I'm going to disappear, before pulling back.

My eyes flutter open when I feel the light brush of his fingertips slide through my hair. His dark teal eyes are hooded as he simply watches me, or the remnants of me after he lit my entire body on fire and made me explode.

"What?" I murmur, and a soft smile plays on his lips.

He stays silent for a moment, his fingers still stroking the edge of my hair, leaving tingling trails on my forehead with every move.

"I always thought that when I left Dawnlin, I wouldn't ever want to look back. All I would remember is this room, and this ship, and be reminded of how lonely I was despite being surrounded by a group of people I cared for and who cared for me."

I stay silent, waiting for him to continue, not wanting to interrupt whatever confession he feels he needs to share.

"But now, this room has brought me some of the best memories of my life. Leaving now, I see only you."

Tears fill my eyes, and I blink rapidly, cursing them when they fall. "I can't take those away from you."

His fingers stroke again, his hand shifting farther down so the pad of his thumb rubs across my cheek.

"But I would give them up for you, so that you could keep them. I'd give them up so you could have the future you always wanted."

I swallow hard, the lump in my throat aching as my voice cracks. "You are the future I wanted, Weston."

"Then we'll figure out how to make it happen. I swear it."

I nod quickly, my eyes never leaving his, but I have to clamp my jaw shut to hide the quivering. He leans forward, pressing a soft kiss to my lips before sliding out of me, and my body already aches with his absence. Settling behind me, he tugs me against his front, wrapping me in his arms so one cages me across my chest. The other hand slides between my thighs, cupping me where I'm still throbbing and dripping from both of our releases, before he lets out a heavy sigh.

I close my eyes and clutch his forearm, nuzzling my head into the bulge of his muscles, when I feel the press of a kiss to the back of my head.

"We'll come up with a plan tomorrow. Right now, you need to sleep. Everything will be alright, Lennox. I won't stop until it is."

I want to believe him, but nothing is ever that simple.

Not when you're the queen.

CHAPTER
FORTY-FOUR

*S*oft breaths punctuate the still room as I lie watching Weston sleep peacefully. His lips are parted slightly, and every worry line and tense muscle is smooth and relaxed, making me want to brush my fingertips across them. It's been hours, and I haven't been able to close my eyes, or drift to sleep, even after this seemingly endless day of being pushed to exhaustion and consumed by so many emotions.

My thoughts are a chaotic storm, creating every possible scenario, every possible worry, and living through it, dragging me deeper into tumultuous waves of anxiety until I feel like I'm drowning. The only thing that has kept me from falling off the deep end of despair is watching Weston sleep. A ghost of a smile plays at my lips to see him, clearly exhausted from loving me so deeply, after waking multiple times in the night to remind me again and again.

I can't close my eyes. I need to soak up every second of him before I shatter my heart into unsalvageable pieces, and this man that I have come to cherish over everything else in my life is no longer part of it.

There is no reality where he allows me to let go of my mother, not after spending over twenty years here trying to save her. I can't find any option where he would allow me to talk him out of it, where we would let her go. Knowing we are both worthy and hold the vials of healing waters in our hands eliminates any chance that he would. He would sacrifice himself for me, the same way he repeatedly did for the Castaways, for my father, for my mother.

But I can't let him.

I tried to find a solution. I spent all night praying to the gods to give me an answer, using all of my critical thinking, plotting and strategy skills. I examined every outcome, every possibility, every choice, just as Edmond taught me. I looked at everything I have before me, and have to use it to make the best decision I can.

I am the queen. It's my responsibility to do what is best for everyone. The kingdom and my people come before my own wants and needs, and even though he will never admit it, he is one of my people.

He's right. This choice falls on my shoulders. I have to choose what is best for him. I know he won't see it. He'll fight me and demand I see it differently, but he won't change my mind. Living another meaningless, wasted life, tied to an oath that brings him nothing but pain and hardship and sacrifice isn't what is best for him.

How could I choose that for someone I love?

How could I condemn him to a life of loneliness and pain, watching me live without him, not remembering everything that brought us here, and everything we shared? Why would I ever cause him such torment?

The world needs Weston, and stripping him of the man he has become as the captain would leave a gaping hole in the lives of so many. I would rather lose myself than lose him. I would rather lose everything I've ever wanted than have him live another twenty years serving a crown and living every day miserable and alone.

Because I know if our roles were reversed, that is exactly how I would feel.

I can't do to him would I would never want done to me. I can't harm the one person who has chosen me, and loved me, even though it may hurt him in the process.

I need to show him how much I love him by letting him go.

Violent pain erupts in my chest as my eyes graze over his features one last time, trailing down over his slowly rising and falling chest until I reach the hand that lays loosely wrapped around my forearm. I can't wake him, so I have to move carefully. If I do, I'll never be able to go through with it, and I need to do this. There's no other choice.

My fingers don't stray from the smooth metal as I grasp the ring that has caused me so much heartache. Sinking my teeth into my lower lip, I bite so hard trying to hold back the cascade of sobs that I taste blood. Agonizingly slowly, I slide the ring off his finger, squeezing it firmly in my palm, and my heart shatters. He doesn't stir, just continues to sleep peacefully with no knowledge of what is happening on the other side of his consciousness and the pain coursing through my body.

Be strong, Lennox.

Lifting the sheets just enough so I can wiggle out from under them, my bare feet are silent against the floorboards as I gently slide off the side of the bed. I pad across the room, slowly opening the door of the armoire and begging the island not to let the hinges creak. It opens noiselessly, and I close my eyes with a small sigh of relief for the set of clothes that awaits me there. I pull on the undergarments and pants quickly, but leave the rest there, because there's something that I can't leave this world without.

Tiptoeing around the bed, I keep my eyes trained on my goal, not on the sleeping form next to me, and round the foot, pausing to gently raise the lid of the trunk. Weston's scent overwhelms my senses, and the tears I've kept at bay almost break loose. Lifting one of his shirts from the pile inside, I hold it to my face, breathing deeply before sliding it over my head, and tucking the ends into my waistband. Crouching down, I pull out the only gift he gave me, my vest. The one he wanted me to wear to ensure I was protected. When I left it behind the first time, it was because I knew I'd have him protecting me, but now, I can't part with it. In a way, it will be like he is still beside me, and I want to always have that piece of him, even if I don't remember.

I slide my arms through the holes and lace it up tightly before tucking his ring into one of the pockets. Sneaking a glance over my shoulder, I check to see that he hasn't moved, and find him still sleeping gently, completely unaware of the heartache he is going to wake to.

And the pit in my stomach deepens further.

You have to, Lennox. It will be easier for him if he hates you.

Turning my back to him, I cover my mouth and stifle a sob. I can't look at him again. The pain searing in every limb and the sinking in my stomach that tells me to run to him, to beg him to make it go away, that tells me to turn around and stay, to ignore everything, to give up my kingdom and my duty for him. It's all too much. I can't handle it.

You can. You are the strongest person I know. You have survived worse than this.

Weston's words echo in my mind. If only he knew. If he thought facing death multiple times, losing my father and my friends that had become family, and becoming queen was the worst I had faced, he has no idea what it feels like to walk away from him right now.

I feel anything but strong.

The first step toward the door is the hardest, but I make it, and every heavy one after. With each movement, it feels like my world is pulling me backward, like I'm caught in a war between what my heart and head tell me is right.

I snatch my dagger off the desk and slide it in place, then swallow the thick lump in my throat as my eyes are drawn to the glittering, glowing vials in front of me. Reaching out, I wrap my fingers around the cool, smooth glass.

Of both vials.

I slide them into my vest, then drop to the floor, shoving my feet in my boots and lacing them quickly. I need to get out of this room, out of his vicinity, off of this island, because if I don't, I don't know what I might do.

The world feels like it is crashing down on me as I stand and walk to the door, pulling it open just enough that I can slip through and shut it silently behind me.

I let out an aching sigh as I halt, my back pressed against the closed door of the Captain's quarters, when I realize.

The magic didn't stop me.

Then I run.

I barely register the pounding of my feet as they pull me through the ship, up the stairs, and down the gangway. I barely feel the chill of the wind off the sea as I flee across the jagged reef for the last time, through the black sands and up the stone steps.

Edmond. I need Edmond.

Just like Sig taught me, I think repeatedly about what I need. I don't know how it can take any more, but my heart aches again as I realize I won't remember her either. The pain pushes me forward, toward the plateau, as I beg the island to bring me the Guardian.

I run as if in a trance. My chest heaves and burns with every breath, and I know it's not only from the exertion. My sole focus is on needing Edmond to return home, because I can't waste time. When I climb the trail and come around the curve through the trees, my steps slow until I'm walking toward the figure that waits for me with a knowing smile on his face.

"I felt your call, Your Majesty."

"I need to leave, Edmond. Now."

He nods slowly. "I see. I imagine that you have assessed all possibilities?"

My eyes well with tears. "Just like you taught me."

He makes a sound of approval that I've heard so many times over the years. "Well then, just as I have always said, you are well prepared for the challenges that lie ahead of you. I have no doubt that you are ready to be the queen of Blackwood. But as the Guardian, I will return you to your kingdom now, if that is your wish."

"It is." My voice is weak and watery, and the finality of the words echoes through my already hollow body. They feel like a lie. It isn't truly my wish. My wish is that I didn't have to make this decision, that I didn't have to choose between duty and love, that I could have it all.

But I was stupid. Naïve. Inexperienced. I thought my life would be different once I became queen, that I would get to make my own choices and change it to be everything I had always dreamed of. I thought that once I had no one to answer to but myself, things would finally be happy.

I didn't know that the queen doesn't get to decide for herself. Every decision is for the betterment of everyone else, and it's my duty to bear it all on my shoulders. I thought the crown was heavy before, but now I feel crushed beneath its weight.

My mother has held on for twenty-three years, her health unexplained by anything other than the strength of her love for me, and I can't ignore it. I won't give up on her. I won't let her survival go unanswered, and I won't let Weston make yet another sacrifice for me. He had already done enough.

This one is mine to make.

"When you are ready, Your Majesty."

I walk toward Edmond, slowly closing the distance between us as I soak up the bit of dawn that is coming over the horizon. It's the last one I will see for a while. Possibly ever.

With only a handful of steps left before the end of the plateau and the waiting Guardian, a sound echoes in the distance, pulling me from my fantasy of the heat on my skin. My steps falter, and I look around, trying to place what it is, when I hear it.

"Lennox!"

My head falls back, and my eyes squeeze shut as despair erupts in my chest. Even though there's only one other person on the island, I would recognize that voice anywhere. Weston's footsteps pound as he roars my name again, and I turn back to the same path I ran along, just before he rounds the corner. His feet skid across the slick dirt and grass as he almost tumbles to his knees, his clothes disheveled as if he barely threw them over his body before racing out of the room. His hair is the same mess after last night, from time after time of me running my fingers through it.

Chest heaving and skin glistening with sweat, he rights himself, and his gait turns from frantic to furious. His jaw is tight as his eyes narrow on me, standing helplessly before the wrath I know I'm about to incur, the same one I fought against so many times back when I was convinced he was my enemy instead of the best thing that has ever happened to me.

But this time, I don't have the strength to fight back.

"I'm really fucking tired of waking up alone on my godsdamned ship." He stalks toward me, and I watch the fury rise in his face as he gets closer.

"Weston, stop," I say, my voice cracking as everything that I have been holding in surfaces.

Tension hardens his shoulders and the curve of muscle in his arms as he points at me. "You have something that's mine." His voice is low, and the growl in his throat makes me shiver. "Give it back."

"Weston—"

"Give it back, Lennox." His long strides have closed almost half the distance, and my breaths start to increase as panic takes over.

"Weston. Stop." My words are firmer than before, but he ignores them. He can't get any closer. He can't touch me. Because I know with one brush of his skin I'll collapse, and take back everything I already decided.

"No." He stomps forward, now barely a few paces from me, but I need him to listen.

"I command you to stop!"

"You're not the queen here, remember? You wanted me to treat you the same as everyone else, and now is no different!"

"Weston, please," I plead, begging that he will see what I see, see the despair etched into my face, and understand why I had to walk away. "Please don't make this harder."

"You promised you wouldn't take it from me."

My fingers itch to touch the pocket in my vest, because I know exactly what he is talking about.

His ring. The promise I made him on the beach, when he told me that golden band was the only thing ensuring he could stay near me.

I remember the promise, and that's the exact reason I had to break it.

"I have to."

"Whatever you think you have to do, you're wrong."

I take a hesitant step backward, my body finally able to move under the hold of his commanding gaze, but it doesn't matter. He closes the distance, reaching for me, and before I can stop him, his hands wrap around my face, the momentum of his walk causing me to stumble backward as his body crashes into mine.

A soft whimper escapes my lips as my face crumbles when I look into his fierce eyes. "You're getting a second chance, Weston. Don't waste it."

"Listen to me," he growls, and his grip tightens. "I don't care what anyone before me has ever told you or made you feel, I need you to hear me right now. You are not a waste. There is no second chance because I didn't lose anything. Spending my life beside you, whether you remember me or not, will never be a waste."

"I can't let everything you sacrificed be worthless—"

"I sacrificed nothing, Lennox."

"You lost everything for me!" My hands grip his wrists, squeezing tightly as I scream at him, but he doesn't flinch. He holds firm, the unwavering pillar I've relied on for support, who even when I walked away from him, still holds firm, letting me rage at him, letting me hurt him.

And I need to hurt him. I need him to be able to move on with his life, to find happiness and not be trapped in the lost world we created here. The only way to do that is by replacing all the love with something else, and making the last thing he feels toward me be pain and hate.

"Saying you sacrificed nothing? That's bullshit, Weston, and you know it! You gave up your life for mine. You gave up time with my father, your only friend, and you'll never get that back! He's gone! You lost your mother, then gave up your life with your father! You walked away from your family here that you could have built a life with, all to serve a crown! How could you say that wasn't a sacrifice? Everything you let go will not be in vain. I refuse to let it be. And I will not let you continue to lay yourself down for everyone around you. I *am* choosing you! I'm choosing your happiness over mine because you shouldn't be the only one who only gets to do that!"

His shoulders heave, and his jaw tightens, but his eyes don't leave mine.

"I won't stop you," he grinds out. "I told you it was your choice, but please. Give me my ring back."

After all that, after throwing everything I could at him to get him to see why I need to do this, he still doesn't care. He fully accepts it—this stubborn, frustrating man—and can only see the part that will keep him bound to me, living in misery for the rest of his life.

If he can't see it, then I have to give him no choice. I know what I need to do. Nothing I said has worked, and he needs to be angry. He needs to hate me. I want it to be easy for him to walk away and never look back, to move on and find love. I want him to have happiness, even if my heart is absolutely shattering.

I pull his hands off my face and step out of his grip, putting distance between us and trying to breathe. Squeezing my eyes shut, completely unable to look at him, I pull my shoulders back, holding my head high, and ignore the hot tears streaming down my face as I grit my teeth and push the words out.

"Weston Rowe—"

"Lennox."

"I release you." I choke on a sob.

"Lennox, stop."

"From your oath."

"Don't do this."

My voice holds firm as I muster all the strength I have left to open my eyes and meet his as I deliver the final blow. "Thank you for your service to the kingdom of Blackwood. You are free to live your life."

"My oath wasn't to the fucking kingdom. My oath was to you!" His roar echoes in my ears, and I flinch. It's filled with the anger I needed, the anger that I will be able to walk away from.

"Then, as your queen, your devotion is no longer needed."

"You can say whatever you want, but nothing will ever change for me. Ever."

I sink farther into myself as I take a step back, my lip quivering slightly before I clamp my jaw together to stop it.

"Goodbye, Weston," I whisper, but as I turn my back on him to face Edmond, his hand catches my arm, spinning me around until my body slams into his, followed by the grip of his hand in my hair and the crush of his lips.

And I break.

Every wall, every bit of strength I had disintegrates the moment his mouth is on mine, and I sob against him. Body shaking, limbs weakening, chest heaving. Everything I've held back surges through me. I try to fight it, but I can't. His grip is crushing, his movements rough, his lips and tongue demanding as he forces me to remember the depth of his feelings.

He kisses me until my body is consumed by sobs and tears, and barely slows even as he swipes them from my cheeks. But as fierce and stubborn as he is, I know I am too. He can't stop me with his kiss. He can't erase everything I've thought through and decided. He can only make it harder. With everything I have left, I raise my hands, placing my palms flat on his chest, and push him away until I have enough room to breathe.

"This isn't over," he growls, repeating my words back to me, back when I thought he was saying goodbye on the night Dane stole all our hope.

The hope for a life together at home returned with Edmond's lesson. Light always finds a way, but not this time. The hope is gone once again. At least for me.

"This time it is," I whisper. My vision blurs as I look up into his eyes. All I see is pain, and it makes me choke on my breath.

Weston told me that people come in and out of our lives, and while there are some who we wish would stay longer, it sometimes isn't meant to be. When he said it, I never thought he was talking about us. But just like Fin, and Sig, and Jorn, and Stass, and Mara…just like Edmond, I'm so grateful that my determination to change my life brought them all into it. Even though I might not remember, each of them has changed me to my core, and I wouldn't be the queen I know I can be without them.

"Promise me you'll find them," I cry. "Promise me you'll give them all their chance."

The muscles in his cheeks tick as his jaw clenches shut, and I wait in silence before he finally responds.

"I promise."

Pushing against his chest harder, I lean back, putting a little space between us before I reach down and grasp his wrist. His other hand presses firmly into the small of my back as he tries to tug me back in, to hold me in his arms as I fight against him. But he lets me move his arm, and I flatten his palm across my chest, his fingers splayed over my skin as I cover his hand with mine.

"I'll always feel it."

"Don't walk away." His voice drops to a murmur, and the defeat I'm now watching creep over his face is evident. "Don't. Please."

Rivulets of tears stream down my cheeks, and I mutter the last words I want him to hear.

"I love you, Weston. You gave me everything. Thank you for saving me."

His eyes fall closed, his chin dropping to his chest as the arm wrapped around my waist squeezes tighter, trying to pull me in again. I push him away, twisting out of his grasp and turning my back to him so I can't see the helplessness that I know he's feeling.

I feel it too.

I storm toward Edmond, my gaze focused on the man who practically raised me, who just watched me break his son's heart, and I silently beg the gods that he doesn't hate me.

"Take me back," I command, but my voice shakes until the last sound.

I fist Edmond's cloak, clutching onto him while dropping my chin to my chest and squeezing my eyes shut to block out every piece of the world around me. I sob into Edmond as the familiar pull of magic washes over me.

And I leave Weston and Dawnlin behind forever.

CHAPTER FORTY-FIVE

My knees give out the moment the magic dissipates, and I crash onto the cold stone ground. This time, Weston isn't here to catch me. I can barely feel the chill in the air despite my thin clothes and lack of a cloak. I don't know or even care what time of day it is because I can't open my eyes.

Falling forward onto my hands, the jagged surface bites into my skin as my body collapses in on itself and a piercing wail shreds my throat. My nails dig into the stone, cracking and breaking as I claw at it, trying to gain purchase as I heave through the sobs. Chaos churns in my belly, threatening to spill all over the ground in front of me as the gravity of what I've just done washes over me.

I left Weston alone on the island that he had tried to escape for so many years, with the promise that I would forget him.

For his own good.

My stomach heaves, and I can't stop the burning sickness that erupts from my throat. Every limb shakes as my body continues to dry heave, trying to rid itself of the pain, but nothing can take it away.

I need him.

He's the only one who has ever been able to calm me when I feel like this, like my world is out of control, and I'm spiraling deeper and deeper until I can't pull myself out of it.

Warm, familiar hands wrap around mine, and there's a flicker of hope in my chest that is dashed when I remember they are the wrong man's hands. The father, not the son.

Edmond lifts gently, helping me to my feet as I struggle to remain upright. My hands shake as I push into his grip, but he holds me steady.

"It pains me to see you like this, Lennox," Edmond murmurs, and all it takes is for him to completely disregard my title and all the formalities, to see me as a person, one who he watched grow up, for me to throw away all my inhibitions. I fall into him, digging my forehead into his chest, and wail. I cry like I have never been allowed to in this kingdom, and I don't give a fuck who might see or hear their queen have a moment of humanity. Edmond's arms wrap around my shoulders, and he hushes me in a low, soothing voice, stroking my hair and holding me like a father should. Like my father never did.

I fight all the thoughts flying through my mind, all the regrets, all the fears, all the pain, and sob into Edmond's understanding embrace. My shoulders shake, my chest heaves, and my voice is strangled when I choke out my justification.

"I had to hurt him. I had to. He wouldn't listen to me." Every word is stuttered by a shuddering sob, and the strain in my voice makes it barely recognizable, but Edmond's comfort doesn't falter.

"My son is a man who knows what he wants. It is difficult to change his mind once it is made up. His mother and I tried time and time again when he was a boy, and his stubbornness did not leave him in adulthood."

"I can't let him live in pain, Edmond. I can't condemn him to that fate." I tilt my chin up and pry my swollen eyelids apart until I can see the face of my beloved tutor. His expression is exactly as I would have expected. He's calm and thoughtful, but intense in his own way.

"As someone who loves you both very much, I don't want to see either of you live a life filled with unhappiness and regret."

"Please, Edmond, please," I beg, fisting my hands in his cloak. "You have to make sure he lives a good life. Make sure he is happy. Please. Don't let him give up everything he could have because of me. He deserves so much more." I search his eyes, trying to find agreement, but all I see is the same all-knowing gaze Edmond has had since the day I met him.

"The promise of a joyous and fulfilled life is all a parent ever truly wants for their child."

I grit my teeth against another sob. How I wish I had grown up with a father who had only wanted what was best for me. I never experienced the unconditional love of a parent, the kind where I didn't have to prove myself or earn whatever sliver of attention they were willing to give me.

Until now.

Because I have the healing waters, and a mother who only ever wanted to love her daughter.

I suck in a deep breath, trying to slow the shake of my shoulders and calm down my racing thoughts. Forcing away the pain, I focus on feeling nothing, willing my body and mind to go numb. I will not let the sacrifice I made be in vain. I will not let giving him up and causing him such pain be for nothing.

I pull away from Edmond, straightening my shoulders and wiping the tears from my puffy eyes.

"Will you come back with me? Just for a little while? I—" I stammer, because when you are queen, it doesn't feel you should ever utter these words, but I do, because he might be the last person I can trust with them.

"Edmond, I need your help."

CHAPTER FORTY-SIX

The walk down the hallway to my rooms feels like it stretches on for an eternity. My eyes are still swollen, my jaw aches from clenching my teeth, and my limbs are so heavy that I feel like I could collapse at any moment. Edmond and I spent the last few hours in the library, the place we shared, for possibly the last time. When we finally decided it was time, and that our affairs were as complete as they could be, we said our heart-wrenching goodbyes.

I don't know when or if I'll ever see him again, and even though walking away from him felt like tearing through an already fatal wound, at least if our paths ever cross again, I will remember the time we spent together, from before.

Unlike anyone else who has been touched by the magic.

I'm tired of goodbyes.

I thought I knew loneliness before I sought Dawnlin, back when I wished for love and friendship that wasn't bound to my duty as the future queen, but that feeling is nothing compared to what I feel now. To finally have it, then feel it ripped away, leaving you only with an empty pit of loss and an aching heart, far surpasses any feeling I had in my previous life. Because that is how it feels, like I lived two lives: before Dawnlin, and after, and one of them is about to be lost to me forever.

Rubbing my hand over my chest, and wrapping the other around my middle, I try to soothe the ache threatening to swallow me whole, when my fingertips brush the lump in the leather. The vials, tucked away safely in my pocket, beckoning me to put them to use.

I'm coming, Mother.

But I'm not ready yet. There are still things I need to finish first.

The door swings open silently, and I glide into the darkness, almost flinching at how final the loneliness feels when the click of the closing door echoes through the room. I keep my eyes trained on the floor, because I know if I look around, all I will see is Weston. In the grand scheme of things, he was only here for a small part of the time I spent in these rooms, but he branded them with his presence like the mark on a barrel of liquor.

I float through the space as if I'm a phantom of my old self, without even a shred of my energy or drive left. Once I reach my vanity, I lower myself onto the stool, and my eyes catch on the book I stowed there long ago. Covered in a thin layer of dust, my mother's journal sits in the same place I left it, completely untouched for all this time. It started this entire adventure, this quest to bring her into my life. The grief I felt when I heard the healers tell my father it was time to let her go felt so immense, but now, as I stare at the leather cover, I almost chuckle at how little I knew.

I pull open the top drawer and look inside, shoving the jars of makeup and hairpins around until I find what I'm looking for. A long, thin gold chain is curled up in the corner, the pendant hanging from it one I wore to match a dress made for an early birthday. Undoing the clasp, I slide the pendant off and stuff it back in the drawer, shutting it firmly before my fingers dig into the bulging pocket of my vest.

The vials shimmer as I set them on the polished black wooden surface, but I ignore them. They aren't what I am after right now. When I reach in again, my fingertips brush the smooth metal of Weston's ring, and my breath snags in my throat. Another wave of pain courses through me as his face flashes in my mind, when he begged me to give it back.

But I couldn't. This ring in my possession is the only thing that ensures his freedom. It will be my daily reminder of him, one that will stay close to my heart, even though I won't remember what it means to me. I slide it onto the chain, then lift both ends around my neck and close the latch. My palm rests over it, pressing it to my chest, and my eyes flutter shut.

Please forgive me.

My movements are stilted, each one feeling like it is happening to me instead of me controlling it as I slowly unlace my vest and stand. Pulling it off my shoulders, I stow it away with my training clothes. I will use it, I know I will the moment I can bear to go back into the training ring, after I can find a new First Guard to replace him and Brynne. Wearing it will be like he still is protecting me, even if he isn't.

Yanking one of my simple gowns out of the closet, I quickly change, tossing my pants in with the training clothes, but clutching Weston's shirt tightly to my chest. Crossing the room to the bed, I press the shirt to my face and inhale deeply, breathing in his scent until silent tears soak the fabric. A sob wracks my shoulders, and I cover my mouth, trying to stifle the sound, although there's no one at risk of hearing it. I shove the shirt under my pillow, and turn back toward the room, just as my eyes fall on the glimmering vials.

This is it. It is time.

I only need one. The other I only took from Weston as assurance that he wouldn't try to circumvent my decision and heal my mother himself. He carved her name into the mountain's walls the same as I did, so I know it would work if he tried. I couldn't give him the chance.

I slip one into the top drawer of my vanity and close it with a slam before grasping the other firmly in my hand and gliding out of the room.

If I don't do this now, I might never.

The castle is silent, the halls empty, and I don't even know what time it is now. I haven't been able to think about anything other than the devastating decision I have to make, and I know that in the end, time doesn't matter anymore.

At least it won't in a few moments.

The handle of my mother's door clicks as I turn it, and I slip inside to find the room exactly the same as it has been every time I have entered. She lies in bed, so still and peacefully asleep, as if I only need to shake her shoulder to rouse her.

Lowering myself into the chair beside her bed, it doesn't escape me it is the same one my father used the night he cried over letting her go, and now I'm here to fulfill his long-awaited hope.

What would have happened if he had decided to after I had already left? What would have happened if he had lost hope?

I'd be living my life with Weston, not sacrificing it for him.

But as my gaze trails from her serene face and down the quilt-covered body that has survived for so long, I remember why I made the decision I did. Whatever fight my mother is fighting, she never gave up on the life she wanted with me, so I can't give up on her. Even though it is costing me the unconditional love I've always dreamed of, I've always dreamed of having her, too.

I reach out and grasp her hand, the warmth of it startling until I wrap my fingers around hers. My breath quickens as I realize this is it. The last moment before everything disappears. I look down at the sparkling liquid in my other hand, and feel panic rising in my chest.

I have to find strength in my weakness and have hope that this was all meant to be.

Tears well in my eyes as I release her and pull the cork from the vial before setting it down on the bed.

Never in my life have I had anyone worth sacrificing for, so maybe the gods did truly give me everything I had always wanted. Maybe Weston's love was only meant to be fleeting, not meant to be with me forever. Maybe I was right, and that kind of love isn't really meant for a queen.

I love you, Weston.

I think it hard, repeating it again and again as I clutch the healing waters in my hand, hoping that the magic of Dawnlin will let him feel it one last time.

Reaching out, I raise the vial toward her, when a sob erupts from my chest, shaking my whole body. I lower the vial back down onto the bed so as not to spill a drop and slam my palm over my mouth.

Breathe.

Thoughts of everything I'm going to lose berate my mind, and guilt slices through me when the whisper of a thought breaks through, that everything I'm going to gain doesn't outweigh the loss. Flashes of memories blind me, and I can't see the room, only him, and the faces of the others, the island, the light, the heat. Everything overwhelms me as I war back and forth. The entire reason I sought Dawnlin was for this moment, for this final task that I need to complete.

I open my eyes, looking between her calm face and the swirling healing waters in my hand before I squeeze my eyes shut once again.

I hope I'm making the right choice.

EPILOGUE

Two months later

I thought the last time I wore this dress was the most important day in my life. I never expected I would be wearing it again so soon after, because I was wrong. *Today* is the most important day of my life. After the disaster that was my birthday ceremony, I couldn't let it go to waste. No one got to see the billowing silk skirt covered in glittering silhouettes of the Blackwood trees, and after all the work Tila and her ladies put into it, I wanted to honor her by wearing it again.

What better way than to wear it for my coronation?

Smoothing my hands over the silk bodice, I press out any wrinkles as my fingers glide down the soft fabric. This time, I refused the gloves, much to Tila's disagreement, mostly because I didn't want to sweat through them with all the nerves coursing through me. Although, there are worse things that could happen in front of the entire attending audience.

I invited them all. Royalty and representatives from every other kingdom, every member of our staff, significant leaders from the city and throughout Blackwood. They will all be in attendance, watching me be crowned as the queen.

The castle gates are not closed, not like when my father was king, and I can't explain the joy and freedom it brings me, knowing I am no longer trapped behind these walls. I upheld the promise I made to myself, never to live a life hidden away again.

Today should feel monumentous. I'm finally able to officially act as queen, and make all the choices for my life I always desired. I'm surrounded by people I have been longing to to meet, and I get to be the one to determine what impression I make. But as I stare at myself in the floor-length mirror, my eyes trailing over Tila's handiwork, I can't help but feel frustrated on top of the already overwhelming nerves.

So much depends on today, for the future of this kingdom, and for me. Everything needs to go according to plan.

The sound of the door opening and firmly closing behind me pulls me from my thoughts. I don't bother turning around. I'm not worried about who is entering my rooms unannounced, because I know there's only one person who is comfortable enough to do so.

"You look stunning."

A small smile plays at my lips, and warmth blooms in my chest at the voice. I glance over my shoulder and meet the sparkling eyes that are a mirror of mine. My mother stands behind me, gazing at me, her hands clasped tightly to her chest clad in her own gown newly made by Tila just for the occasion.

No one can explain what happened the night she woke. Alone at her bedside, I clutched her hand, ready to say goodbye, when her eyes opened as if she had merely been asleep, not lost to us for my entire life. I startled her when I screamed for the healers, who came immediately to her room, baffled to find her sitting up in bed with me crushed to her chest, both of us sobbing.

Mother and daughter, finally united after all hope had been lost.

Our reunion was overwhelming, filled with joyous tears and fierce hugs, but was overshadowed the moment she asked for my father, and I had to explain his death.

The month-long mourning period was somber, but while she took the loss of my father so deeply, it didn't affect the joy she held onto at finally meeting me. The healers helped her come to understand how much time she had lost. Standing in front of her, I clearly was the vision of it, but just as I saw in her diary and her letters to me, she didn't let lost time stop her. Instead of wallowing over missed stages and experiences, she made every moment we had together count.

I finally got to know my mother during that month of mourning, having spent every waking moment together. This time, I got to be the one telling her stories of my life, of Edmond and Tila, of growing up in the castle. It was difficult for her to comprehend the difference between the parent she thought my father wanted to be and the one he became, but I could see by the look in her eye that she didn't want my life to continue that way.

And it hasn't.

Meeting her was like meeting a stranger who understands and accepts every piece and part of me without question, and just as I thought when I read her diary, it was everything I had always hoped for. She is everything I always needed. I didn't know what a mother was, didn't know what I was missing, but now I realize I had a hole in my heart that only she could fill.

"What's troubling you, darling girl?" She closes the distance between us, coming to stand just behind me so I can see her hovering over my shoulder.

I let out a sigh. "How'd you know?" My eyes meet hers in the mirror, and she shoots me a look.

"You're my daughter. I know." Her face softens with a warm smile. "Tell me."

My hand rises as if on its own and presses to my bare chest, rubbing the empty space there. "I can't find my necklace. I didn't take it off, but when Tila brought the dress in this morning, I realized it was gone."

"Did you remove it to bathe? Set it somewhere out of the ordinary?"

I shake my head. "No. I never take it off. It doesn't feel right to."

Her brows contort with concern. "Maybe Addy has seen it. We can check with her."

"I'm afraid I lost it on the training grounds, or somewhere in the city, and there isn't time to look for it. I just…need it. Especially for today." Nerves tumble in my belly, and I wring my hands together.

If this was the first issue I had to deal with today, it probably wouldn't be affecting me as much as it is. Somehow in the chaos of my father's death and funeral, I lost the dagger I received at my ceremony, and in the time since I buried him, I haven't been able to find it, despite searching everywhere on the grounds. Mother and I went to the royal blacksmith who created it at my father's request, and he immediately began work on a new one, but late last night I was informed that it would not be ready for the coronation today. An entire element of the ceremony would be left out, already putting a stain on my first real traditional event as queen.

Edmond would be disappointed in me.

I can't remember how I lost it, or where I even had it last. I just know it's gone. And now, with my missing necklace, it seems like the day is testing me, throwing every hurdle at me I have to navigate in a way fitting for my new official role.

"There's still a bit of time," she says. "It's likely nearby."

I huff out a breath and stare at the space where it normally lies on my chest with the ring pendant tucked into the top of my bodice. I have no recollection of when I got it or where the ring came from. There's something about it though, a feeling that it gives me, that it's mine, and I never want to be without it. Sometimes I think it could be my father's, the last gift he gave to me before a traitorous citizen murdered him, but he isn't here any longer to ask.

Neither is Edmond. The blow of his departure happened only the day after my mother woke. A letter arrived the morning after, detailing his resignation because of his acceptance of a position in another kingdom, to raise and coach their future heir, as I would no longer need his service as a tutor. His loss during this turbulent time cut like a deep blade, especially because he disappeared without so much as a goodbye, leaving me alone to navigate becoming the queen my kingdom needs from the very start.

Not even Brynne is around, having disappeared unannounced. If it weren't for my mother's miraculous wakening and Tila's constant involvement, I would feel completely alone, lost and trying to find my way with no one who was supposed to be by my side.

But I can't say I would be completely alone. Once the news of my father's death spread to the other kingdoms, many of them reached out, offering condolences or assistance. Even Berrendahr, our closest neighboring kingdom and partner in trade, immediately sent a representative to stay at the castle as one of my ladies. Signee may be the princess of her own kingdom with duties and responsibilities of that she has pushed aside, but over the past month, especially with the preparations for the coronation, she has become a friend, stepping in and filling the void Brynne's disappearance left.

I can't even describe how it feels to finally have a friend, one who isn't bound to me by duty or obligation. As princess of Berrendahr, she's not obligated to be here at all. She stays because she wants to, and her kind and caring yet sarcastic and direct nature is exactly what I need to pull me through all of this. It's the kind of friendship I've always wanted, despite my father never allowing it.

My mother's fingers trail back and forth across my bare shoulders in a movement I've come to know as her way to comfort, and I lean into her touch.

"I have missed thousands of moments I wanted to experience with you, and I know the significance of this day means I've lost Rem, but despite all that, I am beyond grateful to be here with you on this day."

A lump forms in my throat, and I try to swallow it down as tears pool in my eyes. "Me too, Mother."

She swipes at her own eyes. "Ach. None of that." Shuffling around until she faces me, she dabs my eyes with a cloth she pulls from a secret pocket in her skirts. "Tila will never let us hear the end of it if she has to fix your eyes before the ceremony. Gods know she's done it for me too many times."

My laugh is watery as I feel deep down how similar we are, and in just a few weeks we have only scratched the surface. We have a lifetime together now.

She shoves the cloth in her pocket and lets out an uplifting sigh. "Let's get a move on. We can't keep the other kingdoms waiting."

I don't bother taking another look in the mirror, because I know there's nothing I could or would change, anyway. Turning on my heel, I stride through the room and out into the hallway, trying to push down the incomplete feeling caused by my missing necklace.

Every corridor is empty as we weave through the castle. All the staff are probably already seated and waiting in the throne room as a musical ensemble entertains them until the ceremony begins. That was my mother's idea. She hated the dreary silence of the castle that I had become accustomed to, and it was one of the first things as queen mother she suggested we change.

We descend the steps down the main staircase, arm in arm, and weave through the halls until we approach the throne room from the opposite side. Whenever I have had to use it, I typically enter from my private entrance on the side, but not today. Not when I have to follow the ceremonial steps and allow everyone the chance to gawk at the queen they've never seen. Just before we round the corner of the final corridor leading to the black wooden doors that await my arrival, I spot Addy briskly walking toward me.

"Addy!" I call out, releasing my mother's arm as I approach her. "Have you seen my necklace? I can't find it anywhere, and I need it."

She drops into a deep curtsy before righting herself again, and I can see she's mildly out of breath. "No, Your Majesty, I haven't."

My stomach sinks, and it takes all my focus to keep my hands relaxed at my sides instead of worrying my fingers. It isn't queenly behavior, especially right now. I can't let anyone see the current of nerves surging just beneath my skin.

"Alright," I sigh. "If you find it, just bring it to me, please."

"Yes, Your Majesty."

"We'll see you inside, Addy," my mother says with a smile.

Addy drops into a nervous curtsey, her hands clutching in her skirts. "But oh, I'm so sorry, Queen Mother." She worries her lip and then turns back to me. "Your Majesty, I was actually coming to find you. We have a bit of an issue in the entrance hall."

My head quirks and my brows draw in as I process her statement. There should be no issues to deal with right before the coronation. Everyone who has been invited should already be seated. Mason made sure of that. "What do you mean? What's going on?"

"There's a man here. He says he needs to speak to you."

I huff a laugh. There's nothing anyone could need to speak to be about in this moment that couldn't wait until the end of the evening. "He can speak to the guards. If he doesn't have an invitation to the first part of the ceremony, he can wait on the grounds for the ball."

She shakes her head. "I tried, Your Majesty. He was insistent. He says he will speak only to you. He's claiming to be the First Guard."

Another wave of irritation washes over me. I need to be focused on the ceremony right now, not dealing with a delusional man showing up at my doorstep, demanding to see the queen.

"I haven't chosen a First Guard," I say through gritted teeth. My mother clears her throat softly behind me, and my eyes fall closed as I take a deep breath. I can't let something this simple fluster me, despite the other inconveniences that have already altered my mood. When I think about what my mother would do, how she always prioritized time for those in our kingdom, I decide to lock away my feelings and take care of it. At least if I do, I won't spend the entire ceremony wondering what is going on in the courtyard.

"Fine," I concede. "Take me to him."

"Thank you, Your Majesty," Addy breathes. She drops into another swift curtsey before turning on her heel and leading us through the empty corridor and toward the entrance hall.

Just before we reach the giant black doors that lead into the entrance hall, Signee steps through the archway beside them, a look of relief on her face. "There you are. Everything's ready, Lennox. We're just waiting for you."

"I know. I'm sorry. I need a few minutes. Someone is in the entrance hall demanding to see me, claiming he's the First Guard."

Signee's mouth closes abruptly, her features schooling to indifference before she takes a few quick steps forward and falls into place behind me. "I'll come with you."

"It shouldn't take long. You can go. Just wait for me at the doors."

She shakes her head firmly. "Nope. I want to see this."

I shoot her a confused look, but shake it away as Addy opens the door before us. She drifts through the opening, and I hear her announcement echo off the stone walls.

"Her Majesty, Queen Lennox Holt."

I hope my face doesn't show the frustration I feel at having to address whatever concerns he has, especially now that Signee said everyone is in place and waiting.

But when I step into the room, I'm no longer worried about frustration showing on my face. My body jolts to a halt when my gaze trails through the room and falls on the man in question, the man claiming to be the First Guard. I don't know what I expected. The man my mind concocted that could halt the commencement of the coronation was one that frequented the taverns, one well past his prime, who would do anything to relive his youthful days.

That is not at all who stands before me. My eyes slide up his body, catching every detail of his formal armor and uniform, complete with the seal of Blackwood and the insignia of the First Guard. But the shock of his attire matching his claim isn't what halts me.

I can't tear my eyes away, because he is the most attractive man I've ever seen.

His intense focus is trained on Addy, but when she steps back out of the way, her announcement of my entry now over, his head turns in my direction. The moment our eyes meet, his stoic expression falters. His throat bobs with a hard swallow, and it's as if time is frozen as we stare at each other from across the hall. I can barely take in his other features in my peripheral vision: dark wavy hair, a thick beard, broad shoulders and corded muscles that fill out every inch of the uniform he wears.

But his eyes.

The teal is enchanting, and I can't look away.

So it takes nothing for me to notice when he does. My skin heats as his eyes slide down my body, blazing a trail over every inch of me in this gown, before gliding back up to my face. The muscles in his cheeks flicker as he clenches his jaw, his throat bobbing once again before he clears it.

The harsh sound snaps me out of whatever ensnared us in a trance, and I hope no one noticed my clear perusal of his features. Remembering that I have a coronation to attend, I step forward, slowly closing the gap between us, trying to pretend as if my body didn't react so obviously at the sight of him.

When I'm just beyond his reach, I halt, and hear Signee and my mother filing into the hall over the swish of my skirts. A sharp gasp from behind me makes me turn, and my gaze falls on my mother, her eyes wide and hand covering her gaping mouth as she stares at the man. I glance between them, confused, but he isn't looking at her. His gaze is still locked on me.

"I'm sorry, sir, but you've come at a very inconvenient time. The coronation is about to begin, and I simply cannot hear your concerns until after it is complete." I try to hide the irritation in my voice, but with as flustered as I feel after losing my necklace and the anticipation of all eyes being on me, I know some of it slips through.

One corner of his mouth turns up in a smirk, and I'm startled by the way my stomach flutters, deep and low. I shift on my feet.

"I disagree, my queen. I think I came at the perfect time." The low rumble of his voice with that hint of a smile makes my skin ignite again, and this time I'm the one clearing my throat to regain my composure.

"You did not. My handmaiden says you claim to be the First Guard, but seeing as I have not appointed you to that position, you are not."

His eyes don't stray from mine, and I am doing everything I can not to squirm. "Again, I disagree, my queen. I can provide you with proof of my position."

He reaches into the pocket of his uniform and pulls out a piece of folded parchment before extending his hand. Addy crosses in front of me, taking it from his grasp before bringing it straight to me.

"The position of the First Guard can be passed down from the previous First Guard. You'll find the details of Blackwood's law in that letter. I assume you will recognize the handwriting."

I eye him warily, but he only smirks back at me, and the smugness grates on my already overworked nerves. Prying the seal open, I turn my attention to the parchment before unfolding it and reading the first few words.

I'm unable to stop the sharp intake of breath as I immediately recognize the writing. I don't even need to see the signature. He's right. I would know that handwriting anywhere. My eyes fly over the words, consuming them as quickly as I can before my head snaps back up to his.

"Where did you get this?" I demand.

"Do you have no objection to the contents, my queen?"

"'Your Majesty' is just fine, thank you," I say, trying not to sound rude but completely flustered by how intimate the words feel coming from this stranger's mouth.

His smirk deepens, and I seethe further. "I think I'll stick with 'my queen'."

I huff a laugh, holding the letter up so he can see it. "When did Edmond give this to you? And how do I know it isn't falsified?"

"He assured me you would know it came from him, because you've seen his writing throughout your childhood."

"How…how did you…" I stammer, trying to find the right words and still processing what he's telling me while mentally noting that he did not answer one of my questions. He never said when he received it from Edmond, and that makes me more wary of lies. "There's nowhere in our laws that states the position can be passed down. It has only ever been chosen by the king or queen."

He shrugs his shoulders. "My grandfather disagrees."

My mouth falls open, and I snap it closed again. "Your grandfather?"

He nods toward the parchment in my hand. "You read his words yourself."

"Edmond is your grandfather?" I say, unable to hide the shock in my voice. "I didn't even know he had a son."

"He did." My mother's voice is soft from behind me, and when I turn to look, her focus is still locked on the man. "You look so much like him, I can hardly believe it."

He turns to her then, his face softening as he hinges into a deep bow. "Queen Mother, he had nothing but great things to say and fond memories to share about you."

A quiet cough comes from the far wall, where Signee is leaning against it, trying to conceal a smile with her hand. The man glances at her before turning back to me.

"This letter does nothing," I say, folding it back up and shoving it in my pocket. "And I don't have time to pull the law books from the library right now, so if you'll excuse me, mister…"

"Rowe. Weston Rowe, my queen."

My traitorous stomach flips again at the sound of his name.

I blame it on the nerves.

"Mister Rowe," I say curtly. "Like I said before, I am unable to discuss this at this time, so if you will please excuse me—"

"I have more proof of my position than the letter." The shock at his arrogance and nerve in interrupting the queen flares in me, but it's gone the moment he raises his hand and a flash of gold flickers in the torchlight.

My hand flies to my chest as my eyes zero in on the ring circling his finger, the thick band stamped with a design I could recognize anywhere.

"The seal of Blackwood, and the ring of the First Guard, my queen."

I storm toward him, my steps angry and aggressive, before pulling myself to a halt. I don't know this man, and I can't get too close to him. I can't trust anyone who just walks into the castle making unsupported claims, no matter who he knows or who he looks like.

"Where did you get that?" I cry. My palm flattens against my skin where the missing necklace used to lie until this morning. "That's mine."

"No," he says firmly, his eyes sparkling with challenge. "It's mine."

My mouth gapes as I try to make sense of how he could have the ring I've worn around my neck every moment until now. How could any of this have happened? How could he have spoken to Edmond? How did he come to have the armor of the First Guard?

I shake my head in disbelief, and look to my mother, silently pleading for her thoughts on the matter. She must see the desperation in my eyes, because she doesn't hesitate.

"The Rowe men are trusted and cherished by the royal family. If you are who you say you are, the son of my late husband's most loyal friend and protector, and by the looks of you, I would assume so, then I believe you have the best interests of the kingdom at heart." She slowly turns to me, giving me a slight nod.

I clench my jaw tightly and turn back to Weston, sending him a glare that I hope conveys how annoying his appearance is today of all days, but my stare is only met with a smirk and sparkling teal eyes.

It is infuriating.

"I will look into the laws the moment the coronation ball is over, understood?" I snap. I barely get the last word out before something slams into my legs, almost knocking me off my already aching feet, and I look down to find…a child?

I stare down at the top of his head, mouth agape, as this child squeezes me as tightly as he can through my billowing skirt. It's only then that I finally look around and notice Weston is not the only one waiting in the entrance hall. A small family stands off behind him. The man, who looks to be the father, holds a small infant. The mother's arms are laden with what looks like a set of staff uniforms, and a beaming smile lights up her face.

"Hello," I say hesitantly, and the boy tilts his head back, looking up at me with a wide, toothy grin. I can't help but smile at him, warmth blooming in my chest at the pure joy in his childish expression. Unwrapping his hands from my dress, I crouch down, and his eyes widen.

"So *you* were the princess," he says, his boyish voice filled with wonder.

I chuckle softly. "I was. But now I'm the queen. What's your name?"

"Fin," Weston grumbles, and both the boy and my head snap toward the sound. Weston shakes his head slightly before jerking it backward, toward the family near the doorway.

"Oops! Sorry!" the boy, Fin, says before shrugging his shoulders to his ears and smiling sheepishly up at me. "I forgot." He steps backward before waving shyly at me, then turns and runs straight for the man at the back of the room. I watch in disbelief as he waves wildly across the hall, and turn to see who he is looking at, only to find Signee, shaking her head with her arms crossed over her chest, a smile playing at her lips.

I press my fingertips to my forehead, rubbing at the ache I can feel coming on. "I don't know what is going on here, but it all needs to end. Now. I have a coronation to attend."

"I'll lead the way, my queen," Weston says, taking a step toward me, but I react, holding my hands out to halt him.

"No. No. You can stay here and wait. I will have someone collect you after."

He shakes his head. "As you are aware, the First Guard has a role in the ceremony, and since that is my position, I will be going in with you."

I gawk at him in disbelief, and the hold I had on my heavily practiced queenly decorum snaps. "Who do you think you are, showing up here and demanding to take part? You don't even know what to do!"

"I'll explain," Signee calls out from the side of the room, and my eyes shoot daggers at her for her quick betrayal.

"It's for your protection, my queen." The depth of his voice sends shivers down my spine, and I hope no one can see how affected I am by it. "I will not let you walk into a room filled with representatives from other kingdoms completely unguarded."

"Fine," I grind out, my teeth clenched tightly as I try to figure out how much time we have spent in here, leaving everyone in the throne room waiting.

"Aren't you forgetting something?" Weston grunts, and I roll my eyes, no longer caring if my response to his challenging nature looks bad to anyone around.

"What could I possibly be forgetting after you show up unannounced and force your way into my court?" I snap.

Burning sparks in my chest when his smirk expands into a dazzling smile.

"My oath? You can't have a First Guard complete his duty without swearing it."

I clench my teeth because I know he's right, and the fact that he looks so content to have bested me makes my blood boil. Giving him a curt nod, I track his movements as his hand hovers over the hilt of his sword, his head tilting in the first acknowledgement of needing my permission before he draws his weapon.

"Yes, fine, just make it quick," I say, and his sword sings as he pulls it from the sheath.

Weston steps forward, eliminating almost all the space between us as he digs the point of the blade into the stone floor and sinks to one knee. My breath catches in my throat when he looks up at me, his expression filled with something I can't quite place, and I feel my irritation lessen slightly.

"I, Weston Rowe," he starts, and any noise in the entrance hall dims as my body squares with his, as if on its own. "Pledge my service to the kingdom of Blackwood. I give my sword, my body, my life…" He pauses, swallowing hard, but still holding my gaze. "Everything…to my queen. I swear my loyalty to her, Lennox Holt, and vow to stay by her side, no matter what she commands, however or whenever she will have me, despite her duty or her choice, until the breath stills in my lungs."

The breath stills in my lungs, and I barely notice the hand I have pressed against my chest, over my heart.

"Long live the queen."

My chest heaves, and my body feels paralyzed as I'm pinned to this spot by his smoldering gaze and scorching voice. Lips parting slightly, I know if I try to speak, my voice might not cooperate. But I have to say something.

"Those aren't the words."

"Those are the words, my queen."

I don't know how long we stay like this, locked in a heated trance that makes the rest of my worries and responsibilities fall away. It breaks the moment he rises from his bent knee, his tall, broad frame towering over me so I have to crane my neck to look at him.

"One more thing." Weston reaches into the belt at his back, and the slice of metal rings through the air. I gasp as he closes the remaining distance between us, stepping forward, his armor-clad body no doubt poised to attack.

I knew I couldn't trust him. I should have listened to my years of training. He's going to kill me before my coronation. The story, the letter, the oath—it was all a ruse to get close to the queen.

He extends a blade in front of him, and before I can even think, I move. Wrapping my hand around his wrist, I wrench it down and slide the hilt of the weapon into my fingers, flipping the blade in my hand so it's ready to strike.

But I don't strike.

I stare.

I've never moved like that before. I never truly learned how to use a dagger before Brynne disappeared. But it isn't just the movements that have caught me completely off guard.

My eyes widen and my mouth falls open as I take in the hilt that rests on my palm and the glitter of the sharp blade that points at Weston's abdomen.

My dagger.

He had *my* dagger.

My head snaps up, and the dazzling grin that spreads across his face makes my chest squeeze and my heart race. I look up at his sparkling and heated gaze, but notice he doesn't at all look surprised.

His voice drops, low enough so only I can hear it, and my knees threaten to collapse as he leans forward ever so slightly.

"There she is."

BONUS CHAPTER
WESTON

The air glitters just out of reach as I watch the only woman I've ever loved disappear before my eyes.

Gone. She's gone. And it was her choice.

Every muscle in my body seizes, ready to burst. My breath is trapped in my chest as chaos wreaks havoc inside me, and the storm that has been brewing since I opened my eyes and found empty sheets beside me is threatening to erupt.

Watching her turn her back and walk away was the first time I've truly felt helpless and completely out of control. Everything inside begged me to move, to take the situation into my own hands and bend it to my will.

But I knew there was nothing I could do.

The instant the last speck of dust dims, the dam inside me snaps. My knees slam into the ground, cracking beneath the full weight of my fury and despair. I fall forward onto my hands, my fingers digging into the soil, clutching the earth of this place that was supposed to give me hope.

The roar that erupts from my chest sounds as if the island has concocted a new monster that's coming to put me out of my misery, but I know there isn't. Nothing and no one else is here.

I'm alone.

It took every shred of control I had to stop myself from completely ignoring her command, from chasing after her. I wanted to grab her, to hold her, to fight her. To refuse to let her leave until we came up with a plan. A solution.

I would beg that woman for anything if I knew begging would work. But I know her, and I know there is no changing that beautiful, stubborn mind once it is made up. At least, not with words. I've done this once before, and it worked then. Now I know I have to do the same thing again.

I have to show her.

Show her I meant every word I swore to her. Show her that there is no life for me outside of her. Show her she may be my queen, but she's more than that.

She's *mine*.

I will fight for her, just not in the way she or anyone else would expect. Not at this moment. Not after she had already decided to crush me because she thinks it is what's best for me.

It's not.

She is.

She thinks she is the only one who is bound by duty, but I am bound by much more than the oath I swore to her. I promised her father I would protect her and make sure she lives her life, that she is loved. I refuse to break the promise I made to my best friend with his dying breath. Call it selfish, but I know he saw the love I hold for her, because he's lived it too.

There's only one problem.

My throat is raw as I sit back on my heels, my arms falling heavy at my sides, and yell again.

"Please. Please let her remember!"

I've always thought the island hears us. Too many things supported that theory, but even if it doesn't, the magic somehow knows. The moment I saw her, the day she arrived in Dawnlin, I thought the magic was playing some sick game. Maybe it was. But now, after everything, we know the whole reason. Dawnlin was trying to heal itself, and everything came back to her.

She almost died, and everything that was wrong was righted again.

So now I need it to give her back to me.

"I'm fucking begging you," I cry out into the air. "Please let her remember!" Scrubbing my hands through my hair, my fingers grip the strands as a deep ache settles in my chest. "I never wanted to use more of your magic. I never doubted you. I always had hope. Give it to me now. Let me have her back."

The still calm remains unchanged, except for the rustle of the leaves in the breeze, and the distant crash of waves on a nearby beach.

I know it heard me. It always does. But, the same way it's been for the last twenty-two years, there isn't a reply. Only silence as a reminder of my part in this, the island's requirement to hold on to hope, and blindly trust.

I can do both. I *will* do both.

But that doesn't mean I will fucking do nothing else.

Rising to my feet, I storm through the tunnels, straight back to my ship. I barely register the crack of the door against the wall as I shove it open and walk straight to my desk. Slamming my hand down, I stab the point of her dagger into the smooth surface, splintering the surrounding wood from the sheer force.

I took it. There was no way I was going to let her leave with it. When I left that castle, I knew there was no remaining threat to her, so at least I can breathe, confident she won't need it. Not yet, anyway. I needed the leverage, and when the time comes, I'll use it.

I can't look at the rest of the room. I lived here for so long, alone, but the years of memories were insignificant once she stepped foot into it. Now, all I'll see is her. Her golden hair cascading in untamed waves over the pillows, the sound of her soft breaths and noises as she sleeps. Her tight body laid out over the wooden surface.

I need to get out of here.

I grip the edge of the desk so hard that either it will break, or my fingers will, but something catches my eye. A blank packet and roll of empty parchment sit on top of the desk, and I feel a glimmer of hope.

Maybe it heard me. If it did, if this is its sign that what I am planning is the right choice, then I won't give up yet. I roll out the parchment, grab a charcoal, and get to work. I'm keeping the promise I made to her. I had no intention of breaking it, and it's one thing that kept me standing there with my feet planted into the ground instead of chasing after her.

A rough map of the kingdoms forms on the blank page as I quickly sketch, drawing in landmarks and cities, before smoothing out a new sheet and marking the right spots on the map. Every name. I write the names of every person who was here, in my crew, or back at camp. I am going to go find every person and bring them back for their chance at the healing waters that was stolen.

I don't know how long I spend pouring over the map, plotting out my course, my method. It will take time, because I don't know how many fountains there are, or how far everyone lives from them, but she was right. Only I can do this.

Folding the lists up and shoving them in my pockets, I stomp around the room, keeping my eyes focused only on what I need, and nothing else. I slide my vest over my shoulders, lacing it tightly, then wrap my belt around my waist and cinch it down. My sword is still in Blackwood. I didn't bring it back with us when we returned, so I rip her dagger from the desk, putting it in its place in my vest before storming down to the armory to load myself up.

I barely register my last moment on the ship as I barrel down the gangway, heading straight for the plateau. I don't know whether he's back yet. I don't even know how long it has been. I just know I need my father.

"Pop!" I call out, over and over as my feet carry me to the same place I watched him take her away from me. "Pop!"

Rounding the last curve in the path, I'm not surprised when I look up and find him standing in front of me, the same knowing smile I saw constantly growing up on his face.

"I don't care what she told you," I growl, "don't try to stop me."

"Weston, all your mother and I ever wanted in life is for you to be happy. You are the only one who truly knows what or who will do that."

I cross my arms over my chest and give him the surest look I can. It has been a lifetime since we truly spent time together, but I know he hasn't forgotten a second of it, or a bit of me, and he know's I would tear the world down to fulfill my promises and get back to her. "I'm going to need your help. There are a lot of people who never got their chance."

He nods once. "Then as the Guardian, I will be happy to give it to them."

"Thank you, Pop."

His eyebrow quirks, and he eyes the weapons slung across my body. "I assume we are not headed to Blackwood?"

"No," I say, shaking my head and striding toward him until I'm close enough to be engulfed by the dust that he led me to after all that time.

"Take me to Berrendahr."

499

Don't lose hope.

Light always finds a way,
even through the blackest woods.

ACKNOWLEDGEMENTS

Dawn of Hope changed my life. Before sitting down to write it, I never thought I could have an idea fully fleshed enough to write an entire book, let alone three. Now, it feels so surreal to be writing this just a few weeks before the one-year anniversary of publishing Dawn of Hope.

Unless I challenged myself to do something creative, I never would have found out that I was capable. I never would have found out that I loved telling stories, or that I could actually get all the pictures that have plagued me over the years out of my head. But I did, they're gone, and now they are with all of you.

The series is over. The story is done. And somehow I have to find some new people to think about every single day.

Young Amanda would never have believed that this would be her life over twenty years later. She never would have believed that after growing up being expected to do something prestigious, something that required years and years and years of expensive education, something that would make you rich, that instead, she would turn away from all of that and do something that she loves. Can it still be all of those things? Sure. But that isn't the reason she's doing it. Grown Amanda can look back and tell the younger one that all the years of being made fun of for reading, of having my hobby dismissed, and my dream of making my own stories shoved off as unimportant, were worth it. Because now I'm here, with my own books, my own readers, my own stories, and my pride in what I have accomplished and what I have created.

A piece of my heart will always hold Lennox & Weston. It's very hard for me to say goodbye to these characters. If any of you know me as a reader, you know I very rarely finish the last book in a series, because I hate the finality of it all being over. Well, I had to for this one. I didn't have a choice. I hope it left you with every feeling and emotion I wanted these characters to give you, and you'll remember it as a series that sticks with you.

None of this would have been possible without my husband. I know I have thanked him in every acknowledgements section, and will continue to do so in every book that I write. I'm dead serious when I say I couldn't have done this without him. He pushed me, he encouraged me, he held me when I cried, or laughed, or cried and laughed. He reminded me why I started, and most of all, he loved me in a way that inspires the love I give to my characters. And that's not to mention all the work he does to actually create the book and run the business with me.

Dawn of Hope was the beginning of this new life of ours, but now that the series is finished, I know I can do it. Even more, I know I *want to*. I want to keep going, to keep writing, and keep getting all these ideas out of my head, even though reading back my writing literally makes me throw the book across the couch and cringe every time I have to choose a quote to try to make people want to read it.

Lots of you have asked, "What's next?" Something is. I promise.

Of course I can't end the series without thanking some very specific people. My sister Jennifer, (not) sorry I made you cry so much. My amazing PA Taylor, thank you for all your work, day and night, on promoting this series! My beta readers, even though I sent it to you all very late. Morgan (illustratedbymorgan) for continuing to bring my characters to life, even when it hurt. My editor Kay for being understanding when this bad boy took me a lot longer than I expected. My Street Team, thank you for caring about the series so much!

Very grateful doesn't even begin to describe how it feels to write this acknowledgements section or respond to messages and comments from all of you.

Every single one of you who has read this series, who has loved my story and my characters, who has trusted me to give you something worth spending your time on, who has cried over them, have made my dreams come true. The sleepless nights were worth it.

ABOUT THE AUTHOR

Amanda Briar has been an avid reader of romance, both fantasy and contemporary, since middle school, and loves to watch a good rom-com or fantasy series. After starting a family and deciding her career wasn't for her anymore, she took a chance to fulfill a lifelong dream to write books. As a self-proclaimed Disney Adult who grew up craving a happy ending, she now writes them herself. She currently lives in California with her family, and still loves reading, baking, movies, and going to Disneyland.

@authoramandabriar

@authoramandabriar

www.amandabriar.com

www.ingramcontent.com/pod-product-compliance
Lightning Source LLC
Chambersburg PA
CBHW021328310726
48971CB00001B/33